THE ATOM BOMB

ADELBERT SCHOLTZ

THE ATOM BOMB

A PIECE OF ROMANTIC SCIENCE FICTION

RESOURCE Publications • Eugene, Oregon

THE ATOM BOMB

A Piece of Romantic Science Fiction

Wipf & Stock
An Imprint of Wipf and Stock Publishers
199 W. 8th Ave., Suite 3
Eugene, OR 97401

www.wipfandstock.com

PAPERBACK ISBN: 978-1-6667-4361-6
HARDCOVER ISBN: 978-1-6667-4362-3
EBOOK ISBN: 978-1-6667-4363-0

READ THIS FIRST

This story is a work of fiction. Some of the characters mentioned in this book really lived, but most of the actions and words ascribed to them are pure fantasy. The other characters are purely the inventions of the author. If a photograph of a certain person appears in this book, then it may be assumed that that person existed. The places where this story unfolds are real places. The Sixth Mountain Division of the German Waffen-SS really existed and a youtube video about its exploits during the Second World War can be viewed at
https://www.youtube.com/watch?v=igXHovv566c.

The secret German Uranium Club also did exist.

Liberties were taken with certain historical events to achieve a more dramatic effect, although care was taken to make this story as credible as possible.

A glossary of German words and expressions with their English equivalents is to be found at the end of the book. The rank structures of the Waffen-SS and the German military medical service are explained in another annexure. A list of illustrations and their sources also appear at the end of the book.

PART 1

BERLIN

The Story of David and Willem Scholtz

Atlantic Ocean, Tuesday, 3 January 1933

David:

The German steamship Usambara is gathering speed as she sails into the Atlantic Ocean from Table Bay. We – that's me and my twin brother Willie – stand near the stern of the ship, staring at Table Mountain and Cape Town at its foot as we start our voyage to Germany.

Near us a long, thin and somewhat older gentleman with dark hair and spectacles on his nose is standing. He approaches me: "Is this the first time that you are travelling to Europe?"

"Yes, we have never been overseas and I and my brother are looking forward to see some of Europe. We are on our way to study in Berlin."

"Now, that is remarkable. I also plan to study in Europe, but in Amsterdam. In which fields to you wish to study?"

"I want to study medicine and my brother, Willie (while pointing at him), intends studying physics."

"So, your brother wants sit at the feet of the famous Otto Hahn?"

My brother Willie interjects: "How do you know of Otto Hahn?"

The stranger answers: "I read newspapers and I remember everything that I have ever read."

I cannot help but to ask: "But who are you, if I may ask?"

"My name is Gerrit Scholtz. I have a master's degree in history and I want to obtain my doctor's degree in this field."

My brother Willie smiles broadly: "Well, well. Pleased to meet you! I am Willie Scholtz and my twin brother is David. It is possible that we may be related. Are you perhaps a descendant of Joachim Scholtz who emigrated to the Cape from Germany more than two centuries ago?"

"Yes, indeed. It is quite possible that we may be somehow related. My father, who is a lawyer in the Free State, is also called David." He looks at me: "Are your full names perhaps David Johannes Philippus?"

I exclaim: "Yes! Yes! I am named after one of my father's brothers who also had this name. Willie's full names are Willem Charl Andries, and he is named after another brother of our father. Our father is Pieter Ernst Scholtz. He's a lawyer in Kimberley and a member of Parliament for the electoral district of Barkly West."

"My, my. Because I read newspapers, I certainly know of him. His father was Gerrit Daniel Jacobus Scholtz and this grandfather of yours was a brother of my great-grandfather. I am indirectly named after your grandfather, although I am only Gert Daniel Scholtz. So, my dear cousins, please take my hand!"

Both of us are pleased to have a distant family member on board and I declare with a great grin: "I may just ask the purser to seat us at the same table in the dining room. How do you feel about that?"

Our distant cousin Gerrit replies: "Let's hope that I don't become too sea-sick, otherwise I will gladly join you at your table."

We continue staring at the disappearing Table mountain. The ship sails in a north-westerly direction in order to pass the big bulge of West Africa. We continue staring at the disappearing Table Mountain.

Willie points at Table Mountain: Have you ever climbed Table Mountain? We were there yesterday to say good-bye. Our father has a dwelling in Camp's Bay where he stays when attending Parliament. It is not too far from the foot hills of the mountain. We used the opportunity to have a last look at the Cape from the top before we embarked today. "

Gerrit shakes his head: "Today was my first visit to Cape Town and I only arrived by train this morning. I have spent my whole life in the Free State, although I was born in the small Karoo town of Philipstown. No, I never have had the pleasure of looking down on Cape Town from Table Mountain."

I join in: "We both studied in Stellenbosch until last year. We belonged to the university's mountaineering club, the BTK, which is the abbreviation for 'Berg– en Toerklub' (Mountain and Touring Club). We love the mountains of the Boland."

The hills around Saldanha Bay are also disappearing behind the horizon. After we have reached the open ocean with no land in sight, we all retreat to our cabins to prepare for dinner, which starts at six-thirty. It transpires that Gerrit shares a double cabin with a Dutchman, while I and Willie also share a double cabin, not far from Gerrit's cabin.

The SS Usambara leaving Table Bay with Table Mountain in the background

On our way we stop at the purser's office with the request that the three passengers with the surname of Scholtz be seated at the same table in the dining room – a request that is granted

During dinner we continue our conversation with cousin Gerrit. I declare: "We are very fortunate to have a learned father who is a lawyer and who understands the value of a good education. That is why he sent us to the Stellenbosch University to attain a scientific degree each. Unfortunately, Stellenbosch does not offer courses in medicine and advanced physics – the fields in which we wish to study.

"We, therefore, both got a Bachelor in Science degree to prepare us for our chosen fields of study overseas. I studied chemistry and zoology and with this background the University of Berlin has agreed to allow me to start the second year of the course in medicine. Actually, I will start in the middle of the second year since the academic year in Europe starts during their autumn, which is during August."

Willie adds: "I obtained my degree in chemistry and physics. The university of Berlin also allowed me fall in with the second semester of the second year. We are fortunate that our father can afford to pay for our studies. As a member of Parliament, he earns a sizable salary. Apart from that, he still practices as lawyer part-time in Kimberley and we also have a farm in the southern Free State, called Klaverfontein."

Gerrit replies: "Although my father also has a law practice, as well as a farm in the district of Ventersburg in the Free State, he could not afford to pay for my studies. I had to work as a civil servant in the Department of Justice and studied part-time through the University of South Africa. Since I wanted to follow in my father's footsteps by becoming a lawyer, I attained a law degree and I was then appointed as a state prosecutor. That helped me to save some money to pay for my studies in Amsterdam. I also applied to become a member of the Free State Bar as an advocate, but they required of me to swear an oath of allegiance to the British crown – which I flatly refused."

I exclaim: "Hurrah! That is also our sentiment. To hell with the English king! That is why we are on our way to Germany and not to Britain. Our father fought the British during the Second Freedom War of 1899. He fought initially at the battle of Spioenkop as a member of a Free State commando but later joined the commando of General Jannie Smuts. My father's brother, also called Willie, together with his two eldest sons, joined the Boer forces at the battle of Magersfontein while being a citizen of the Cape Colony and, therefore, a subject of Her magnificent Majesty, Queen Victoria. That made him, technically, guilty of high treason and a prize was put on his head and he had to flee to Holland for the duration of the war until he was granted amnesty only in 1904. So, you can see, we cannot in any way like the bloody British and, therefore, we refuse to study in London, Oxford or Edinburgh."

Gerrit looks puzzled: "But your father is a member of Parliament for the South African Party, the party of Smuts. This party has the policy of supporting Britain in all respects. Jannie Smuts even declared that South Africa only has a future as part of the British Empire. How does your father reconcile this with his war experiences?"

"He was requested by Clever Jannie to stand as candidate for the SAP in the 1921 elections. Out of respect for his old commander and comrade-at-arms, he complied. He also knew Smuts from his student's days in Stellenbosch, although Smuts was his junior. But he told us that he does not want to fight another election as member of the SAP because he cannot agree with Clever Jannie Smuts on our country's relationship with the British."

Willie adds: "It is well-known that the Dutch and the Germans were very sympathetic towards the Boer Republics during the war with Britain, although it was not possible for them to send any military units to join our forces. For this reason, we are very well disposed towards the Germans and the Dutch. The

Germans and the British fought each other during the Great War. We like to declare: our enemy's enemies are our friends! I gather this is also the case with you."

"Exactly. My father was born as a British subject in the Cape Colony, but he got Free State citizenship when he joined a commando during the war. Unfortunately, he became seriously ill and could not fight any longer. As a child I witnessed to a skirmish between government soldiers and a rebel who joined the rebel commandos in 1914 at the outbreak of the Great War in an effort to regain independence for the Free State from British domination. I can never regard myself as a friend of Britain and that is why I want to continue my studies in Holland. I am glad that you two Afrikaner boys are strengthening our ties with our countries of origin in Europe. Perhaps you may even marry two nice German girls to strengthen our numbers!"

My twin brother responds: "That's a great idea. But first, I want my doctorate in advanced physics and learn all I can from Otto Hahn. But tell me, why do you want to study history in Amsterdam if you are actually a qualified lawyer?"

"As I told you, I refused to declare my loyalty to the British crown to become an advocate and, therefore, I decided to pursue another career. I later obtained my master's degree in history and I hope to become a professor in history after I have obtained my doctorate."

"Do you already know what the subject of your dissertation will be?"

"Yes, I have already agreed that with professor Brugmans in Amsterdam. I will do research on the relationship between the Boer Republics and the European powers during the war. For that reason, I will have to work through the archives in The Hague and Berlin to read all the correspondence in this regard. I will also have to interview people who were involved at the time and who are still alive."

I smile: "Congratulations! I wish you well with this noble endeavor. With that, you will prove that we, Afrikaners, can achieve anything. We are not inferior to the British, although they regard us as rubbish and refer to us as 'dirty Dutchmen'."

"Thank you for you good wishes. When I go to Berlin to peruse the documents in the imperial archives, I hope to see you during my stay there."

"That will be great. By that time, we will know Berlin rather well and we will be able to show you around. We may even introduce you to a beautiful German girl!"

With a frown on his face Gerrit asks: "But how will you two guys get along in Germany? Can you speak German?"

"Of course. German was one of our school subjects. Our father insisted that we take it. Of course, you will not have any trouble with Dutch since we Afrikaners still read the Bible in Dutch. I believe that you can also read and speak German?"

"Certainly. I even know a little bit of Latin, which I got from my father, the lawyer. He speaks Latin fluently. It is actually his second language."

Atlantic Ocean, Thursday, 5 January 1933

Willie:

The ship has docked for a short stay at Walvis Bay on the coast of the former German colony of South West Africa to take on passengers and freight. This territory is now being administered by South Africa. We three members of the Scholtz family decided to take the bus to the nearby town of Swakopmund, where most of the inhabitants are still Germans. We want to practice our German on the locals.

The Adolf Woermann, sister ship of the Usambara, at Walvis Bay

We enter a "Kneipe", which is the German for a saloon. We order some local beer and start chatting with the men who sit at their "Stammtisch", the table reserved for the regulars.

When they hear that we are on our way to Germany, one guy with a scar on his cheek declares: "I hope that you will soon learn to shout 'Heil Hitler!'"

We look puzzled and he explains: "Adolf Hitler is due to become the next leader of Germany. As you probably know, Germany lost the last war and the English and Americans have bled the country dry to pay for the losses they claim they have suffered during the war. Hitler declared that he will put a stop to this nonsense if the people vote for him. Whenever his followers, the Nazis, greet each other they shout: 'Heil Hitler!' They also raise their right hands like this to salute each other."

I respond in my best German: "I think I will like this gentleman."

After having looked around, we return to our ship in time for her departure shortly before dark.

He next stop is due to be in Lobito Bay in Angola, the Portuguese colony.

Dinner is being served after the ship has reached the open ocean. A friendly young man who embarked at Walvis Bay joins us at our table. He introduces himself as Stefan Strauss and we enjoy a conversation in Afrikaans.

Stefan is – just as the other three of us – on his way to study in Europe. He wants to study maritime science and engineering in the German harbor town of Bremen. Since his mother is German, he can speak German fluently.

Atlantic Ocean, Sunday, 8 January 1933

David:

We are meeting Father Neptune today. As everybody knows, he is the boss of the oceans. And whenever a ship crosses the equator, he is invited aboard to initiate all mariners who cross this line for the first time.

Of course, the three members of the Scholtz clan are part of those who have to meet this illustrious figure. The ship slows down briefly to allow a guy with sea-weed in his long white hair and beard and with a trident in his hand to appear on the main deck. He commandeers a few seamen to assist him.

All the new-comers to the equator have to line up and receive a douse of shaving cream from the visiting deity, which has to double as foam from the waves.

After old Neptune has again disappeared the Captain calls for refreshments, including frothy beer from a barrel. All the Germans aboard start singing – as they often do – and we join in with the songs that we have learnt as members of the BTK at Stellenbosch. Even the stiff Gerrit Scholtz unwinds and joins in with the festivities. The shipboard band consisting of two accordions, a trumpet and a clarinet accompany the singing.

It appears that these Germans are in good spirits, in spite of the fact that they have lost the Great War in 1918. We hear from them that they are hopeful that a great future awaits Germany under the leadership of this Herr Adolf Hitler.

I wonder what type of man this Hitler is. Will we ever have the chance of meeting him?

Rotterdam, Tuesday, 17 January 1933

David:

At last! We are entering the harbor of Rotterdam, the biggest port in Europe. The last three days were harrowing while we were passing through the "Biskaja", the German name for the Bay of Biscay, where stormy seas tossed the ship up and down.

The farewell dinner last night with the Captain was attended by only a few passengers. Most of them were too sea-sick to leave their bunks. Me and my brother, though, seem to be good sailors. Our father kept a small yacht in the fishing harbor of Camps Bay and we used to sail on her during many a weekend or a holiday and, therefore, we are used to be on a moving vessel.

A train journey through the day brought us to Berlin, the capital of glorious Germany! The train glides slowly the last few kilometers after we have passed the outskirts of the city and it comes to a graceful stop at the Hauptbahnhof, the main station, exactly on time. It is Wednesday today and the sky is overcast.

We grab all our belongings – two suitcases, as well as a rucksack each – and walk to the exit, following our fellow passengers. Announcements are blared through a public address system. We find it strange to hear that the announcer mentions "Gleis Zwo", instead of "Gleis Zwei" when announcing platform two where our train halted. We have learnt in school that "two" in German is "zwei" – not "zwo".

At the exit of the train station, we find a taxi that is willing to take us to a cheap hotel in the vicinity of the university campus. After a few minutes the driver informs us that we are passing the Alexander von Humboldt University, one of the most prestigious institutes of learning in the whole world of which all people in Berlin are rightfully proud.

I retort: "We are here to study at this university."

He grins: "Herzliche Glückwünsche!" (hearty congratulations!). He stops in front of a neat building with a sign board: Hotel Krone (Hotel Crown). The taxi driver gives us a hand with our luggage and we pay him. Fortunately, we have German Reichsmarks in our wallets.

We get a double room and I explain to the hotel manager, Herr Max Busch, that we are looking for permanent accommodation in the vicinity of the university. He smiles: "My nephew is just the right person to help you. He has an "Immobiliengeschäft" (estate agency). I will give him a ring and ask him to come along tomorrow during the afternoon to aid you in your search."

Berlin, Wednesday, 18 January 1933

David:

After breakfast, we venture into the city. We have been so used to being in moving vessels and vehicles for a long time and we have to adjust to a stable Mother Earth under our feet. It is freezingly cold and we are grateful for the warm coats we have brought along.

A short walk brings us at the university campus and we enquire from a passer-by where the administration building is. We enter a grey edifice and look for a sign to lead us to the registrations section. We keep our correspondence with the university, as well as the letters certifying that we are accepted at the university, ready at hand.

The main building of the Humboldt University

A friendly "Fräulein" (Miss) at the registration office offers to help us. We announce that we must register as new students and we hand over all our documentation in this regard. It seems that the registration process can be dealt with swiftly – we only have to complete a "Formular" (application form) each and we receive cards with our names and student numbers. The friendly girl advises us to go and visit our respective faculties to find out where and when our lectures are to be held.

The Science Faculty is nearest and Willie gets a schedule of lectures at the office of the dean. The clerk immediately recognizes him as a foreigner and tells him to go and meet the faculty dean the next day before attending any lectures. The lectures actually started two day earlier, on Monday morning, but that will not create any real difficulties for Willie.

The next stop is at the Faculty of Medicine, which is situated at another campus of the university. I am also advised to go and meet the dean. The clerk lifts his telephone and gets a connection to the dean's secretary. After explaining that a foreign student from far-way Africa has arrived, the clerk tells us where to find the dean's office. We are immediately admitted and the dean, a Herr Professor Doktor Friedrich Falke, greets us with a warm handshake. I explain that I am the foreign student and that my brother, next to me, will be studying advanced physics.

Herr Professor Doktor Falke is pleased to see me: "Young man, very welcome to our illustrious university! I feel flattered that you chose to study here. I am already familiar with your academic record through our correspondence. As I recall, you will be admitted to the second semester of the second year. It is possible that your fellow students have already dealt with certain topics with which you are still unfamiliar, but I am sure that you will be able to catch up easily. When you start your lectures tomorrow, find out when your professors and "Privatdozenten" (tutors) have their visiting hours and go and talk to them. They will tell you what study material will have to be purchased."

I can only stammer a barely audible "Danke". I find Herr Professor Falke intimidating. He has a powerful presence and sits upright and stiff, just as one would expect of a Prussian officer.

He continues: "Have you given any thought whether you would like to specialize in any particular direction after having completed your basic medical training?"

"This is something that I haven't thought about yet. I think I will only be able to decide that when I reach the end of my basic medical training. By that time, I will know what interests me most."

Falke replies: "A sound approach, Herr Scholtz (he pronounces the name as a German would pronounce it).

"Don't jump the gun too early. Perhaps you will choose surgery, which is my field. Let's wait and see. Anyway, 'Danke schön' (thank you, very much). It has been a pleasure meeting you and your brother. It is possible that we will see more of each other in future."

We exit the building of the Medical Faculty. It has started to snow, a new experience for us.

While we studied at Stellenbosch it happened a few times during winter that the peaks of the Boland mountains were covered in snow. But this is the first time that we experience real snow at street level. Some has already gathered on the ground and I cannot resist the temptation the pelt my brother with a snow ball. He immediately responds in kind.

With all the snow falling the world suddenly looks different and we have to ask our way to the Hotel Krone more than once. We suddenly remember that we are hungry and fortunately we see an "Imbiβstube" (refreshment bar) where we order some" Bratwurst" (grilled sausage) and Sauerkraut with a glass of beer each.

In our hotel room, Willie shakes my frozen hand: "My dear brother! We are at last students in Germany! We have realized our dream!"

"Not so fast. This is only the start of our dream. Lots of hard work awaits us before we can say that our dreams have been realized. It is still a long way before people can call each one of us Herr Doktor Scholtz! But we will get there."

Herr Max Busch's nephew, Moritz, arrived on the dot at two o' clock to help us find accommodation. He shows us a list of possibilities and describes each of them.

I thank him for his trouble. "We don't need anything fancy. We are two poor students and we are used to share a bedroom. Only a small apartment with a kitchen and a bathroom. And, of course, it must be furnished. We don't like sleeping on the floor."

"Then this one in the Dorotheenstraße (Dorothy Street) is just what you need."

We go by foot to the Dorotheenstraße and struggle to stay upright on patches where the snow has not yet been cleared. We find the apartment on the second floor with a living room, single bedroom, kitchen and shower to our liking. One drawback is that the toilet is on the "Treppenhaus" (stairway) that the apartment shares with another apartment on the same floor. Moritz assures us that the price is reasonable. We can move in on the first day of February. I sign the contract on behalf of both of us. It is valid for a full year with the option for another year if both parties agree. We like the fact that the apartment overlooks the Spree, the river that runs through Berlin. The Museuminsel, the island in the river where most of Berlin's museums are located, is on our doorstep and we promise ourselves to go and visits these museums in due course.

In the meantime, we decide to stay at the hotel and we arrange with Herr Busch that we stay at a reduced price till the end of the month.

Berlin, Thursday, 19 January 1933

Willie:

After breakfast we depart for the university campus to find the office of the dean of the Science Faculty. We wait in his secretary's office for half-an-hour before the learned Herr Professor Doktor Siegfried Stiglmair is ready to see us.

"Ach, Herr Scholtz! Here you are at last. I remember from our correspondence that you are to start with the second semester of the second year. You already seem to have a god working knowledge of physics and chemistry. You may structure your own course and you may choose from a variety of subjects: inorganic chemistry, organic chemistry, biochemistry, Newtonian physics or mechanical physics, Einsteinian physics and nuclear physics. Have you heard of the theories of Albert Einstein?"

"Yes, indeed, but I understand that there are exponents of the so-called German physics who do not accept his theories because he is a Jew. I would have liked to attend his lectures."

"Professor Einstein is, unfortunately, visiting America at the moment. He mentioned more than once that he is afraid of the Nazi movement here in Germany and it is possible that he will not return to us. So, it seems that you will not have the opportunity of hearing this former winner of the Nobel Prize. Anyway, I recommend that you also take some courses in mathematics. One cannot do physics without a thorough knowledge of maths."

"I have done mathematics up to second year level. But I agree, it will certainly be to my advantage to deepen my knowledge of this discipline."

"You will have the opportunity to attend lectures by members of the Königlich-Preußische Akademie der Wissenschaften (Royal Prussian Academy of Sciences). This body of scientists is closely associated with our faculty, although it is not part of the university."

"That is the most important reason why I decided to study in Berlin – and not in Göttingen, Tübingen, Heidelberg or Munich."

The dean smiles: "A good decision, indeed. When your studies have advanced far enough you will also work at the Kaiser Wilhelm Institut für Chemie (Kaiser Wilhelm Institute for Chemistry) in Berlin-Dahlem."

"That is another reason why I came to Berlin."

"Excellent choice. You must go and meet your professors and tutors. They will inform you of the study material that you will require."

My brother feels that he also has to say something: "Herr Professor, we also chose Berlin because our distant ancestor, Joachim Scholtz, emigrated to the Cape of Good Hope in 1719 from these parts. He was a Prussian."

Professor Stiglmair gives a wry smile: "We Bavarians don't like the Prussians very much. They are far too stiff and formal for us. They don't seem to have a sense of humor. But I have reconciled myself with the fact that I live and work in the Prussian capital."

When we are outside again, we congratulate each other on what we have achieved so far. We decide to attend our first lectures tomorrow, Friday, and meet our lecturers.

Berlin, Sunday, 22 January 1933

Willie:

Today is Sunday and we decide to go to church. We feel that we can take it easy today because we have been very busy the last two days.

On Friday we attended our first lectures. I was in a class where inorganic chemistry was taught and another class where nuclear physics got attention. I met four of the professors, including Otto Hahn, and I have received a reading list for this semester, together with material I have to master to catch up with the rest of the students.

David also went to meet his professors and he attended lectures in anatomy, physiology and bacteriology. Yesterday we hunted an academic bookstore down and bought all the books and manuals we need.

The Reformed Church in Berlin

And now we are on our way to church. We were surprised to hear from Herr Max Busch that there is a Reformed Church in Berlin and that is where we are headed. We have nothing against the Lutheran brand of Christianity, but we were raised as staunch

Calvinists in the Dutch Reformed Church in South Africa and we feel that we will feel more at home at a reformed church.

After the service we wait for the pastor to come out of the vestry and we introduce ourselves. Pastor Lothar Coenen is surprised to have had visitors from Africa in his church and he invites us to enjoy some coffee at his parsonage.

He informs us that we arrived in Germany at a crucial moment. There has been much political instability the past few years and it seems as if the National Socialist German Workers' Party, also known as the Nazi's, are about to assume power. There are rumors that Reichspräsident Hindenburg will ask Herr Adolf Hitler to form a new government when the present government fails.

David asks him: "How do you feel about this Herr Hitler? Will he be a good leader of the country or will he prove to be a disaster? At Swakopmund in South West Africa and on the ship, there were people who felt enthusiastic about him. They described him as the savior of Germany."

Pastor Coenen looks concerned: "Nobody knows what really to expect. It is certain that Hitler will help us Germans to regain our self-respect after the inglorious defeat in 1918 during the Great War. He has promised to stop paying reparations to the French, British and Americans. I applaud that. But we as Christians cannot agree with his policy of persecuting the Jews. After all, Jesus Christ and his disciples were Jews. Until now, we have lived peacefully with our Jewish neighbors, but there are Nazi thugs who want to beat all Jews up. I don't like that."

David continues: "I have also heard that Herr Hitler is against all the Communists. As far as I can gather, these Communists are atheists and anarchists. It will certainly be a good thing to keep them in check."

"I agree. The church is being persecuted in Communist Russia and we don't want that to happen here. At least, Hitler professes to be a Christian. He grew up in Austria in a Roman Catholic home. That makes him more preferable than the Communists."

I change the subject: "Can you tell us why there is a Reformed Church here in Berlin? I thought that all the Protestants in Germany were Lutherans?"

"The Lutherans are certainly in the majority. This congregation was founded by a group of French Huguenots who settled in these parts in the late seventeenth century after they were subjected to persecutions for being Calvinists. You will find quite a number of French surnames in these parts. I have Dutch forbears who settled in Prussia during the eighteenth century and that explains my Dutch name. My family has always been members of the Reformed Church. Nowadays, the reformed congregations and the Lutheran congregations are united in the EKD, the Evangelische Kirche in Deutschland (Evangelical or Protestant Church in Germany), with the exception of a few reformed congregations along the Dutch border that have ties with the Church in Holland."

After having left the parsonage, we wander about the city. We find the famous Brandenburger Tor (gate) at the end of the main street of Berlin, Unter den Linden. Not far from it the German Parliament, the Reichstag, is situated in all its glory. We find that the Dorotheenstraße, in which our new apartment is situated, leads directly to the Reichstag, which lies about two kilometers from our apartment.

Berlin, Monday, 23 January 1933

Willie:

Today, Monday, is my first lecture with Professor Otto Hanh, the famous expert on chemistry and physics. He is known for the fact that he discovered some new chemical elements, previously unknown to mankind. He discovered thorium, ionium, proactinium and two isotopes of uranium. Apart from his position as professor, he is also the director of the Kaiser Wilhelm Institute, here in Berlin. Indeed – an illustrious man and I feel humbled to be one of his students.

Otto Hahn

Today's lecture deals with radio-activity. Directly after this lecture, there is a lecture by Frau Professor Lise Meitner, a close collaborator of Hahn. I struggle to understand her German since she speaks with an Austrian accent.

One of the students whispers to me: "It is uncertain how long she will still be with us if the Nazis gain power. She is a Jew and, as you probably know, they hate the Jews."

During the afternoon I attend a practical class in the chemistry laboratory. I am familiar with today's task, since I have already performed it in Stellenbosch.

David:

My first lecture in anatomy takes place today. My knowledge of zoology helps me somewhat, but it is a struggle to remember all the Latin names for the different body parts. Our professor stresses the fact that we must be able to make drawings of all the organs and body parts from memory during the exam.

We are also told that we must attend a practical class this afternoon in the anatomical laboratory. Each one is to receive a cadaver, which he has to dissect and learn to know intimately. Fortunately, I am not averse to cutting into flesh since I have often helped on our farm to slaughter sheep. My knowledge of the innards and skeletons of sheep also help me to identify the corresponding organs and bones in a human body.

After the lecture in anatomy, we receive a lesson in bacteriology. Bacteria are those tiny bits of living matter that can make people sick. They are called germs by ordinary people. We are informed that we must attend a practical class tomorrow afternoon in the bacteriological laboratory to look at slides of all sorts of bacteria through microscopes.

Berlin, Monday, 30 January 1933

David:

Nobody attends lectures or practical classes this Monday afternoon. All the students and even some of the professors stream to the city center. Reichspräsident Paul von Hindenburg, a Field Marshall of the Great War, has asked Herr Adolf Hitler to form a new government. After the previous elections, no party got a majority in the Reichstag, the Parliament, but the National Socialists or Nazis came out as the strongest party and they managed to form a coalition with a like-minded party to be strong enough to control the Parliament.

Hitler, at the window of the Reich Chancellery, receives an ovation on the evening of his inauguration as chancellor

There is a parade of the Sturmabteilung or SA, the storm troopers of the Nazi party. They wave their banners and flags and the crowds cheer them on.

Later, Hitler and his new cabinet – consisting partly of his old cronies, including Hermann Göring, an air ace of the Great War – are sworn in at the office of the President. Hitler becomes Reichskanzler or Chancellor. Afterwards, he waves at the crowd assembled outside the building. Of course, I and my brother cannot resist the temptation to witness all these momentous events and, together with the crowds, we applaud Hitler as he appears at the window.

At last, Germany will become great again and we don't want to miss a single minute of this historic moment. It is also our wish that our people, the Afrikaners, can experience a rebirth after the humiliating defeat by the British during the South African War of 1899 to 1902 when the British managed to gain control of our gold mines.

That night, both of us write long letters to our parents to inform them of the excitement of this day.

Berlin, Tuesday, 31 January 1933

Willie:

We attend classes again today and we have already made some friends with our fellow students. They are enthralled with these two boys from far-away Africa with German names and who speak a passable German. My name Willem is somewhat foreign to them and they transform it into Wilhelm or Willi (pronounced: "Villi"). They all know of the late President Paul Kruger of the Transvaal Republic and they call him "Ohm Krüger" (Uncle Kruger). Everybody is still excited about the glorious events of the previous day, but some are concerned about the fact that the Sturmabteilung of the Nazi party consists mostly of rowdies. But we cannot dwell too long on that because our academic activities need attention. After the completion of our practical classes in the afternoon we return to our hotel.

We borrow a wheelbarrow from Herr Max Busch and we transport our belongings to our new apartment in the Dorotheenstraße, after having paid him for the time we spent under his roof. His nephew, Moritz, has left the keys with his uncle for us to collect.

The apartment has enough furniture – two beds, two cupboards, a dining table, a kitchen table, a gas stove, some upright chairs and two sofas. There are curtains in front of the windows and central heating.

We discover that there is absolutely no linen or blankets. Also, no cutlery and crockery. We run to town to purchase these items but the shops are already closed. We have no choice but to go back to the Hotel Krone and beg Herr Busch to accommodate us for another night. We complain that we are afraid of freezing to death without blankets and he complies with a huge grin. We have dinner for the last time in his dining room and plan to have a final breakfast tomorrow morning.

Herr Busch asks us what we think of the events of the previous day. I cannot help but to say: " We are both very excited. We are glad for Germany that a new future awaits you. We are proud to be part of it. We hope that your new Chancellor will be able to kick the British King under his ass."

"For that, he will need a very long leg because he is in Berlin and His Majesty resides in London. But if he achieves that, I will rejoice. Hitler may even order the British King: 'Leck mich am Arsch' (lick my ass)."

We all laugh at this well-known citation from Goethe, the famous German author.

Berlin, Monday, 27 February 1933

David:

As we are cold, we decide to go for a walk along the banks of the Spree in the direction of the Reichstag in the hope of getting some warmth into our cold limbs before we go to bed. It is about nine o'clock on a Monday night.

No modern city is silent at night. There is always traffic and other noises. But suddenly the relative calm is disturbed by the clanging of fire brigade bells. It sounds as if the fire engines are racing along the Dorotheenstraße and Unter den Linden, which run parallel to each other. We wonder where the fire is, but suddenly we see that the Reichstag is on fire. A huge cloud of smoke is hanging over the spot and we can see flames lighting up the sky.

Being very inquisitive Afrikaner boys, we cannot resist the temptation to see what is happening. Crowds gather at the spot and the Police have a busy time keeping everybody at a distance to make it possible for the brave firefighters to do their job. Only after almost three hours the fire is finally extinguished.

However, the building is gutted and it is clear that the Parliament will have to find another meeting place. When the fire engines start to depart the crowds cheer and applaud their brave efforts. Slowly, we walk back to our apartment.

Berlin, Tuesday, 28 February 1933

Willie:

I walk to the University along the Dorotheenstraße, which brings me to the backside of the central university campus. On the way, I buy a newspaper to read about the events of last night.

It transpires that the police have arrested a Dutch Communist, a certain Marinus van der Lubbe. He is to be charged with arson.Everybody in my class wants to hear my version of the events of the previous evening. Most of the students saw the smoke from far away but they did not take the trouble of walking to the burning Reichstag.

My best friend, Paul Plisch, declares: "You just watch and see. Hitler will use this as an excuse to clamp down on the Communists! He hates them." Most of the students agree.

When walking home after the completion of my practical classes in the afternoon I see posters of a special edition of the Nazi newspaper, Die Völkische Beobachter (The Peoples' Observer). I buy one to read at home.

The main news is, of course, still the Reichstag fire. But we also read that Hitler has convinced Reichspräsident Hindenburg to declare a state of emergency. All civil rights have been abolished and the Communist Party has been banned.

Frau Elisabeth Drammen, our elderly neighbor on the other side of the Treppenhaus, knocks on our door. She is terrified. She asks us whether we have a radio. We don't, but we give her our newspapers to read. She has a nephew who belongs to the Communist Party and she wonders what will become of him. Will he be arrested?

Of course, we don't have any answers but secretly we are relieved that the godless Communist scourge has been removed from the country in which we are guests.

After Frau Drammen has left, we decide that we must buy a radio. We need to hear all the news directly. Things are happening so rapidly that we have to stay on top of everything. Both of us write long letters home to tell our parents of our exciting experiences.

Berlin, Tuesday, 21 March 1933

Willie:

On my way home from the campus, I buy a copy of the Nazi newspaper to read at home. We switch on our new radio to hear the youngest news. There is a recording of a speech by Hitler earlier the day at the opening ceremony of the new Parliament. There were new elections a fortnight ago on 6 March and the Nazis and their coalition partners, the DNVP, the Deutsche Nationale Volkspartei (German National Peoples' Party), achieved a comfortable majority, although the Nazis only achieved 44% of the vote.

Since the Reichstag building has burnt down the opening ceremony was held in the Garrison Church in the town of Potsdam, a few kilometers to the west of Berlin.

During his speech, Hitler emphasized that his movement supports the military establishment of the country, together with the aristocracy, which still dominates the officers' corps of the armed forces. The newspaper contains a photograph of Hitler, dressed in a neat suit, greeting President von Hindenburg before the ceremony with a respectful bow to show his respect for this aged Field Marshall and member of the aristocracy.

Although Hitler could not prevent the Communists from participating in the elections, despite having banned the party, his friend Hermann Göring, who is minister of the interior for the state of Prussia and who controls the Police in this state, ordered the arrest of all 81 Communist members of the Reichstag before the Reichstag constituted in Potsdam. These arrests were effected in accordance with the state of emergency, which was declared after the Reichstag fire. This step removed the most vociferous opposition to his party from Parliament and gave him a great majority.

Berlin, Friday, 24 March 1933

David:

We heard over the radio last night that Hitler has in effect achieved full power over the country. He convinced the Reichstag that assembled in the Kroll Opera House to adopt a law, called the "Gesetz zur Behebung der Not von Volk und Reich" (Law to Remove the Distress of the People and the Reich). This law gives him the power to issue decrees with the force of law, without consulting the Reichstag. The act was adopted by a vote of 441 for and 84 against.

We students discuss this development during the lunch period on campus. All agree that this law actually abolished democracy and that Hitler, in effect, became a dictator. Susanne Schmidt argues that this is not so bad. After all, Russia, Italy and some South American countries also have dictators. Napoleon Bonaparte was the dictator of France and he is still the hero of most French. The Roman emperors were also dictators and the Roman Empire endured for centuries. As long as the dictator has some common-sense things will work out beautifully.

On the other hand, Stephan Stein is of the opinion that the Nazis are a bunch of thugs, criminals and hooligans and that they will only bring disaster to the country. He heard that a large detachment of SA rowdies intimidated Parliamentarians before the session started during which the new law was passed. Susanne Schmidt warns him not to talk too much like that since it could bring him into serious trouble. Democracy boils down to the rule by the mob and one can be sure that mobs do not know what is good for them.

Fritz Fittig doesn't agree. He mentions that Roman emperors like Nero and Caligula were disasters and fools and madmen. It is always possible that a dictator could make serious mistakes and cause heaps of misery as Josef Stalin did in Russia.

I can only quietly listen because I, as an outsider and foreigner, really has no say in the matter. However, secretly I think that Germany needs a strong leader after the chaos of the years after the Great War and to reverse the misfortunes brought about by the Great War.

After my practical anatomy class with my cadaver, I walk home. I tell Willie about the discussion our class held during lunch. He finds that interesting because a similar debate happened in his class during lunch.

Potsdam, Friday, 14 April 1933

Willie:

Today is Good Friday and there is a short Easter break. After I and David had attended church this morning, we picked up two of my class mates, Annemarie von Czapiewski and Josephine Semmel.

Now we are relaxing on a rowing barge on the Templiner See, a lake in the nature reserve of the Potsdammer Wald und Havelseegebiet (Forest and Havel Lake Area of Potsdam). Potsdam is a town a few kilometers west from Berlin. The lake is formed at the spot where the Spree joins another river, the Havel. The girls brought a basket with refreshments and we enjoy the spring sunshine and beautiful surroundings.

This is the first time that we are dating girls in our life. During our years of study in Stellenbosch we had many female friends but we never actually dated any of them. I made friends with these two girls in the class for mathematics and they agreed to come with us on this outing.

After a lazy afternoon we find a Pension (guest house) in Potsdam where we rent two double bedrooms. My idea was that I and David share one room and the girls take the other room. After dumping our few bits of luggage, we look for a restaurant for dinner.

The girls inform us about all the customs of the people of the Province of Brandenburg, the heart of Prussia. They speak to each other in the local dialect, called "Plattdeutsch" (Flat German) or Platt for short. It sounds rather similar to Dutch and we easily understand them.

Josephine, who knows some history, tells us that Ohm Krüger, the old President of the Transvaal Republic, visited Chancellor Otto von Bismarck in 1884. They communicated initially through an interpreter but very soon Bismarck found that he could understand the Dutch and Afrikaans of Krüger and he switched to Platt, which the old President could follow.

During dinner we finish three bottles of red wine from the Rhine region and we are in a very mellow mood when we return to our Pension. When we want to say good-night to the ladies before they disappear into their room, they stop us. Annemarie says: "No, boys, this will not work. I and Josephine decided that we like you two. I will spend the night with you, Willi, and Josephine will share the room with David."

The wine causes any possible resistance from our side to evaporate. That night, both me and David loose our innocence and I suspect that that was also the case with the two girls

Potsdam, Saturday, 15 April 1933

David:

The next morning, during breakfast, I and my twin brother briefly discuss our experiences of the previous night in Afrikaans because we do not want the girls involved in our conversation. We agree that we will definitely and certainly not report our experiences to our parents when we write our next batch of letters. We can only imagine how they, with their staunch Calvinistic morality, will fail to understand the excitement and pleasures we were subjected to.

Sanssouci Palace in Potsdam

After breakfast and enough coffee to drive any lingering headaches away, we explore the old town of Potsdam. King Friedrich der Große (Frederick the Great) of Prussia sometimes lived here in the Sanssouci Palace, a beautiful baroque edifice, which we visit with our new girlfriends. The girls inform us that the common folk often referred to their king as "der Alte Fritz" (the old Fritz). The guide tells us that the king was a lover of music and that he regularly held concerts at Sanssouci in which he often played the flute. We are impressed.

Annemarie looks serious: "Let's hope that Hitler will bring glory to Germany, just as Old Fritz brought glory to Prussia. I have the feeling that he will complete the job left unfinished by Bismarck."

I ask: "What do you mean?"

"Bismarck succeeded in unifying a number of German kingdoms and principalities and duchies into the German Reich in 1871 after a victory in the war with France. Since the other German states formed an alliance with Prussia against France it was easy to get them to agree to form a German Empire with the King of Prussia as Emperor. There are still German-speaking parts of Europa that did not unite with Germany in 1871, such as Austria and parts of Czechoslovakia. I hope that Hitler will achieve unification of all the German-speaking people."

Josephine adds: "Many people dream about that ideal."

We also visit other old buildings and beautiful parks in Potsdam. When we rest under shady trees Josephine gives me a hug and a long kiss, of the same sort that we practiced last night. Annemarie follows her example with my twin brother.

At the end of the day, we board the train for Berlin. In Berlin we want to take the girls to their places of abode, but they flatly refuse. Josephine announces: "Certainly not. The holiday period is not over yet and we will spend the rest of the time with you two boys in your apartment."

Willie stretches his eyes wide open while he looks at me and grins. All I can do is to nod and with that the matter is settled. We actually hoped to spend Easter Sunday and Easter Monday with our books, but this endeavor becomes totally impossible. In Afrikaans we agree that we actually need the break and the pleasure.

Josephine smiles: "With our knowledge of Platt we can understand much of what you say to each other! Anyway, we have also earned some rest and relaxation after a few hectic academic weeks. The world is chaotic enough. So, let's make the most of this time."

We draw lots to decide who will get the bedroom and who will sleep in the living room. The girls still have their luggage from the visit to Potsdam and just after eleven we switch off our lights. It is my good fortune that I may occupy the bedroom with my sleeping partner, while my twin brother and his sleeping partner have to be satisfied with the sofas in the living room.

Berlin, Tuesday, 2 May 1933

David:

The radio informs us tonight that Herr Hitler has banned all trade unions. Their leaders, who were deemed to be Communists, were arrested.

In the place of the trade unions a new organization was to be created, called the "Reischsarbeitsdienst" (Labor Service of the Reich).

It becomes clear to us that Hitler is cleaning the country of the godless Communists. We find it incomprehensible that any enlightened person of the twentieth century can support a Communist movement if one considers all the misery, persecution and poverty caused by the introduction of communism in Russia.

We remember that our father told us that there was a Communist plot in South Africa in 1922 when a number of miners went on strike. Their efforts to sabotage the mines were quickly suppressed when the Army was called in. We were only ten years old at the time and we didn't take notice of these events at the time.

Berlin, Wednesday, 10 May1933

Willie:

My practical lecture on electrons and electricity came out a little early and I start walking to at the Medical Faculty to wait for David to appear.

Suddenly I smell smoke and I hear singing and shouting. The clamor seems to come from the library building. I walk in that direction and see a horrifying sight: a few dozen members of the Nazi Sturmabteilung or SA with their swastika armbands on their left arms are piling books on a huge bonfire.

I ask one of the students watching the event: "What's going on? Why are they burning books?"

"These Nazi brown shirt hooligans decided that books written by Jewish academics contain degenerate information and they have taken it upon them to get rid of that so-called filth. I, however, am horrified by this. If they start burning books the next thing will be that they start burning people. We can trust them to start burning Bibles as well because all the authors of the biblical books were Jews. Where will all this end?"

"Does Reichskanzler Hitler know about this? Has he approved it?"

"Who knows?"

I catch the eyes of Annemarie, my current girlfriend, where she watches the bonfire with fear in her eyes. I join her and she borrows her face in my jacket while she whispers: "I hoped that Germany will become great again. These people are dragging us back to the dark ages. This reminds me of the burning of the library of Alexandria because a few fanatics thought that the books in there contained ideas with which they did not agree."

Later, I return to the Faculty of Medicine but it seems that all the students have already left. I accompany Annemarie to her lodgings and return to our apartment where I find David.

"What a horrible day!" he exclaims. "What is becoming of this country?"

Berlin, Monday, 5 June 1933

David:

The semester ended Friday and our long summer holiday started. We are satisfied with the results of our exams at the end of the semester and it is clear that we have been able to catch up with the rest of our classes.

Today is Monday and we are on our way to collect our girlfriends, Josephine and Annemarie. They suggested that we explore the Rhine region with its romantic castle ruins and beautiful towns and villages during our vacation. We all joined the Youth Hostel Movement and we will stay over in youth hostels along the way. We plan to start in Cologne and hike down to Koblenz on the western bank of the great river. We calculated that we will need at least a fortnight to complete the route.

Fortunately, the two girls like the outdoors and love to go "spazieren" (hiking). Berlin lies in a very flat part of the country and we long to see some hills and mountains. We are assured that there are many hills along the Rhine and beautiful hiking routes through ancient villages and virgin forest.

The train leaves the station exactly on time – as everything happens in this country. The girls boast that babies in this country are born with clocks in their hands and they are able to read the time before they can walk and talk and, therefore, everything works like clockwork.

Annemarie declares: "This is the first time that I visit the city of Cologne, although my mother has been there many years ago. She said it was a most interesting city, which was founded by the Romans. The name Cologne is derived from the Latin name of *Colonia Claudia Ara Agrippinensium* and it became the capital city of the Roman province of Germania during the first century after Christ."

"I cannot wait to get there," I say with a smile, "Especially if it is in the company of the most beautiful and charming guides."

Josephine punches my arm: "What are you thinking about? Who are these guides? Have you organized something behind our backs?"

Willie laughs: "Who do you think these guides are? Please, use your intelligence, of which you seem to have enough!"

Berlin, Friday, 23 June 1933

Willie:

We are back in our apartment in Berlin after we have escorted the girls to their home town of Brandenburg an der Havel, where they are to spend the rest of the summer holidays.

The time has come to report back to our parents about the holiday. We have sent a few picture postcards along the way, but we are sure that they want a full account.

We tell them of the interesting city of Cologne with the biggest medieval cathedral in the country. There are even some ruins from the Roman times. We also visited the city of Bonn, a sleepy place on the banks of the Rhine. We hiked through vineyards, drank some wine at places where we had meals and bought milk from dairy farmers along the way. We ascended many a hill and we were glad that we brought our mountaineering boots along to Germany. We were accompanied by two charming German girls with blonde hair and blue eyes. We slept in youth hostels in dormitories where ten or more people shared the same space (and we hoped that our parents would conclude from this that there was no opportunity to become naughty in such a set-up, although we purposefully neglected to tell them about the opportunities where we swam naked in the pools of forest brooks and made love to our girlfriends in the forests, away from prying eyes). We saw many ancient churches and we attended services in Roman Catholic churches on Sundays because there are very few Protestant churches in the Rhineland, although we did not take mass.

Berlin, Friday, 30 June 1933

David:

It is just after lunch on the Friday. I and Willie have bought our books for the next semester and we are busy perusing them in order to be ready for the new semester that starts in August. We plan to take some time off during the month of July and enjoy the sights and pleasures of Berlin and surroundings.

There is a knock on our door. I am the nearest and stand up to open the door, but before I can reach the door it is opened from the outside. It appears that we have forgotten to lock the door this morning after having come back from our outing to buy our books.

To our surprise, Josephine steps inside and she is followed by Annemarie. Josephine announces: "You are wasting the beautiful weather by sitting here inside. Let's go to the Tiergarten (Zoo) and eat something there afterwards."

We both find this proposal very enticing and a few minutes later we are on our way. The Tiergarten is not too far away, only a few blocks along Unter den Linden, the main street of Berlin and on the other side of the Brandenburger Gate.

After a most enjoyable day where we greeted a number of animals from Africa and with the sun only setting at ten o' clock, we return to our apartment. On the way I ask: "And where are you two girls staying tonight?"

"Stupid question! I refuse to answer stupid questions." That comes from Annemarie. The only logical conclusion is that the girls intend staying with us as before.

Berlin, Saturday, 1 July 1933

Willie:

Today is Saturday. The girls require of us to accompany them to the book store where they plan to buy their prescribed books and other learning material for the new semester.

That chore is completed rapidly and the girls dump their new books in our apartment. Josephine hugs my brother while she asks: "What are we going to do with this beautiful weekend? Let's go rowing again at Potsdam as we did at Easter. I have fond memories of that time."

Annemarie chimes in while looking at me: "Any better ideas from your side?"

Of course, I have no better idea and it is rapidly decided that we again spend the weekend at Potsdam. The following program is agreed upon: this afternoon we visit the parks adjoining the town after we have secured lodgings for the night and tomorrow, we go rowing on the lake.

We don't have timetables for the trains to Potsdam but we take a chance by leaving immediately for the train station.

Potsdam, Monday, 3 July 1933

Willie:

We enjoyed Potsdam so much that we stayed a second night. We didn't get as much sleep as we wanted because the energetic girls could not get enough of our love making. We were quite willing to comply.

We leave for the train station after breakfast and we buy the Nazi newspaper at the station. After the train has left the station, we start to look at the newspaper. Josephine reads aloud for the others. It appears that while we were very busy during the weekend to enjoy Potsdam earthshaking events took place.

The "Schützstaffel" (Protection Squadron) or SS, the unit of body guards of Hitler, together with the Police, raided the homes of the leaders of the SA. Hitler became wary of these supporters of his and he had intelligence that they planned to stage a "Putsch" or coup d' etat against him. There are, after all, enough brown shirts to take over a city like Berlin if their leaders should have decided to do so. When these leaders resisted arrest and even started to defend themselves with guns, they were shot down. The most prominent victim was Ernst Röhm, the leader of the SA. The newspaper gave a name to the night of 30 June to 1 July: "The Night of the Long Knives."

Annemarie declares: "You will all remember that it was the SA thugs that took books from our university library to pile them on a bonfire. I am sure that Hitler came to the conclusion that this type of behavior is unacceptable and that the ringleaders had to be stopped and even punished. I am glad that he has ended this criminal behavior."

Josephine concurs: "We need order in this country. It seems as if sanity is slowly being restored and this nonsense is being eradicated. But let's forget about these things and concentrate on the rest of our holiday." All agree with this proposal.

Berlin, Friday, 14 July 1933

David:

It appears that the year 1933 is a year of great events. I and my brother have completed our first semester at the university of Berlin and we have fallen in love with two beautiful Aryan girls. In addition, the National Socialist Peoples' Workers' Party of Germany or Nazi Party took over the power and their leader, Adolf Hitler, became the Chancellor or Prime Minister of the country. We even glimpsed Hitler when he rode through Unter den Linden yesterday, Thursday, on his way to the Reichschancellery. Crowds were cheering him as he gave the Nazi salute. We both wonder whether we will ever have the opportunity of meeting the leader of Germany personally.

We listen to the news on our radio while we also try to prepare for the next semester. The Cabinet has decided in terms of its emergency powers to outlaw all other political parties with the result that the Nazi party becomes the only legal political party.

Berlin, Friday, 15 December 1933

David:

In contrast with the first part of this year the second part progressed relatively peacefully. Today, Friday, is the last day of the semester and we prepare for the Christmas holidays.

In the past, Josephine and Annemarie were the ones to make suggestions about our destinations, but this time I and my twin brother take the initiative. We simply tell the girls that we love the mountains. The nearest mountain range to Berlin is the Harzgebirge and that is where we want to spend our holiday. They are welcome to join us.

As usual, Josephine has the last word: "No. that is not quite how it will be. There is a little more than a week left before Christmas. We are going to enjoy the Christmas market here in Berlin this weekend and then we all depart for Brandenburg an der Havel where our parents live. Both of you are invited to spend Christmas with our families. You, David, is going with me to my parents."

Annemarie adds: "Willi, you are to stay over with my family. It won't do if you spend Christmas on your own in a strange spot."

I smile: "All right, girls. I am sure that Willie will agree with me. We are grateful for the invitations and we accept gracefully and gratefully. But what happens after Christmas? The Harz mountains?"

Annemarie: "That is oekee (the way the Germans pronounce OK). We will teach you how to ski in these mountains. Or do you already know how to ski?"

"I cannot think of any better ski instructors than the two ladies who are sitting opposite us."

"I bet that you don't know any other ski instructors. But then that is settled. We depart on Wednesday, 27 December to the Harz. You do the bookings."

Brandenburg an der Havel, Monday, 18 December 1933

Willie:

The four of us arrive at the railway station of Brandenburg an der Havel. There we move into opposite directions to the respective homes of the two girls.

Annemarie's parents live on the outskirts of the town and we take the "Straßenbahn" (tram). The house has a small garden in front. Her father, Herr Waldemar von Czapiewski, opens the door when we ring the bell. He welcomes me and gives me the assurance that he has only heard good things about me. I thank him for the compliment. Frau Heidemarie von Czapiewski also appears and shakes my hand. I have learnt that the Germans expect people to bow a little when shaking the hand of a lady or an important person and that is what I do. In my best German, I thank them for their hospitality and the invitation to spend Christmas with them. Annemarie's two younger sisters are introduced to me.

I am shown to the guest room in the house where I leave my luggage.

It is almost time for dinner and I am invited to sit with Herr von Czapiewski next to the fire and drink a beer. I have learnt that the Germans who live along the big rivers, such as the Rhine and which was part of the Roman Empire, are wine drinkers. Those who live away from the rivers and never fell within the borders of the Roman Empire, are beer drinkers. Although Brandenburg lies on the Havel, the town lies outside the old borders of the Roman Empire. There are no vineyards on its banks and, therefore, no wine is made in these parts.

During the dinner – consisting of Gulasch, Sauerkraut, "Bratkartoffeln" (fried potatoes) and "Salat" (salad) – I must tell my hosts all about my family and my country. Herr von

Czapiewski is glad to hear that my father is a lawyer. "I am also a 'Rechtsanwalt' (lawyer)," he assures me: "Apart from that, I am also a member of the Town Council."

"So, you are also a politician?" I ask.

"Only a tiny little bit. That is no full-time job."

"Well, I never. Annemarie never told me anything of the sort. But I must confess, I never told her either that my father is also a politician. Or, more accurately, a retired politician. There were parliamentary elections in my country earlier this year and he decided not to be available for another term. He wants to concentrate on his law practice and his farm."

This revelation from my side seems to please my hosts because that puts me in the elite class in my country, while they also see themselves as members of the elite in Germany with their aristocratic family name.

The conversation, inevitably, turns to politics. Herr von Czapiewski felt forced to join the Nazi Party to be able to keep his seat on the town council. "But, I must tell you in confidence, I don't know whether Hitler is the right leader for this country. He isn't even a real German. Neither is he a Prussian. He was born in Austria, although he fought in the German Army during the Great War. But he never rose higher than a "Gefreiter" (lance corporal). He never even fought in any battles because he was a mere messenger between headquarters and the front line, as well as a stretcher bearer in the "Sanitätsdienst" (medical service). He was, though, awarded the Iron Cross First Class for bravery under enemy fire. But now this person of low birth sees himself as the successor to Frederick the Great. Preposterous!"

Frau von Czapiewski feels that she has to help her husband: "But he brought some order to this country. We can already see some changes and the unemployment rate has dropped. So, he can't be that bad."

David:

Josephine's parents live in an important-looking house in the "Altstadt" (old city), the historic canter of the city. The house is situated directly on the street and consists of three stories. When we ring the bell a maid with a white apron opens the door. When she recognizes Josephine, she immediately makes way for us to enter. We leave our luggage in the foyer for her to take up and we ascend the steps to the living room where Herr Joseph Semmel and Frau Grethe Semmel await us.

I greet both of them with a slight bow to show my good manners and I am invited to sit down on a sofa. Josephine sits on another sofa, although I would have preferred to have her next to me. I suspect that she does not want to show her parents how close we are.

After having inquired about our train journey and our studies, Herr Semmel immediately starts to explore my background. I believe he wants to make sure that I am a suitable suitor for his daughter. "Josephine has told us that your father is a farmer," he starts. I suspect that he does not have a high regard for farmers and I decide to play along for a little while.

"Yes, he has a farm in the southern Free State in South Africa. He breeds sheep for their wool and the mutton. My parents are good but humble God-fearing people."

"And how big is this farm?"

"Oh, about three thousand hectares. It is in a rather dry part of the country and that is why it is rather big in comparison with European standards. In terms of South African standards, it is a rather average farm."

"And does your father get a good price for his wool and the mutton?"

"The markets have slumped during the recent economic crisis. But things are improving."

"So, you wish to become an 'Arzt' (medical practitioner)? How do you pay for your studies?"

I do not wish to give the game away too soon and I merely reply: "Fortunately, I and my twin brother are able to come by. We haven't gone to bed hungry and we are able to pay our tuition fees."

I get the feeling that Herr and Frau Semmel don't feel too positive about their daughter's boyfriend. He adds: "Fortunately, we are more than able to pay for Josephine's studies. I own a paper mill that has been in our family for more than a century. Her brother will inherit the business when he finishes his engineering degree."

"Will Josephine play any future role in the business?" I ask, knowing very well what she has told me.

"Yes, she is studying mathematics and economics and she will become the financial director after she has completed her studies. Will you return to Africa after you have completed your studies?"

"Not immediately. I plan to specialize in some or other branch of medicine after that."

"And why have you chosen to study in Germany and not in England?"

"Because my family hate the British. My father fought with General Smuts, our present Prime Minister, during our war against the British during 1899 to 1902 when they invaded our country. An uncle of mine had to flee to Europe during that time for having aided the Boer forces at the Battle of Magersfontein where the British were thoroughly humiliated. He was, however, a subject of Queen Victoria at the time since he lived in the Cape Colony. He was sentenced to death in absentia and, therefore, he and his family had to settle in Holland for the duration until he was granted amnesty. Some of my family members died in British concentration camps due to the horrible conditions that prevailed there, including an aged uncle of my father."

"I never had the opportunity of fighting the British during the Great War. Our paper mill was declared "kriegswichtig"" (essential for the war effort) and I had to continue managing it. My younger brother, though, was a "Kapitänleutnant" (naval lieutenant) on the cruiser Wiesbaden during the Battle of Skagerrak – the British call it the Battle of Jutland – which we won because twice as many British ships than German ships were sunk. He, unfortunately, lost his life when his ship was sunk."

The girl with the white apron appears and announces: "Dinner is to be served."

We sit at a large dining table and Herr Semmel indicates that I should sit at his right-hand side, with Josephine next to me. Herr Semmel continues while spreading his napkin on his lap: "So, your family are no friends of England?"

"My father refused to join the South African Army that invaded the German colonies of South West Africa and Tanganyika. I believe that your General von Lettow-Vorbeck gave our General Smuts a very hard time in Tanganyika."

"Indeed!" Herr Semmel smiles for the first time. "Von Lettow-Vorbeck is one of our national heroes. But you said that your father fought with General Smuts against the British?"

Dinner is being served by a man-servant and it consists of Eisbein, potatoes and vegetables. We drink red wine in glasses with the family crest. I am impressed. Josephine never told me how grand her family was.

I decide it's time to divulge more about my family background: "Yes. My father knew Jannie Smuts when both of them studied law at the Victoria College in Stellenbosch during the nineties, although Smuts was my father's junior."

"So, your father studied law? How did he become a farmer?"

"Yes, he is a lawyer. He has a practice in the town of Kimberley, the town with the biggest diamond mine in the world.

Our farm is in our family for almost a century now and my father inherited it. My eldest brother manages the farm when my father is in Kimberley or when he has to attend Parliament in Cape Town."

"Oh, and what does your father do at the Parliament? Is he a member of Parliament?" Herr Semmel's eyes betray his surprise.

"Not anymore. There was a general election earlier this year and he decided not to stand again for election, although his friend, General Smuts, requested him to be available."

"Well, well. So, your father and the Prime Minister are friends?"

"Yes, and no. They fought together in the war and they belong to the same political party. But my father does not agree with the policy of Smuts of supporting Britain."

"And that is why you chose to study in Germany and not in England."

"Exactly."

Brandenburg an der Havel, Tuesday, 19 December 1933

David:

After having drank a tot of Schnaps and smoked a cigar with Herr Semmel, I was allowed to retire to my bedroom in the attic. I suspect that there are better rooms on a lower floor, but that I was allocated this room, being the son of a humble farmer. This room is, actually, the best place to be in this patrician home. About fifteen minutes after I have covered myself with the "Oberbett" or eiderdown and switched the bed lamp off, my door opened silently and a figure in a white night gown crept in and slid into my bed.

"Please hold me tight because it is so cold," she whispered. I did so willingly.

"Vati and Mutti cannot hear us here because they sleep on the floor below. You must please forgive Vati for interrogating you so much. The biggest disappointment in his life is the fact that the Kaiser never elevated him to the nobility. There were rumors that he would be given the title of 'Freiherr' (baron) but the end of the war and the flight of the Kaiser to Holland made that impossible. Anyway, he is a stiff old Prussian and social classes means much to him and Mutti. I purposefully never enlightened them about your background because I wanted them to hear it from your own mouth. You were brilliant to keep them guessing for a time."

"My love, thank you for telling me this. Do you think your parents will accept me as a suitor?"

"I could see that Vati was very impressed with your pedigree. You are indeed acceptable. When you become Herr Doktor Scholtz some day you will have a title, which he doesn't have, apart from Herr Direktor. I am actually relieved that my father was never elevated to the nobility. Can you imagine how the family name of 'von Semmel' would have sounded?"

"What is wrong with that?"

"You haven't been to Bavaria yet. What we call a 'Brötchen' (breakfast roll) is called a 'Semmel' down there." She giggled softly and added: "Now, give me a long kiss and if I like that kiss you may do with me whatever you wish. Nobody will hear us."

At breakfast table this morning Herr Direktor Semmel announces that he has to be at his office at nine. He hopes to continue our conversation this evening.

During the day, Josephine takes me for a "Stadtbummel", a sightseeing tour through the old city. We buy Christmas presents. Josephine's father arrives home at six and we settle down at the hearth in the living room. "You told me something about your interesting family yesterday, Herr Scholtz. What can you tell me more?"

I have been waiting for this and I tell him that I descend from a long line of warriors. My first ancestor in Africa, Joachim Scholtz, hailed from these parts in Germany and he was a soldier at the Castle in Cape Town. His son was a field corporal in the Roggeveld, a remote region of the Cape Colony. His great-grandson, also called Joachim, was married to the daughter of the field commandant of those parts. This rank is more or less the equivalent of an "Oberstleutnant" or lieutenant colonel. This Joachim was a Field Cornet in the district of Graaff-Reinet – the equivalent of "Hauptmann" or captain. He was my great-grandfather. One of his sons, Pieter Ernst Scholtz (after whom my father was named) became acting commandant general of the Transvaal Republic during the fifties of the previous century. There was constant war against the Hottentots, Bushmen and blacks over the possession of parts of the country and every able-bodied burgher had to double as warrior.

"With respect, but I believe that I have much reason to be proud of my family," I declare. I conveniently stay silent about the fact that my great-great-grandfather died in prison in 1805.

During dinner the Herr Direktor speaks his mind about the current political situation and also asks my opinion. I am careful not to give offence and explain that I, as a foreigner, cannot really judge.

Willie:

Of course, there was not the slightest possibility that I and Annemarie could have shared the same bedroom last night in her parents' home. She slept in her old bedroom and I had the guest room. She did not even say good night with a kiss. Herr and Frau von Czapiewski wished me a good night's rest with a formal handshake each. I thought: "How Prussian!"

Herr von Czapiewski isn't at home during the day since he has to attend to business at his office. I and Annemarie go shopping in the old town center and I have to look for Christmas presents for my hosts. Annemarie advises me on appropriate presents.

During dinner. Herr Rechtsanwalt von Czapiewski continues with the conversation of the previous evening:

"I suppose that my daughter has told you that I fought in the Great War. I was in command of an artillery battery against the Russians when we gave them a thorough beating during the battle of Tannenberg.

General der Arillerie Friendrich von Scholtz

"Thereafter, I became commander of an artillery battalion under General der Artillerie Friedrich von Scholtz on the Bulgarian front. I should have been promoted to Major but got stuck with the rank of 'Hauptmann'. Unfortunately, my old General does not live anymore. I hold the name of Scholtz in high regard. There you can see his portrait against the wall."

He continues: "Did your father also fight in the Great War?"

"Certainly not. That would have meant that he would have joined the British forces, which would have been unthinkable. He fought in our Freedom War against Great Britain during 1899 to 1902 as part of the commando of General Jan Smuts who is the present Prime Minister of our Country. He and Smuts are close friends."

Herr von Czapiewski's eyes widen visibly and his wife blinks her eyes a few times.

It is clear that they are already considering me a good prospect as a future son-in-law.

Brandenburg an der Havel, Wednesday, 20 December 1933

Willie:

Herr Von Czapiewski stays at home today and he has given his secretary also off till after Christmas.

After breakfast, he invites me to go "spazieren" (hiking) with him in the woods outside the city. He points to some interesting spots in the landscape. Suddenly he asks: "When do you plan to get engaged to my daughter?"

This is something I have not expected. I can only answer: "Herr von Czapiewski, I cannot think of that at the moment. I must finish my studies first and that will take me at least five more years more years before I receive my doctorate in physics. But I must confess, I have thought in that direction more than once, although I haven't discussed it with your daughter as yet. She hopes to become a teacher after completion of her studies and our future relationship will also depend on where she gets employment."

This seems to satisfy him. He continues: "May I believe that your intentions with my daughter are respectable and honorable in all respects?"

"Oh, certainly. I won't do a thing to harm a hair on her head. I am indeed deeply in love with her and she is all that I wish from a woman."

David:

Herr Direktor Semmel invites me to view his paper mill. We set off in a chauffeur-driven sedan and arrive a few minutes later at an industrial complex.

He introduces me to his second-in-command, a mechanical engineer. I am shown around from the spot where consignments of logs are delivered to the point where long sheets of paper are being rolled onto huge rolls. These rolls are to be inserted into printing machines at newspaper offices. There are also big white sheets on which books are to be printed.

Afterwards we retire to his office where one of his employees serves us with coffee and "Keks" or cookies. When we are alone, he asks me: "When do you plan to get engaged to my daughter?"

This question catches me unawares, but I manage to answer: "Herr Semmel, there are, as yet, no such plans. I still have to study a few more years before I can complete my medical studies and then I can, perhaps, think about an engagement. But I may assure you, I have only honorable intentions regarding your charming and beautiful daughter. I have dreamt about such a girl all my life and she is the answer to all my prayers."

Herr von Czapiewski loses his stern expression and smiles the first time this morning: "I am relieved to hear that. It seems that there is still lots of time left before we can make plans for you two together."

I can only conclude that he has decided to accept me as a future son-in-law.

Brandenburg an der Havel, Sunday, 24 December 1933

David:

It is Sunday today, as well as Christmas Eve. I accompanied the Semmel family, including Josephine's brother Johannes who has arrived yesterday, to church. We attend the service in the Katharinenkirche (St Catherine's Church) in town. It is a beautiful medieval building with rich furnishings. There is beautiful organ music with a small orchestra on the organ balcony.

Interior of the Katharinenkirche in Brandenburg an der Havel

Afterwards, we return home to gather around the Christmas tree where we exchange presents and enjoy "Stollen", a type of cake with raisins and almonds.

Willie:

The von Czapiewski family attend a Christmas service in the Katharinenkirche in the old town of Brandenburg an der Havel. I see David, Josephine and her family sitting a few pews from us. This is my first experience of a German Christmas. At home in Kimberley or on the farm, Christmas was always spent in a quiet way. We went to church on Christmas morning and had a good meal afterwards – almost as if it was a Sunday. We never had Christmas trees and decorations because my father thought that it was an English invention. We only held a feast on New Year's Day when all our friends and family would gather for a day of fun and sports.

After a beautiful "Gottesdienst" (divine service) in the church we drive back to the von Czapiewski home. We gather around the garishly decorated Christmas tree with golden balls and "Lametta" – long thin strands of golden paper. We sing a few carols and then exchange presents. I get a kiss on the cheek from Frau von Czapiewski and from Annemarie. Her two younger sisters follow this example. This makes me feel part of this family already.

I make the mistake of asking when the Germans took over the English custom of decorating Christmas trees. Herr von Czapiewski snorts derisively and utters a grunt: "The British only learned about Christmas trees when their Queen Victoria married a German prince, her cousin Prince Albert of Saxe-Coburg and Gotha in 1840. Victoria was actually half-German herself. Her mother was Princess Victoria of Saxe-Coburg-Saalfeld. Victoria and Albert taught the British about Christmas trees. So, you see, the British are actually the copy cats."

Goslar, Sunday, 31 December 1933

David:

The four of us are celebrating "Silvester" (New Year's Eve) in the youth hostel in the old town of Goslar on the fringe of the Harz mountains. There are a number of young people around and the "Glühwein" (cheap red wine that is heated on the log fire to evaporate most of the alcohol) flows freely to keep the chill away. It has snowed yesterday, the day after our arrival, and we are ready for our first ski lessons tomorrow.

The respective fathers of our two girlfriends have only agreed on this holiday on condition that we stay in youth hostels where we sleep in dormitories with other young folk. That will make any monkey tricks impossible.

Goslar in the Harz

While sitting in the gathering room of the hostel with the others, I ask my girlfriend how her family got the family name of von Czapiewski. It doesn't sound German.

"We have a long family history. It goes back to the 1500's in Poland. But somehow or other a branch of the family settled in Prussia and were given noble status by the Prussian king. My father has a distant cousin who was a "Graf" (count). He was the German ambassador to America, but he and his family were killed when their airplane crashed. My father doesn't have a noble title, but we are entitled to use the von Czapiewski family crest."

"I must find out whether my family also has a family crest. Our ancestors came from Prussia, the district of Altmark. Perhaps we must go and investigate our family roots some or other time."

"If you want, I will gladly help you. I am sure that Willi and Annemarie will also like to aid us."

Berlin, Monday, 15 January 1934

Willie:

We sit in the lecture room for mathematics. That is, me and Annemarie. Our holiday in the Hartz is only a memory and we must start a new semester.

While we wait for the professor to appear, we reminisce about the holiday. Annemarie remarks: "Do you also agree that we had a delightful holiday in the Harz? You and your twin brother proved to be naturals when it comes to skiing. You got the knack almost immediately after we have given you some instructions."

"Thanks. But I must say that you are also a natural when it comes to making love. You proved to be a first-class instructor."

She manages to blush: "You know very well that you are the first man with whom I got into bed. And you are to stay silent about the fact that we spent the last two nights in Goslar in a Pension (guest house) where we had the luxury of being on our own."

"Ah, Goslar, what a beautiful old town! We have nothing of that sort in South Africa. We have only one relatively old town, namely Stellenbosch where we studied before coming to Germany. This town was founded in 1685. It is charming, but nothing compares to beautiful Goslar…"

The professor enters and our conversation ends.

Berlin, Sunday, 3 June 1934

David:

We foursome have developed the custom of visiting the Lutheran and the Reformed Churches alternatively. That is, if we don't take some or other trip to a destination outside the city on a weekend. That cannot happen too often, due to the pressures of our studies. We actually utilized only the Easter break to hike in the Naturpark Märkische Schweiz, a nature reserve with beautiful forests, east of Berlin. Otherwise, it usually happens that the girls join us in our apartment with their books over a weekend to study.

Our girlfriends are both of the Lutheran persuasion, while I and Willie are, of course, of the Reformed confession. We even joined Pastor Coenen's Reformed Church officially.

On this Sunday, it is the turn of the Reformed Church. Pastor Coenen informs the congregation during his sermon that he came back from a very important synod in the building of the Reformed Church of the town of Barmen on the border between Westphalia and the Rhineland. It was held far away from Berlin in order not to attract the attention of the authorities and the rowdies of the SA. An important declaration was adopted, which boils down to the principle that the Christian Church cannot accept the Nazi ideology and that it has to be rejected that the State has the right to prescribe to the church what it has to believe. It is to be expected that some Nazi Christians will reject this declaration and that the Nazi party will not like it. It may even eventually lead to persecutions, but Christians must be prepared to endure that if they want to stay true to their faith and to the teachings of the Bible.

After the service, the members of the congregation start discussions all over the place and reluctantly leave the church building. We foursome decide that we applaud this declaration and we go to the vestry to inform Pastor Coenen of our feelings. He gets tears in his eyes when we inform him of our sentiments and he grabs our hands. We assure him that we are all pro-German, but that we have our reservations regarding the Nazis.

Afterwards, we realize that did not even introduce our girlfriends to the good pastor.

Brandenburg an der Havel, Sunday, 10 June 1934

Willie:

Our girlfriends have manipulated their parents to invite me and my brother to visit them in Brandenburg an den Havel a few days during the summer break at the university. I and David are sitting in the Semmel abode after attending the service in the Katharinenkirche and we discuss our plans with Herr Semmel and explain to him that we want to explore our roots in the Altmark region of the province of Markt Brandenburg.

Herr Semmel listens carefully to our explanation and then replies: "I propose that you start in Stendal, the biggest town in the Altmark. You might just find something in the archives of the civil authorities or the records in one of the churches. But it is not so easy to reach Stendal from here. Brandenburg an der Havel and Stendal lie on different railway lines. If you want to travel by train to Stendal, you will to go back all the way to Berlin and get another train."

I interrupt him: "Although the university vacation is two months long, we don't have so much time because we plan to go mountaineering in Bavaria later on. It will take a whole day from our program just to travel by train via Berlin. Perhaps we must choose another time to go to the Altmark."

Herr Semmel smiles: "I think I can help you. I will ask my chauffeur to take you in my automobile tomorrow morning to the station in Rathenow, north from here, and there you can catch the train to Stendal. When you have spent enough time in Stendal, you may phone me to inform me on which train you are returning and then my driver can meet you again in Rathenow to bring you back. How about that?"

We accept this generous offer with gratitude and we decide to depart the very next day.

Rathenow, Saturday, 16 June 1934

David:

We have arrived back at the station in Rathenow and now we are returning to Brandenburg an der Havel. Herr Semmel drives his automobile himself because it is Saturday and his driver has the day off. He brought Josephine along. They are very inquisitive to hear what we have found out and we report back eagerly.

My brother fires away: "Stendal is a very fine old town. There are beautiful old buildings from the Middle Ages. We inquired at the Rathaus (city hall) first of all after we have found lodgings in a Pension. The clerk there was very helpful and allowed us to inspect tax returns from the early eighteenth century. It appears that there were various families with the surname of Scholtz. We found three cases where an individual was called Joachim Scholtz.

Stendal: St Mary;s church and town hall

"If we consider that our ancestor's eldest son was named Johannes, we argued that this boy was named after his grandfather.

"In that case, we found a Joachim Scholtz occupying the same address as a Johannes or Hans Scholtz in the village of Lübthin. Lübthin lies to the west of Stendal. We took the bus there and checked with the church records and indeed found a Joachim Scholtz whose parents were Hans (or Johannes) Scholtz and Catharina Lafrenz. Hans was born in 1652 and his son was born on 1 July 1690. The father of Hans was Joachim Hans Scholtz. who was born in 1613.   I add: "We fortunately had four eyes to scour the records. We also found on the church floor the gravestone of Joachim Hans who died on 5 February 1668. I made a drawing of the family crest. It appears that our ancestor was the youngest son of his father and since he could not inherit the family estate, he joined the Dutch East India Company as a soldier and arrived at the Cape in 1719. According to family tradition, he later acquired a farm in the Piquetberg region."

I carefully take out a large piece of paper out of a folder: "I went to a stationary shop to buy good quality paper – which I believe comes from your paper mill, Herr Semmel – as well as good pencils, pens and an eraser. Here is my drawing of the family crest of the family Scholtz."

Josephine takes the paper: "There are two Prussian eagles as well as six armored arms holding a triangle each. The triangle seems to be the balancing point of a pair of scales – the symbol of justice. Your ancestors seem to have been warriors who were involved in the administration of justice. They were likely judges or magistrates. The name 'Scholtz' also suggests some-thing of the sort."

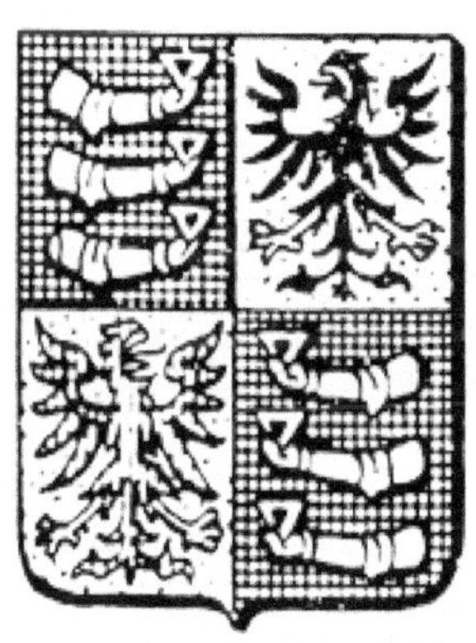

Herr Semmel smiles: "Well, I never!"

Josephine also smiles: "We must invite Annemarie and her parents to come for dinner tomorrow so that we can show them your results. Is that in order, Vati?"

Vati nods his head in affirmation and grunts his approval.

Josephine continues: "I heard that your ancestor's mother's maiden name was Lafrenz. That sounds French. She must have been a Huguenot refugee who emigrated to these parts. There were many Huguenot families in Berlin, as well."

My brother retorts: "That is what Pastor Coenen also told us."

I conclude that the information we gathered impresses Herr Semmel and he must have decided that I may be an acceptable future son-in-law. However, I wonder how a marriage will work out if I want to become a surgeon in South Africa and Josephine is being groomed to become the financial director of the paper mill.

Oberstdorf, Thursday, 28 June 1934

Willie:

The four of us are looking down on the world – other mountain peaks, pastures (called an "Alm" in these parts), villages and glaciers. This is a dream come true for me and David. We have scaled one of the highest peaks in the Bavarian Alps, the Mädelegabel in the Allgäu, one of the most southerly districts in Germany and adjoining the Tyrol in Austria. This peak is 2 645 meters above sea level.

The girls' parents only gave permission for this trip if we again stayed in youth hostels. Fortunately, we got accommodation in the hostel in Oberstdorf, a village in the Allgäu. We plan to spend three weeks in these parts and a week of that has already passed. The last part of July will be spent in Berlin when we have to acquire our study material for the next semester, which starts in August.

Here in Oberstdorf, we have attended more than one "Kurkonzert" (promenade concert) by a group of local musicians. They played classical music, as well as folk music with traditional songs from these parts. We rapidly learnt how to dance with our girlfriends.

We also cannot wait for the autumn symphony season to start in Berlin. Our girlfriends have introduced us to the Berliner Philharmoniker (Berlin Philharmonic Orchestra) under the baton of the famous Wilhelm Furtwängler. We have learnt to appreciate Bach, Beethoven, Mozart, Schubert, Wagner and other German and European composers. The girls boast that the English don't have anything to compare with German art and culture. Since we have never been to Britain we cannot agree or disagree, but we gladly take their word for it.

On our way up to the peak of the Mädelegabel we passed many mountain dairy farms where we bought large jugs of fresh milk to quench our thirst. We also drank water from clear mountain streams emanating from the bottom of glaciers. Whenever we passed an Alm, we heard the melodious bells tied to the necks of the brown cows. The bells chime whenever a cow moves her head. The bells tell the farmers where their cows are, should they get lost at night or during a snow storm. We, as farm boys, are very much interested in these animals.

We also passed a German soldier leading a mule. After having greeted him with the traditional Bavarian "Grüssgott" (greetings in the Name of God), he informs us that he is a member of a mountain regiment of the German Army. He showed us with pride the Edelweiss badge on his sleeve to demonstrate that he belongs to an elite mountain unit.

The Rappenseehütte, with the Mädelegabel peak in the background.

David said afterwards: "If I ever have to serve in the armed forces, I will prefer to be a mountain soldier. Willie, you and I love the Boland mountains and perhaps the South African Army may have a similar unit."

I agree wholeheartedly.

Since it's already late in the afternoon, we plan to stay the night in the Rappenseehütte, a hut built by the German Mountaineering Club, before starting the descent tomorrow. It is also necessary to get shelter for the night because a thunder storm seems to be brewing. According to the locals, a thunder storm high up in the mountains is much more violent than down in the valleys since the thunder bolts crash down on the nearby peaks with great fury.

Berlin, Saturday, 4 August 1934

Willie:

Berlin has come to a standstill today since it is the funeral of Reichspräsident Paul Ludwig Hans Anton von Beneckendorff und von Hindenburg who died the day before yesterday. Since he was a Field Marshall, he is to be buried with full military honors at the site of his biggest military victory over the Russians, at Tannenberg in the east.

We read in the newspapers that Hitler had a law passed while von Hindenburg was lying on his deathbed from lung cancer. This law stipulates that the offices of Reichspräsident and chancellor would be combined in one person, should von Hindenburg die. Hitler assumed the title of "Führer und Reichskanzler" (Leader and chancellor of the Reich) two hours after Hindenburg's death was announced. With that, he combined the offices of head of state and head of government in one man.

We join the crowds that watch the hearse with Hindenburg's coffin go by.

Berlin, Monday, 21 August 1934

David:

Germany was again brought to a standstill on the day before yesterday, a Sunday. I and my brother stayed at home because we had no business of taking part in the referendum that Hitler had called.

He wanted the approval of the German nation for assuming the combined title of "Führer und Reichskanzler" since the German constitution doesn't make provision for such a state of affairs. Everybody expected an overwhelming vote of support for Hitler and last night the radio announced the result. More of less 88% of the votes went in the Führer's favor.

During the lunch break the students in my class discuss the results. It seems that those who were critical of Hitler in the past changed their opinions about him. One has to agree that the economic situation of Germany has improved dramatically with unemployment plummeting and the standard of living rising.

After my practical class during the afternoon, I walk back to our apartment. Willie informs me that his fellow students felt the same as my fellow students.

Arnsberg, Monday, 31 December 1934

Willie:

We are sitting next to a huge log fire in the lounge of the hotel in Arnsberg, a beautiful little town in the hilly district of the Hochsauerland in a sparsely populated area of western Germany. All the guests are awaiting the church bell to announce midnight and we are celebrating Silvester with a number of strangers with Schnapps in our glasses. We are ready to call "Prost!" (cheers!) and "glückliche Neujahr!" (happy New Year) at the stroke of midnight.

Arnsberg in the Hochsauerland

We spent Christmas with the families of our girlfriends in Brandenburg an der Havel. Unfortunately, they could not accompany us on our skiing holiday in the Sauerland. Josephine has to help in the financial department of the paper mill where some difficulties are being experienced. Annemarie had to accompany her parents to a family gathering of the von Czapiewski family.

We are very satisfied with the exam results of the previous semester. We already have four semesters in Berlin behind us. David needs three more semesters to qualify as an Arzt and I need three more semesters to receive my diploma as scientist. After that, we plan to proceed to our doctorates.

In the meantime, we love the skiing in these parts. There is a ski lift at Winterberg, which we often use. Otherwise, we hike with our rented skis to the top of other hills to start our "Schilauf" downhill.

A number of the guests in our hotel are from Holland and we practice our knowledge of Dutch on them while awaiting the midnight chimes from the church bell. Arnsberg is a lovely little town with a number of historic buildings and a "Zwiebelturn" (onion-shaped tower) on its medieval parish church. After we have tasted the Schnapps, we decide that it is nothing but old-time "witblits", a very potent traditional distilled spirit in South Africa.

Berlin, Sunday, 3 February 1935

David:

The four of us are attending church today – that is, the Reformed Church of Pastor Coenen. We sit silently in a pew and listening to the organ music before the service starts. Suddenly we hear an unfamiliar voice addressing us in Afrikaans: "May I join you?"

We look up and see our distant cousin Gerrit standing in the aisle. We move up to make room for him. We greet him with whispering voices and introduce him to Fräulein Annemarie von Czapiewski and Fräulein Josephine Semmel. He greets them with a passable German.

After the service we cannot wait to start a conversation with him. While we are leaving the church I remark: "So, you did make it to Berlin! Have you already started in the State Archives?"

Gerrit smiles: "I thought that I would find you here in the Reformed Church. I arrived a fortnight ago and I have already started my researches."

Willie places his hand on Gerrit's shoulder: "We have an apartment here in Berlin and our girlfriends have agreed to cook our lunch. I am sure that there will be enough for you as well. Please join us."

Josephine smiles: "This is not the first time that we hear Afrikaans because you two boys often address each other that way. I could more or less understand what your cousin said with our knowledge of Plattdeutsch. If he doesn't want to speak German, then it will be oekee if he speaks Afrikaans."

Gerrit, the gentleman, gives a slight bow: "Gnädiges Fräulein, of course I will speak German to oblige you."

For lunch we enjoy pork sausages, tomatoes, carrots, potatoes and Rosenkohl (Brussels sprouts).

Gerrit, who reads newspapers and knows his history, keeps us occupied with his explanations of the political situations in

Germany, Holland, England, America and South Africa. According to him, Hitler is the best thing that could have happened to Germany, but one cannot be too happy about the SA hooligans who support him. Although he has gotten rid of the leadership of the SA, there are still enough brown shirts to make trouble. Many of them are disgruntled soldiers from the Great War who are looking for revenge on the French and the British, as well as the Communists whom they blame for the disastrous end of the Great War. The story they repeat over and over is that the Communists organized strikes at the end of the war in the factories and desertions in the Imperial Navy. That paralyzed the country and forced the Kaiser to abdicate.

We agree to keep contact and to take our distant cousin along to concerts of the Berliner Philharmoniker.

Berlin, Tuesday, 19 March 1935

Willie:

It is lunch time and I and a group of "Kommillitonen" (fellow students) are sitting in the students' club to discuss Hitler's announcement of the previous day, which we heard on the radio last night and which is reported in this morning's newspaper.

Hitler has decided to enlarge the German Wehrmacht – until recently known as the Reichswehr – to 600 000 members. There will be an Air Force and the Navy is to get capital ships. Until now, the Reichswehr was restricted by the Allies of the Great War to 100 000 men.

We expect the League of Nations and other countries to condemn this move, but our student friends laugh it off. One of them, Stephan Schneider, snorts: "What can they do but make a lot of useless noise? They do not have the means to send their armies over to Germany to stop Hitler from doing what he is doing. It is also clear that Hitler is preparing to restart the Great War and win this time."

Semmering, Thursday, 20 June 1935

Willie:

I and my brother are holidaying alone. We have visited the family homes of our girlfriends during the first week of the summer holidays. We were all downhearted when we had to say good bye. My Annemarie has completed her studies to become a teacher in mathematics and she has procured a position in a gymnasium in Magdeburg, to the west of Brandenburg an der Havel.

Her father had to take her there in his automobile to meet the head master and look for lodgings. There was, therefore, no opportunity to accompany us on our holiday.

Josephine took up her position as financial director of her father's paper mill and, although David had pleaded, she could not disappoint her father by absconding.

The Semmering Pass

A few weeks ago, I asked Frau Professor Lise Meitner, who hails from Austria, which was her favorite spot in the Alps where we could go mountain climbing. She immediately replied: "Go to Semmering. It is not too far from Vienna and there are beautiful mountains all around, especially the Rax and the Wechselgebirge. The town of Semmering is in a valley with the Semmering Pass between the provinces of Niederösterreich (Lower Austria) and the Steiermark (Styria). Take the train from Vienna."

And now we two brothers enjoy what we like most: ascending and descending mountains.

Berlin, Tuesday, 6 August 1935

David:

My medical studies have gone into a new phase at the start of this semester. I am to do practical work on living patients, albeit under supervision, in the Charité–Universitätsmedizin Berlin, the University Clinic. I am supposed to do rounds in the wards while wearing my white "Kittel" (dust coat) and a stethoscope around my neck.

The two subjects I enjoy most are pharmacology and surgery. The pharmacology seems to be not too difficult since I have studied chemistry at Stellenbosch.

I and Willie went to Brandenburg an der Havel last weekend to visit our girlfriends. I stayed at the Semmel home and Josephine was also there. We both lamented the fact that the distance between Magdeburg and Berlin makes it difficult to keep our romance going. She was not in a position to visit me in Berlin over a weekend since she does not have a place to stay. Her father would never allow her to stay over in our apartment – although it did happen in the time while she was still studying, but without her parents knowing, of course.

Willie:

When I visited the von Czapiewski home the first time, I was assigned a room in the attic. Later, when Herr Rechtsanwalt von Czapiewski decided that I came from an acceptable social class I was "promoted" to the guest room on the floor with all the other bedrooms – and that is where I was sleeping again during my visit the previous weekend. It was impossible for Annemarie to sneak into this room during the night because it adjoins her parents' bedroom.

Nevertheless, it was most pleasant to be in her company during the day. Her father declared that I was welcome to come and visit his daughter over weekends whenever I had the time. My studies have entered a very difficult phase, though, and there would be little opportunity of taking the train to Brandenburg an der Havel.

From this semester, I am supposed to do some work at the Kaiser Wilhelm Institute in Berlin-Dahlem, one of the southern suburbs of the city. That was where all the important scientific work in the fields of chemistry and physics was being done and I regarded it as a privilege to be allowed into this temple of learning. I hope to bump frequently into the famous Otto Hahn, as well as Lise Meitner, two of the most illustrious scientists in the German Reich.

The Kaiser Wilhelm Institute in Berlin-Dahlem

Brandenburg an der Havel, Tuesday, 24 December 1935

David:

The Semmel family, of which I am almost an honorary member by this time, are attending the Christmas Eve service in the Katharinenkirche in Brandenburg an der Havel. It is glorious to see my Josephine again. Of course, we sit tightly next to each other.

Yesterday, I asked her to marry me. We went for a walk in the woods outside the city and there, on a wooden bench under an oak tree, I popped the question. We are so lonely without each other that I could not stop myself from proposing to her. Of course, she immediately accepted.

We agreed to keep it a secret for the time being. I still have a semester to go before I can call myself an Arzt. It would be an appropriate time just after my graduation to become officially engaged.

Josephine assured me: "I don't know how Vati will react. But my life with you is more important than my career as financial director of a stupid paper mill. How much time will you still need to complete your training as a specialist surgeon after you have graduated as an Arzt?"

"Impossible to say. I must work in the university hospital during this time, as well as attending lectures. I will also have to do research for a thesis and that may take time. But I will be earning money during that time."

"And when will we get married?"

"I hope within a few months after our engagement. Perhaps next year, this time. That is, to say, if you can get a job in Berlin so that we can live together. I am sure that your father will be able find a good replacement for you at the paper mill. And then – after

I have become a specialist surgeon – we go back to my Fatherland."

"I know I will love it there. I feel as if I know the place already because you have told me so much. I cannot wait to meet your family because they almost feel as if they are already my family. You must start to speak Afrikaans with me so that I can get used to the language."

And now we are sitting in the church, listening to glorious Christmas music. I decide that I really want to get married in this beautiful church. I am sure that Josephine's parents will agree with that since it is their parish church.

Willie:

Of course, I am spending Christmas again with the von Czapiewski family and we are on our way to the Katharinenkirche for the Christmas Eve service. I feel on top of the world because the most wonderful girl in the world, Annemarie von Czapiewski, has agreed today to become my bride.

I didn't really plan it that way. We were enjoying coffee in a "Konditorei" (confectionary shop) in town when I could not stop myself. I just asked: "When are we getting married? Are you willing to become Frau Scholtz?"

She got a huge smile on her lovely face: "Willi, why have you waited so long to ask me that question? I would have agreed a whole year ago if you had asked me then."

"Is that a 'yes'?"

She smiles: "What do you think, Dummkopf (stupid)? Do you really think that I wish to have any other man than you?"

We agree to keep it quiet for the time being, although Annemarie assures me that her father has already told her that he would like to have me as a son-in-law, provided that I stay and work in Germany because he does not want to lose his daughter.

"Let's get to that point regarding our future abode when the time comes," she says wisely: "But I am sure that I will be able to persuade Vati that there is a good future for me as a teacher in Africa."

"You will be able to teach Mathematics, as well as German. I am also sure that you will be able to find a position in the foreign department of a bank with your knowledge of economics and German."

We enter the Katharinenkirche and we find seats just behind the Semmel family. We greet each other heartily. Josephine is Annemarie's very old friend from school days. That ties the two families together in a certain sense.

While we are listening to the glorious German Christmas music, I ask Annemarie softly: "When do you want to get married?"

She giggles: "How about tomorrow?"

"Do you really think that is possible?"

Before she can answer her father gives us a stern look for behaving inappropriately and without the necessary decorum in church. I decide to continue this conversation tomorrow morning. It is anyway clear to me that we will only be able to marry after I have graduated and started to work towards my doctorate. I wonder what my twin brother's plans in this regard are.

It is the intention of the four of us to go skiing in the Harz again during the remaining holiday period. Both fathers of our girlfriends have given the green light on condition that we stay in a youth hostel with its big dormitories. This time, we will be staying in the ancient town of Quedlinburg with its fairy-tale castle and medieval town center.

Berlin, Tuesday, 20 March 1936

David:

Germans all over the country are celebrating. Hitler has removed another humiliating restriction placed on their country by the victorious Allies of the Great War by sending a few units of the Wehrmacht into the Rhineland – in violation of the Versailles Treaty that ended the Great War. The Allies had stipulated that no German soldier may tread on soil of the most western parts of the country adjoining France and Belgium in order to make the people of the countries feel more secure from possible attacks by the "Huns" or the "Boches", as the German soldiers were popularly called.

According to newspaper reports, Hitler was careful not to provoke the erstwhile Allies by sending in massive concentrations of troops. He only ordered a few infantry regiments to move into the Rhineland. Of course, there were protests from the former Allies, but nothing more than hot air was produced.

And the average German went about his business with a smile on his face. The country was becoming prosperous again. The unemployment rate has dropped dramatically, from six million in 1932 to one million. The standard of living was considerably higher. Great public works programs were initiated, including the erection of a motor car factory in the new town of Wolfsburg and the building of "Autobahnen" (freeways) to connect all the major cities in the country.

My fellow students in the Faculty of Medicine hoped that all these public works would include the building of new hospitals.

Brandenburg an der Havel, Sunday, 14 June 1936

Willie:

I, Willem Charl Andries Scholtz, graduated with honors as a scientist in physics and chemistry last week. My twin brother, David Johannes Philippus Scholtz, also graduated cum laude a day later. He may call himself an Arzt from now on. We got a telegram from our parents to congratulate us.

Both of us have been accepted to study for our doctorates and we will start with our advanced studies next semester. I will specialize in nuclear physics and David aspires to become a specialist surgeon. Our courses will take three years or more.

But today, a Sunday, is a far more important date than the dates on which we graduated. We both are getting officially engaged today at the home of Herr and Frau Semmel. We have decided to make it a joint occasion and both families thought that it was a good idea. Before that, we both had to convince our future parents-in-law that we dearly love their daughters, that we will be able to provide for them and that our families will welcome the new daughters-in-law wholeheartedly. The question regarding our marriage dates and our future abodes were left hanging in the air, for the time being.

Berlin, Saturday, 1 August 1936

David:

Now we are back in Berlin, in time for the start of our first semester, which will start in the middle of August. We had a glorious holiday in Salzburg in Austria, together with our girlfriends – or rather, fiancées.

While we were away in Salzburg and enjoying a Mozart festival, as well as exploring the nearby mountains, we never touched a newspaper, nor listened to the radio. Nothing of importance seems to have happened in this time.

Berlin is in a festive mood today. Today was declared a public holiday and the foursome of us are sitting in the brand-new gigantic Olympic Stadium in Berlin where the Führer is to open the Summer Olympic Games. We are here to support the South African team with its thirty-two members.

Hitler at his seat of honor at the Summer Olympics of 1936

There is a parade of all the athletes taking part, a ceremony to light the Olympic Flame and a speech by Hitler. The city of Berlin is decorated with hundreds red swastika flags. This is an occasion where Germany can boast about her achievements for all the world to see. Our girlfriends feel proud to be Germans and we are also proud of our Prussian ancestry.

Afterwards, we locate the South African team. We enjoy seeing folks from our own country again and we wish them luck.

My fellow medical students are enthusiastic about the Olympic Village that was built for all the athletes to stay. It was announced that the buildings will be converted into a hospital and military barracks after the games.

Berlin, Tuesday, 1 September 1936

Willie:

The news broke today that that Hitler has decided to send a contingent of soldiers to Spain, including a few squadrons of the "Luftwaffe", the new German Air Force, to help the Spanish leader, General Franco, in his fight against the Communist rebels. This German force was called the "Condor Legion" and the first soldiers arrived in Spain already towards the end of July. "Oberst" (colonel) Walter Warlimont was placed in command of the operation.

The newspapers in Berlin agree that this step would provide the Wehrmacht with valuable experience of a combat situation.

My fellow students argue that it was about time that Germany started to flex her muscles by becoming involved in international affairs, especially since Soviet Russia started to help the Communist rebels in Spain.

Oberstdorf, Thursday, 31 December 1936

David:

We liked Oberstdorf in the Allgäu so much during a previous summer holiday that we four decided that this town will be our holiday destination this winter holiday. It is Silvester tonight, but today we are enjoying the snow on our skis.

Ski lift at the Nebelhorn, Oberstdorf

Today, we are racing each other on the "Idiotenhügel" (idiot's hill), the easiest ski slope where beginners (idiots!) get lessons. But because it is such a gentle and safe slope, we decided that to use it as a racing track. We slalom downhill and repeat the procedure several times. When the sun disappears behind the Nebelhorn at three o'clock, we decide it is time to get dressed for the festivities tonight.

We are staying at the youth hostel, which was a condition set by both our prospective fathers-in-law for allowing the girls to accompany us.

Brandenburg an der Havel, Saturday, 3 July 1937

Willie:

David and I are sitting in the Katharinenkirche in Brandenburg an der Havel, each dressed in a "Frack" (tail-coat). We are waiting for our brides to enter the church on the arms of their respective fathers.

We are actually already legally married, since we got married yesterday, Friday, at the "Standesamt" (registry office). But for upright Christian folk that is not enough. The marriage has to be solemnized in a church and, therefore, we are seated in the front pews of the church. All the guests of our respective two families are sitting behind us, listening to the organ music coming from the organ balcony. Unfortunately, we miss our parents because we know that they would have loved to be here.

The organ suddenly switches to Wagner's wedding march (the wedding march of Mendelssohn is no longer played since he was a Jew). That is the sign that the brides are entering. My Annemarie, on the arm of her father, is in front since her father is of a somewhat higher social standing than the father of Josephine.

I hear nothing of the pastor's sermon since my thoughts are only with my Annemarie. She looks beautiful and her face is radiant with love for me.

The wedding reception is to be held in the "Ratsaal" of the local "Rathaus" (council hall of the city hall) dating from the fifteenth century. Herr Rechtsanwalt von Czapiewski, who is also a member of the town council, was able to organize the wedding reception in this illustrious space. We are to be driven in two horse-drawn carriages to this venue.

Our plan is to spend our honeymoon in the Alps so that we can do some mountaineering again. We have booked two double rooms in a Penson in the village of Kufstein on the border between Germany and Austria. Unfortunately, we are not able to stay away too long, only a fortnight, because the work for our doctorates keeps us very busy.

Brandenburg an der Havel: Rathaus

I am doing research on the proton and I am investigating the possibility that this fundamental particle may, perhaps, be not fundamental, after all. I theorize that it is possible to divide this particle into yet smaller components. I am working at the Kaiser Wilhelm Institute in conjunction with Otto Hahn and Lise Meitner who have, so far, discovered ten new elements heavier than uranium. They bombard uranium with protons to produce new elements, some of which exist for only a fraction of a second before disintegrating.

David is also very busy in the University clinic where he is experimenting with new techniques to perform knee operations as a surgeon.

We have been able to procure the apartment opposite ours, the apartment that was occupied by our late neighbor, Frau

Elisabeth Drammen. Her family has cleared the place out after her recent death and I and Annemarie will move in there, while David and Josephine will remain in our present apartment.

Both our brides have been able to find work in Berlin. Josephine is to be employed by the Dresdner Bank and Annemarie will teach mathematics at a local gymnasium.

Suddenly, Annemarie tugs at my arm and I awake from my reverie. I hear that the Pastor asks me a second time: "Wilhelm (!) Karl (!) Andreas (!) Scholtz, what is your answer?"

Fortunately, I know the answer and I proclaim with a clear voice: "Jawohl, das verspreche Ich" (yes, I do so promise). The same question is levelled at David Johannes Philippus Scholtz and he answers without hesitation.

Kufstein, Tuesday, 13 July 1937

David:

While on our honeymoon in Kufstein, we meet an Afrikaans-speaking German, Karl Krause, who is on holiday with two friends and their three girlfriends. He grew up in South Africa and is presently a pilot in the German Air Force, the Luftwaffe. The lot of us do a few day trips into the mountains together and I enjoy speaking Afrikaans with him.

Berlin, Tuesday, 8 February 1938

David:

It is Tuesday morning early and I am operating in the "Krankenhaus Moabit" (Moabit Hospital) in Berlin as assistant to Professor Septimus Schneider (an appropriate name, since "Schneider" means "Cutter"). We discuss the latest news, while we are also tending to the patient who is under anesthesia.

The Professor, who is known for his strong opinions, growls: "That madman proclaimed himself chief of the Wehrmacht. Bah! He was only a Gefreiter during the Great War and he never even fired a single shot. All he did was to carry messages to the front line. What does he know about military matters? I was a 'Stabsarzt' (staff physician with the rank of Captain) during the war and I know how much suffering a war can bring about. And now he…, he has fired a whole bunch of Generals, including the commander of the Wehrmacht and installed himself in that position. It is clear that he is making ready for war. He is a madman! 'Sheiße!' (shit)!"

One of the nurses tries to calm him down: "Herr Professor, it is dangerous to speak like that. Fortunately, we all know each other well. But what will happen if somebody reports you to the Gestapo (Geheime Staatspolizei – Secret State Police)?"

The professor smirks: "They need me. They cannot fire me or shoot me."

Berlin, Tuesday, 15 March 1938

Willie:

We have fond memories of our holidays in Austria. And now Austria is suddenly part of Greater Germany. There has been a coup d'état in Vienna by the Austrian Nazi's and they have requested Hitler to take over the country. And that is exactly what he has done. It is called the "Anschluss" (joining) of Austria with Germany.

The newspapers are full of photographs showing Hitler driving in his special automobile through the streets of Vienna, while the crowds are cheering and applauding him. Austria is to be called "Ostmark" henceforth. The "Wochenschau" (newsreel) in the cinema, which we often attend, gave much coverage to Hitler's triumphant drive through Vienna.

Dr Lise Meitner during a lecture

I cannot but discuss this development with Otto Hahn and Lise Meitner.

She is extremely concerned since she is an Austrian, but also a Jew. She declares: "I cannot stay in this country. Many Jews have already fled and perhaps I have stayed too long."

Otto Hahn assures her: "Don't worry, my dear. There are enough people here who will protect you. If needs be, I will be able to help you to get out of the country. Perhaps you can join Albert Einstein in Princeton."

Neuberg an der Murz, Thursday, 14 July 1938

Willie:

The four of us are sitting on a rock, high in the mountain above the village of Neuberg an der Murz in the province of Styria, eating our lunch that we have taken along.

Annemarie sighs: "There is so much talk about war. It is hard to believe that we are heading to a war when it so peaceful here. Look at that village, down there. Simple God-fearing folk. They have a very old church, which they attend regularly. They love their priest. They love their children. They love their animals. They love their neighbors. I would have loved to live in such a beautiful and peaceful place."

Neuberg an der Murz

Josephine agrees: "These people are now part of the Greater Germany. If we should get into a war their sons will be called up and trained to shoot other people. Horrible!"

I add: "We certainly live in a horrible world. One of my professors, Lise Meitner, who has recommended this spot as a beautiful holiday destination – as you may recall – fled Germany just before we left Berlin. She does not feel safe in Germany anymore, simply because she is a Jew. She has a very sharp mind and she and Otto Hahn are a formidable team. He and some of his colleagues has helped her to reach the border with Holland and from there she went to Sweden where she got a job at the

University of Stockholm. Otto Hahn got a card from her saying that she arrived safely there. Our loss – and Stockholm's gain.

Berlin, Thursday, 29 September 1938

David:

We sit in our apartment for dinner. It is my and Josephine's turn to prepare the meal. Next week it will be the turn of Annemarie and Willie.

While we are busy in the kitchen, we listen to the radio news. We hear the Führer's voice. He is jubilant because he has reached an agreement with Joseph Chamberlain, Prime Minister of Great Britain, Édouard Daladier, the French Prime Minister and Bennito Mussolini, the Duce of Italy, that Sudetenland, a part of Czechoslovakia, is to become part of Greater Germany. Sudetenland was part of the Austro-Hungarian Reich before the Great War and most of the inhabitants regard themselves as Germans.

We also hear that Chamberlain proclaims his satisfaction regarding the agreement that was reached after a one-day conference in Munich because the agreement will mean peace in our time.

It is clear to our minds that Hitler threatened with a military invasion of the Sudetenland if the other powers did not agree with his demands. This agreement simply means that nobody will come to the aid of little Czechoslovakia if Hitler simply annexes the Sudeten districts and make them part of the Third German Reich.

I think aloud while looking at the two girls: "We certainly don't like everything the Nazis do. But it is clear that Hitler has achieved much for the German people. I am sure that he will visit the annexed parts of Czechoslovakia in the foreseeable future and that the people will greet him with enthusiasm – just as happened in Vienna. You have regained your national pride. I hope that our people in South Africa will achieve the same."

There is applause for my short speech.

Berlin, Thursday, 10 November 1938

*

David:

The four of us are sitting in our apartment in the Dorotheenstraße. All are ready to help with preparations for dinner, which is to take place in our place this week.

But before we can proceed, I produce a letter from my father that I have found in our post box at the entrance of the building. I open the letter and read aloud for all to hear:

> Kimberley,
> 5 November 1938

> My dear sons and daughters-in-law,
> Thank you for your letter of 1 November. I am very proud of you for the progress you are making towards the attainment of your doctorates. If you are able to realize your dreams some or other time next year I and your mother wish to attend those occasions. You will be the first members of our direct family to achieve doctorates, although I have read in the newspaper that your distant cousin, Gerrit Scholtz, has received his doctor's degree in Amsterdam already two years ago. He works presently as a journalist at Die Volksblad, the Afrikaans newspaper for the Free State.

Willie interjects: "So, he hasn't realized his ideal of becoming a professor of history yet. Sorry."

> Anyway, it will be fairly easy for us to attend your graduation ceremonies. As I have told you, the German airline, Deutsche Lufthansa, has started with a weekly service

between Berlin and the coastal city of Durban and that will be how we will travel to Germany.

Please find enclosed four tickets for you to travel to South Africa early in December. The laying of the cornerstone of the planned monument to the achievements of our forebears, the Voortrekkers, will take place on 16 December in Pretoria. The festivities will already start two days before the time.

And then you are to spend Christmas with us at the farm before you return to Germany.

This will be a wonderful opportunity of meeting our German daughters-in-law. I repeat: we are extremely glad that you have managed to capture two beautiful Protestant Germanic girls – to judge from their photographs – to strengthen our Afrikaner stock.

Your loving father and mother,
Pieter and Isabella Scholtz

Directly after I have completed, Josephine exclaims: "Wonderful! I have understood more or less everything. So – we are to travel to your country during December! Annemarie, I can see on your face that you are also excited. Very, very nice."

Annemarie smiles: "I cannot wait to meet your family and see your father's farm!" She grabs me and we make a few dancing movements.

Our excitement evaporates a little later when we switch the radio on to listen to the news. It is reported that dozens of SA men have attacked Jewish businesses and synagogues throughout the country last night. They smashed windows and looted the shops. According to the newscast, this step is well-deserved since the Jews have to be blamed for all the ills that have befallen the German people. Now they are receiving their just reward for their purported crimes. Due to the fact that so much broken glass lay strewn on the sidewalks, the event was dubbed the "Kristallnacht" (crystal night).

The eyes of the two girls are suddenly filled with tears. Josephine wails: "I feel utterly ashamed. These SA hooligans don't represent the German people. Poor Jews. What will happen to them and their children?"

Willie embraces his sobbing wife: "I think that we must leave this country directly after we have received our doctorates. We cannot stay here. We love Germany and the German people. We have only experienced friendliness and love here. But if things continue this way, we cannot raise our kids here. When will war break out so that we will get stuck here?"

I add: "It seems as if war is inevitable. I only hope that Hitler will be able to humiliate the hated British if it comes to that."

Pretoria, Friday, 16 December 1938

Willie:

The whole Scholtz family – that is, my parents, my elder brothers and sister, together with the "German" branch of the family – are enduring the heat of the December sun at the outskirts of Pretoria, the capital of South Africa, where the cornerstone of the Voortrekker Monument is to be laid by three elderly granddaughters of leaders of the Voortrekkers.

The tent village outside Pretoria during the laying of the foundation stone of the Voortrekker Monument, December 1938. People wore the clothes of a century ago

We are staying in tents in order to copy the lifestyle of these pioneers who trekked into the wild interior of South Africa to flee the British administration of the Cape Colony and to establish two free republics – which were invaded by the power-hungry British during the South African War of 1899 to 1902. The Voortrekkers defeated the perfidious Zulu king, Dingane, on 16 December 1838, exactly a century ago and, therefore, today is a fitting occasion to commemorate this event. During the past two days we heard much about our past and the Voortrekker heroes.

Our two wives enjoyed the flight to the port city of Durban very much. It was our first experience of flying. Our parents met us at the airport and we took the train from Durban to Pretoria. Our parents were overwhelmed by their new daughters-in-law who could understand Afrikaans and could even speak a few sentences of Afrikaans. When they got stuck, they switched to Plattdeutsch, which my family could more or less understand if spoken slowly. My father repeatedly voiced his satisfaction with our good taste in women.

The atmosphere during the festival is electric. Everybody is proud of our Afrikaner heritage and it is clear that we have gotten rid of the humiliation of the defeat of the two Boer republics by the English four decades ago. We can shrug it off should an Englishman refer to us as 'dirty Dutchmen'.

Josephine has picked up this atmosphere: "What is happening here reminds me of the Olympic Games two years ago. Then, suddenly, it was pleasant to be a German. We were all proud of our accomplishments. I get the same feeling here."

Annemarie adds: "I am sorry that we didn't bring our folk costumes along. All these people wear their traditional clothes. We would not have been out of place if we wore our "Dirndls" (folk dresses)."

Suddenly a voice behind us greets us in German. We turn around and, to our surprise, our distant cousin, Gerrit greets us with a broad smile and gleaming teeth: "And what you doing here? Have you fled Berlin to get away from the Nazis?"

I reply: "Of course, we are very concerned about what happened on Kristallnacht. But we didn't flee. We still have to complete our studies before we can settle in this country again. But, let me introduce you to Frau Scholtz and Frau Scholtz. That one is my sister-in-law and the other one is my brother's sister-in-law."

Gerrit looks puzzled.

I add: "And the two girls are also sisters-in-law of each other.

Before Gerrit can say anything, Josephine suddenly gives him a hug, which he didn't expect: "Gerrit, you are also my distant cousin now. Of course, we are now two married couples. Annemarie, who is my best friend, is also my sister-in-law. In case you have forgotten, we have met in Berlin a few years ago. And what are you doing here?"

"I cannot stay away. This is a big occasion for us Afrikaners. But I am also here for the wedding of my younger sister. A number of couples are to be married here on this auspicious day. My sister is marrying a young minister of religion whom she met at Stellenbosch."

We all four echo simultaneously: "Herzliche Glüchwünsche. Are you going to be the best man of the bridegroom?"

"Yes, and that is why I am dressed like a Voortrekker and have grown a beard."

Over Africa, Tuesday, 27 December 1938

David:

We are airborne again on our way from Durban to Berlin. The flight takes two days with the stops in-between. Before our departure, I happened to approach one of the pilots and asked him why they do not start the flight in Johannesburg or Pretoria, but from the coastal city of Durban.

His reply made sense: "The air here down at the coast is much thicker than in the interior. That makes it easier to become airborne and then we use less fuel. Simple, isn't it?"

We are staring at the African bush below us through the port-holes of the Focke-Wulf 200 Condor, a giant aircraft with four engines – the pride of the German aircraft industry.

Josephine remarks: "My bottom is still sore from the saddle on your father's horse. It was my first time that I sat on the back of a horse in my life."

"My bottom feels the same. It is many years since I have ridden a horse. But when we go back to the farm sometime in the future, I will teach you how to handle a horse properly. We only rode at a walking pace while exploring our father's farm."

"I loved those open spaces with hardly any sign of human habitation. I suppose, that is more or less how the world looked when the Voortrekkers settled in those parts a century ago."

"Actually, my forebears settled on that farm even before the time of the Voortrekkers. The Cape Colony could no longer provide farms for all the sons of the farmers and these sons simply trekked across the Orange River and settled on empty land beyond the Orange River, which formed the border of the Colony in those days."

"Now we must get used to the cold of the German winter again when we celebrate Silvester with my parents in a few days' time. I have never experienced such harsh sunlight than during our stay at Pretoria or the farm. You have promised to take me to Cape Town when we come back to your country. It is my wish to climb Table Mountain with you. Do you promise again?"

"Of course, my love. I always keep my promises."

Berlin, Friday, 6 January 1939

Willie:

We came back to Berlin three days ago. I started working again at the Kaiser Wilhelm Institute the day before yesterday.

This morning, Herr Professor Otto Hahn called the whole research team on nuclear physics to his laboratory. He held a copy of *Die Naturwissenschaften*. the German scientific journal. in his hand: "You may congratulate me and Herr Professor Strassmann. We have published an article in this journal regarding the results of our experiments. Actually, you should also congratulate Frau Professor Lise Meitner, who also collaborated on this project, but no German journal will publish anything with her name on it, due to this mad prejudice against the Jews. Anyway, this article describes that we have managed to split atoms. Democritus, the old Greek philosopher, coined the name 'atom' for the smallest bits of matter that cannot be divided into anything smaller. The word 'atom' actually means 'that which cannot be cut up'. But we have proved Democritus wrong. We have bombarded a uranium atom with protons and it broke up into two atoms of barium. This process is called 'fission' and I believe that this introduces a new chapter in the history of nuclear physics."

We all applaud Otto Hahn and proceed to shake his hand. This article certainly makes him the second most famous scientist in the world, after Albert Einstein. I feel proud to share this moment and to be one of Hahn's disciples.

Hardanger, Monday, 3 July 1939

David:

Last month I proposed that we don't go mountaineering in the Alps again. There are other jolly interesting destinations. How about Norway?

The other three immediately looked interested and my Josephine exclaimed: "Then we can go and explore the land where our Germanic gods had their abode!"

Willie added: "Hurrah! You just demonstrated that you and I are capable of original ideas – not only on a scientific level, but also on a personal level. I second your proposal. Any votes against this proposal?"

The Hardanger Fjord

No objections were raised. And now were are having the biggest adventure of our lives. We are exploring the mountains and fjords of the Hardanger region of southern Norway. We got here by train via Copenhagen and a ferry between Skagen on the northern point of Denmark and Kristiansand on the southern point of Norway.

Norway is a beautiful, wild and rugged country. There are mountains, rivers, lakes and waterfalls all over the place. Most people are able to speak some German. Although Norwegian is supposed to be a Germanic language, we don't understand a word of it. The people are generally poor, but very friendly and hospitable. Their log cabins resemble the chalets of the Alpine regions.

Unfortunately, we cannot stay very long. We can only afford a holiday of ten days. I and my brother are getting nearer and nearer to our ideal of achieving our doctorates. We have both started to write our theses and our dear wives help us with the German grammar when we sometimes struggle. We hope to graduate during September or October after our referees have scrutinized our theses and we have defended our theses before our respective faculties.

Berlin, Friday, 1 September 1939

Willie:

The four of us arrived more or less at the same time at the doors of our apartments. I and Annemarie are supposed to prepare dinner, but it is not really possible. All look downhearted and I propose: "I think you will all agree that we ought to have an official family meeting, right now." Nobody protests and we all enter our living room.

I start the meeting formally: "'Bitte, meine Damen und Herr' (Please, dear ladies and gentleman), I can understand that today was a very bad and shocking day for all of us. I would like to hear what you have experienced."

Annemarie sobs: "I really have a sad story. But do tell us your sad story first."

"All right. On my bicycle en route to the Kaiser Wilhelm Institute I could not help but to see the newspaper placards telling the whole city that war has broken out and that the Wehrmacht has invaded Poland. When I arrived at the Kaiser Wilhelm Institute, I found a note on my desk from Herr Professor Otto Hahn that a meeting was to be held in the common room. Only researchers involved with nuclear physics were invited."

My curious brother wants to know: "Did he tell you that all of you have been called up for service in the Wehrmacht?"

"Almost something like that. He told us that the commander of the 'Heereswaffenamt' (Munitions Office of the Army), General der Artillerie Karl Becker, phoned him early this morning and requested that his research team develop an atomic bomb under the greatest secrecy. We are to cooperate with the 'Abteilung Sondergerät' (Department of Special Tools) to develop this weapon. For that reason, his research team is to be code-named the 'Uranverein' (Uranium Club) henceforth. Another meeting with researchers from other universities is to be held in a few days' time where plans are to be made how our research has to be parceled out. By the way, this is secret and I am not supposed to tell you this. So, keep it under wraps."

My brother's astonishment is clearly visible on his face: "And he invited you, although you are not even a German!"

"That's correct. I asked him at the conclusion of the meeting to see Otto Hahn for a moment in his office. There I told him my dilemma. How can I, as a foreigner, be involved in this highly secret project? He looked me in the eye and said: 'Herr Scholtz, your doctoral dissertation has already been approved. The only formality is that you will have to defend it before the Faculty of Natural Sciences and then you will become Herr Doktor Scholtz. You have so much knowledge of our research up to this moment that it is unthinkable that we can allow you to return home.' He added that it is to be expected that Britain will declare war against Germany within the next few days and that South Africa will follow. He knows that I am married to a German woman and my anti-British feelings are well-known and, therefore, he automatically assumed that I would agree to cooperate with the Uranverein."

Annemarie cannot believe what she heard: "So, you are actually going to help the Wehrmacht? What is going to happen with our plans to go to South Africa after your graduation? What will happen with your parent's plan to attend tour graduation?"

"My dear wife, those plans will have to be shelved indefinitely. Unfortunately. It just can't be helped. We don't know how long this war will last. I assume that all the borders have been closed, except for people with special passes. All I know is that I will graduate next week and that I have no choice but to fall in with Professor Hahn's plans."

"So, you have no choice in the matter?"

"No, unfortunately not. Professor Hahn told me in no uncertain terms that if I don't cooperate, I will be thrown into a concentration camp since I am a citizen of a country at war with Germany. I told him that no concentration camp will see me. The idea of a concentration camp is a British invention, which they used during the war of 1899 to 1902 to keep thousands upon thousands of innocent civilians captive and that thousands of those innocent women and children died in those camps. An aged uncle of my father was one of the victims."

David asks: "How did he react?"

"He simply said: 'Then you stay a member of the Uranverein. I will inform General Becker that I wish to have you , that you are eager to work with us and that he has no choice in the matter'."

Annemarie sobs: "Then we are stuck here for the duration. I have already sent in my letter of resignation to the Dresdner Bank. I will have to retract it. Will we be able to keep these apartments?"

"Yes, we are staying just here in Berlin so that I can continue my post-doctoral work at the Institute and aid the development of the German atomic bomb. Actually, I am not too unwilling to do that because I will aid the Germans to take revenge on Britain, that perfidious Albion."

Josephine asks her husband: "And what did you experience today?"

"On my way to the University Clinic I could not help to notice the newspaper placards that war has broken out. Because I still had some time before I had to be at the Clinic, I went to the dean of our Faculty of Medicine, Herr Professor Friedrich Falke. He was relieved to see me. He said: 'Herr Scholtz, this is a sad day for our country. We are again at war. And this concerns you intimately.' He pointed out that I am not a German citizen and it is likely that my country, together with the British, will declare war against Germany for invading Poland. I, as a foreigner, will most probably end up in a concentration camp.

"I must have looked very downhearted and he tried to console me. His words were: 'I will do my best to keep you out of a concentration camp.' One argument that he could use is that my dissertation has been accepted by the referees and all that still has to happen is that I defend it before the faculty next week. After that, I am supposed to be a highly qualified specialist surgeon. It is just possible that I can be of service of Germany during the war. In wartime there are many wounded civilians and soldiers and it might perhaps just be possible that he can convince the authorities that I don't deserve to go to a concentration camp. He told me to come back on Monday and that he might have some news for me then."

Josephine says: "So there is a chance that you won't be thrown into a concentration camp?"

"Let's hope so. I also told the honorable dean that my people suffered far too much in British concentration camps during the South African War. Our women and children died like flies due to malnutrition and epidemics sweeping the camps. There were funerals almost on a daily basis."

I add: "That was also my point. So, your dean thinks that you as a surgeon may aid the German war effort?"

"Yes, that seems to be the case. Therefore, I and my dear wife are also stuck in Germany for the duration. God knows how long that will be. At least, I will be able to get my own back at the British for what they did to our people, albeit in a very indirect way."

Josephine grabs me around my neck: "I am greatly relieved that you will be spared a concentration camp. I will also retract my resignation from the gymnasium. Our school will certainly need all the teachers we can use because I suppose that most of our male staff members will be called up for military service."

It is Annemarie's turn to speak: "I want all of you to help me with dinner. David, you can lay the table and remember to take out the 'Sekt' (champaigne) glasses. Josephine, will you please peel the potatoes and wash the salad? I will roast the sausages and the potatoes. Willi, you will run out to the Konditorei and get some 'Schwalzwälder Kirschtorte' (Black Forrest Tart) for pudding? We must celebrate the fact that you won't go to concentration camps and that you are to receive your doctorates next week.

PART 2

SS SURGEON

The Story of David Scholtz

Berlin, Tuesday, 5 September 1939

Yesterday, Monday, I went back to Herr Professor Falcke before I had to report at the Clinic for the day's operations. Yesterday was also the day on which Britain and France declared war against Germany.

Falcke told me briefly: "You are to report to the headquarters of the Schützstaffel or SS tomorrow at eight o' clock sharp. Ask for 'Generalstabsarzt' (medical practitioner with a rank equivalent to Lieutenant-General) Grawitz. He is awaiting your visit."

It is with a fair amount of trepidation that I walk to the SS Headquarters at 8 Prinz-Albrecht-Straße in the inner city. The SS is notorious as the bodyguard of Hitler and the guards at concentration camps. It is also a quasi-military force with uniforms and fire-arms. If they want me to become an Arzt in a concentration camp then I will do my best to wriggle out of such a position. It is an open secret that conditions in the German concentration's camps are hideous. There is, for instance, such a camp at Brandenburg an der Havel, not too far from Annemarie's father's paper mill.

It is ten minutes before eight o' clock that I enter the building and I show my "Personalausweis" (identity document) to the sentry, who directs me to the reception desk down the passage. I tell the uniformed clerk there that I have an appointment with Generalstabsarzt Grawitz. He also checks my Personalausweis. He lifts his phone and dials a number. After mumbling a few words, he orders me to wait. I remain standing on one side.

A few minutes later another uniformed orderly comes to fetch me and I enter the office of Generalstabsarzt Grawitz. He smiles – and I don't know whether to feel relieved or afraid – and he invites me to sit down opposite him. He orders the orderly to bring us some coffee, and I interpret that as a good sign.

After having shaken my hand, he starts: "Herr Scholtz, or should I rather say, Herr *Doktor* Scholtz, thank you for taking the trouble of coming to see me. My old friend from university days, Herr Professor Falcke, has informed me about you. I gather that you are willing to help our glorious war effort against the forces of evil that confront us. I was also told that you harbor no love for the British. We can use you in the medical service of the SS. Where would you like to serve?"

"Herr Generalstabsarzt, thank you for giving me some of your precious time. I can imagine that you must be very busy at this crucial time in German history. Yes, I am no friend of the British and I certainly would like to see them humiliated. You are certainly aware of how they robbed our two Boer republics of their independence and made sure that our gold mines and diamond mines came under British control."

Grawitz smiles: "I also heard that you have Prussian ancestors and that you are married to an Aryan German woman. Wonderful. Am I correct in assuming that you are very eager to join our war effort?"

"Yes, you are correct," I assure him, while secretly telling myself that I have absolutely no choice in the matter.

"All right. Let me give you some information about the SS. We started simply as the 'Leibstandarte' (unit of body guards) of Adolf Hitler, but we have grown into the police force of the National-Socialist Party. Our members also receive military training. We are planning to put some SS regiments in the field, together with the Wehrmacht. Four SS regiments are already fighting right now in Poland. Of course, our men will be the elite troops. We need medical officers for these regiments. What type of regiment would you like to become part of? Infantry, artillery, Panzer, transport, 'Pionieren' (sappers) or communications?"

"Are there any SS mountain troops? I and my twin brother are avid mountaineers. We also learned how to ski."

"I am sure that will be possible. The 'Heer' (Army) has a number of 'Gebirgsdivisionen' (mountain divisions) and the SS will certainly also have mountain units in future. But, first of all: you will have to get your graduation done with. I heard that that will happen later this week.

For the time being, you continue with your work at the University Clinic and the Krankenhaus Moabit and on Monday, 2 October, you are to report at the SS barracks, here in Berlin. There you will be trained as an SS medical officer. Your call-up papers will be given to you immediately after this. Since you are not a German citizen you cannot be drafted into the Wehrmacht. There is, though, nothing to prevent you from becoming a member of the SS."

Generalstabsarzt und SS Gruppenführer (Lieutenant General) Ernst-Robert Grawitz, head of the SS medical corps

"Will I be required to fight against Britain?"

"That may certainly be possible."

"I would rather not, please. I hope you understand my position. I would very much like to take revenge on the British for all their crimes against my people. But should it happen that I be captured by British soldiers – and it happens all the time during a war that men get captured – then I will certainly be shot or hanged as a traitor. I hope you understand that I would like to prevent such a situation."

"I have never thought about that. I am sure that there will be other fronts. I suppose our men will be fighting against the French soon. Perhaps we can deploy you there. But that can be sorted out in more detail after you have completed your training. I wish you luck with your work on behalf of our glorious Fatherland! Or do you perhaps prefer to be kept in a concentration camp for the duration of the war as a national of a country at war with us?"

He leaves his chair behind his desk and I take that as the sign that I am dismissed and I do not reply to his last question. I interpret that as a threat that I had better do my bit.

That afternoon I report back to the other three: "You will not believe it, but I am going to become a member of the SS! That, or an inmate of a concentration camp…"

My wife does not smile.

Berlin, Monday, 2 October 1939

I arrive at the SS barracks on the western outskirts of Berlin. These barracks turn out to be part of the Olympic Village of 1936 that has been converted for use by the SS Medical Academy. I had to take a bus to reach this point. I have taken the minimum luggage since I suspect that I will be supplied with everything I need.

I queue behind a long line of young men who all wish to become part of the SS Sanitätsdienst. I suppose that most of them will become medical orderlies, stretcher bearers and ambulance drivers. I also see a few faces of students who have graduated from the Faculty of Medicine of the Berlin University. Presumably, there are also a number of qualified medical practitioners who studied elsewhere.

At a desk two burly SS officials sit and check our call-up papers and identity documents. I am told to proceed to Block A where all the medical practitioners are to congregate. The rest of the men are distributed throughout the rest of the barracks.

We are a group of about fifty men in Block A. We stand around, not knowing what to do and we start to introduce ourselves to each other. Most of them have only recently completed their training as "Hausarzt" (family physician), but three of us are specialists. I am the only specialist surgeon, while the other two, who come from Munich, are gynecologists. I suppose that the SS needs gynecologists because there may be female SS members and nurses in the hospitals who have to be kept healthy.

Suddenly we hear a loud voice at the entrance: "Achtung! Achtung!" (Attention! Attention!). We are called to form three rows outside and then we are marched to the quarter-master's store. The loud voice belongs to an individual who introduces himself as "Hauptscharführer" (Staff Sergeant) Dralle. "I will be in charge of you silly lot for the foreseeable future. I am to lick you into shape. You will always address me as 'Hauptscharführer.' Verstanden? (do you understand?)" Nobody replies and he scowls.

We are kitted out with full uniforms, toilet kits, blankets, pillows, linen, a lock to secure our metal lockers and writing materials (supposedly for the lectures that we will have to endure). Each has his photograph taken for his SS membership card.

After this we are marched back to Block A. Hauptscharführer Dralle shouts: "Get dressed in your uniforms! Report to the recruits' mess in half-an-hour from now!"

We scramble to secure beds and metal lockers to store our belongings. I get a bed as far as possible from the entrance and from the bathrooms, which are placed next to the entrance. It will certainly be quieter here at the back. While I get dressed in my new charcoal uniform the chap next to me remarks: "If we were in the Army, we would have had the rank of 'Fahnenjunker' (Assistant Candidate Officer). It is the equivalent of an 'Unteroffizier' (Corporal). This is what our shoulder straps tell me. I wonder what the SS calls this rank. I suppose we will hear shortly."

We are served lunch in the mess. The other recruits, who presumably would become medics, stretcher bearers and ambulance drivers in due course, sit at their own tables. They do not have any rank insignias.

After we have gobbled up our lunch, Dralle appears and orders us out. It is time for roll-call: "Now that you have eaten the grub the SS and the Reich have given you and also that the SS and the Reich have clothed you, you are the property of the SS. As I read your names out, you are to step forward and form a long line. SS-Junker Albrecht, Jonas!" Herr Doktor Albrecht steps forward. "SS-Junker Andreas, Wilhelm!" Herr Doktor Andreas joins Herr Doktor Albrecht. "No, you idiot! To his left! Do you know which side of you is right or left? If you don't know, I will knock that into your square skull! You are supposed to know a little bit of human anatomy, or am I mistaken?"

It takes a long time before "SS-Junker Scholtz, David!" is called. By this time everyone knows that we have the rank of SS-Junker.

Dralle yells again: "Now you are to form three ranks! Every second man is to stand behind the first man and the third man is to stand behind number two! Number four shifts up and gets next to number one! I hope you imbeciles are able to count properly! And you continue along these lines!"

It takes a few minutes for us to form up as ordered. Dralle yells again: "Now you, slime balls! Listen! Every time you are to form a 'Schar' (squad or troop), each one is to occupy exactly the same place as today! Verstanden?"

No one replies. Dralle becomes white in the face. "You useless lumps of shit, every time I ask you a question, you are to shout, 'Jawohl, Herr Hauptscharführer!' And remember, every time you address me you stand at attention with your eyes fixed on a spot a meter above my head. Verstanden?"

We all shout: "Jawohl, Herr Hauptscharführer!"

"Do that again! You were not together. You sounded like a lot of bloody kids from a third-rate Kindergarten. Behave like SS men! Verstanden?"

We all shout again, this time in unison: "Jawohl, Herr Hauptscharführer!"

"Now we are going to teach you how to march. Scholtz, do you know which foot is your left foot? Show me!"

I shout: "Jawohl, Herr Hauptscharführer!" I lift my left foot up.

Dralle continues: "Plose, do you have enough brain cells inside your thick skull to distinguish your right hand from your left hand? Show me your right hand!"

Plose complies in the correct manner.

The rest of the afternoon is taken up with marching up and down. Later, Dralle's voice gives in. One of our guys in the back row shouts: "Herr Hauptscharführer! I have some bonbons in my locker. Would you like some for your throat?"

Dralle becomes red in the face and he croaks: "Who is that fucking idiot who spoke out of his turn? Come here, immediately." The poor guy gets out of the ranks and walks leisurely forward. Dralle manages to screech: "You rotten piece of horse dung! Whenever you move around in uniform you march properly by swinging your arms! Who in hell are you?"

The poor victim answers: "Krebs, Herr Hauptscharführer!"

"Now, if you don't behave properly in future, I will see to it that you contract a severe case of Krebs (cancer). Verstanden?"

"Jawohl, Herr Hauptscharführer!"

"What type of medical phenomenon are you?"

"Herr Hauptscharführer, I am a specialist gynecologist."

Dralle is utterly speechless. And we others can't help to grin.

"Quiet, you lot!", he manages to get out.

We shout in unison: "Jawohl, Herr Hauptscharführer!"

"And what is a gynecologist doing in the SS?"

"My job is to catch babies and help ladies with their health, Herr Hauptscharführer!"

Dralle does not know how to respond and he orders with a funny voice: "Get in line, Krebs." After he has done that, Dralle demonstrates to us how we are to dismiss and he tries to bark with a squeaking voice: "Schar, do your duty, dismiss!"

Berlin, Tuesday, 3 October 1939

After dinner last night, we were ordered to go to our blocks. After breakfast, this morning, we march again for an hour around the grounds. We have to practice the Nazi salute by raising the right arm to 45 degrees and shout "Heil Hitler!" We do it twenty times before Dralle is satisfied.

Then Dralle, who has regained his voice, shouts: "Form a long line, alphabetically! Verstanden?"

As a trained choir, we respond: "Jawohl, Herr Hauptscharführer!"

"Now you are to enter that door in front of Albrecht! In single file! And then you go and sit down in the lecture hall! Alphabetically! Verstanden?"

We respond again in an appropriate manner.

In the lecture room a senior officer awaits us. He dismisses Dralle and he introduces himself: "Gentlemen, I am 'Oberstarzt (Colonel Physician) Michael Meinhardt. My rank is equivalent to that of a SS 'Standartenführer' (colonel). I am the commanding officer of the Academy. I want to welcome you here. I need not remind you of the state of affairs in which Germany finds herself at the moment. We need your expertise dearly and thank you for volunteering to join the SS Sanitätendienst. You will receive lectures in military medicine. You will do practical work in hospitals that will count as your internships, if you haven't done that yet. As you might know, the other half of this former Olympic Village was converted into a hospital where we help out. You will also get some training to become combat soldiers. Although you will mostly work at field dressing stations behind the battle lines, it may sometimes be necessary to defend yourself. Any questions at this stage?"

Nobody ventures a question. Robert Rohwald, who sits next to me, whispers: "It is nice to be treated as a professional by a fellow professional." I nod in acknowledgement.

Oberstarzt Meinhardt introduces us to "Stabsarzt" (staff physician) Willi Janeke who will give most of the lectures in military medicine. He explains that his rank is equivalent to that of "Hauptsturmfüher", which is the same as "Hauptmann" in the Army.

Janeke thanks Meinhardt for the introduction and immediately proceeds: "I have looked at all your files. It appears that we have a specialist surgeon in our midst. Herr SS-Junker Doktor Scholtz, please stand up so that we can all see you."

I stand up for a moment and all turn their heads to see who I am.

"It is, indeed, fortunate that we can have you. You will help these men to become better surgeons on the battle field. I understand that you are a specialist on knees and legs. We can use that expertise very well. Please be ready to take some lectures. You will also demonstrate your techniques on patents for all of us to see. Are you ready for that?"

I can only nod my head, too astonished to utter a word.

Berlin, Monday, 6 November 1939

It is Monday morning and a rather chilly autumn wind is blowing across the parade ground. Dralle is marching us up and down and makes us perform all sorts of difficult manoeuvers. All the exercise helps us to keep warm. After an hour Dralle announces a smoke break. We may sit down on the parade ground and those of us who are smokers are allowed to light up their cigarettes. It is clear that Dralle has a hang-over, most probably due to drinking too much over the weekend and that is why he announced this pause.

Krebs, the gynecologist, asks with a friendly tone: "Herr Hauptscharführer, if I my ask: which type of liquor would you, in your expert opinion, recommend to us if we want to go on a binge? Wine, Schnapps, beer, vodka or what?"

It is clear that Dralle likes this subject: "I only drink Schnapps. Vodka is bad for you because the Russians drink it and look what has become of their country! No, Schnapps is best. It is a pure German product and I love it. To tell you the truth, I emptied two bottles yesterday!"

Krebs looks interested: "Herr Hauptscharführer, that must be a wonderful achievement. I am sure that I will never be able to keep up with you."

"My boy, I am sure that few people will be able to keep up with me when we celebrate. Over this week-end, I had to celebrate the victories of our glorious Wehrmacht in Poland."

Krebs looks concerned: "Herr Hauptscharführer, our Schar really doesn't want you to get health problems. Are you aware of the fact that your fallopian tubes can get seriously damaged or blocked by drinking too much Schnapps? Scientific experiments have shown this time and again to be the case."

"What can I do to protect my fucking fallopian tubes?"

"Medical experts have found an antidote. Take lots of dehydrated water, three times a day."

"Thank you for that generous advice. For a blooming recruit you do seem to be not too stupid."

It takes lots of self-control not to grin.

Berlin, Tuesday, 7 November 1939

It is Tuesday morning and we get into line again for our morning parade.

Dralle appears with an evil look on his face: "Today all of you medical people are going to get a taste of what the results are when you make fun of a senior non-commissioned officer, like me! You are all going to shit bricks! Krebs, you wise guy, I went to our medical post and asked the orderlies for dehydrated water to help my fallopian tubes, as you advised. You friggin frog's ass! You and your mates who are accomplices will sweat today! Half of you will beg for mercy after an hour and the other half will have passed out by that time!"

Krebs shouts; "Herr Hauptscharführer! We only have your welfare at heart!"

"Quiet, you stupid toad! You will wish that you never studied gynecology if I am finished with you!"

Krebs, nonetheless, ventures: "Herr Hauptscharführer! You can count on me and my mates to give you sound advice. We don't want you to drop dead."

"Krebs, you look like a bloody fairy! You are only to speak when spoken to! Please tell me where my fallopian tubes are situated, you imbecile! In case you as an idiotic medical specialist didn't know – only fucking women have bloody fallopian tubes! And I dare you to drink a shitty jug of dehydrated water! That blinking jug will be totally empty! So, all of you quacks, lie down on your stomachs! Leopard crawl to the other end of the blooming parade ground!"

We have no choice but to comply but nobody can keep his smile a secret.

Berlin, Monday, 4 December 1939

We are back at the barracks on this Monday morning after we did some cross-country marching the past four days. We are still stiff and sore of carrying heavy rucksacks with supplies for four days, together with a heavy machine gun and ammunition and heavy coats for the cold winter wind with heavy steel helmets on our heads. We had to sleep under trees to simulate battle conditions.

And now we are standing ready for our daily parade with Hauptscharführer Dralle, awaiting his orders for marching us around. One of our men, Karl Niehaus, calls out: "Herr Hauptscharführer! Permission to speak?"

Dralle does not seem very eager to hear what Niehaus has to say, but he cannot ignore the request either: "Yes, what is it? Do you have another complaint? Do you want to report sick?"

"No, Herr Hauptscharführer. No complaints. I am not sick, either. But a few of us have noticed that your cheeks are very white and pale this morning. We have discussed your condition and we are of the opinion that you must have an overabundance of white blood cells."

"What in hell is that? What's so bad about that?"

"Herr Hauptscharführer, an overabundance of white blood cells can cause blindness or sexual impotence. I am sure that you don't want that to happen!"

"Yes, wise guy, what do you recommend to get rid of this problem?"

"Herr Hauptscharführer, it's advisable that you take some anorexia syrup twice daily, with meals. Another option is an autopsy, but you are entitled to refuse that type of operation."

"Is an autopsy painful?"

"In most cases, no."

"Ha! If you are making fun of me again you will regret it."

Berlin, Tuesday, 5 December 1939

We all wait in suspense to see what the reaction of Dralle will be regarding the medical advice dispensed to him yesterday. We stand at ease in our formation and await his arrival.

"Achtung! Achtung! You stupid lot! Today you will shit a mixture of syrup and white blood cells! I am going to give you a special type of exercise that you may need when you are on a battle field. Imagine that your right leg has been wounded and you cannot use it. You have to hop around on your left leg. We are going to practice that maneuver now! All of you medical scum! Stand on your left legs and lift your right legs so that the upper part of the leg is horizontal. Verstanden?"

"Yes, Herr Hauptschardfüher!", we all shout in unison.

"Then do it at the count of three! One! Two! Three!"

We obey.

"Now, hop one step forward on your left legs!"

We obey.

"Another step on your left leg – and, stay in formation, you crippled lot!"

We obey. And the angry Hauptscharführer keeps us going for the next fifteen minutes in this fashion. A few men just cannot go on anymore and fall over, too exhausted to use their left legs anymore. Dralle stops the exercise.

"Now, you silly lot, you slimy bits of excrement! Get into line again, but stand at attention. Verstanden?"

"Yes, Herr Hauptscharführer!"

"I notice that Niehaus is one of those who fell out, too much of a softy to carry on. My dear chap, you will never do in a war situation. Niehaus!"

Niehaus replies: "Yes, Herr Hauptscharführer!"

"On the double! You are to run as fast as possible, without falling, to the first aid station and fetch some bottles of anorexia syrup for all those of you sorry lot who have fallen down during the exercise! Get going!"

Niehaus doesn't know what to do and grins stupidly.

"You stupid idiot! You paralyzed ape! Get going! We need twelve doses of anorexia! You will know where to get them! Get moving!"

Niehaus has no option but to start limping towards the first aid station. The rest of us cannot help to grin widely. Good for old Dralle! He got us back!

Dralle shouts: "Wipe those stupid grins from your faces, you brainless oafs! The next idiot who grins again, will hop on his left leg for the next ten minutes!"

Niehaus returns after five minutes and stands at attention in front of Dralle: "Herr Hauptscharführer! I have just been informed that they are out of stock. The next batch is only expected after Christmas!"

We cannot help but to laugh out loudly.

Dralle gets a cruel grin on his face: "On you left legs! Hop one step forward, all at the same time on the count of three! One! Two! Three!"

Berlin, Friday, 30 August 1940

Today, Friday, our passing-out parade is to take place. It has been a long and difficult eleven months of training, studying, working and training. I am extremely fit, due to all the marches that we had to undertake and the manoeuvers in the countryside that we had to attend, often in the snow. Apart from knowing how to treat wounded and sick soldiers on the battle field, I am familiar with the use of various types of fire-arm. We were also taught how to manage hygiene in the field.

I got very little leave. I saw my Josephine for the first time just before Christmas and after that only for another few weekends. We visited her parents on Christmas but I had to report back for further training on 2 January. During the eleven months, we were steadily promoted from being "SS-Junkers" to "SS-Oberjunkers" and eventually to "SS-Standartenjunkers". This last rank is the equivalent of a "Fähnrich" (ensign or candidate officer) in the Army and the rank insignia are the same as for "Oberscharführer" or "Oberfeldwebel" (sergeant).

Today, the members of our Schar are to be promoted to officer status, namely "Assistenzarzt" (Assistant Physician), which is the equivalent of a "Untersturmführer" or second lieutenant. We will be given shoulder straps with a small golden staff with a snake and our corps color is blue.

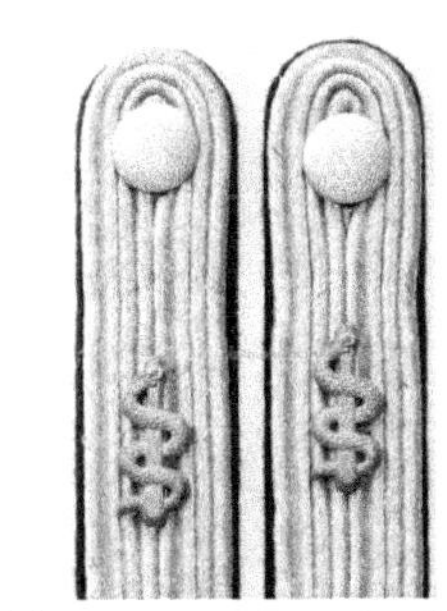

Shoulder straps of an Assistenzarz

We were told that the SS regiments that took part in the campaign in Poland were grouped together in a SS division and that this fighting branch of the SS is henceforth to be called the Waffen-SS. We are to join new units of this Waffen-SS, which fall under the administrative command of Reichsführer Heinrich Himmler, but under the strategic command of the Army.

The passing-out parade is witnessed by my dear wife, my brother and his wife. We swear an oath of allegiance to Adolf Hitler, Führer of the Reich and Commander-in-Chief of the Wehrmacht. This oath is called a "Fahneneid" (banner oath). I am granted a week's leave and then I must report to the SS "Gebirgsjäger" (Mountain) Artillery Regiment 6, which has its barracks at the Ordensburg in Sonthofen in the Allgäu, a few kilometers north of Oberstdorf – a region with which I am already familiar. This is a new unit and the recruits are in training.

Sonthofen, Tuesday, 10 September 1940

I arrive at the Ordensburg in Sonthofen. Part of the journey was undertaken by train to Ulm and the last part was on a military truck taking provisions and ammunition to Sonthofen. I am told that the Ordensburg was originally built to house a training camp for the Hitler Jugend, the Nazi youth movement.

Sonthofen in Bavaria

I report to "Obersturmbannführer" (Lieutenant-Colonel) Franz Müller, the commander of the regiment. He informs me that there are four battalions in the regiment and that each battalion is comprised of three batteries. Each battery has four field guns. I am to man the dressing station of the fourth battalion when we are in the field, but at the moment I am to be part of the "Lazarett" or field hospital. The fourth battalion uses 105 mm mountain howitzers, while the other three battalions use a lighter 75 mm mountain howitzer.

Müller also reminds me that the Wehrmacht has invaded Denmark and Norway in April. "I expect that this regiment will join the units already there since Norway is a very mountainous country."

"I know, Herr Strumbannführer. I and my wife and my brother and his wife had a beautiful holiday on the Hardanger Plain in Norway last year."

"Can you speak Norwegian?"

"No, unfortunately not. But many locals know some German."

From him, I am sent to Sturmbannführer Lothar Nöthling, the officer commanding the fourth battalion. He sends for Oberarzt Julius Dettering, my immediate chief.

After a cup of coffee in Nöthling's office, Dettering shows me around and introduces me to the medical staff of the battalion – the nurses, medical orderlies, ambulance drivers and stretcher bearers. He also takes me to Stabsarzt Leopold (also known as Poldi) Wiese, the chief medical officer of the regiment. Wiese tells me that he has read my file and has noticed that I am a specialist surgeon. "Wunderbar!" he exclaims: "Our medical staff regularly helps out in the local hospital and you will be assigned duty days. In the meantime, you are also to train with the recruits by trekking through the mountains and taking part in manoeuvers. You must earn the Edelweiss badge on your sleeve and cap – it cannot be given as a gift."

I retort that I actually look forward to the manoeuvers in the mountains and I wonder if it will be possible to visit the Rappenseehütte just below the Mädelegabel, where I have spent a night a few years ago. He looks surprised: "So you know these parts?"

"I have spent two holidays here while I was still a student."

After that, I am assigned a cabin where I am to sleep when not on duty. It seems that I will have a very busy time ahead of me

Sonthofen, Monday, 11 November 1940

The whole regiment is ordered to attend a parade in front of regimental headquarters on this Monday morning. A dais with a public address system was placed on one end of the parade ground. Franz Müller, his second-in-command and an officer in a foreign uniform ascend the dais.

Müller addresses us: "Men, we have a very important visitor today. He has come all the way from far-away Argentina to study military tactics in a mountain setting. He has spent a few months in the Italian Alps and now he wants to get familiar with our methods, especially artillery tactics. He is to stay with us for a week and all men are to treat him with the utmost respect and afford him all the assistance he needs. I want to introduce you to Oberst Juan Peron."

Peron also addresses us and he has an interpreter. He thanks us for the honor of witnessing our parade and he hopes to accompany us into the mountains.

After the parade all the officers are called to our conference room where each of us gets the opportunity of shaking the Argentinian's hand. Müller announces that full field exercises are to be held during the next few days and that Peron will attend those. He will move from battalion to battalion and even visit the support units, such as the company of Sanitätstruppen.

Oberstdorf, Thursday, 14 November1940

Colonel Peron arrives at our regimental first-aid station in the mountains above Oberstdorf on horseback. It has not snowed yet and it is still easy to move around.

The Colonel comes to me, together with his interpreter: "I have been told that you are a volunteer from far-away Africa. How did you land here?"

I explain that I actually had very little choice. The declaration of war caught me at a very bad moment, just before I received my doctorate in medicine to become a specialist surgeon. I am from a country at war with Germany and I don't know what my country's government will do with me after the war has ended.

"Ever thought of settling in Argentina when that time comes?" he asks.

"That is something I have never contemplated. But, thank you for this invitation."

Sonthofen, Tuesday, 4 February 1941

The war is in full swing, and still, our regiment has not yet a fired a single shot in the direction of an enemy. German forces have overrun France and the British Expeditionary Force in France had to flee back to their island with their tails between their legs. British efforts to throw the Wehrmacht out of Norway failed dismally. The Luftwaffe flies daily sorties over England and Scotland, dropping bombs on air fields, railway facilities, harbors and factories, almost at will.

We have not been idle. Our troops have been trained and trained and then more trained and they are more than battle-ready. I attended many field exercises to be at hand whenever an injury should occur. There were few injuries and I volunteered to be trained as a gunner in command of a howitzer.

Mules pulling a 105mm howitzer through a Bavarian village

We often had to pull our howitzers up into the mountains or through the fields. For that, we have teams of horses and mules. A veterinarian is attached to our regiment's Sanitätsgruppe to tend to the health of these animals. As a farm boy who grew up with horses, I sometimes help the vet with the animals and I sometimes teach the troops how to work with these valuable animals, although quite a number of them also grew up on farms in Bavaria.

My involvement with all the activities of the regiment has the result that the soldiers seem to accept me, although it is widely known that I am a South African and not a German. By this time, my German is more or less perfect and I am even able to speak Plattdeutsch, which I used in Berlin, as well as the Bavarian dialect, which I use here.

Our regimental commander, Obersturmbannführer Franz Müller, noticed my activities and he recommended that I be promoted to "Oberarzt", which is the equivalent of "Obersturmführer" or "Oberleutnant" (full Lieutenant).

My promotion was approved by Gruppenführer (Lieutenant-General) and Gene-ralarzt Dr Karl Genzken, the new chief of the Waffen-SS Medical Service, came through during early December while I was on a fortnight's leave in Berlin to see my Josephine who was extremely grateful that I was safe in Upper Bavaria.

I display my Edelweiss badge on my uniform sleeve, as well as on the side of my cap, with pride to demonstrate that I am a fully qualified mountain soldier.

Willie seems to be envious of this distinction because he also loves the mountains.

Our regiment also has a chaplain, titled a "Militärgeistlicher" (military spiritual advisor) or "Kriegspfarrer" (military pastor), who is a member of the staff of the "Feldlazarett" or field hospital. We became good friends, although he is a Catholic priest and I am a staunch Protestant. He is Pater Josef (Sepp) Heibl, a native of Bavaria, just as most of the soldiers in our regiment. He is addressed as "Pater" (Father), although he is barely older than the troops and will never become a father since it is a requirement for the priesthood that he stays unmarried. The troops often make fun of him and suggest that he chooses a bride from one of the nurses. He responds by maintaining that he is already married – to the Church. His main job will be to conduct funeral services for soldiers who have fallen – which did not yet happen with our regiment. Otherwise, he helps the medical orderlies and has become a proficient nurse in the process.

At five o'clock, Obersturmbannführer Franz Müller calls all the departmental chiefs and his staff together in the officer's mess. "Gentlemen, I have just received a signal from OKW (Oberkommando der Wehrmacht, the supreme command of the whole Wehrmacht) that we are to proceed with utmost haste to Norway where we are to join other Waffen-SS units in guarding the coastline against possible raids by the British. You are to pack all your equipment, starting tonight. Three special trains have already been dispatched to load our guns, animals, equipment and vehicles at the Sonthofen station. We will travel via Ulm to Cologne and from there to Denmark where we will board ferries to take us to Norway. We have two days to get ready. Inform your troops immediately. Any questions?"

"What happens with our mail?" one of the battery commanders ask.

"You are sternly warned not to write to anybody about these plans. Your incoming mail will be sent to a central mailing depot that will see to it that you still receive letters from home. As in the past, your postal address will just be SS Gebirgsjäger

Artillerieregiment 6, together with your name, rank and force number."

Trondheim, Friday 28 March 1941

It took us a full three weeks to reach the port city of Trondheim in central Norway and we arrived on 25 February. Our batteries are now spread out along the escarpment of Djupvika, a hill overlooking the sea to the west of Trondheim's harbor. This harbor is important for the German war effort because it is home to a U-boat flotilla.

It is our task to deter any raids by British commandos on the harbor and its installations, although nothing of this sort has happened yet. However, we are powerless to do anything about air raids by the Royal Air Force against the submarine base since our guns can only fire at targets on land or sea. There is a flak battalion to our rear that has the task of keeping the British bombers away. The result is that our troops are idle most of the time and they chase the Norwegian girls in town when they are off-duty.

The construction department of the Reich, the so-called Todt-organisation, has built an inpregnable bunker of reinforecd concrete to house the submarines when they are not at sea and no bomb will be able to penetrate this shield.

Our medical detachment is, on the other hand, not idle. We tend to the medical needs of the locals, free of charge. We hope to win some goodwill in this manner since we get the clear impression that the Norwegians do not like our presence. It appears that not a few girls got pregnant from German seamen or soldiers here in Trondheim and the locals do not take kindly to this state of affairs.

And today, I attend to a somewhat surprising case.

As I often do, I talk to myself in Afrikaans: "Bliksem! Hierdie outjie lyk bleddie sleg (Bloody thunder! This guy looks bloody bad.)" The patient immediately replies in Afrikaans: "En wie de hel is jy? (And who in hell are you?)"

Me: "Did I hear correctly? Did you reply in Afrikaans?"

Ja. I did. And what in hell am I doing in this place? Where am I?

"You are in the 'Lazarett' (military hospital) in Trondheim. You were pulled from your sinking aircraft by a patrol boat of the Kriegsmarine. You seemed to have tried to make it to the Ørlandet air base, but you didn't get there. According to your navigator, you passed out just at the moment when your fuel gave out. You must have passed out due to blood loss. As you can see, you are linked to a bag of blood to replenish your blood circulation system."

"What did you do to me?"

"Patched up your leg."

"So, I didn't lose a leg or something?"David Scholtz of the Sixth Mountain Artillery Regiment of the Waffen-SS. I see on your admittance file that you are Oberleutnant Krause. Are you also from South Africa?"

"Yes, From Rustenburg. But I'm actually a German, although I was born in the Transvaal. That's why I can speak Afrikaans – as well as German."

"And how did you manage to become a pilot in the Luftwaffe?"

"I completed an application form."

"Yes, of course. But how did they accept you?"

"My application was approved."

"How did it come that you applied in the first place?"

"Because I wanted to fly."

"And who introduced you to the Luftwaffe?"

"My brother-in-law, who was an instructor in Berlin."

"And how did he become you brother-in-law?"

"That's a stupid question, really. I married his sister."

"And how did you get to know his sister?"

"You sound just like the guys from the Gestapo – interrogating me like this."

"Although I am with the Waffen-SS, I have no time for the Gestapo. I'm only curious how an Afrikaans-speaking member of the Luftwaffe landed on my operating table."

"OK. I competed in the Olympics in thirty-six when I met my wife. She was a member of the German team. And then we got married after I qualified as a pilot. Simple. And how did you become a member of the SS?"

"By accident. I was studying medicine in Berlin when the war broke out. I had to choose between a concentration camp and the SS. I chose the SS. But wait, didn't we meet before the war? In Kufstein?"

"Yes, yes. That's it. I remember now. We became friends then. You were on your honeymoon, together with your brother. Three guys of us were there with our girlfriends."

"Nice to see you again. Never expected to encounter you again. And, as I told you, you were badly wounded. Fortunately, I am a specialist surgeon and I specialize on legs, feet and hips. That's why the other quacks asked me to take you on. I am going to book you off and send you home to recover. That wound has to heal totally and you will have to learn to walk again."

"Will I be able to ride my bicycle again?"

"Take it easy at first. But that will be excellent exercise to regain the use of your leg."

Afterwards I think that this was the first opportunity I had of speaking my mother tongue in many months. When will that happen again?

Trondheim, Thursday, 15 May 1941

Our commander calls for a conference of all section leaders. I was recently promoted to Oberarzt and I am in charge of the fourth battalion's medical station. Obersturmbannführer Müller informs us that we are no longer an independent regiment; we are to be incorporated into "SS-Kampfgruppe" (battle group) Nord, which is officially of brigade strength.

This unit seems to be a formidable force. We are informed that our strength is in excess of 10 300 men and comprised of 22 battalions. There are three infantry regiments, an artillery regiment (us), a "Panzerjäger" (tank hunter) battalion, a flak battalion, an engineer battalion and other support units.

With the addition of our regiment, the Kampfgruppe is to become a full division.

Gruppenführer und Generalleutnant der Waf-fen-SS Karl-Maria Demelhuber

A new divisional commander has taken over as from today and he is Gruppenführer und Generalleutnant der Waffen-SS Karl-Maria Demelhuber. He previously commanded the "SS-Standarte" (regiment) Ger-mania and is a veteran of the Great War. Obersturmbannführer Müller announces that the new commander will visit us soon to inform us about our future deployment.

He adds that he gets the feeling that all of us are bored because we have not yet fired a single shot in anger. That might change soon. We all wonder what that means. Are we to be transferred somewhere else again?

Trondheim, Tuesday, 10 June 1941

I am still helping at the military hospital in Trondheim. A naval officer with an ugly broken leg appears on my operating table. On his admission card he is identified as a certain Oberleutnant zur See (sub-lieutenant) Stefan Strauss. The name rings a bell in my mind. I scrutinize the man carefully and I realize that it is the same man who voyaged with me and Willie on the Usambara to Europe.

After he has woken up, I address him in Afrikaans to see how he reacts: "Hey! Are you awake? How do you feel?"

He opens his eyes widely and he grasps around him. He grips the sheets and blankets.

I smile and talk again: "Stefan, do you remember me? David Scholtz. We sailed together on the Usambara to Europe many years ago."

"Yes, really! David, is it really you? What on earth are you doing here?"

"I asked that question first. How the hell did you land here, you bloody blinking Nazi?"

"Got hurt. I believe I broke my bloody leg. That's how."

"Yes, of course you did. I fixed it and I had to install a piece of steel with screws because you got hurt badly. But how is it that you are sailing around in a blooming submarine? In Norway, of all places?"

"It's because I am helping in the war against England."

"And then you got hurt and landed on my operating table."

"Ah, yes. You went to study medicine in Berlin? Are you the quack who patched me up?"

"Yes, that's me. And – I am not an ordinary quack. I am a qualified surgeon and that is why I was called to work on your ugly leg. I specialize on knees and hips. Your leg broke just below the knee. Rather badly broken. I see on the admission card that your Sanitäter completed on your behalf that you have the job of being a submarine captain and that you have the rank of Oberleutnant zur See. How the devil did you get to that point? If I remember correctly, you had the intention of studying nautical engineering in Bremen and that you planned to return to South West afterwards."

"That's right. And after I had received my diploma, I joined the Kriegsmarine. I fell in love in the meantime with the daughter of the Director of the Nautical College and that is why I never returned to South West Africa. We got married and we have a beautiful baby daughter. But – what in hell are you doing here, here in Norway at a military hospital, of all places?"

"The same as you – fell in love and got married. And shortly before I completed my studies the war erupted and prevented me from getting out. I was given a choice – join the Waffen-SS or becoming an inmate of a concentration camp."

"And then you chose the SS? Do you also guard concentration camps?"

"No, stupid. I am with the Waffen-SS, a fighting unit. I am a medical officer in an artillery regiment and we are sitting around, waiting for something to turn up. In the meantime, I help here at the Lazarett to keep busy because my division, the sixth Waffen-SS Mountain Division, must help to guard Trondheim. It seems that everybody is healthy and strong – except for the men who sometimes get a hangover."

"Well, well. When can I get out of here?"

"Not so hasty. I am going to book you off for two months. And then you fly home to rest."

"To South West Africa?"

"What do you think, you idiot? To your home in Germany with your wife and kid."

"Oh."

Trondheim, Saturday, 28 June 1941

Action at last!

We heard the news that three massive German army groups invaded Russia a week ago and made spectacular progress in just a few days' time. It is called "Blitzkrieg" (lightning war). Whole Russian divisions surrendered or were wiped out. The operation is called "Unternehmen Barbarossa" (Operation Barbarossa), named after a famous medieval German emperor of the Holy Roman Empire.

Finland also declared war against Russia for the second time three days after the invasion of Russia by the Germans with the object of regaining their lost province of Karelia, which the Russians have annexed. The Finns were obliged to negotiate a peace settlement with the Russians fifteen months ago at the conclusion of the so-called Winter War. Now that Hitler has ordered the invasion of Russia, the Finns have grasped the opportunity to get their own back on the Russians.

Our division is today being moved to Finland and we are to become part of the Finnish Third Corps under General Hjalmar Siilasvuo, and that we are to take up positions at Louhi, Kiestinki, inside the polar circle. Our operation is called "Unter-nehmen Polar-fuchs" (Operation Polar Fox).

Our division has received a number and a new badge, which we display with pride. We are now officially the Sixth Waffen-SS Gebirgdivision Nord. That means that we are the sixth division to be formed in the Waffen-SS. We regard ourselves as the elite of the German armed forces.

Fortunately, it is summer and not cold at all. In Trondheim, we had to get used to sunsets at a very late hour. Here, inside the Polar Circle, the sun never sets at this time of the year and it completes a full circle around the horizon. That means that we have to stay vigilant at all times since the Russians may attack at any time, day or night. Fortunately, their attention is focused on countering the German invasion to the south and there are relatively few units available to withstand the Finnish and German attack.

Lapland, Tuesday, 30 September 1941

Winter is descending upon us and it has already started to snow. The combined Finnish and German forces have conquered the whole of East Karelia and the situation has stabilized to a certain extent since the Finns only want to guard the old frontiers of Karelia. The attention of the Russians is elsewhere. The commander-in-chief of the Finnish forces, Field Marshall Carl Mannerheim – he has German ancestors, hence his German name – enjoys the confidence of all the Finns and he is regarded as a hero because the Finns have regained Karelia under his leadership.

However, our division was tasked, together with some Finnish units, to try and capture the northern Russian port city of Murmansk and to cut the railway line that connects the city with the rest of Russia. For that reason, we are moved again and our division's sector of the front is just south of Murmansk. So far, we have not been able to achieve our goal by plugging the supply route from Murmansk, although we have taken the little town of Salla in Lapland.

My field dressing station is fairly busy, patching up wounded men. The terrain is very difficult and is filled with mosquito-infested swamps and lakes. Our casualties are not only due to wounds inflicted by the enemy; many men break arms or legs when they lose their footing in the muddy and water-logged fields and forests. Some soldiers on their skis fall through the ice on frozen ponds and get injured in the process – and then I have to patch them up so that they can fight again.

Lapland, Thursday, 25 December 1941

This is certainly the worst Christmas that I have ever experienced. It is absolutely freezing with snow a meter thick. There is very little daylight and I have to keep kerosene lamps burning in the Lazarett tent where we have to operate on wounded soldiers. There are many of them and we barely get any rest.

It is so cold that we cannot afford to switch the engines of any of our vehicles off; they have to remain idling, otherwise their engines will freeze tight and have to be defrozen with blowtorches.

There is no thought of celebrating Christmas, although this morning we called "Frohe Weihnachten!" (Merry Christmas) to each other, but that was that. We just have to carry on as on any other day because the war does not stop. This is the first Christmas I spend away from Josephine and I cannot help but to think of her the whole day while pottering around in the field dressing tent.

Captured Soviet equipment in Karelia

Josephine writes to me very regularly, no less than once a week. The delivery of mail to these parts is intermittent and I often receive five or six letters at the same time. Willie also keeps contact through regular letters. I have no idea how frequently and effectively my letters are delivered to Berlin, although – to judge from Josephine's letters – most of them seem to have gone through.

The wounded men – Germans, Finns and even captured Russians – tell me of their ordeals. It does seem as if the Finns and the Germans are able to inflict very heavy casualties on the Russians, but we also suffer. The Russians are not so mobile as we are because our men can dart around on their skis, an art the Russians have not mastered. The infantry on their skis are difficult targets, but the artillery, which cannot move around so easily, are easier targets.

Although our artillery regiment does not fight directly on the front line near Murmansk, we are frequently targeted by the Russian artillery. One whole battery of my battalion was almost wiped out during a three-week period. Our regiment has to back up infantry attacks against the Russian supply lines and our guns have to be moved frequently to prevent being shot at by the Russian artillery.

Franz Müller has more than once requested Army headquarters that our artillery regiment be outfitted with 88 mm guns since our light guns do not have a long enough range to counter the Russian artillery. Furthermore, we are fighting on a flat terrain where heavier guns can be operated easily. His requests have been turned down on account of the fact that these guns are in short supply and are needed in the defense of the Reich against Allied air raids and against the Russian armor on the Eastern Front.

Our horses and mules suffer terribly. There is nothing to eat on the vast snow fields and we cannot provide enough fodder. Fortunately, divisional headquarters has realized our plight and they have called for mechanized gun tractors, of which we have already received a few and we are to become a fully motorized division.

I cannot do much more than patch up our wounded men temporarily. There is nowhere for them to be taken care of and they have to be evacuated by plane. A Junkers Ju 52 transport plane, lovingly known as "Tante Ju" (Aunty Ju), flies every second day between the Nautsi base of the Luftwaffe near our headquarters and an airport near a military hospital in Finland. When Tante Ju flies back to come and fetch yet another batch of invalids, she brings some reinforcements and medical supplies so as not to fly empty.

A Junkers Ju 52 ambulance aircraft on the snow

I have asked myself more than once: "David, what on earth are you doing at this dump? You are a son of sunny South Africa. How did it happen that you are working your ass off, a stone's throw away from the dark North Pole?"

All I know, is that I was trained to treat wounded and injured soldiers and that is what I do every day.

Lapland, Sunday, 22 March 1942

Fierce gunfire wakes me up. I glance at my watch and I see that it is supposed to be three 'o clock in the morning. It is totally dark and bitterly cold with snow still lying everywhere outside. The sun is expected to rise in a few hours' time and shine feebly.

There have already been many skirmishes and even minor battles along our front since our arrival, but this battle seems to be bigger than anything we have experienced so far. My medics, stretcher bearers and ambulance drivers are all awake and we prepare our operating tent, as well as the tents in which the expected casualties are to be housed, before they can be evacuated.

After about an hour the first wounded men appear and I start removing bomb fragments and bullets from wounds, patching up cuts, treating burns and amputating legs and arms that have been shot to pieces.

I ask a young Rottenführer: " Do you know what's going on, out there?"

"Herr Oberarzt, it's wholesale slaughter. I have killed at least fifty dozen Ivans with my machine gun – or so it seems. That's before I got this bullet in my shoulder. A blooming stray bullet."

I talk to a Hauptsturmführer, the second-in-command of a battalion, whose nose has been shot off. He tells me: "This is our first real battle. In the past, we were able to run over the Russians. We could have advanced further, but the bloody Finns didn't want to invade Russia proper. They only wanted to liberated the parts of their country held by the Russians."

Me: "How large is the attacking force?"

"Difficult to say. In our division's sector, I'd say, at least a corps. Easily fifty thousand boys. They keep on running into our guns. If they keep on coming like this, we will run out of ammo shortly and then they will run over us. But we shoot them down, whole battalions at a time. The bodies are just piling up."

At about ten a wounded capture Russian officer is brought to me. He introduces himself as Captain Andrei Metelski, commander of a cavalry unit. In broken German, he tells me that this attack is Stalin's method of getting rid of unwanted elements in the Soviet Union – Jews, Muslims, Uzbecks, Volga Germans and so forth. Conscripts from these minorities are organized into special battalions. They are forced to charge the German and Finnish positions in massive waves with the expectation that they will all be shot down. Problem solved.

This inhumane, barbaric and cruel strategy almost makes me sick. It's cynical. Stalin doesn't seem to have the slightest respect for human life and he sends thousands upon thousands of boys to their deaths without batting an eyelid. And then he hopes we, the enemy, will do his dirty work for him.

25 December 1942

Lapland, Friday, 25 December 1942

Another Christmas has arrived. Although it is again extremely cold, things have stabilized somewhat. The siege of Leningrad to our south continues and the combined Finnish and German forces cannot breach the defensive lines around Murmansk, although some of our patrols have succeeded in blowing up parts of the railway line – which is simply repaired a few days later by armed Russian working parties.

Brigadeführer Matthias Kleinheisterkamp (here with the rank of Gruppenführer)

We are certainly one of the biggest divisions in the Waffen-SS and our strength is more than 21 000 men. We have a new commander since 1 May: Brigadeführer und Generalmajor der Waffen-SS Matthias Kleinheisterkamp. He was a professional soldier since the Great War and the previous commander of the SS-Division "Das Reich".

Two months ago, I received very welcome home leave of three weeks. Josephine was overwhelmed by joy to see me suddenly at the doorstep of our apartment in Berlin. Willie and Annemarie were rapidly inform-ed of my presence and we celebrated my safe homecoming with abandon.

It seemed as if life in Berlin is becoming difficult. There is not so much to eat anymore and the blackout at night makes movement after dark virtually impossible. Willie, though, is still working full-steam as a member of the Uranium Club.

A month ago, I had to take over the task of temporary "Divisionsarzt" (divisional physician), in charge of all the medical units in the division. I was promoted to Stabsarzt, which is the equivalent of Hauptsturmführer due to the fact that I am a qualified specialist surgeon. Some of my colleagues have been transferred somewhere else or have suffered nervous breakdowns and had to be sent home. I can understand that it may become too much even for the strongest man to be confronted daily by wounded, crying, home-sick, weeping, crippled, maimed and dying boys. Although we hoped for a rapid end to the war, that hope seems to be over-optimistic. The Russian resistance has stiffened and we cannot make any more progress. It seems as if the front lines have become frozen, just as frozen as the snow fields surrounding us.

There are skirmishes almost every day somewhere and there is a constant stream of wounded men carried to the divisional Lazarett where I am in charge. This position is meant for a Oberstabsarzt with a rank equivalent to a Sturmbannführer or Major, but I can't be promoted yet since I have not been serving long enough.

One perk of my position is the fact that I have a Volkswagen Kübelwagen (literary: bucket car) with a driver with which I can visit all the field dressing stations throughout the divisional sector.

Our division doesn't have any horses or mules anymore. We had to slaughter them months ago because it became impossible to feed them. That gave us a good supply of horse meat for a number of weeks. I did not want to witness the killing of the animals, although I have helped my father's workmen to slaughter many a sheep on our farm when I was younger.

Volkswagen Kübelwagen

Our men are often supported by the Junkers Ju 88 bombers of KG 30 (Kampfgeschwader – bomber wing no 30) from the Kemi and Nautsi air bases of the Luftwaffe when the weather is not too bad. These bombers also have to sink ships carrying supplies to the Russians before they reach Murmansk.

It happened more than once that crew members of these bombers landed in my Lazarett tent after they had been shot down by the Russians and crashed near us.

Lapland, Saturday, 25 December 1943

It is my third Christmas in Karelia with the 6th SS-Gebirgsdivision Nord and my third Christmas away from my beautiful wife. It is, of course again exceedingly cold where we are trying to cut off the supply lines between Murmansk and the interior of Russia.

The German Kriegsmarine with its battleships, cruisers and U-boats are doing their very best to prevent American and British convoys from reaching Murmansk with supplies for the Red Army, but with limited success.

A week ago, we received yet a new divisional commander, Gruppenführer Lothar Debes, another veteran of the Great War. We all hope that he will, perhaps, be able to break the deadlock on the Murmansk front.

Gruppenführer and Lieutenant General of the Waffen-SS Lothar Debes (here in the uniform of a Brigadeführer or Major General)

It is also our task to prevent these supplies from reaching our enemies, a task that becomes increasingly difficult and even impossible. We are often pushed back and then we push forward again. At this point of time, our division is still more than 20 000 men strong. We have received many reinforcements to replace our casualties, including a battalion with Norwegian volunteers. There is a special battalion to train these men to become proficient mountain troops before they are assigned to one of the regiments. any of them are young boys who are terrified of dying in a far-flung corner of the world and Pater Sepp Heibl and his colleagues do sterling work to console them and take confessions.

Often when a young wounded soldier lands on my operating table, I have to help him by drying his tears. It is a terrible disappointment to lose an arm or a leg and many of them don't know how they are going to face life as cripples. I try to cheer them up with the promise that the horrible war is over for them and that they will be sent home. We also have to treat many cases of frostbite in this terrible cold. Many a soldier has lost a foot, a hand, a penis or a nose due to the freezing temperatures. Of course, they cannot take part in any battles after having suffered these mishaps.

A field dressing station in the forests of Karelia during winter

There is a directive of the OKW forbidding soldiers to urinate in the open during winter where their private parts get exposed. It is so cold that the hot urine freezes before it reaches the snow and one can hear the icy crystals twinkle and crack as they drop on to the snow. But in the process, the poor man's manhood also gets frozen and can often not be saved.

Lapland, Monday, 1 May 1944

A letter from Willie, dated 15 March, reaches me today with very, very bad news.

Willlie isn't working in Berlin anymore because the Uranium Club of the Kaiser Wilhelm Institute was relocated to southern Germany due to all the bombing raids on Berlin by the US Army Air Force during day-time and the Royal Air Force at night. During one of these raids on 11 March our block of apartments was flattened, including the cellar where the inhabitants of the block were hiding after the air raid alarm had sounded. Our two wives were under the fatalities. It was possible to bury them in their home town, Brandenburg an der Havel.

Waffen-SS soldiers with their camouflage summer outfits

The irony is that Josephine's last letter, written the day before her death, has also reached me simultaneously with Willie's letter. In her letter, she assured me again of her love and how she was longing to see me again. I read this letter first, before Willie's letter, but I read and reread it again afterwards while the tears from my eyes made smudges on the paper.

I feel like walking back to Germany to go and visit my dear wife's grave. But that is, of course, totally out of the question. We are almost as far north as one can go on land. My division needs me too much. We are suffering setback upon setback on account of the enormous number of troops the Soviets are able to throw at us. We shoot them down by their thousands with our machine guns, mortars and howitzers, but they still keep coming. Russia is such a big country that they can easily absorb these losses – which we cannot do.

Tante Ju taking on a wounded soldier with medical personnel looking on

It is my team's job to patch up as many wounded men as possible and send them back to the front. Although I am supposed to be in charge of all the medical staff of the division, I feel that I am walking around in a dream. I can fully understand how our men feel when they get bad news from home. Many of them just don't think about their own safety anymore and charge into the murderous fire of the Reds – with dire results. Whenever our stretcher bearers are able to retrieve the wounded and bring them to the dressing stations or the divisional Lazarett, they get the best treatment we can give them. But many of them have just given up the will to live, despite our best efforts. The cases that have a chance of living are still evacuated by the ambulance plane, but the hopeless cases are left in the care of Pater Sepp.

Although I have previously declared that I would prefer not to fight against the hated British, I have had a change of heart. After the building in the Dorotheenstraße in Berlin has been bombed I have a very personal reason to shoot back at the British and the Americans. But I also diagnose myself as a serious case of shell shock.

Lapland, Saturday, 22 July 1944

Gruppenführer und Lieutenant-General of the Waffen-SS Lothar Debes, GOIC of the 6th Waffen-SS Gebirgsdivision Nord, stands with a stern and even sad face in front of us – that is, all the section chiefs of the division. He has called us for a very urgent conference.

"Meine Herren! I have very tragic news. Something happened to besmirch our good name as Germans. There was a case of treason of the utmost gravity in the highest levels of the Wehrmacht, involving a number of Generals and senior officers. A signal has been sent from OKW to all field units informing them of this treason and I must tell you about its contents."

I can see the puzzled expression on the faces of my fellow officers. Treason by generals of the Wehrmacht? Unthinkable!

Our commander continues after a moment of silence in which he collects his thoughts: "Yes, there was a dastardly and despicable attempt to assassinate our beloved Führer and Chief of the Wehrmacht, Adolf Hitler. A bomb was placed under the table at a conference of Generals at his headquarters at Rastenburg in East Prussia. Fortunately, he was not killed, only slightly injured. It seems that the bomb was not strong enough to kill anyone. Those who are responsible for this conspiracy are at this moment being hunted down and they will be dealt with appropriately.

"It appears that those who wanted to remove the Führer planned to negotiate a separate peace agreement with the Western Allies. They wanted to install Field Marshal Erwin Rommel as head of government. As you may well know, the Allies landed a huge task force on 6 June on the beaches of Normandy in France. Our valiant soldiers were not able to throw them back into the sea. Now the Allies have already driven our forces from large parts of France and it is clear that they want to invade our Fatherland. The

Russians are also pushing our divisions back and they have already taken Lithuania and are advancing into Poland now.

"Thus, meine Herren, the situation looks rather grim for us. The Russians are also forcing us back here in Karelia and the Finns have lost quite a bit of territory. But I want to state to you unequivocally: The Waffen-SS will not give up so easily! Our division will not run away!"

Applause is given.

"Yes, we are the elite. There never has been a fighting force like ours. And we can certainly be proud that our division has shown more courage than any other division. We have endured unspeakable hardships. We have held out against everything that the Russians could hurl at us. We can hold our heads high! We will not be guilty of treason! Heil Hitler!"

I drive back in my vehicle. On the way I pass a column of infantry in their camouflage outfits on their way to the front to relieve their comrades who have been fighting there. They are standing at attention and are awaiting orders. I cannot but stop and ask the

"Oberstabscharführer" (sergeant-major) in charge of the machine gun company if I may address these boys. Permission is granted and I tell them of the news of the treason of a number of Generals. They listen with attention, but I can see that they are determined not to budge a centimeter if they can help it.

Lapland, Friday, 4 August 1944

We experience something rather strange today: an air raid by Russian light bombers. Their target seems to be the nearby Nautsi airfield of the Luftwaffe, but a few bombs also fall near our headquarters. No real damage is being done, except for a bomb splinter that got lodged in my left buttock. One of my colleagues operates on me and applies stitches to the wound because I cannot reach the spot myself. He gives me sick leave of three days. That is not enough for me to go anywhere and I just continue with my work, even with a thick bandage on my bottom. I must either stand on my two feet, or lie down on my stomach because it's impossible to sit down.

Our anti-aircraft boys shoot two of the Russian bombers down.

Lapland, Saturday, 2 September 1944

The days are becoming shorter and we have some darkness at night, which helps me sleep somewhat better – that is, if I don't have to work during the night to effect some repairs on wounded and injured men. The fighting just goes on and on and there is almost never silence. Big guns bark and grumble, machine guns chatter, small arms fire sounds like crackers and the howling of aircraft engines – from our Luftwaffe, but more often of the Soviet Air Force – sounds like the roar of hungry tigers.

I went to bed last night while my medics kept looking after the wounded in our field Lazarett. Just after dawn one of them shakes my shoulder: "Herr Doktor, get up! We are surrounded by Russian soldiers!"

It takes me ten seconds flat to put my boots on and I venture outside. A Russian captain, who can speak a little bit of German, comes to me: "Are you the doctor?"

"Yes, I am."

"You are to treat my wounded men. They got shot by your soldiers."

"Bring them to me."

I have no choice since my medical ethics forbids me to refuse to treat anybody in pain. Three men are brought to me by their comrades. One has a head wound; another one cannot use his left foot because it is shot to pieces and the third one is unconscious with a chest wound – perhaps due to blood loss. I decide that number three has very little chance of survival and, therefore, I won't waste my time on him and concentrate on the other two.

My operating table is brought into readiness and I tackle the head wound first. The wound merely has to be cleaned and stitched up since it is superficial. The poor boy with the wounded left foot will have to say good-bye to that foot, since it is badly mangled, probably by a land mine.

After I have done what I can for these two men, I look at number three with his chest wound. He is gone and I gesture to his friends to take him away. While I clean my hands, I think that I have seen so many corpses since arriving on this front that I have become totally immune to this horrible, horrendous, and horrific state of affairs.

Suddenly, I think: how will that man's mother feel when she gets the news that a German bullet killed her son and that a German doctor did not even try to save his life? Too bad, too bad, nothing can be done about it. But, on the other hand, she must feel the same way as I did when I got the news of Josephine's death. Poor mother.

The captain approaches me and offers me a tot of vodka – which I gulp down, together with the captain. We sit down and stare at each other in silence. In the distance, the guns – big and small – continue their conversations in German and Russian.

The vodka makes me drowsy and I lie down on one of the field beds in the operating tent. The captain does the same.

Lapland, Sunday, 3 September 1944

Last night I asked the captain to accompany me while I was doing my rounds in the Lazarett to check on my patients, German and Russian. After that, the captain invited me to share his dinner, which consisted of black bread, cheese and vodka. We both drank too much and fell into a stupor.

This morning I wake up with one of my medics shaking my shoulder: "Herr Doktor, wake up! We are surrounded. By our own men!"

It takes me ten seconds to get my boots on and I rush outside. It is indeed true. German soldiers of the Waffen-SS are guarding a bunch of Russian soldiers whom they have captured during the early morning hours. My new friend, the captain, is amongst them.

I walk over to the captain and ask him if he is OK.

"Thank you for your help when you were my guest. Now I am again your guest. Shitty luck."

The Russian captives – about eighty of them – are taken away an hour later and I am again part of the Sixth SS Gebirgsdivision Nord.

Three men in SS-uniforms are brought to me. One has a head wound, the second one has part of his right foot blown away and the third one was shot through the stomach. They received these wounds in an effort to free me and my medics. They tell me that about six of their comrades fell in the skirmish. Ten Russians died.

When will this madness end? My brain refuses to register any sorrow, sympathy, or sadness. I can only see my Josephine's beautiful face in my imagination and that keeps me going. I must keep going in honor of her memory.

Lapland, Tuesday, 19 September 1944

Our new divisional commander who took over from Debes on 1 September, Gruppenführer und Generalleutnant der Waffen-SS Karl-Heinrich Brenner, calls a conference of all section commanders. I, as chief medical officer, also have to attend.

He looks worried: "Grüßgott, meine Herren! We are undoubtably the finest German division in Finland. As you may know, there are three whole corps comprised of divisions of the Wehrmacht and the Waffen-SS here in Finland. Our overall commanding General is General der Infanterie Emil Vogel, who is a trained mountain soldier himself. As SS mountain troops, we are the best. "We have been given a very special task because General Vogel has very special confidence in us.

Gruppenführer und Generalleutnant der Waffen-SS Karl-Heinrich Brenner (here as a Brigadeführer)

"You may not have heard, but the Finns have given up the fight. Field Marshall Mannerheim has signed a secret armistice agreement in Moscow this morning. He thinks that this war is going nowhere and before the Russians conquer back more of Karelia he has decided to throw in the towel. His government agreed with him."

Somebody mumbles: "The swine!"

"And what does that mean for us? General Vogel informed all the divisional commanders earlier today that we are no longer welcome in this country and we have to pull out as fast as possible. The Finns will probably fight us because we are no longer allies and because the Moscow Treaty stipulated something of the sort.

But we will also have to fend off the Russians who will pursue us all the way back to Norway, which is still in German hands. This operation is called 'Unternehmen Birke' (Operation Birch)."

The same voice utters again: "Donnerwetter! Scheiße (bloody thunder, shit)!"

"And that is where our special task comes in. General Vogel has ordered our division to form the rearguard and make it possible for all the other units to reach safety in Norway. So – we are going to fight the worst battle of our whole time in Karelia and Lapland, because we will be forming the shield for all our other comrades. Any questions?"

Standartenführer Alfred Röhrs, one of the regimental commanders, raises his hand: "When do we leave?"

"Immediately. We start tonight. And then we retreat twenty kilometers where we dig in. Hopefully the Russians and Finns will be caught napping by our sudden departure and it will take some time before they attack. And then this Gebirgsdivision will be ready for them while our comrades get away."

I raise my hand: "What happens to our wounded? Are they to be sent ahead, or do we leave them here to be taken care of by the enemy?"

"Of course, we cannot leave them here. Herr Doktor, evacuate them as speedily as possible. But most of you and your medical staff stay behind with the rest of the division because we will constantly need you with all the fighting that will certainly erupt. It is to be expected that our casualties will be high."

Franz Müller of the artillery regiment stands up: "With respect, Herr Gruppenführer, our ammo will all be used up within a few days if we have to do all the fighting while the others get away. That will leave us in a tight fix."

"General Vogel has already ordered that our division shall be kept supplied with all the supplies we need, including ammo.

The other divisions have been ordered to keep their surplus stocks ready to be transported to us immediately when we need anything."

The same voice from earlier yells: "Kreuzitürken! (crucify the Turks!)" while we are rising.

Somebody at the back shouts: "So, we are losing the war, are we?"

"No, certainly not! The Wehrmacht still has a number of powerful cards up its sleeve. The Luftwaffe is getting the most advanced fighters in the world – jet aircraft. They can fly circles around anything the enemy has. Rockets are raining down upon London. The Kriegsmarine is due to get the most modern U-boats the world has ever seen. There are other nasty surprises still coming with which we will beat all our foes!"

Silently, I say to myself: "And atom bombs..."

Opel Blitz WW2 German truck

I leave the conference tent immediately and run to my field hospital. I gather my staff: "Pack up everything and load everything onto our trucks and ambulances. We are leaving for Norway. Evacuate all the wounded men with an escort of ten drivers and ten orderlies and drive as hard as possible to the

Norwegian border. See to it that you don't stray over the border into Sweden. The rest of you are to await further orders."

I race to my Kübelwagen to drive to all the dressing stations of the various regiments to order them to pack up and move all their patients to divisional headquarters and the divisional Lazarett.

Lapland, Thursday, 21 September 1944

Our boys dug in yesterday afternoon. It was no easy job since we had to cover a wide front, which is interrupted by various rivers, swamps and lakes. The region is filled with forests and there is only one passable road. We have, however, to be vigilant because the enemy might try to outflank us by cutting through the forests and swamps. The autumn rains turned everything into a muddy mess.

There are two defensive lines along the main road, the one behind the other. The idea is that when it seems that the first line is to be overrun, these men are to retreat to the safety of the second line and dig in for yet another defensive line behind that.

The first line is formed by the infantry and the Panzerjäger with their rifles, machine guns, "Panzerfausts" (bazookas) and grenade throwers. The artillery is situated behind the second line of defense from where they will be able to bombard the approaching Russian or Finnish forces. The "Pionieren" (engineers or sappers) have dug mines under the road to create havoc amongst all vehicles coming that way.

My medical team is distributed behind these lines and we are ready to receive the first casualties. Until now, nothing has happened yet. I drive around to inspect every first aid station and check whether they have all the supplies they need.

My second in command as Divisionsarzt, Oberarzt Heini Söhnge, corners me: "If I don't make it, will you please send this letter to my wife in Graz – that is, if she is still alive. Let's hope we will all make it, but I am not very optimistic."

I pat him on the shoulder: "Please remember, we are the elite and proud of it. I am the descendant of a long line of Boer warriors who also fought to the bitter end against fierce tribes and the hated British. We won't give up! I will, anyway, keep this letter in a safe place. If we both survive the war, I will return it to you."

It is the autumn equinox today. From now on, the days will become shorter and shorter and the nights longer and longer. The whole wide world is also growing darker and darker.

Lapland, Saturday, 23 September 1944

Nothing happened yesterday. The onslaught of the Red Army started early this morning and our boys were more than ready. The Russians were not able to breach our lines at any place, although they almost succeeded at a few spots in the forests to our left and right. The wounded and dead are taken to our bandage stations, from where they are transported in ambulances to the rear.

Our ambulances struggle in the muddy conditions and I decide that we will have to use the half-tracks tomorrow to reach the men in the forests.

Mercedes Benz type L 1500 E ambulance

In the meantime, Karl-Heinrich Brenner informs me that most of the divisions have already managed to retreat a respectable distance to the rear. Tonight, we are to abandon our front-line positions and also retreat to the rear after having again mined the road leading to our new positions.

Lapland, Sunday, 24 September 1944

Today is a repetition of yesterday. The Russian soldiers throw themselves at our positions and they are cut down like a scythe mows down a wheat field.

Fortunately, it is still raining and that means that we are safe from attacks by the Soviet Air Force. Our flak battalion is ready for them, in any case.

The muddy conditions make it impossible for the heavy Russian tanks to attack us from the flanks. They will simply sink into the mud if they tried to advance and we count that as a blessing.

I have received a few armored half-tracks that can be used as ambulances and we hastily paint red crosses on their sides. They are actually meant to be gun tractors, but Franz Müller graciously lent them to me on condition that they be returned at night to tow his howitzers further to the back.

Lapland, Sunday, 1 October 1944

It is a week since our retreat has begun. The Russians kept coming during the day. The Finns have joined in with their onslaughts. At night we retreat to new positions. It happened twice that our forward positions were breached but the brave men could in most cases reach safety behind the second line.

Although it is far too early for snow, a light snowfall has occurred last night. Our men were prepared for the cold and most of them quickly donned their winter outfits. At least, the snow also kept the Red Air Force grounded.

Franz Müller – in the meantime promoted to Standartenführer – and his second-in-command were killed by a Finnish rocket yesterday.

Karl-Heinrich Brenner comes to me: "Herr Doktor, there is no experienced officer left who can lead that artillery regiment. I understand that you have trained with these men as a gunner yourself. Can you take over? Your second-in-command at the field dressing stations seems to do be doing a marvelous job and your skills as surgeon are not needed at the moment because all the wounded are evacuated as soon as possible to the rear and to Norway. How about it?

I cannot believe my ears: "But, Herr Gruppenführer, I have never completed a course as regimental commander!"

"But you have proved your capabilities as officer-in-command of the Sanitätsgruppe of our division. That is a battalion-sized unit. You are a capable administrator. You have successfully filled a position that actually requires a more senior officer. I have nobody else to take this job. Anyway, the regiment has suffered quite a lot and lost a large part of its equipment. There are little more than two battalions of the original four left. Three of the batteries are commanded by nothing more than a Hauptcharführer. I have nobody else to take over."

"But then you have to tell the remaining officers and senior NCO's in the regiment of your decision yourself. I cannot do that."

"Well, jump into my truck and we go there."

The men of the artillery regiment didn't know how to address me when I joined them. The older members still remembered me as one of their medical officers, way back in Bavaria. At that time, they addressed me either as "Herr Doktor" or "Herr Assistenzarzt". Now they alternate between "Herr Stabsarzt" and "Herr Hauptsturm-führer".

I couldn't care less what they call me. After all, I am not a stiff Prussian.

Fortunately, I can still remember how the howitzers are to be operated and aimed. Our forward observation posts inform us by radio of possible targets and also tell us whether these targets have been hit.

After a few rounds have been shot, we have to move the guns again before we become targets of the Soviet artillery. Their aiming capabilities are poor, but their volume of fire is such that they often cause much damage – men, guns and vehicles get blown to pieces.

Rovaniemi, Thursday, 12 October 1944

Yesterday, our rearguard reached Rovaniemi, the capital town of Lapland. It is the terminus of railroads from the south and the east. Parts of the German forces advanced from the south and the east to this spot, but they will have to depart for Norway by road.

75 mm Mountain gun 36

As acting commander of the artillery, I am informed that a train with ammunition is awaiting us at the station of Rovaniemi, with which we must continue the struggle.

The town is situated on the south western banks of a broad river, the Kemijoki. Our sappers have already placed explosives on the road bridge and the railway bridge across the river to blow them up as soon as our last troops have crossed the river and to stop our pursuers.

Suddenly, we hear an enormous explosion. A shock wave shakes us where we have halted just outside and on the southeastern side of the town. My first thought is that this explosion was meant to destroy the bridges. But then I look in the direction from which the explosion came – the loudest bang that I have heard during the whole war. I see parts of railway trucks flying into the air.

One of the men next to me cries out: "There goes our ammo train!"

Another guy shouts: "It is these bloody Finns who have blown up all our ammo! Where will we find bombs for our guns?"

Instinctively, I call my men: "We must go and help! I am sure that many of our men have been seriously hurt."

Although we are gunners, a few dozen of us start running. We gaze upon a scene of indescribable destruction. The goods train station to the west of the town has been wiped off the face of the earth. Large parts of the town consisting mainly of wooden houses were totally destroyed.

We find a number of wounded men and we throw them over our shoulders to take them to the first aid stations. Other wounded men struggle on their own to get there.

In the meantime, I hear how the guns of my regiment start to spit fire. After I have put down a wounded man from my shoulders I run back to the spot where my gunners have started to hammer the Finns on the other side of the river. Our infantry follow suit with machine guns and mortars. A few hundreds of Finns, nevertheless, are able to reach our side of the river.

The only conclusion I can make is that the loads of explosives on the bridges have been blown off by the force of the explosion and landed in the river. I order my gunners to concentrate all their fire on the bridges. After having fired for about ten minutes, my men succeed in blowing the bridges to pieces, leaving the Finnish soldiers on our side of the river stranded. They rapidly see their difficult situation and try to flee, but many of them are shot down.

Rovaniemi, Friday, 13 October 1944

The remnants of my artillery regiment are leaving Rovaniemi this morning. A few skirmishes took place during the night, but we succeed in getting away while our pursuers are caught on the other side of the river.

Rovaniemi after the explosion

Gruppenführer Karl-Heinrich Brenner arrives with his vehicle to inspect our losses. Fortunately, we were sufficiently far away from the explosion and the ensuing firefights and our losses are, therefore, relatively light. Brenner tells me, though, that there were hundreds of casualties – mainly men who were busy loading ammunition from the train onto our trucks. According to him, the battle of Rovaniemi was the fiercest and bloodiest battle our division had to fight since our retreat started.

In order to ensure the safe transport of the supplies stored in Muonio, our Division receives orders to create a defensive position south of the town and hold our ground until the evacuation was complete. The Finns, who are pursuing us along the Tornio-Muonio and Rovaniemi-Muonio roads, see an opportunity to inflict some damage on us. The Finns manage during the afternoon to take advantage of the difficult terrain to infiltrate between some of our units in an effort to block the road. Standartenführer Franz Schreiber, who commands the rear guard, immediately orders my artillery to fire on these Finns in support of an infantry attack. In a three-hour night fight, we manage to eject the attacking Finns and clear the road for passage. The Finns suffer quite heavy losses against minor casualties to our troops.

After the fighting had died down during the night, Schreiber comes to thank the batteries under my command for making it possible to repulse the Finns.

Northern Norway, Saturday, 14 October 1944

We have managed to reach the safety of the border of Norway after fighting our former comrades, the Finns, as well as the Russians, for 23 days. Or, that is what we thought. We see the Norwegian town of Helligskogen in front of us and we hope to be safe there.

Our hopes of being safe after having crossed the border of Norway proves to be grossly mistaken. Although the Finns have stopped pursuing us, the Russians simply carry on with their attacks and we are forced to by-pass Helligskogen.

Lyngenfjord, Sunday, 15 October 1944

We did reach safety today in the vicinity of Lyngenfjord. Our Waffen-SS and Wehrmacht comrades, who have managed to get away while we protected their retreat, have taken up defensive positions and they let us through. The Russians give up the fight and return to where they came from.

We hoped to be able to be taken by train from Fauske to the south but we are informed that partisans have wrecked the rails. No trains are running and we will have to travel on our own to the town of Mo i Rana, twelve hundred kilometers to the south over mountainous terrain.

Karl-Heinrich Brenner calls a conference of section chiefs: "Meine Herren, please congratulate your troops for a job well done. We have covered our division with glory. We have achieved our goal of forming the rear-guard for the retreat of the German forces from Finland. We have suffered serious losses, but these comrades will live on in our memories. I want to thank especially our Sanitätsgruppe. They have done a wonderful job of taking care of all the wounded.

"We will proceed from Mo i Rana by train down to the southern tip of Norway and from Kristiansand we will cross the Baltic Sea to go to Denmark. There we will enjoy a welcome period of rest where we will regroup. We are needed in the Fatherland to stop the Americans from reaching our towns and cities.

"But, unfortunately, it will take some time before we can reach the railroad. On our way there we may be harassed by air raids from Scotland and by partisans. So, be vigilant!"

Mo i Rana, Friday, 20 October 1944

It took us another week to reach Mo i Rana where two trains awaited the first batch of the division to be taken to the south. We have marched 1 600 kilometers, mostly on foot, from our front position in Karelia to this point – certainly no mean feat. One of the men calculated how long we fought against the Russians: 1 214 days of combat against the Soviet Army.

Pater Sepp asks me to call the survivors of the artillery regiment together on a parade. I willingly oblige.

When all the men are assembled in platoons or batteries on an open stretch alongside the station, Pater Sepp shouts at the top of his voice: "Meine Herren, please bear with me. I am in no position to give you any orders. But I request you humbly that we all go on our knees. I will lead you in prayer." And with that, he provides the example by going down on his knees.

Nobody refuses to comply and the whole regiment – or what is left of it – kneels on the Norwegian soil. Pater Sepp does a moving prayer of thanks at the top of his voice. If I am not mistaken, quite a few of the boys got tears in their eyes.

I secretly think that the priest will make a marvelous Oberscharführer or Feldwebel with that volume of his voice.

After his "Amen!", everybody is allowed to stand again. I start to go through the ranks and I shake the hand of every man and boy. Although I am not a real German, these guys have become my family. I still mourn the loss of my wife and my sister-in-law, but these chaps have accepted me as a second father, although I am only thirty-two years old, younger than some of the NCO's. They are truly my family. We have gone through so much together; we have lost many comrades and we have learnt to trust each other. I also mourn the loss of many a friend in the regiment.

I am to get onto the last train, together with all the section chiefs and Karl-Heinrich Brenner. The bulk of the division is to go ahead as soon as possible.

Oslo, Monday, 30 October 1944

Our train stops in Oslo, the capital of Norway. Gruppenführer Brenner is called over the public address system of the station just when the train comes to a stop. He is the only person who is allowed to get off the train. SS guards surround the train to prevent anybody from going AWOL (absent without leave), although nobody seems to have that wish.

After half-an-hour Brenner comes back with a list of names in his hand. He hands this list to a Stabscharführer who walks from carriage to carriage and reads out the names on the list. Those who are called are allowed to step onto the platform. To my surprise, my name is also called out.

All those who were summoned are ordered to line up in three rows. We march to a waiting bus outside the station. The bus takes us to the Wehrmacht headquarters for Norway. We are required to get out of the bus and form a long line from the most senior to the most junior on the parade ground next to the headquarters. I am almost at the end of the line.

And then Generaloberst (Colonel General) Lothar Rendulic, commander-in-chief of the German forces in Norway and a native of Austria, appears.

Generaloberst Lothar Rendulic

He has the edelweiss badge of a trained mountain soldier in his cap. He addresses us and thanks the division for the excellent work we have done.

Then Gruppenführer Karl-Heinrich Brenner is called upon to step forward.

The General's adjutant reads a citation, conferring the Knight's Cross of the Iron Cross on Brenner. Brenner salutes the General, who returns the salute. Then he hangs a multi-colored ribbon around Brenner's neck with a fancy Iron Cross hanging from it. Brenner salutes again and the General returns the salute. Brenner steps back into the line.

Standartenführer Franz Schreiber is next. He also receives the Knights Cross. Other recipients of the Knight's Cross are Sturmbannführer Gottlieb Renz and Hauptsturmführer Günther Degen.

And so, it goes on. All the other officers and NCOs on parade receive the Iron Cross, First Class. It never occurred to me that I may receive a German decoration for bravery when I joined the Waffen-SS four years ago. All I wanted to do was to be a medical practitioner and to stay out of a concentration camp.

When the last man has received his Iron Cross, the adjutant requests me to step forward again. I salute once more, which the General reciprocates. Then a citation is read out that I am promoted to "Oberstabsarzt" (Senior Staff Surgeon) – the equivalent of a Sturmbannführer or Major. This is another sign of the gratitude of the Wehrmacht for my sterling service as chief of the division's medical service and temporary commander of an artillery regiment – in spite of the fact that I have not yet served long enough to be promoted to this rank.

I salute again after my new rank insignia have been slided onto myshoulder straps and the old ones had been removed and Rendulic returns the salute. When we are marched back to the bus to take us to the station, I feel exceedingly sad. How I wish to have been able to tell my Josephine of this honor! I will, though, write to my parents-in-law with whom I have kept contact and inform them of what has befallen me.

Shoulder straps of a Obersstabsarzt

Of course, it is totally out of the question to let my parents in far-away South Africa know of what has happened. We have had absolutely no contact since war was declared. I am sure that they will surely not believe what their two sons have achieved in far-away Germany. For all they know, both of us are languishing somewhere in a concentration camp and performing slave labor.

Kristiansand, Tuesday, 7 November 1944

The trains carrying the remnants of our division stop at the station of the port city of Kristiansand. We disembark and are taken to barracks where we are to await the ships and ferries that are to take us to Denmark after the whole of the division has arrived.

I have fond memories of Kristiansand. The four of us disembarked here during the summer of 1939 on our way to the Hardangerfjord and surrounding mountains. I am thankful for wonderful memories but I would have preferred much rather to have had my Josephine still alive and well.

Kristiansand, Sunday, 12 November 1944

We are resting at Kristiansand for a few days.

A film crew appears. They are to entertain us with a propaganda film with the title of "Ohm Krüger". The division is to watch the film in shifts – battalion by battalion. Gruppenführer Brenner sends a messenger to summon me.

He smiles after we have saluted each other: "Herr Doktor Scholtz, this film we are to watch deals with the life of somebody with whom you must be familiar. The film was shown to audiences a number of years ago, but it was reissued to bolster the morale of our troops. What can you tell my about 'Ohm Krüger'? I believe he was the last President of one of your Boer republics?"

"Herr Gruppenführer, yes, he was indeed the last President of the Transvaal Republic. Actually, he is very distantly related to me. My great-grandmother, Anna Jacoba Kruger, whose father was the commandant of the militia in the Roggeveld district of the Cape Colony during the eighteenth century, was a far-off cousin of the old President. So, there is some sort of a link. I don't know how this film will deal with his life but I expect it will accentuate the crimes the British have perpetrated against my people during the war of 1899 to 1902. I find it somewhat strange that the old President is given the title of 'Ohm'. We have the custom in South Africa to call any elderly person 'Oom', which means 'uncle', although we may not be related. But I doubt whether my people would have dared to call the old President 'Uncle Paul'. He would have been addressed as 'Herr Präsident'".

"That is also what I have heard. Go and watch it with your regiment. And – when we reach Denmark in a few days' time where we will rest and regroup, you will return to your old job of Divisionsarzt. We will get a replacement to command the artillery regiment. Thank you."

I was correct. The film is indeed about the life of the old Boer president. What I find funny is the fact that the film was clearly made in Germany with the snow-covered Alps in the background. The British concentration camps where so many Boer women and children died are featured prominently. It was, though, strange to hear the actors depicting our Boer women and children speak German fluently.

Suddenly I think: I haven't spoken Afrikaans for a very long time, except with Stefan Strauss and Karl Krause. Will I still be able to speak my mother tongue when I reach my own country, if ever?

Afterwards, members of my regiment tackle me to hear more about the South African War in which the two Boer republics lost their independence. That elevates me to hero status – much more than the Iron Cross First Class and the promotion that I have received.

Oberscharführer Desmond Dumm, one of the temporary battery commanders, asks me earnestly: "Herr Sturmbannführer, do you think that we will be sent to fight the British when we go back to the Fatherland? I am sure that you are very eager to take revenge on them for what they have done to your people."

"Herr Oberscharführer, I haven't got the faintest idea what our future role will be. All I know, is that we are to get refitted in Denmark and get some reinforcements. Heaven knows where we will be able to dig them up."

Kristiansand, Tuesday, 14 November 1944

I help in the military hospital In Kristiansand. One of the local doctors asked me to help with a certain patient. It might be an appendix, but then it may also be a tumor or food poisoning – but he was not sure.

It transpires that the patient simply had an inflamed appendix. When I check his admission card, I see that it is Korvettenkapitän (lieutenant-commander) Stefan Strauss, the same chap I operated upon three years ago in Trondheim and was a fellow passenger on the Usambara, many years ago.

I address him in Afrikaans after he has woken up: "Is this that bloody guy from South West Africa again? What on earth are you doing here, my friend? Last time I saw you, you were a big shot on a submarine."

Stefan smiles at me: "I must rather ask you what you are doing here. When I last saw you, you were in Trondheim with a bunch of SS butchers."

"Don't insult my regiment. We are elite troops, mountain troops. And if you want to know, we shot the shit out of the Russians. This is what we have done until the fucking Finns decided to throw in the towel and chase us away. Now we are back here."

"Are you the quack who worked on me?"

"Don't insult me, you miserable fool! I am not a quack! That is something that I explained to you three years ago. I am a specialist surgeon."

"OK. What did you do to me?"

"Ever heard of an appendix? We butchered yours out of your body. It was rotten and could have killed you – just as effective as a Russian or British bomb. Only slower."

"Thanks, man."

"When you are better you are going to pay me a visit. And then we can gossip about these blooming Germans. The stiff Nazis give me a pain in the ass."

"The same here. Tell me, what do you hear from your brother Willie? Does he also fight the Russians?"

"No, he has a civvie job. Research, or something. He's working, I believe, on some or other wonder weapon."

"I also work with a wonder weapon."

"Oh, yes?"

"Yes, I wonder every day what the poor conscripts in my flotilla will achieve when the enemy really strikes. The poor sods were only partly trained and then let loose."

"Yes, we can only wonder. We are supposed to get some reinforcements when we get to Denmark, some or other time. But I wonder where they will come from."

"You mentioned to me when we saw each other the last time that you married a German girl – just as I did."

"She was killed last June in Berlin by an American bomb."

"Sorry, man. My wife and little daughter were also blown up by an American bomb, two years ago."

"So – both of us are widowers."

"Officially, I am one. But, in the meantime I have made a Norwegian girl pregnant. I think a lot about her. But I will only be able to take her away after the war has ended."

"That is, if you don't kick the bucket before that time. You naughty boy!"

"This appendix is perhaps the punishment for my sins. But – I will struggle to kick the bucket, because I only have one-and-a-half feet after having lost three toes on my left foot."

It feels strange to conduct a conversation in Afrikaans again.

Just before I leave, Stefan's father-in-law and his son arrive to visit him. I am introduced as Oberstabsarzt David Scholtz to

Kapitän zur See (Navy Captain) Joachim Graf von Czapiewski. While I am shaking the nobleman's hand with a slight bow, I exclaim: "Von Czapiewski! Then we must be distantly related, somehow or other."

The Kapitän zur See frowns: "Yes?"

Me: "My twin brother was married to Annemarie van Czapiewski. She, unfortunately, died last year when an American bomb flattened the building in which she and my late wife lived. Her father is Waldemar von Czapiewski of Brandenburg an der Havel."

"Well, well, I never! I know him. He is a cousin once removed of my late father."

"So, there is a link, however distant."

"We must get together, some or other time, to continue our chat."

Kristiansand, Sunday, 19 November 1944

Yesterday, Saturday, I visited Stefan Strauss for the last time in hospital and discharged him. He is certainly not yet fit for service and I give him another fortnight to regain his strength. The medic in their sick bay must remove the stitches a fortnight after the operation. I also asked him, whether he would like to attend a religious service as my guest today – something he could not refuse.

After breakfast at the officers' mess, I go to fetch him. Pater Sepp leads the service in the open air. It seems as if the whole regiment has turned up voluntarily for the service. Pater Sepp as a Catholic priest says mass and delivers a short but inspiring sermon. Stefan, and I, who are staunch Protestants, do not take mass but we find the rest of the service uplifting.

Me: "That priest is a wonderful man. He has withstood all the hardships with the men and he proved to be a capable medic who helped me in the operating tent. That's why these men have the greatest respect for him and attend his services willingly. I think he qualifies for sainthood."

After the service, I invite Stefan to have lunch with me and my officers in our temporary lodgings where we are housed before taken over the Skagerrak to Denmark in a few days' time. Because the men would certainly never see Stefan after this, he deems it safe to divulge that he is actually a compatriot of their medical officer who hails from South Africa. We sit next to the Catholic priest and I assure Stefan that we are best friends, although we adhere to different brands of Christianity.

After lunch, Stefan and I go outside to sit on a rock where we can watch the harbor. I produce a bottle of vodka: "I have kept this for a special occasion. I carried it all the way from Finland where a Russian officer, whom I tended to in my medical tent, presented this to me out of gratitude that I had saved his life."

"And now you want to share it with me?"

"Yes, and then we can talk nonsense and shit while none of these stupid Nazis can understand what we are telling each other. We are going to finish this one-liter bottle while we are conversing in our mother tongue, Afrikaans."

"Marvelous. It seems as if you don't have a high regard for the Nazis."

"Let's take each a swig from this bottle to accentuate that profound insight you have."

Both of us take a mouth full of this fire water and Stefan gets tears in his eyes. He wonders what half-a-bottle of this strong stuff will do to him, but he cannot insult me, his new friend, by refusing to drink with me.

We start gossiping about the Nazis. We both agree that Hitler is a fool, a megalomanic idiot. It is actually a pity that those generals didn't take him out last July. By this time there is no chance whatsoever that Germany can win this war.

We drink another generous toast to another profound insight.

Me: "We were told that the Russians are barbarians and that Stalin is a near cousin of Satan himself."

Stefan: "And I have been taught that Churchill is a drunkard and that Roosevelt is a secret criminal Jew."

"And yet, I have found that the Russians are just ordinary folk who speak a strange language and who love this stuff (and he holds the bottle up in the air). I have operated on quite a number of wounded Russian prisoners and they have the same feelings and aspirations as we have."

"And I had lengthy conversations with two Canadian airmen whom we captured after having shot down their plane in the Atlantic. I found them to be very decent guys. If we weren't waging a war against them, I could even have befriended them."

"Let's drink on that piece of deep wisdom!"

Me: "And yet I hate the Americans and the British. The Brits allowed thousands of our women and children to die in their concentration camps during the South African War. And an American bomb killed my dear wife and my brother's wife."

Stefan: "My dad fought in the South African War against the Brits. Since he was an inhabitant of the Cape Colony, he was a subject of Her fucking Majesty, Queen Victoria. He was a member of the commando of Commandant Golding that operated in the mountains, south of the Karoo town of Fraserburg. They didn't know that peace was declared on 31 May 1902 and a few days later they shot and killed a few British soldiers on patrol in the mountains. He was sentenced to death in absentia for being a murderer and a so-called traitor and he and a few friends fled to German South West Africa where the Brits couldn't catch them. That's where he met my German mother. During the previous war, he helped the Germans in South West against the troops of Louis Botha and Jannie Smuts when they invaded the country."

"So, your folks were always anti-British. Was it an American or a British bomb that killed your family?"

"It was a bomber of the Royal Air Force. It's called 'Royal' because these guys are supposed to be loyal to His fucking Royal Majesty, King George."

"This information makes us almost blood brothers. Here, take another mouth full."

He does so and I follow his example.

Me: "Now that you mentioned the king, I can remember something we kids sometimes sang. It goes like this:

> 'God save the King
> With a bottle of paraffin.
> Out came a flame
> And away with the King!'"

Stefan starts laughing out loudly at this hilarious rhyme and he holds his belly with the operation wound. We both swallow another mouth full of fire water. After that he says: "I can also remember a silly rhyme from long ago. Here it is:

> 'King George flies in his aery,
> The people see his canary.
> He gets his parachute,
> And shouts: let us shoot!'"

I rock to and fro as I almost laugh my head off: "Wonderful! How does the King's canary look like? Do you know?"

We fall silent again.

Stefan: "Tell me about your wife, please? What type of person was she?"

I start telling how beautiful she was, about her wonderful family and then I start crying. He pats me on my shoulder and the sobs subside somewhat.

Me: "How did you and your wife get to know each other?"

Stefan waited for this question and he starts telling how they met and what happened after that. He takes out her photo to show to me and suddenly the tears start running down his cheeks.

I pat him on the back and I take out a photo of my wife. We both agree that we had married beautiful and wonderful girls.

None of us can talk any further and we finish off the last few drops in the bottle.

Me: "How in hell are we ever to get back home after this fucking war?"

Stefan: "Heaven knows. You must ask that priest pal of yours to pray for a miracle."

Both of us remain sitting on the rock, watching the harbor and feeling very sorry for ourselves.

Zweibrücken, Wednesday, 27 December 1944

We are back in the Fatherland, at last. The division was fighting in Finland for the past three years, almost non-stop. Our period of rest in Denmark was very welcome and we received reinforcements. Our manpower strength is said to be at more or less 15 000 at present. We were down to 12 000 from a high of 22 000 – a loss of 10 000 casualties consisting of those who were captured, have fallen or were crippled for life. I am thankful that I could have saved the lives of quite a number of wounded. That is, after all, my calling to lessen suffering and pain and preserve life.

Of course, it was never easy to amputate a limb or cut away part of an internal organ that got shot to pieces by shrapnel. It happened more than once that a young man lost an eye or got brain damage from a head wound and nothing could be done to remedy those situations.

I feel sorry for these new boys who join our regiments. They are not real Germans, but German-speaking Russians or "Volksdeutsche". Their fore-fathers settled along the Volga in the time of Empress Catherine the Great, but retained their German language and traditions – even their Lutheran faith. And now they are being pressed into military service with the Waffen-SS after some rudimentary training.

I can only guess what will happen to them, should they be captured by the Russians who will regard them as traitors.

We spent Christmas on the road. We were moved piecemeal to the lower Rhineland to a spot opposite the point where the borders of Germany, France and Luxemburg meet.

And now we await orders to attack the Americans in the mountainous and hilly parts of the north-eastern corner of France. Our skills as mountain soldiers are sorely needed there.

Zweibrücken, Sunday, 31 December 1944

As usual, Silvester in Germany is accompanied by snow. In these icy conditions, to which we have become used beyond the Arctic Circle, our boys have to attack the Americans and there is no time for festivities. We lie ready at the small town of Zweibrücken, adjacent to the French border, and we await the signal to start "Unternehmen Nordwind" (Operation North Wind) early tomorrow morning. Some wise guy cracks the joke that Division Nord will be the north wind that sweeps the American Seventh Army away. Our infantry battalions are supposed to be the spearhead of the operation – and they are again required to bite off the hardest bit.

Of course, my divisional medical section is not far behind. My colleagues, the medics, ambulance drivers and stretcher bearers were all glad to see me back after having been a temporary commander of the artillery regiment.

This part of the world is rather mountainous – we are to operate in the Upper Vosges Mountains – and therefore the infantry regiments of our Gebirgsdivision are called upon to carry out the attack. The few artillery pieces we have left are to back up their assault.

Wingen, Monday, 1 January 1945

It is to be expected that the inexperienced American soldiers we have to attack are still asleep when our men descend on them in the dark early morning hours. It is clear that they are totally unprepared and during the day a few hundred of them are captured. When darkness descends, we have secured the town of Wingen. I set our main medical post up in the ruins of an old castle outside the town.

Ruins of the Château du Grand-Geroldseck near Wingen

The American wounded are brought to our bandage station and these men are surprised to hear my excellent English – which I, as a South African, am supposed to know well enough, although I don't disclose that fact. After they have been tended to as well as possible, they are taken under guard to the Catholic Church, where they are kept together with the other prisoners of the 70th Division of the US Army . There is just no other building big enough to hold them all. We simply don't have the means to transport them to POW camps deeper inside Germany. Father Sepp assures me that God will forgive us for desecrating a holy church building in this time of need. He asks me to warn the prisoners in my best English not to steal anything from the church since that will bring a painful curse upon their heads. They can expect their eyes to become blind, their tongues to rot, their private parts to fall off, their lungs to perish, their fingers to turn black and break off and their noses to turn into stone.

We cram almost a whole battalion into the church.

Interior of the church at Wingen

Wingen, Sunday, 7 January 1945

The valiant fighters of our division are forced to retreat today – and our medics with them. We have been promised support of armor and more artillery, but that never materialized and, therefore, we could not advance any further. Our men defended the town against a terrible onslaught by the Americans – infantry, artillery and armor. The American attackers suffered serious losses in the process but after seven days our men have to give up and return to safer positions, fighting rear-guard actions through the snow-covered hills of the Vosges. Our ammunition stocks and food supplies are almost depleted and we are not likely to receive new supplies soon.

Storckenkopf in the Vosges Mountains, covered with patches of snow

We leave our American prisoners in the church behind and we presume that their comrades will find them and feed them, which we could not do. My medicinal supplies also ran out and it becomes more and more difficult to treat the wounded.

Vosges Mountains, Monday, 15 January 1945

After a week of fighting and fleeing there is a slight lull in the struggle. We get the impression that the Americans are also exhausted and that they have to regain their breaths.

Gruppenführer Brenner hastily calls a conference of section leaders: "Meine Herren, the Americans seem to have lost some steam. I suppose their supplies have run out and they want to regroup after the heavy losses we have inflicted upon them. This is our chance to strike back. Tomorrow morning at 06:00 our infantry is to attack and to inflict as much damage as possible. We have to keep these Yanks away from our German borders. I leave the particulars to the different regimental commanders. I have full confidence in your abilities. Unfortunately, you all know that we cannot rely on any armor support, but this hilly country is, anyway, not suited for armored warfare. We don't have much artillery left, but you won't need that support because you will strike swiftly and unexpectedly."

Afterwards, Brenner corners me outside, just before I get into my Kübelwagen that I have brought along, all the way from Finland: "Herr Oberstabsarzt, you are one of the veterans of this division and you have seen much. How is the morale of the men?"

"Herr Gruppenführer, we are very proud to be mountain troops of the Waffen-SS. We are the best. That is what the Americans also thought. When I was treating American soldiers at Wingen they told me that they would not have given up so easily if they were against regular German units. But when they realized that they were attacked by the terrible SS, they simply gave up and allowed themselves to be captured. Our men got a great morale booster from that. But, on the other hand, we have suffered so many losses since we started fighting the Americans that the men wonder whether it is still worthwhile to keep on fighting. Many of them ask whether there is still any chance of us winning the war, in spite of the fantastic wonder weapons we have been promised. They also wonder whether it was worthwhile to attack at Wingen since we lost all the ground that we have gained."

"I can understand their pessimism. It is true that we have suffered many losses. We set out with full divisional strength when we left Denmark. We had about fifteen thousand men. I don't know what our exact strength is at the moment but I guess that we are down to nine or ten thousand. Most of our losses were these boys that joined us in Denmark. We have lost much equipment and we don't have transport for all the men. Fuel for the vehicles is also a problem. We have lost the oil fields in Rumania to the Russians and I don't know how the Wehrmacht will be able to go on fighting without fuel for the tanks, trucks and airplanes – if we have any left. But anyway, let's see what tomorrow brings. Thank you for your time."

Vosges Mountains, Tuesday, 16 January 1945

Our infantry, under the direct command of Standartenführer Schreiber, the present second-in-command of our division, started their attacks early this morning. I, with my surviving medics, followed them to be near enough to treat any wounded men.

Throughout the day we hear the machine guns bark and rattle as they mow Americans down and the Panzerfausts howl and bang as they destroy American vehicles. It is clear that the Americans did not expect this attack. I also surmise that most of the Yankees are not accustomed to this cold, especially since it has started to snow again and the temperatures are below zero. Our men know how to deal with freezing temperatures. By midday, our first aid station is overflowing with wounded men – Germans and Americans. The Americans inform me that they were surrounded by the SS fighters and had nowhere to go. They were told by their generals that it would be a cake walk to reach Germany and overrun the Wehrmacht, but now they see that it is not the case.

I tell more than one wounded American officer whom I treat that it is clear that the Yankees are much softer than our men.

We have endured three winters inside the Arctic Circle and we don't surrender as easily as the Americans. We are as tough as leather. These officers cannot but agree with me.

Vosges-Mountains, Thursday, 18 January 1945

I hear from the American prisoners who are brought to my medical post that six American companies, almost two battalions, have surrendered to these terrible SS soldiers.

Standartenführer Schreiber visits my medical post to see his wounded men and to hear how many will be able to fight again. I hear from him that his men have captured valuable supplies, including medical equipment and food, from the Americans. He also tells me that he does not know what to do with the Americans who have surrendered. There are hundreds of them. There is no transport to take them into Germany and he cannot spare men to guard them while they are taken on foot to the rear.

I come to his aid by proposing that a number of our wounded men, who are not able to man the font line anymore but who are still able to move around, are able to guard these prisoners. He finds that a marvelous idea and about forty men with bandages are tasked with guarding the prisoners while they all march to the rear. The Americans will then be taken to POW camps and the wounded men will hopefully convalesce in a safe place.

Vosges Mountains, Monday, 22 January 1945

It is a miracle, but our men of the 6th Waffen-SS Gebirgsdivision Nord were able to push the Americans back for six whole days after we started the attack. I and my medics followed them and we had to shift our position every day, deeper into territory previously held by the enemy. We were able to capture much equipment.

However, the Americans have been able to organize a terrible counter-attack. The wounded who are brought to us report that our men were digging in but that the odds against us are just too much.

When darkness falls, we are ordered to retreat, back to the old line of fortifications – concrete bunkers, tank traps and tunnels, built a decade ago to protect the German border from attacks from France. We call it the Westwall, but I hear from wounded American prisoners that they call it the Siegfried Line.

A few of them even sing a song to oblige me:

"We're going to hang out the washing on the Siegfried Line".

Steinfeld, Wednesday, 14 February 1945

We have held out behind the Westwall for a whole fortnight since we retreated here on 30 January, but the sheer numbers of the Americans were too much. The Westwall was breached on several spots and what is left of our division has to retreat, deeper into Germany. I and my medical team have to move to the rear of the protected front formed by the poor battered infantry soldiers. We camp at a village called Steinfeld.

Tank traps on the Westwall, called "Drachenzähne" (Dragons' Teeth). The Allies called the defensive line the Siegfried Line

I am informed by Brenner that we are probably down to seven or eight thousand men. Our losses are due to men who have fallen, were wounded or got captured. We cannot be called a real division anymore because we are only of brigade strength. Although we have lost the Westwall, there is still the Rhine that can be used as a defensive line. Brenner tells me that our Pionieren will mine the bridges over the Rhine as soon as our troops have crossed the river and blow them up before the Allies can cross the river.

Karlsruhe, Thursday, 8 March 1945

The past three weeks went by in a blur. I got very little sleep due to the numbers of wounded men – Germans and Americans – who were brought to our medical posts. My position of Divisionsarzt is supposed to be mainly an administrative position, but there is just too much pressure on my colleagues and our medics that I can concentrate solely on managing our medical teams. In between operations and short periods of sleep I give orders that our supplies have to be checked, that new supplies have to be procured from somewhere and that our few ambulances have to be kept in a working condition. Fortunately, my men know their jobs and it is not necessary to supervise them closely.

I amputate limbs, patch up wounds after I have removed pieces of shrapnel or bullets, give blood transfusions, dispense medication and hear the woes and wails of suffering boys. I apply an old folk remedy that I got from my mother, namely to treat burn wounds with the albumin of a raw egg and my colleagues tell me that it works miracles – if we can get eggs. I was warned during my training, way back in 1940, that this sort of horror may be expected under battle conditions, but at that time I was not able to imagine what it would be like to work under so much pressure. It is worse than anything we experienced in Finland.

We have sent away all the female nurses we had since our stay in Denmark. It is simply too dangerous for them to stay with us while we have to move around almost on a daily basis. It has happened more than once that the American artillery has targeted our medical tents, even if they are marked with huge red crosses on a white background. I have lost two colleagues and several medics in this manner, including my colleague Heini Söhnge. I still have the letter he gave me to deliver to his wife in Graz.

Food is a problem. We have to feed our patients while they are still in our care but supplies are only coming through in a trickle. I suspect that all people in Germany are starving and I am actually glad that my dear Josephine is spared this hardship. I shudder to think what will happen when we lose the war, which seems certain. There is very little to be seen of the wonder weapons that were supposed to win the war.

More than one wounded man lying on my portable operating table tells me that the soldiers have totally lost faith in the Führer. One of them, a battalion commander, says: "He got us into this war. In the beginning everything went well, but it was a lousy decision to declare war against Russia and America. We simply didn't have the resources to take them on and keep them away from our borders. Our Wehrmacht is a shadow of what it used to be due to all our losses. The British and American bombers flatten our cities at will and our Luftwaffe seems to have disappeared. When we discuss the Führer, we have given him the nickname of 'Gröfaz' – which is the abbreviation for 'Größte Feldherr aller Zeiten' (greatest commander of all times) – as the Propaganda Minister Goebbels has given us to believe. Hmff. Look at all the mistakes he has made. It is actually a pity that those Generals didn't take him out last July."

I know that I am supposed to report him for this treacherous and defeatist outburst, but the men know they can trust me not to betray them. And, in the meantime, that is exactly how I already felt a long time ago.

And in the meantime, our men were fighting a desperate rearguard action against the Yankees in the area to the west of Karlsruhe.

Gruppenführer Brenner comes to me: "I have received an insane order from the OKW. They want us to pull back to go into reserve for a week and then go back to fight the Russians in Austria since we are a mountain division and supposed to be familiar with the Alps."

"Is it in any way possible to pull out at this moment?" I ask.

"We will leave a gap in the front if we pull out. But we actually have no choice. The Americans have managed to capture an intact bridge on the lower Rhine at Remagen yesterday and they are swarming into central Germany. If we stay here, we will be cut off. So – off we go, even if it leaves a gap in the front. And – as soon as we pull back, we can count on the Amis (German slang for Americans) to chase us. We have few vehicles left and most of our men will have to use their tattered boots to keep running."

"Fortunately, I still have my Kübelwagen. I can take three Sanitäter along with me."

Kufstein, Tuesday, 3 April 1945

We reached Kufstein yesterday morning – Easter Monday. I have fond memories of this place because the four of us have had a memorable holiday here, many years ago. This is where we had our respective honeymoons. I almost cannot remember those happy times anymore; my whole world is just filled with shattering and exploding bombs, screeching machine guns, howling fighter aircraft engines, the growls of bomber engines, the cries of boys in pain and a lack of sleep.

We plug the gap in the mountains where the railroad and the highway pass between Bavaria and Tyrol. The Yankees seem to regard it as a waste of time to force this gap and they by-pass us. It might also be that they do not want to take chances with the terrible Waffen-SS.

On the way we suffered horrible losses. The American infantry, tanks and guns harassed us constantly. It was not even possible to reach our wounded men and bring them back to our medical posts. There was no time to pitch our medical tents and we had to leave those injured and dying men to be taken prisoner with the hope that the American doctors would treat them before they were taken away to POW camps.

Yesterday was a particular hard day, just before we reached the gap in the mountains. American fighter planes strafed our struggling convoys and rows of weary foot-sloggers. One of the casualties was Karl-Heinrich Brenner, our divisional commander, who was seriously wounded.

I had to treat him as well as I could with the meagre medical supplies we still had. A bullet was lodged in his stomach and it was a dangerous operation to remove it without damaging his internal organs. It was so serious that he had to be operated upon immediately in order to save his life. Before I gave him chloroform to anesthetize him for the operation, he asked me to call Standardtenführer Schreiber to the medical post.

Standartenführer (colonel) Franz Schreiber

When Schreiber appeared, he addressed us both: "Men, this war is history for me. I cannot go on and you must leave me here so that the Amis can take me. There is no way in which I can be evacuated to a German Lazarett. Schreiber, you are the most senior officer I still have. You must take command of what is left of the division. I guess that we have a little more than two thousand men.

"And you, Herr Doktor Scholtz, you must take over command of a battalion. We have merely three battalions left if we reorganize the remaining men. That is your task, Schreiber. You may decide which battalion to give to this good Doktor."

I frowned: "Herr Gruppenführer, you are asking too much of me. I have never been trained as an infantry soldier. I am in the first place a medical officer. As a favor to you, I have taken command of my old artillery regiment. I knew how to deal with big shooting machines. But of infantry tactics, I don't have any blinking idea."

Schreiber looked me in the eyes: "Herr Oberstabsart, what you say may be true. But after me, you are the most senior officer we have left. You know how to lead men. They are well trained and know how to do their bit and all you have to do is to manage them and motivate them. We have one other Sturmbannführer and one man of the rank of Hauptsturnführer left. These men will have to lead the other two battalions."

Brenner nodded his head: "Herr Scholtz, you have no choice. It is my wish. There are two trains waiting for our men at the station in Kufstein and with that you are to be transported to the east. And now you may operate on me and after that you report to Standartenführer Schreiber to await your orders."

And now, the day after Easter Monday, I become the commanding officer of the third battalion of what is left of our glorious division. I get three subalterns to lead three of the companies and a senior NCO to lead the fourth company.

Standertenführer Schreiber calls a conference of all battalion and company commanders: "Meine Herren, our orders are to proceed to the eastern front and stop the Russians. You have seen the trains at the station that will take us to Graz and beyond. I haven't got the faintest idea how we will do it and where our services will be needed, but when we travel further, we will certainly find a place where we can do some good before everything in Greater Germany comes tumbling down.

"As I see it, we must keep the Russians as far away from our towns and villages and when the end comes, we must be able to surrender to the Americans. I suspect that some American units will enter Tyrol after we have left Kufstein. I believe that you will agree with me that it will be better to be prisoners of the Yanks than of the Ivans."

I ask: "Herr Standartenführer, it seems that we will have to leave most of our big equipment and vehicles behind. There is just not enough place on the trains for all that. May I request that the remaining members of my old Artillery Regiment be allocated to my new battalion?"

"Sturmabannführer Scholtz, that's a reasonable request. And, will you please request your friend, Pater Sepp, to conduct a short service for all the troops before we leave here? Tonight, will do. We need all the help from heaven that we can get."

Graz, Friday, 6 April 1945

It took us three days to travel by train to Graz through the Alpine valleys in-between. It happened twice that we had to hide in tunnels when American aircraft flew overhead. There are many troop trains moving to and fro and the stations and towns are overcrowded with refugees fleeing the Russians. All that slows down our progress towards the east.

At the station of Graz, a Wehrmacht General and his staff await us. He asks us who our commanding officer is and he is pointed to Standartenführer Schreiber.

Before our train gets going again, I call an elderly man in the uniform of the "Reichsbahn" (Railways of the Reich) to my carriage window. "My good man, will you please post this letter for me? I cannot get off the train, but I see a red post box over there. Will you please drop it in there?" and with that I hand him the letter that my late colleague Heini Söhnge entrusted in my care.

I could not hear what the General and Schreiber were discussing, but when the train gets going again, Schreiber holds a conference in his compartment. "Meine Herren, here I have orders from the corps commander under whose authority we will operate for the foreseeable future. I have the idea that he doesn't know much of what is going on in his sector. He was greatly relieved that three battalions of Gebirgsjäger are at his disposal and we are given the task of stopping the Russians from entering the 'Gau' (province) of Styria. We have to plug two passes – the Semmering Pass and the Wechsel Pass, the only routes into Styria from Lower Austria. Does anybody here know any of those places?"

I hold up my hand: "I've spent a holiday a decade ago at Semmering where I ascended the Zauberberg. I also spent time in the region of the Murz river. I think I have a good idea of the lie of the land there."

"Excellent, then you and your Battalion Number Three will go there. Number One Battalion will guard the Wechsel Pass and Battalion Number Two will act as our reserve. Thank you, gentlemen. When this train stops at Semmering, Battalion Number Three will disembark there and dig in. The First Battalion is to march to the Wechsel Pass and dig in there. Battalion Number Two will take up positions at Murzzuschlag."

Semmering, Sunday, 8 April 1945

The Semmering Pass is rather narrow and long and it is fairly easy to plug. Our troops dig in next to the highway and the railroad beyond the railway station, as well as between the trees on the slopes on both sides. There are enough rocks and trees to hide behind, but it was also necessary to dig trenches and machine gun pits.

Our arms consist of rifles, machine guns, Panzer-fausts, hand grenades and even a flame thrower. We preserve the few mines we have left for future use. We disable the railway tracks to prevent any trains of using it. I decide to deploy two companies and rest the other two companies. After a few days they are to be rotated. My company commanders agree with my plan. And now the waiting starts. According to the news we can pick up on our radios, the Russians are advancing on Vienna and it is expected that they will take the city soon.

The few locals who are still left in these parts help us with victuals – milk, cheese, bread and some vegetables and fruit. They are but too thankful to have our protection.

Late in the afternoon the first Russians appear. These chaps seem to have by-passed Vienna and are carrying on in the direction of Styria. Since they have encountered little resistance in Lower

Austria, they seem to think that it will be a piece of cake to enter Styria through the two passes.

But a very nasty surprise awaits them. When their vanguard was almost through the pass, we spring the trap. We wipe a whole battalion out within half an hour of firing on the suddenly disorganized and disorientated troops. It is almost as if we are shooting at targets on a shooting range. A few of them manage to shoot back and a few of our men get wounded, but we suffer no fatalities.

The units following this vanguard fall back in disarray. We expect them to be back tomorrow.

Semmering, Friday, 13 April 1945

I have decided to rotate the companies last night. The men inside the pass are exhausted after non-stop fighting over the past five days. They endured artillery fire and the Russians also tried to send tanks through the gap in the mountains. Fortunately, we mined the road the day before the tanks appeared and the blown-up tanks block the road. The enemy was repulsed every time with heavy losses. We allow their stretcher parties with white flags to remove their dead and wounded.

We also suffered casualties. Although the artillery fire of the Russians is far from accurate, they did manage to inflict some damage on our positions with their high volume of fire.

During the first two days the Russians only attacked once per day, but after that they tried twice every day, but they did not manage to gain a single centimeter. We are too well fortified. We hear over the radio that Vienna has fallen to the Russians. That means that there will be so many more Russians to attack our positions in a few days' time.

One of the company commanders comments: "I almost enjoy this operation. We have never inflicted so much damage on the Ivans when we were still in Finland!"

Towards late afternoon something happens that we all find amusing: a Russian artillery piece comes rolling and bouncing down the right-hand slope towards us and comes to rest on the railway tracks. One of its wheels became unattached and found its own way down the mountain. I am at that moment doing an inspection tour of our boys on the front line when a lull in the fighting occurred.

The only explanation we can find for this happening is that the Russians must have pulled one of their guns with great effort to the top of the mountain to shoot at us from above, but that they lost control of the heavy piece of metal and that it came tumbling down.

To prevent this of happening again I decide to place two sections of ten men each on the mountains on both sides. The have to block any attempt by the Russians to try something of this sort again with their rifles and machine guns. We keep radio contact with them.

Semmering, Saturday, 14 April 1945

It becomes clear that our men cannot survive more than two days at a stretch in the ambush. Conditions are terrible. It rains almost every day and then the men have to wait in their holes and trenches for the Russians to attack. They are cold and hungry and tired due to lack of sleep because the artillery fire does not stop at night and it often happens that the Russians try to slip past our positions in the dark.

Some of the men tell me that it is at its worst when fog envelops the mountains. It restricts their vision to, perhaps, twenty meters. The mist tests the mens' vigilance to the utmost because the Russians may come marching along through the nebulae at any moment and there are only a few seconds left to start shooting at them before they reach our positions.

Semmering, Thursday, 19 April 1945

Unexpected reinforcements arrive this morning. A company cadet from the artillery school in Graz appear and I greet them with open arms. They come with their own trucks and brought much-needed supplies – food and ammo.

Their commander, an army Hauptmann, reports to me with a salute: "Heil Hitler! Herr Major, I am Hauptmann Wilhelm Liebenberg. The commanding General in Graz, Generaloberst Rendulic, suddenly remembered that we exist. He thought that it would not be a bad idea if we interrupt the training of these cadets for a while by exposing them to a little bit of action here in the mountains."

I remember Rendulic from Norway when he pinned the Iron Cross, First Class, onto my battle dress. Now it seems he is back in his native Austria and in command of the Sixth Army.

I explain to Liebenberg that I am the most unlikely battalion commander he will ever meet in his life since I am actually a medical officer with a rank equivalent to that of a Major, but not really a Major as he mistook me to be. "But anyway, you are extremely welcome. Two of our companies are at this moment waiting for the Ruskies to reappear from Lower Austria in an effort to force the pass. We have repulsed them for more than ten days already. I believe that they count their losses in the thousands. It is my plan to deploy the two resting companies tonight and pull the boys in the ambush out. But perhaps some of your boys can join the two companies that are to go in tonight and dig some more fortified positions. We expect the onslaught to be so much fiercer now that Vienna has fallen and more troops are likely to come this way."

Liebenberg replies: "Our boys are not exactly infantry men. But they know how to handle machine guns and Panzerfausts and they can throw hand grenades."

Later that afternoon a company elderly men arrive – all of them from the Pay Master's Corps. They are only able to count money. Liebenberg agrees with me that they will be more of a burden than a help and I send the poor devils back. I doubt whether any of them has ever shot with a gun.

Still later, Standartenführer Schreiber arrives with an important message: we have received so many reinforcements from units in the south that one can almost say that the Sixth SS-Division was resurrected. The reinforcements are, though, regular Army units, but they are also mountain troops who know how to fight in these conditions. He deployed them higher up in the mountains to prevent the Russians from entering Styria in this way. In the meantime, my battalion, with the reinforcements of Liebenberg, must carry on guarding the Semming Pass.

Semmering, Saturday, 21 April 1945

My time is divided between visiting the men in their trenches and foxholes, patching up wounded men and organizing things at our headquarters – an old barn in the abandoned village of Semmering.

The Ivans have at last managed to get the disabled tanks that blocked the road through the pass out of the way under cover of darkness when we were not able to shoot at the men doing the recovery.

This morning, the Russians sent up some more tanks. Our men shot the first three out with their Panzerfausts and that again blocked the road for the rest. Before more tanks could be destroyed, they retreated.

Hauptmann Liebenberg, who unofficially became my second-in-command, is of the opinion that our stocks of ammunition is due to run out shortly due to the rate of fire that we maintain. "But that need not be too much of a problem. There is an ammunition store at the artillery school that we can go and raid."

"Fantastic. You know the way, but perhaps I will have to come with you. I suppose we will need a few men to help us to load the boxes and trunks."

We set off in a convoy of four trucks to the artillery school. When we enter the ammunition store, the clerk behind the counter wakes up and utters sleepily: "Heil Hitler! And what can I do for the 'Herrschaften' (masters)?"

I reply: "We need ammo. And lots of it!"

"Where is your paper work? I cannot release stocks without a signed requisition order. I have to keep track of every single bullet that leaves this place."

A burly Hauptscharführer, Hans Hansen, steps behind the counter and grabs the clerk by his coat: "Just get out of the way, you stupid asshole!"

I order the men behind me: "Take everything we can use, including cleaning kits for our guns. We don't need brooms and buckets, but everything that we must have to keep shooting. Look for tinned food if there is any."

The poor clerk squeals: "Meine Herrschaften! Please, be merciful. I will get into big trouble for allowing you to do this!"

Hansen simply throws the man out of the way and shouts: "Männer! This way! I have the keys!"

I feel sorry for the poor clerk and take him gently by his arm while the men swarm into the vault: "My good man, nobody will cause you any trouble. In case you haven't heard – the glorious Third Reich is finished. It lies belly-up. It is only a matter of days before the whole country is overrun by the Ruskies, the Tommys and the Yankees. In a few days' time you will be out of a job – and so will all of us because the Wehrmacht will cease to exist. Our only hope is to keep the Ivans out of Styria to protect our civilians with the hope that the Americans reach us in time so that we can surrender to them. Verstanden?"

The poor man has no choice but to shake his head up and down while his bulging eyes are opened wide from shock. I cannot but have sympathy with this poor German (or Austrian) who has to do everything according to the book and always needs official orders to do anything.

It takes about an hour to load the trucks and we are satisfied with our haul. The trucks are refueled and two hours later we arrive at the Semmering Pass where we unload the priceless treasures. We even have four heavy mortars – the 80 mm Granatwerfer – with twenty boxes of mortar bombs. We can use these very well because they extend the range at which we can blast the hapless Ruskies who dare to storm us. We are also grateful for fifteen crates with hand grenades and six crates with illumination flares to light up the night sky.

Semmering, Monday, 30 April 1945

We have managed to keep the Russians at bay for more than three weeks, The men are absolutely exhausted. We get little sleep since the Russians bombard us at night from afar. We have nothing to counter that, except to creep further into our foxholes and dig deeper.

Part of the haul we got from the ammunition store is some spare batteries for our radios with which we keep contact with the world. We report each day to Standartenführer Schreiber to keep him up-to-date. He even visited us a few times and he repeats his confidence in me as battalion commander. We hear over the radio that the Wechsel Pass is not breached, either.

And then we hear very dramatic news: Großadmiral (Admiral of the Fleet) Karl Dönitz, commander-in-chief of the Kriegsmarine, announces that Hitler has fallen while helping to defend Berlin against the Russians and that he was appointed as the successor of the Führer as Reichskanzler.

Schreiber who was at my command post at that moment murmurs: "The war must be over any day now. I cannot see that we can go on. The big shots at the OKW who always bowed before the Führer and executed everything he ordered will simply not know what to do next. Dönitz has his headquarters at Flensburg on the Danish border and there is no way in which he can control those fools at the OKW!"

I cannot but taunt him with a smile: "But, Herr Standartenführer! Do you know that I will have to report you to the Gestapo for your seditious, disrespectful and defeatist talk? How can you, as a fervent Nazi, talk like this? Have you forgotten your Fahneneid, your oath of allegiance to Hitler?"

He laughs: "Which member of the Gestapo will dare to come and arrest me here? I am sure that they are all hiding in their rat holes. That is, if they have not already secretly defected to the

British and the Americans! I expect the total surrender of the glorious Wehrmacht to happen very soon. But, in the meantime, we have to keep the Ruskies from our doorstep. Thank you for your marvelous job. I feel like recommending you for the Knight's Cross to the Iron Cross, but I am afraid that there will be no chance of that being approved before the end comes."

Semmering, Tuesday, 1 May 1945

The survivors of the Sixth SS Gebirgjägerdivison Nord – there are about one thousand and six hundred men left – receive the order from corps headquarters that we have to leave our positions and retreat. I decide to ignore the order. There is no way that we can allow the Russians to enter Styria and terrorize the civilian population. We have heard many stories through the grapevine that the barbarians from Siberia plunder and rape as far as they go – and we won't allow that to happen in Styria if it is in our power.

Schreiber supports my decision.

So – we keep on shooting Russians. A few hundred die or are wounded each day. It is clear that the Russian Generals don't attach any value to human life; they simply sacrifice poor ignorant boys from the Caucasus, Siberia, the Volga regions and the Ukraine by using them as cannon fodder – although we don't have any cannons, only rifles, machine guns, Panzerfausts, hand grenades and mortars. That tells us something about the state of mind of these Communists and we are proud to have fought against that monster.

Semmering, Monday, 7 May 1945

We receive the news that the chief of the OKW, Field Marshall Wilhelm Keitel, is to sign the surrender of the Wehrmacht tomorrow at a ceremony in Berlin, although he has already signed a deed of surrender to the Americans at Reims in France today. Fighting has to stop today.

We see the Russians celebrate on the plain to the north of us. There is a huge parade and a band plays music that we faintly hear. It is clear that they are not prepared to fight anymore. That leaves the road open for us to leave our positions after four weeks of continuous battles.

I call all our dog-tired men of the Third Battalion on parade and I thank them for their sacrifices: " I will always remember your bravery and the fact that you were proud members of the Waffen-SS and of our division. We can be proud of our achievements. We have a wonderful record. We were the best and we did our best. Our country could always rely on us. You are to march westwards to surrender to the Americans who are, by this time, not too far off. Perhaps ten or twenty kilometers. May God protect you all."

We collect our personal belongings and arms. It may happen that the Russians attack us from the rear and then we have to be able to defend ourselves. The wounded men are loaded onto the trucks of the Artillery School. While we are marching in rows of three in their companies the men start singing – something they haven't done for quite a while. There simply was no time or energy for that. I gather that they are relieved that the hell of war is over for them and that they did not fall into Russian captivity.

We reach Schreiber's headquarters and halt. The men with him are also lined up in anticipation of the march to the west.

Schreiber takes me and my friend Pater Sepp aside with a worried look on his face: "My dear Herr Doktor Scholtz, you are now relieved of your command of the Third Battalion. Our division dies today and won't exist anymore. What are your plans for the future? Are you ready to become a prisoner of the Americans?"

"I am really not sure. On the one hand I don't want to be separated from my men. I have been their leader for a month and they have become my dear friends. They were my patients as well. I have heard their sad stories while tending to their wounds. They asked me to sit by and listen when they confessed to Pater Sepp and he advised them on their troubled consciences. I shared their nightmares. I mourn all our dead. They were like family – just as I still mourn the death of my dear darling wife during a 'Bombenangriff' (bombing raid) on Berlin a year ago."

Schreiber looks at me when I fall silent and fight back a knot in my throat: "Is that all?"

"Not really. I was afraid of falling into Russian hands. I have heard stories that they reserve their utmost cruelty for SS officers. And now I am also afraid of falling into American or British hands. I am not a German subject. As you are well aware, I am a citizen of the Union of South Africa. I only joined the SS because I had no choice. If I hadn't joined, I would have been thrown into a concentration camp. But my government won't understand that. I carried arms against the Allies during this war and there is a real possibility that I will face the death penalty after having been repatriated to my country."

Schreiber frowns: "Then you must disappear. Get rid of your uniform and hide somewhere."

Pater Sepp, who has stayed silent, opens his mouth: "I am aware the Holy Catholic Church could not condone everything that the Nazi's did, but the Holy See is prepared to overlook the crimes of the Third Reich because we fought the godless Communists and we have been able to keep them out of most of Europe. Perhaps, perhaps, the Church may help."

I get a sudden brain wave: "The most beautiful convent in the whole of Styria is about a day's walk from here to the south. I have visited Stift Vorau of the Augustinian Order may years ago when I was on holiday at Semmering and I have loved the place. Pater, do you think that it might be a good place to hide until the dust has settled?"

Pater Sepp smiles: "That is a piece of divine inspiration that has struck you. Herr Standartenführer, I and my Protestant friend will say good-bye to you now and start walking to Stift Vorau immediately after that. I don't want to greet my boys again because it will only bring tears to my eyes and I don't have a handkerchief anymore to dry my tears. So – Tschüss! Lebe wohl! (Good-bye! Live well!)"

About an hour after we've started walking, I ask my friend: "Do you want to hear the greatest, deadliest, and best-kept secret of the whole war?"

"I never thought that you were privy to military secrets. Did one of your patients talk in his sleep?"

"No. I happen to know something that very few people ever heard of."

"Yes?"

"Yes. I'm sure that you can recall that I've told you that my twin brother is a scientist, a nuclear physicist?"

"Yes, yes, you told me. Was he working on this secret stuff?"

"The war is over. Germany is defeated. The Wehrmacht has surrendered. The war is over. It won't matter now if I tell you about my brother's secret work. He was a member of a team working on an atom bomb. It's clear they never succeeded, otherwise we wouldn't have been fugitives, but proud conquerors."

"An atom bomb? What's that?"

"Don't ask me what it is. Or how it works. It has something to do with uranium – or that's what my brother told us and requested us to keep it secret. But according to my brother, it would have been the ultimate weapon. If we had it in time, we could have wiped out London, Paris, New York, Moscow, Leningrad, Stalingrad – you name it. Millions of people would have died in one stroke."

"Perhaps the good God in heaven prevented the manufacture of that blasted bomb. You make it sound terrible, terrifying, totally catastrophic. It's perhaps a blessing that your brother didn't succeed. Yes, it's actually a positive blessing. No doubt about it."

Stift Vorau, Tuesday, 8 May 1945

After having walked steadily to the south and sleeping in the woods, we reach Stift Vorau during the afternoon. Fortunately, the buildings do not seem to have suffered any war damage.

We ring the bell at the entrance. After a while an old monk opens the gate: "We are closed," he says with a sad voice when seeing our uniforms.

Pater Sepp looks at him: "My son, I am Father Joseph Heibl and this is my friend, Herr Doktor David Scholtz. He is a medical specialist. He needs to stay with you for a while until the dust has settled after the end of the war."

"Wait here," the old monk orders. After a few minutes, the Prior appears: "What can I do for you, my children? Please step inside. I will lead the way to my office." I instantly like him for the kind manner in which he addresses us.

In his office Pater Sepp explains that he is a secular priest. "The only parish I ever had, was the Artillery Regiment of the 6th

Gebirgsjägerdivision of the Waffen-SS and, more recently, the remnants of the whole division. But this division does not exist anymore since the Wehrmacht has surrendered. And now I have no parish anymore. My last task as Kriegspfarrer is now to help my good friend, Herr Doktor Oberstabsarzt David Scholtz, to reach safety. He is a South African who happened to join the SS because he had no choice. He has rendered sterling service to his fellow human beings by patching up, sowing up and cutting up wounded and injured boys who were wearing a uniform. But he is in grave danger. Because he is a South African who served in a German military unit that fought the Allies, he faces the possibility of being condemned to death as a traitor in his country. Is it possible that you can hide him here for a while until his future is perhaps more secure?"

The Prior, Father Jerome, listens attentively: "God has answered our prayers. We urgently need a doctor in our convent, as well as in the villages around us. Of course, Herr Doktor Scholtz is welcome to stay here. He will, of course, have to get rid of his SS uniform. If he chooses to join our order as a brother, he is always welcome. But we will supply him with a habit in any case so that he will be indistinguishable from our priests and brothers. Welcome, Brother David – if I may call you thus?"

Pater Sepp continues: "God will bless you, dear Father Prior. And now I will have to leave you again. God didn't call me to devote my life to study and contemplation, as your order evidently is called to do. I have a responsibility towards our men who surrendered to the Americans. They will need me more than ever before. Tomorrow, I will walk back to where I came from. That is, if you can give me lodgings for the night where I can rest before I go back."

Father Jerome simply said: "Selbstverständlich" (of course).

And so, I take refuge in the Order of Saint Augustine in the convent of Vorau. What will my Calvinist parents think if they could hear that I joined a Roman Catholic priory? We were constantly warned in church to be wary of all the Romish heresies, superstitions and malpractices.

Stift Vorau, Wednesday, 9 May 1945

The horrible Second World War is over. And suddenly I am part of a very peaceful place that is an island of serenity, sobriety , and sanctity in a restless, rough, and rugged world. I wanted to greet my good friend Pater Sepp before he left, but he has disappeared without saying good-bye. I suspect that he was simply not able to face the inevitable farewell.

Father Jerome supplies me with a habit and takes my uniform away to be destroyed. I am allowed to keep my personal belongings, including my certificates that I am a qualified medical practitioner and a specialist surgeon. I am given my own cell where I sleep.

Father Jerome asks me whether I would like to join the order as a novice. Before I can check myself, I answer in the affirmative. "All right, then you are obliged to attend every service in our church. We are not a silent order and you may converse with the brothers during meal times. One of our main reasons for existence is that we study and educate the world. But we also help people in need. You are a specialist in your field and I am sure that we can benefit a lot from your knowledge and skills. I will make it known in the surrounding villages that we have a medical practitioner who can serve the people. You will simply be known as Brother David."

"Father, I must thank you for this opportunity to be of service of my fellow human beings. That is my calling – to lessen suffering and pain and agony in this world. But – I will need medical supplies and instruments to perform my task properly."

"Yes, yes, selbstverständlich. You are quite correct. I will see what we can do in this regard. I am sure that our contacts in the Church will be able to help, although everything you need will be in short supply after the war. We will also have to provide you with a clinic in which to perform your work. But that will take time. I suggest that you while your time by working in our gardens in the meantime. But, for the interim, we can provide you with our meagre first-aid supplies. There are many refugees wandering through the country and we will have to help them when they come this way."

And so, I become a novice monk – a far cry from being commander of an artillery regiment or a battalion of mountain soldiers. I find it strange that the good Father Jerome did not even ask me whether I am a faithful Catholic, although I have a faint recollection that Pater Sepp called me his "Protestant friend". He also did not ask whether I was married or not. He just assumed that I must be a good bachelor Catholic. I decide not to enlighten him that I am still officially a member of the Reformed Church in Berlin. But, I have grown to love Pater Sepp and I feel myself as a Christian at home in any group that serves Christ.

My first service in the church is tonight and I look forward to see that beautiful space again.

Stift Vorau, Wednesday, 1 May 1946

It is almost a year to a day since I joined the Augustinian Order at Stift Vorau in Styria, Austria. Much has happened in this year.

I enjoyed working in the garden and with the abbey's animals – although I sometimes felt despondent and hopeless. I attributed this state of affairs to the fact that the war is suddenly over and I did not yet know how to relax.

The priory has a farm where vegetables and fruit are cultivated and where the cattle provide dairy products. There are a few horses to draw buggies and plows. My background as a farm boy from the Free State helped much. The brothers accepted me with smiles and without any questions asked.

I often visited the beautiful library of the convent. The shelves are full of old and valuable books. I read up on the history of the

Augustinian Order and held long conversations with Father Michael, the librarian.

Styria is part of the British zone of occupation of Austria. More or less a month after the capitulation of the Wehrmacht, a British major with three troopers appeared at the gate of Stift Vorau and demanded to talk to the prior. Since the major could not speak German and Father Jerome knows only German and Latin, I was called to interpret. Father Jerome requested him to leave all instruments of war outside in their vehicle. I added: "This is a place of worship, peace and salvation. We abhor all signs of violence. I hope you understand."

It is evident that the major did not want to antagonize the Church and he complied. He was then led to the Prior's office and stated his case: "We are hunting down Nazi war criminals. We have reason to believe that the Catholic Church is aiding Nazis to escape justice. May I inspect your buildings to see whether there are any Nazis hiding here?"

Father Jerome smiled while I translated his words: "My good Major, you are welcome to look into every nook and cranny in our buildings. You may inspect our grounds. I will even go further and summon all our brothers to assemble in the refractory where you may inspect them and question them. We don't hide any secrets."

The major was taken aback: "No, no, that will not be quite necessary. Your willingness to open up your convent proves to me that you are an honest man. I will, nevertheless, appreciate it if you could inform me should you hear of any Nazis in the vicinity."

He left the office and we escorted him to the gate. There he turned to me: "And where did you learn to speak English? You have a rather strange accent, or am I mistaken? You are not an Australian or a Canadian perhaps?"

I smiled: "Dear Major, no. I am certainly not a Canadian or an Australian. I am a qualified surgeon who studied in Berlin, as well as being an inmate of this institution. During my medical studies I had to make use of many textbooks in English. Does that satisfy you?"

He grunted a "Yes" and left for his truck.

After the British soldiers had left, Father Jerome turned to me: "Thank you for helping me by being my interpreter. I am convinced that you are not a Nazi and, therefore, I did not utter one word of untruth when speaking to that person. Neither did you."

After postal services with South Africa have resumed about three months after the end of hostilities, I wrote my first letter to my parents. This is what I wrote:

4 August 1945

Dear Father and Mother,

You will certainly be surprised to get this letter from me after so many years. I can imagine that you have had to endure much anxiety about my whereabouts and welfare after war has broken out. But I can assure you, I am alive and well and I am a practicing medical specialist somewhere in Austria.

I cannot tell you much about the war because that will take a long time to relate all. I can only say that I have been able to work as a medical practitioner and specialist surgeon during the whole time.

I must, unfortunately, tell you the sad news that my dear Josephine died during a bombing raid over Berlin in 1944.

1 May 1946

I have no news of Willie, but perhaps you will be able to inform me about his fate.

You may write to me at the address on the back of the envelope.

Your loving Son,

David

About six weeks later the following letter reached me:

24 August 1945

Our dearly beloved son,

Thank you for your very welcome letter that reached us only yesterday. We haste to reply.

We are sorry about your loss, but we are extremely grateful that you are alive and well. It is the answer to our earnest prayers.

We both are still in good health. The law practice in Kimberley has been sold and we now live permanently on the farm.

We have no news as yet of Willie. A soon as we hear from him, we will let you know.

Your loving parents,

Pieter and Isabella Scholtz

A few months later I received this letter:

6 November 1945

Our beloved son!

At last, we have received news from your brother.

He wrote a letter from Argentina to inform us that he is involved in research there, although he could not divulge any

263

details. He thinks it will be a good thing if you could join him there. We agree. The South African government is not well-disposed towards South African citizens who stayed behind in Germany after the start of the war because they argue that those people may have helped the Nazis. We don't know what your role during the war was, but perhaps it will be best not to return to our country for the foreseeable future. We have read in the newspaper that a certain Dr Attie Strauss, who worked as a broadcaster for the German Radio, was captured by British soldiers and immediately repatriated to South Africa. He has received a long prison sentence after pleading guilty to a charge of aiding the enemy, although he never fired a single shot.

So – perhaps it is best if you joined your brother in Argentina. Please keep us abreast of your movements.

Your loving parents,

Pieter and Isabella Scholtz

Some of my patients regularly brought me the daily newspapers and that helped me to know what was happening in the world. The attention of the world was taken up by the trials of top Nazis that started on 19 November 1945. They were accused of so-called war crimes, which included the extermination of millions of Jews and other undesirables in concentration camps, the execution of prisoners of war, the maltreatment of civilians in occupied countries and the use of slave labor.

I was horrified and I discussed this development with the prior: "I was a member of the SS. Here is the tattoo on my arm with my blood group to prove that I was a member of that organization. But I assure you, I was never aware of these horrific crimes that have been committed by our leaders. It is clear that some of them knew what would be their fate and they committed suicide, including Adolf Hitler, Heinrich Himmler and Joseph Goebbels. The SS guards of the concentration camps seem to have been nothing but butchers. But I am not ashamed of my association with a Waffen-SS division. We fought violently, but we also fought cleanly. We did not commit atrocities against civilians. We did not shoot prisoners. On the contrary – I gave them medical treatment if they were wounded."

Father Jerome listened carefully and said: "My son, I have listened to your confessions on more than one occasion in the confessional box. It is clear that you do not have any crimes on your conscience. You are a sinner – as we all are –but I am sure that those sins have been forgiven by the Almighty and All-knowing God. On the other hand, I have gotten to know you as a person who cares for the welfare of others. You are a true servant of Jesus Christ, who was also a healer of the sick."

I feel that I must unburden further: "I feel horrible about the concentration camps that were being run by the SS. But, then, I find it hypocritical of the British to condemn the German concentration camps while they were the inventors of this cruel and evil system. Thousands of women and children of my people died in British concentration camps during the war of 1899 to 1902. The British don't have the moral right to condemn the Germans if they are guilty of the same crimes!"

This talk gave me much relief.

I took note with a measure of unbelief of all the crimes perpetrated by our former leaders during the war. Initially, I thought that Hitler was a good politician, but the disillusionment of my fellow members of Division Nord in their Führer helped me to see him in a better light as a megalomanic fool. My little knowledge of psychiatry convinced me that he must have been a full-blown narcissist. The world became a better place after he had committed suicide.

And now, today, we received another strange visitor at the priory. He asked the Prior whether he could speak to me – a wish that was granted. I take him to my surgery, which is empty at the moment.

He asks: "Can we speak in confidence here? I don't want anybody to hear what we discuss."

"It is my practice never to discuss with anybody what I hear in my surgery. Everything my patients tell me stays confidential."

The person tells me: "I am not here as a patient. I will also not tell you my name. I am here on behalf of an organization that has been formed to help former members of the Waffen-SS. You did wonderful work according to Standartenführer Schreiber. He told us where to find you.

"However, I am also bringing you a message from your brother in Argentina. He was also able to supply us with your address. He is doing excellent work there, but he says that he can only continue if you join him. I am here to help you in this regard. When will you be able to leave?"

"Right now. I have very little personal belongings and I can get everything ready within a few minutes and say farewell to the Prior. But why such haste?"

"There is a ship due in the harbor of Genoa in ten days' time and your passage has been booked on that ship. I have brought you some civilian clothes so that you can get into my vehicle immediately."

"Wait, I haven't decided yet whether I want to go or not. I only said that I am able to leave almost immediately."

"It will be very unwise to stay here. Sooner or later, the British will discover your presence. You seem to have received letters from your parents with your name and address on the envelope and the British may just notice that. They have already dug up the personnel files of the Waffen-SS and your name appears on one of those files. It details your service record, including the fact that you have received the Iron Cross, First Class. I hope that you have gotten rid of that decoration because it may be your downfall. And if you are extradited to the South African government they will press for the death sentence, just as other so-called war criminals have been executed. They will argue that you joined a criminal organization and that you have contributed to the deaths of large numbers of Allied soldiers. In other words: it is dangerous to stay here. You will be safe in South America."

"You leave me no choice. Just as I was forced to join the Waffen-SS in 1939 to escape a concentration camp, you are forcing me to flee. All right, I haven't been inducted as a fully-fledged monk yet. I haven't taken any vows yet. I can go and say 'farewell' to the Prior and just disappear."

"That is certainly wise. I will wait in my motor car outside and you will join me shortly. And then our people will take you to Genoa from where you will sail to safety."

"I suddenly remember that I met an Argentinian colonel five years ago in Sonthofen. He suggested that I settle in Argentina after the war. I have quite forgotten about this man."

"You may perhaps don't know it, but that colonel became a General, as well as the vice-president of Argentina. He recently won the presidential elections and he is to assume this position soon. We have to thank him for his support that enabled us to get settled in Argentina."

Genoa, Friday, 10 May 1946

My love for the mountains and my service with a unit of mountain soldiers served me well on the way to Genoa in Italy.

My mysterious visitor at the priory took me in his motor car to a house in Graz where I stayed two days. Then two former members of the 6th Waffen-SS Gebirgsjägerdivision Nord, who have evaded capture by the Americans, took me on a long hike. I was fitted out with hiking boots, rucksack and more civilian clothes. I also received new forged identity documents and I temporarily assumed the name of one Daniel Jacob Peter Schmidt, a national of Switzerland. I was glad to, at least, have retained my initials.

I clearly remember these two former comrades. Both were senior NCO's of our former division and they fought to the end at the Wechsel Pass. Instead of marching to the approaching Americans, they hid on farms and in the woods, living off the land.

They took me along narrow mountain tracks into northern Italy, into a region known as South Tyrol. We could not risk crossing the border at a regular border crossing point since that could create unnecessary difficulties and even could prove to be dangerous. The people in these parts of Italy speak German since they were part of the Austro-Hungarian Empire until 1918 when Italy annexed that part of Austria. Many of them joined the SS during the war. The result was that I was among friends who wanted to help me.

Two new nameless guides took me in a truck all the way to Genoa where I was taken to the harbor. A familiar-looking ship was docked there and I was taken on board in the guise of a worker who had to deliver supplies to the ship. For that reason, I was given a crate with vegetables to take aboard. My two companions left again.

Now I am on my own and I am shown to my cabin by a seaman. I drop my meagre possessions there and look for the lounge where I might find some company. There is none.

An hour after I have boarded the ship, I hear the harbor tugs sound their horns. The idling engines of the ship pick up revolutions and I can feel that we are moving. I go out on the deck to watch the coast of Italy disappear slowly in the distance. A seaman approaches me and asks me in German whether I am Herr Schmidt.

"That's me."

"Please come to the bridge where the Captain wants to see you."

I follow the seaman and ascend the outside staircase to the bridge. I salute the captain because he looks like a military figure and he returns my salute the navy way and with a broad smile.

And now I am sitting in the captain's cabin. He tells me in German: "I am former Kapitän zur See Karl-Gustav von Lausewitz of the Kriegsmarine and I commanded this ship during the war, which was used as a troop ship. Early in 1945, when it became evident that the Third Reich could not survive, I was directed to sail this ship to Portugal and to paint it underway in civilian colors. In the harbor of Lisbon this ship, the Usambara, was given the name of the Santa Isabella and she was ostensibly 'sold' to a

Portuguese shipping company owned by Germans. I became a civilian and master of an ordinary passenger ship."

"That explains why this ship seemed familiar when I came aboard. I sailed in the Usambara in 1933 on my way from Cape Town to Germany! This is also one of the ships that ferried my division from Norway to Denmark at the end of 1944. I already feel at home."

"Good, I have news for you. Your brother, Willi, was a passenger on this ship when he and a number of friends were taken aboard a year ago from a port in Spain en route to Argentina. And that is where we also are going."

"Herr Kapitän, I thank you for your help. What will my role be here on this ship?"

"I was informed that you are a medical specialist. You may make yourself useful in the sick bay. And, by the way, you are now part of an organization called 'die Spinne' (the Spider). We were formed to help former members of especially the SS and other Nazis who may face the death penalty to get to safety in, amongst others, Argentina. Some people also call the organization ODESSA. That is the abbreviation for 'Organisation der Ehemaligen SS Angehörigen' (Organization of former SS members)."

"Thanks, Captain. You know, I never joined the SS willingly. I was pressed into service by being given the choice between joining the SS or being taken to a concentration camp. So, you can imagine what I chose. But I am extremely thankful for this chance to get to safety because my life was in danger while I stayed in Austria."

"Bitte (please)." He continues: "Herr Doktor, you are to use the forged identity papers that were issued to you when we get to the port of Buenos Aires. Thereafter, you may assume your old identity again when you are with our people. If you mingle with outsiders, you are to remain Herr Schmidt. But please do not advertise the fact that you had an important job in the Waffen-SS.

We never know when that information will reach the wrong ears. You will be taken to a place where most people speak German. But you will have to learn Spanish to get along."

"I have a rudimentary knowledge of Latin that I picked up during my medical studies. That might help me."

"In confidence: we are carrying a sensitive cargo, but our Portuguese flag will save us. I am authorized to inform you that our cargo consists of a number of German political refugees, as well as a number of crates containing gold. Die Spinne needs funds to stay afloat and you can guess where this gold came from. But keep that to yourself. I gather that you will be given an influential position when you reach your final destination and that is why I may tell you all this."

"Herr Kapitän, thank you for your help and your confidence in me."

"Bitte."

While I leave the captain's cabin, I cannot help but to think that, somehow or other, I will get involved in Willie's work to develop a super bomb – even if the war is over. It seems as if a bunch of Nazis cannot accept defeat.

At 18:30 the dinner bell rings and I go to the dining saloon. I look around to see where I can find a seat. Somebody waves his arm to show me that I must join him and I walk that way. I almost fall on my back when I see my old friend Pater Sepp. I grab his hand and pat him on the shoulder before I sit down.

He exclaims: "My old friend, it's good to see you; please be seated. We can converse later on when I can hear your story and you tell me your story."

I gather from this that it not safe to talk where others can hear, although I was told that all the passengers are political refugees. But one never knows – there may be British spies amongst them.

After dinner we walk to the stern and watch the Mediterranean Sea glide past us in the dusk. I ask: "My good friend, what are you doing here? What happened to you since you left me a year ago?"

"That is a very long story and I can go into details later on. The main thing is that I was able to escape from an American POW camp. They mistook me for my cousin with the same name who was a SS Hauptsturmführer and second-in-command of a concentration camp where thousands of people died. I believe that this cousin has disappeared and assumed a new identity somehow. The Amis would not believe that I am a priest and they maintain that I only parade as a Kriegspfarrer to evade justice. I was to be tried and I faced the death penalty for being responsible for all those deaths. I was never able to be united with the members of our old division who could have vouched for me and it was my word against those of my captors. Fortunately, I was helped to escape by friendly people who helped me to get onto this ship. I am supposed to minister to our people in Argentina."

"Well, well. You do seem to have escaped a dangerous situation. I am sure that you thanked God for your deliverance."

"It does help to have God and the Church on your side."

THE URANIUM CLUB

The Story of Willem Scholtz

Berlin, Saturday, 16 September 1939

The first full meeting of the Uranium Club takes place today (Saturday) with scientists from all parts of Germany attending at the Kaiser Wilhelm Institute in Berlin. Herr Doktor Kurt Diebner acts as chairman and leader of the club.

More or less all the eminent German and Austrian scholars in the fields of physics and chemistry attend and I feel overawed by all the great names. My name also appears on the list of attendees and it is the first time that I see it in print after my graduation last week: "Dr Wilhelm (!) Scholtz".

Other eminent scientists who attend, apart from Otto Hahn, are Walther Bothe, Siegfried Flügge, Hans Geiger, Paul Harteck, Gerhard Hoffmann, Josef Mattauch, and Georg Stetter. Diebner outlines the request from General Becker of the Heereswaffenamt or HWA that an atom bomb has to be developed as soon as possible and announces that he is awaiting proposals how the work is to be divided and parceled out. The project is to be financed by the Army. There is much enthusiasm under the attendees and everybody is eager to contribute to the project.

I ask Otto Hahn afterwards to tell me a little more about Herr Doktor Diebner. He informs me that Diebner studied at the University of Halle, about an hour's ride by train east from Berlin. He got his doctorate in 1932 and taught for four years at the University of Halle before he was recruited into government service. The present Uranium Club is actually the second Uranium Club. The first one was established by Diebner a few years ago under the auspices of the "Reichsforschumgsrat" (Research Council of the Reich) or RFR but that nothing really came from it. Now that we are at war, it is very necessary that we continue with all haste to manufacture this important war-winning weapon.

That night I tell Annemarie about the day's events. She says: "You may feel flattered that you were invited to attend. It is a great honor and much better than becoming the inmate of a concentration camp!"

"They simply had to take me on board, otherwise I might have divulged their secrets to the British – or so they thought. I will never do that. There is no way in which I will aid the British."

"You need not to tell me that."

"May I ask you to keep all this quiet, please. I am not authorized to tell even my own wife about our work."

1 October 1939

Berlin, Saturday, 30 September 1939

The second meeting of the Uranium Club takes place today –
again on a Saturday, so as not to interrupt the working week of all
the participating scientists. Several new members join us,
including the famous Nobel Prize winner Werner Heisenberg
and Carl Friedrich Freiherr von Weizsäcker.

Werner Heisenberg, winner of the
Nobel Prize for Physics, 1932

Diebner announces that he was appointed Direktor of the Kaiser Wilhelm Institute in Berlin and that this institute was to become part of the HWA. That means, technically, that all members of the Uranium Club become civilian members of the Wehrmacht and that we are henceforth under military control. All our activities are top secret. It is agreed that every institute and university department continue with the work they have been doing. Eight universities and institute are involved.

The following aspects have to receive attention: the measurement of nuclear constants, the production of uranium, isotope separation, the production of heavy water and the erection of a "Uranmaschine" (nuclear reactor).Of course, I am familiar with all this technical jargon and prattle, but I am glad that I won't need to explain it all to lay people since the project is classified as secret. All in all, about seventy scientists are employed on this project, which is regarded as "kriegswichtig". Institutes and departments that worked on similar projects have to keep contact with each other and share results.

Berlin, Sunday, 1 October 1939

Annemarie invites me to go for a walk through the park at Potsdam after we have attended the Sunday service in the Reformed Church. This is my brother's last day as a civilian and he prefers to spend it with Josephine.

While we are in the open air, my dear wife remarks: "You haven't ever told me exactly what you are doing as member of the Uranium Club. Who are the famous people with whom you are rubbing shoulders?"

"Mein Liebchen (my dear), you know that I am busy with secret work. I may not even tell my wife or other family members what we are doing. It might happen that you talk to somebody who can bring us into serious trouble for divulging state secrets. I have told you a month ago that we are to construct an atomic bomb. I will not tell you what it is and you may never mention this name towards anybody."

"May I at least know who are the people involved with this secret work?"

"I cannot name any people, but I might divulge that we have at least one winner of a Nobel Prize on our list, as well as a titled nobleman."

"Then I am extremely proud to be married to a man who has these illustrious Germans as colleagues and who is accepted into their ranks – although you were born in a country that is part of the British Empire! Marvelous… Wonderful… To be savored…"

Brandenburg an der Havel, Sunday, 24 December 1939

David appeared at our doorstep two days ago in his SS uniform. He got Christmas leave till Tuesday, 2 January 1940. He was looking for Josephine who was in our apartment at that moment where we were discussing our plans for Christmas, which included a visit to Brandenburg an der Havel. David was immediately eager to accompany us for a Christmas visit to our respective parents-in-law.

And now our two families are enjoying the Christmas tree in the von Czapiewski home after we have attended the Christmas service in the church with its beautiful music. We cannot forget that it is war, although David has immediately got rid of his uniform after getting home. He has to tell us all about his training as SS medical officer where we are relaxing after having exchanged presents.

He entertains us with stories about their group's Hauptscharführer who has to teach them how to march and behave as soldiers. This man seems to be very credulous and believes anything from the cadets under his care, all medical practitioners. "One of our guys, Helmuth Holzapfel, told him that his brother, an Oberleutnant zur See (sublieutenant) in the Kriegsmarine, sank with his U-boat. The U-boat dropped to the bottom of the ocean due to a malfunctioning toilet aboard, through which sea water was supposed to have bubbled into the submarine. This guy, Dralle, really believed this story until he happened to talk to a member of the Kriegsmarine who laughed at his story.

"And then my friend, Alois Schwarz, told him that he must make sure that the pen he is using is in accordance with a directive of twenty pages, outlining the requirements for military writing materials, otherwise his pen might be confiscated. Dralle, of course, went to the quartermaster to ask a copy of this directive. The quarter-master only laughed at him. Dralle made us suffer for the pranks we played on him, but we had a good laugh."

My father-in-law remarks: "Poor man. Please, don't be too cruel on him."

"We didn't do anything harmful, really. It is just that we cannot resist the temptation to pull his leg. Fritz von Ledersattel told him a piece of military history he was unaware of. When the Franco-Prussian War of 1870 ostensibly got dead-locked in a stalemate and no side could budge the other, it was agreed that the Prussian chancellor, Bismarck, and the French Prime Minister, whose name nobody can remember or pronounce, had to decide the issue with a game of chess. Needless to say, Bismarck won." These hilarious stories help us to forget the gloom of the war.

Brandenburg an der Havel, Monday, 25 December 1939

I and my SS brother go for a walk through the woods outside the city during the afternoon. We haven't had time with each other since October when his training started.

"It is certain that I will join the war next year as a medical officer. Nobody knows where I will end up. You seem to be active in this war while I am only marching up and down and playing pranks on Hauptscharführer Klaus Dralle. What have you been doing so far? Anything worthwhile?"

"I suppose that I can tell you something, although everything is secret. I am part of a group of scientists known as the Uranium Club. I have mentioned this name to you in the past, so you already know about it. We are all nuclear physicists and chemists and we are working for the Wehrmacht to develop the most powerful bomb the world has ever seen. This project is funded by the Army. So, you are not the only one involved in this war. You are a member of the armed forces. I am also indirectly. That makes us, technically, traitors to our own country because South Africa is at war with Germany. But both of us will like to see Britain beaten. But … we will have to be careful about our positions after the war, whatever the outcome. Do you agree?"

"Totally."

Berlin, Friday, 30 August 1940

Today, Friday, David's passing-out parade is to take place. I have taken the day off and I, Annemarie and Josephine are present to see how my brother receives his commission as a member of the German Armed Forces.

He receives a few days' leave and informs us that he is posted to the SS Gebirgsjäger Artillery Regiment 6 in far-away Bavaria. I believe that we won't be able to see each other frequently after he had left, although we will keep in touch my means of letters.

Berlin, Sunday, 22 June 1941

Today is a memorable day, for two reasons. During the past week, I have bought three tickets for the Sunday concert of the Berliner Philharmoniker and we – that is, me, Annemarie and Josephine – are on our way to spoil ourselves with a bit of German culture.

The second reason is that we heard over the radio this morning that the Wehrmacht has attacked Soviet Russia during the early hours. The operation is called "Undernehmen Barbarossa". We decided that we won't allow this event to spoil our Sunday and after a hearty lunch at a restaurant we proceed to the concert hall.

At the entrance I buy a program and we start studying it after we have taken our seats. The first item on the program is the 1812 Overture of Tchaikovsky.

Me: "This must be a bad omen. Tchaikovsky wrote this overture to celebrate the victory of the Russian Army over Napoleon's French Army. Is this item on the program perhaps a warning of the conductor that our boys are looking for trouble in Russia?"

Annemarie: "I don't think so. The program has already been decided upon weeks ago. Nobody could know that we would attack Russia today."

Me: "I still think they should have changed the program. This overture is a bad sign. And another bad sign is the second item on the program: Siegfried's Funeral by Wagner."

Josephine: "I also don't think the choice of musical items are appropriate for especially today."

Berlin, Thursday, 4 June 1942

We at the Kaiser Wilhelm Institute in Berlin-Dahlem worked steadily on our part of the big project, but our progress is not what we would have wished. Many hitches occur. There seems to be a lack of communication between all the institutes and departments occupied with the work. It is my opinion that there are too many people who display professional jealousy towards each other.

Albert Speer

Today, the Reichsminister for armament and arms production, Albert Speer, visits the Kaiser Wilhelm Institute to hear from Diebner how we are progressing. I attend the meeting, together with the rest of the researchers on the Uranium Club.

Speer is not impressed with our progress: "This is a waste of time and good money. I think that you ought to concentrate on the production of cheap energy by means of nuclear power and forget about your pipe dream to build a super bomb."

Diebner and Hahn try to argue with him and mention that they are sure that the Americans are busy with the same type of research. It became known that Albert Einstein is backing the American effort.

Speer cannot be moved.

Berlin, Tuesday, 9 June 1942

The Führer, Adolf Hitler, today issued a secret decree regarding the reorganization of the Reichsforschungsamt under whose auspices the Uranium Club is working. Reichsmarshall Hermann Göring, the head of the Luftwaffe and the only officer with the rank of "Reichsmarschall" (Marshall of the Reich), is to become head of the RFA. It is hoped that he will blow some life into the RFA.

Werner Heisenberg is to replace Kurt Diebner as Direktor of the Kaiser Wilhelm Institute and he is ordered to expedite the efforts to build an atom bomb.

With his decree, Hitler has effectively reversed Albert Speer's directive of last week.

Berlin, Tuesday, 8 December 1942

Heisenberg informs us today that Reichsmarschall Hermann Göring has appointed Professor Doktor Abraham Esau as his plenipotentiary for nuclear research in the RFR since he has no time to devote to this institution. We hope that Esau, currently a professor in physics in Berlin and previously in Jena, will be able to move things forward.

Professor Abraham Esau

He has experience of management since he previously worked for the radio manufacturer, Telefunken. I like him as a capable person whose lectures I attended while still a student.

Rjukan, Friday, 5 February 1943

Twenty-four of our scientists board a FW 200 Condor passenger aircraft for a visit to Norway to inspect the Vermork heavy water plant at <u>Rjukan</u>, Norway.

A heavy water molecule consists of two heavy hydrogen atoms and one ordinary oxygen atom. The heavy hydrogen atom consists of the usual one proton, but with an extra neutron added. Only about 0.0156% of the hydrogen atoms are of the heavy type and it takes specialized equipment to filter the heavy water out of huge amounts of ordinary water. Such a plant exists in Norway, which is under German occupation. One of the reasons why the Wehrmacht occupied this country was to obtain control of this plant.

Heavy water is being used in nuclear reactors where uranium is enriched to produce the type of uranium that can be used in an atomic bomb.

The Royal Air Force is aware of the importance of this plant for the German war effort and, therefore, this plant was attacked more than once in the past. For that reason, a flak battalion is based in the vicinity.

This excursion is a welcome diversion from our daily toils to study, experiment and calculate how we are to proceed with our super bomb. It is pleasant to chat to fellow scientists from other institutes. I also have pleasant memories of Norway where the four of us had a very pleasant holiday in the Hardanger region during the summer of 1939.

Berlin, Saturday, 27 February 1943

Less than three weeks after our tour of the heavy water plant in Norway, we receive news that Norwegian partisans have managed to sabotage certain cells of the installation. However, production of heavy water goes ahead, albeit at a slower pace.

Haigerloch, June-July 1943

Due to the increased air raids by the Royal Air Force at night and the American Army Air Force during the day on Berlin and other German cities, it was decided to move the staff of the Kaiser Wilhelm Institute and their equipment piecemeal from Berlin to the village of Haigerloch in South Western Germany. Some of the staff members are to stay in the neighboring village of Hechingen. It is a huge disappointment that our wives cannot accompany us. There is just not enough accommodation for them too.

The entrance of the tunnel at Haigerloch, known as the "Atomkeller"

My Annemarie has, therefore, to stay at home in Berlin. In Haigerloch we find a very convenient spot for the erection of a nuclear reactor – inside a tunnel in the hill, which was used by a local beer brewery to store their barrels of beer. This tunnel is quickly requisitioned and the brewery has to find another storage facility. On top of the hill there is a beautiful baroque church and we feel that this sacred building contains our guardian angels.It is a very tranquil and peaceful area and we find that we can work here without interruptions. Work starts in earnest to build a nuclear reactor in our beer cellar where we plan to breed enough atomic bomb grade of enriched uranium.`

Haigerloch, Tuesday, 16 November 1943

We receive more bad news. The Royal Air Force, operating from Scotland, dropped more than four hundred bombs on the heavy water facility in Norway. Dr Abraham Esau orders that all heavy water stocks still in Norway have to be moved to our new facility at Haigerloch.

Entrance to the tunnel with the reactor, Haigerloch

In the meantime, work on our nuclear reactor is progressing slowly – too slowly to my liking. Some of us are getting impatient because we need more progress.

Haigerloch, Sunday, 20 February 1944

We hear yet some more bad news. A ferry that was transporting our last stocks of heavy water across a lake is sunk by Norwegian partisans. A part of the cargo, consisting of barrels that were not full and could, therefore, float on the water, were salvaged.

Berlin, Wednesday, 8 March 1944

The train in which I am sitting suddenly stops in the middle of nowhere. The "Schaffner" (conductor) runs through the carriages and yells: "Get out! Get out! We are being attacked!"

I help two ladies to get to the ground and we run away from the train, into a field. We hear the sound of dozens of heavy aircraft flying overhead. We don't seem to be the target. To my horror I see the planes dropping tons of bombs on Berlin, about twenty kilometers away. Some fighters of the Luftwaffe attack them from high above but a few are shot down by the machine gunners in the bombers. The anti-aircraft batteries of the Luftwaffe in and around Berlin fire with all they have. I see at least twenty heavy bombers being shot down in flames by the flak and the fighters.

An elderly man next to me weeps: "The bloody swine! Look how those Americans are bombing innocent civilians all over the city! They have started with this massive bombing campaign four days ago and here they are again. May God punish them!"

After an hour the battle in the sky is over and we are allowed to get into the train again and I am able to continue my journey to the capital of the Reich. I have taken a week's leave to visit my Annemarie and to gather some books of mine at the Kaiser Wilhelm Institute.

The train stops an hour later in the main station and I rush to our apartment in the Dorotheenstraße and I expect to find Annemarie there since it is already late in the afternoon. On the way I see burnt-out buildings. The men of the Fire Brigade are doing their utmost to put out fires.

To my relief, I find Annemarie alive and well in our apartment. Josephine is there with her. They have decided to abandon David and Josephine's apartment and move in together. Annemarie falls into my arms and sobs: "Thank God! You are still alive!"

Josephine also gives me a hug.

"And what are you doing here?" my wife asks.

"I came to see you because I cannot live without you. And I have to come and fetch some books and papers at the Institute."

"It is a miracle that we are still alive. And it is a pity that I cannot go and live with you in the south."

"That is exactly what will happen. I am staying here a few days and then I am going to take you away. And I suggest that Josephine comes with us. Both of you are to resign from your jobs with immediate effect. I will find lodgings for you in one of the neighboring towns where we work. Unfortunately, Haigerloch, where we are working, is a small village and the place is overflowing with scientists and other staff."

"That will be marvelous. Perhaps there will be more food available in the countryside. We are struggling to get meat, vegetables, bread and even coffee. We have to drink "Muckefuck" (gnat piss or ersatz coffee)."

Berlin, Saturday, 11 March 1944

It was not possible to go to the Institute yesterday, due to yet another bombing raid over Berlin by the Americans. This morning, a Saturday, I went early by bicycle and from the window of my former office at the Institute I witness yet again how Berlin is bombed and burns. I am actually supposed to hide in the cellar as the few other people in the building did but I am too curious to see what was going on outside.

The Kaiser Wilhelm Institute in Berlin-Dahlem

I gather my books and papers after the sirens have sounded the "all clear" and return on my bicycle to the Dorotheenstraße.

When I arrive in our street, I cannot believe my eyes because the building with our apartment is a smoking ruin. The Police and the men of the Fire Brigade keep the bystanders away. Two fire fighters are carrying bodies from the cellar and to my horror I recognize my wife and my sister-in-law. I wriggle through the cordon of policemen and rush to the two bodies as they are laid out on the street where ambulance personnel are waiting to load them into their van.

"How did they die?" I ask one ambulance woman.

"It seems they have suffocated in the cellar due to all the smoke of the burning and collapsed building above them. Do you know any of these people?"

"Yes, this one is my wife and that's my sister-in-law. Where can I collect their bodies for a funeral? I suppose it will be possible to bury them properly."

The woman shakes her head: "Can't say. I have already lost an aunt and her husband this way. They were burnt beyond recognition. We are taking these bodies to the mortuary of the Moabit Krankenhaus and perhaps you may inquire there tomorrow."

In a daze I pedal back on my bicycle to my former office at the Institute and put a telephone call through to the residence of the von Czapiewski family in Brandenburg an der Havel. It takes more than an hour to make the connection and at last I have my father-in-law one the line. It is not possible to keep my tears back while speaking to him. I briefly tell him about the tragedy and ask him to notify Josephine's parents.

He asks me: "Do you think it will be possible to organize a funeral here in Brandenburg an der Havel? I will ask my brother-in-law to help in this regard. We will have to organize an ambulance or hearse that can bring the bodies here. Your mother-in-law will be devastated. I can hear that you are taking it very hard yourself."

Brandenburg an der Havel, Wednesday, 15 March 1944

The bodies of my beautiful Annemarie and David's beloved Josephine are today laid to rest in the soil of their "Heimat" (home town), Brandenburg an der Havel. There was a service in the Katharinenkirche and afterwards the procession moved to the cemetery. Although I try to stay calm I cannot but help to shed some hopeless tears while the caskets are being lowered into the graves. Annemarie's parents are clasping each other's hands and my father-in-law also holds my hand.

The two girls have their graves side by side. The Semmel family is gathered opposite us at the other side of Josephine's grave. This family is suffering their second loss. Josephine's brother Johannes, who had an engineering degree and was supposed to take over from his father at their paper mill, has lost his life as the commander of a U-boat that was lost somewhere in the Atlantic, two months ago.

While the ceremony at the grave is taking place a number of squadrons of American bombers fly overhead, again on their way to bomb Berlin. I vow to myself that those criminals will have to be punished for their war of terror on the defenseless civilians of Berlin and other cities. I decide that our super bomb has to manufactured as soon as possible to strike back. If Berlin is flattened then London must suffer the same fate. New York also deserves this treatment. The boys of the flak battalions are heroes in my eyes for shooting down a number of these murderous aircraft.

I realize that I will have to write to David and inform him of our tragedy. I will spare him the details of how our women died. I believe he has enough to deal with where he is tending the wounded and dying soldiers of his unit, wherever they are.

Haigerloch, Thursday, 15 February 1945

We are making progress with our bomb but despair is setting in that we will not be able to complete the super bomb in time before the end of the Third Reich comes. We have gathered some enriched uranium but by far not enough to be used in a bomb. The Allies are bombing the German cities at will and thousands of civilians have died or are maimed. Apart from that, the German industrial infrastructure is also devastated and nobody in Haigerloch is optimistic that Germany will be able to hold out much longer.

I go through the motions as if in a daze. I mourn the loss of my lovely Annemarie and my antipathy against the Americans and the British grows every day.

My fellow scientists also wonder how our super bomb – if we complete it in time – will be delivered to a target in England. The Luftwaffe has almost no bombers left and a solitary bomber on its way to a target in England will be an easy prey for the Allied fighters who have total air superiority. There are rumors of giant rockets that will be able to deliver such a bomb but we are not sure whether that is fact or fiction.

Today, we hear over the radio news that the British and the Americans have started to bomb the city of Dresden, which is filled with refugees who are trying to stay out of the clutches of the Red Army, filled with barbarians from Siberia who loot and rape as far as they go. The Royal Air Force bombs the city during the night and the American Army Air Force continues with the carnage during the day. The Propaganda Minister, Josef Goebbels, screams bloody murder against the Allies, although we are very pessimistic that the Wehrmacht is in any position to inflict much damage anymore.

Haigerloch, Thursday, 22 March 1945

A mysterious official appears in Haigerloch this morning with orders from the RFA. Selected members of the Uranium Club who are working on the nuclear reactor are to pack up everything and leave by plane tonight to an undisclosed destination before units of the American Army arrive here. A convoy of twelve trucks manned by SS soldiers roll into the village and they load everything they can, including our stock of uranium and heavy water – of course, under our watchful eyes. All our documentation is stored in metal trunks and we are allowed to take our personal belongings. The unfinished nuclear reactor has to stay behind.

Those of us who are married and have families are promised that their families will be looked after and that they will be brought to our destination in due course. But, in the meantime, it is of the utmost importance that the nucleus of the Uranium Club leaves the country to continue its work elsewhere.

The mysterious stranger says: "Meine Herren, I cannot force anybody to leave, but I advise you that it will be in your own interest to do so. If you stay you may rest assured that the Americans and the Russians will do their best to lay their hands on you. Where we are taking you, you will be safe and you will be given all the facilities and the funds needed to continue your great work."

Fortunately, it is overcast after sunset and a soft drizzle seeps down from the clouds. That keeps the Allied aircraft away, at least. I am one of those who has been selected to leave. A few of us don't feel like leaving Germany and their places are taken by volunteers.

At about eleven o'clock, the convoy leaves Haigerloch and picks up a few passengers at Hechingen. We are twenty scientists who start on this adventure. I am glad to get out of Germany because it will be fatal for me to go into British captivity and be extradited to South Africa. There I will be regarded as a traitor and hanged – and I don't want my parents to suffer that humiliation. I also regard my neck as an important body part, which I would like to preserve intact.

About midnight we arrive at the Luftwaffe base of Grosselfingen, a few kilometers south west of Hechingen, where three FW 200 Condor long-range bombers are awaiting us. We get into the first plane and our precious cargo of uranium and heavy water, weighing almost three tons, is loaded onto the other two planes. By half-past-two the aircraft are ready to take off. The pilot of our aircraft welcomes us aboard and announces: "Meine Herren, I am Hauptmann Erich Frölich of the Luftwaffe. Please strap yourselves in. Our flying time will be about six hours. I apologize that we must get airborne at this unholy hour, but we got news that the American forces will reach Haigerloch at the latest by tomorrow afternoon. We cannot wait any longer."

One of my fellow-scientists: "We could already hear gun fire to the west. They must be quite near."

It is very dark outside due to the cloud cover. When we are airborne, I look through the porthole next to me but I cannot see anything below because of the black-out and I feel sorry for those who have to face the inevitable end of the Third Reich.

The flight is rather uncomfortable. It is not easy to fall asleep due to the noise of the engines. We often change direction – certainly to avoid dangerous spots in the landscape. I guess that we are being taken to Spain or Portugal, the only neutral countries in Europa from where we can be shipped somewhere else. It cannot be Switzerland because the Swiss won't allow us into their country.

Bilbao, Friday, 23March 1945

We are still in the air when the day breaks and I see that we are flying over water. That can only be the Bay of Biscay and that means that we are heading towards Spain or perhaps Portugal.

The three Condors land approximately six-thirty on a military airfield. Guards in unfamiliar uniforms surround our aircraft and we are ordered to disembark. One of us who can speak a bit of Spanish tries this on one of the guards and asks him where we are. We hear one word: "Bilbao." That is a port city in northern Spain.

We are led away to waiting trucks. I look for the last time at the Luftwaffe bombers that brought us safely to a neutral country that is well-disposed towards Germany. The crew members of the three aircraft are also taken away.

PART 4

PLANTING THE BOMB

The Story of David and Willem Scholtz

305

Bilbao, Monday, 7 May 1945

Willie:

Since our arrival in Bilbao, we were staying in barracks on the military airfield where we landed. The mysterious gentleman who organized our removal from Haigerloch came to us in our barracks during the first afternoon of our stay.

He called a meeting and said: "Meine Herren, I must apologize for all the inconveniences you must have endured. You are not prisoners, but it is, nevertheless, extremely important that you do not leave this building. It is for the sake of your own safety. We want to evacuate you by ship but at the moment it is not yet safe. Everybody expects the war to end any day and then the oceans will be safe again.

"By the way, I am 'Fregattenkapitän' (Commander) Dieter Döppe and I was, until last week, part of the German intelligence service. My immediate head was Generalmajor (Major General) Reinhard Gehlen, who was chief of intelligence for the Eastern Front. He was fired by Hitler for feeding him with too much uncomfortable information about the Russians. We continue to operate informally and we need your services. Although the Wehrmacht will capitulate within days the fight against Bolshevism must continue and will continue."

We could see the three German bombers that brought us here. They were speedily repainted in the colors of the Spanish Air Force. We speculate that the Spanish authorities were willing to house us for the time being in exchange for the three valuable airplanes. We also saw other German aircraft in Spanish colors: Messerschmidt Me-109 fighters and Heinkel He-111 bombers.

We were well fed and even entertained by watching German films. One of these films was titled "Ohm Krüger". I saw it a number of years ago in a cinema in Berlin but watched it again with interest. This film depicted the life of the last president of the Transvaal Republic and emphasized the criminal behavior of British troops against the civilian population by burning down farms, slaughtering the animals of Boer farmers and herding their women and children into concentration camps where many died. This strengthened my resolve to work on the super bomb to revenge my people.

A week ago, we heard the news that the Führer, Adolf Hitler, had committed suicide in Berlin. We all agree that this event signifies the end of the German Reich. And now, today, we get the news that an armistice was declared and that Field Marshall Wilhelm Keitel, head of the OKW, will sign a deed of surrender tomorrow. That means that the seas are once again safe, for the first time in six years.

Just after dark we are told by Döppe that we are to be transported to the harbor of Bilbao where a ship is awaiting us. When we board the ship, we find that there is quite a number of other Germans aboard. The ship leaves the harbor immediately after we have boarded her.

After about an hour we are summoned to dinner and afterwards the Captain welcomes our group of scientists: "Guten Abend, meine Herren. Welcome aboard the Santa Isabella. We are sailing under the Portuguese flag. I am Kapitän-zur-See Karl-Gustav von Lausewitz of the Kriegsmarine and this ship was previously the troopship Usambara. Before the war she was a passenger liner sailing between Europe and Africa. A fortnight ago she was acquired by a shipping company in Lisbon and the whole crew was taken over by this company. As you can see, the ship is no longer painted in battleship grey and we are to operate between the Iberian Peninsula and South America. En route to Buenos Aires we will dock in Lisbon, but you are friendly requested to stay aboard. We will be shipping some valuable cargo in Lisbon."

This ship has special meaning for me. I and my brother sailed in her from Cape Town to Europe in 1933. And now the ship is named after my dear mother, Isabella Scholtz. I see that as a very favorable sign.

Atlantic Ocean, Monday, 14 May 1945

Willie:

Although Germany lost the war disastrously and totally, most of the Germans on board are in a festive mood today. We are crossing the Equator and old Father Neptune, the deity who reigns over the oceans, visits us this afternoon.

It seems that I am the only passenger who has crossed the Equator in the past. Neptune, with seaweed in his hair and a trident in his hand, appears on deck and initiates all the novices to the Southern Hemisphere of the Earth. The German passengers make a festive occasion of the event. Beer flows by the barrel and many Nazi songs, such as the "Horst Wessel Lied", "Kampflied der Nationalsozialisten" and "Auf, Hitlerleute, schließt die Reihen", are sung with abandon, although not always in tune because the speaking organs of more than one man are affected by the beer.

This is a rather new experience for me because we scientists spent all our time working. There was never time to celebrate or to have parties. I wonder where these singing and beer-drinking Germans are headed.

Buenos Aires, Sunday, 20 May 1945

Willie:

The Santa Isabella docks in Buenos Aires and our group of scientists are looking forward to an opportunity to pursue our investigations.

While aboard, we were briefed by Döppe and told that our efforts to build an atomic bomb must continue at all costs. It seems as if the Americans are on the verge of developing one and it is expected that they will use it on our erstwhile allies, the Japanese.

We are all ready to leave the ship the moment the ship is linked to the quay. Our luggage is ready to be taken off and we were assured that our valuable cargo of uranium and heavy water will be unloaded as speedily as possible. I have a brand-new Argentinian passport, which seems to be genuine enough. While we were still on the Atlantic Ocean, we had our photographs taken to be pasted onto blank passport booklets. New names were invented for each of us. My new name is Werner Carlos Andreas Stamm. At least, I keep my old initials.

A bus awaits us on the quay and we are transported to the main station. A special train has been chartered for us. Quite a number of the other passengers on the Santa Isabella also board the train and we guess that they will travel to the same destination as we are.

Bariloche, Monday, 21 May 1945

Willie:

I look with interest at the Argentinian landscape and I wonder whether I will be able to meet some of my fellow Boers over here. I was told as a child that a number of Boers who refused to accept British domination after the war of 1899 to 1902 decided to settle in this country. However, I have no idea in which area they have settled and how many there are.

We slept in the train last night, quite comfortably. Breakfast and lunch were served in a dining car.

During the afternoon we reach the end of the railway line at a station called Bariloche and we are taken by a convoy of trucks to a location outside the town. Bariloche has a distinct German flavor with Bavarian-style houses. The mountainous landscape also reminds me of Bavaria or Austria and I gather that those mountains must be the Andes, which form the border between Argentina and Chile.

View of the <u>Nahuel Huapi National Park</u> landscape surrounding Bariloche

We get off at a compound and a private bedroom is assigned to each one of us in barracks-like buildings. After having dumped our belongings, we are requested to gather in the mess for dinner. The other Germans from the ship are also there.

Bariloche, Tuesday, 22 May 1945

Willie:

All the German scientists from the Santa Isabella are assembled in the mess after breakfast. An imposing man with a powerfull presence steps in and holds up his hands. We become silent.

"Meine Herren, Guten Tag! I welcome you to the Uranium Club Number Three. I am former Oberführer (senior colonel) Karl Ullrich. I commanded a division on the Eastern Front where I got wounded and was evacuated to the Fatherland. After I have convalesced, I was recruited to be in charge of security on this project. I have a number of former men of the Waffen-SS here to act as our guards and we will be joined later by some more men.

Karl Ullrich

"Their task will not be to keep you in line. This is not a concentration camp! Their duty will be to make sure that everybody in this compound stays safe from possible attacks and outside interference.

"Dear scientists, you are now at your destination after a long and even dangerous journey. Thank you for being here. We are to continue the fight against the Bolshevists and your task will be to continue your good work on the atom bomb.

I secretly think that I, personally, don't have much against the Bolshevists. I have never seen one in my life. But I feel very personal about the British and the Americans.

Ullrich continues: "I understand that you were not very far off from your goal when you had to leave the Fatherland in great haste. Of course, we won't have to start from scratch here. You have done much already and I gather that you have brought all your documentation along. We also have a sizable quantity of heavy water and enriched uranium here.

"Fortunately, there is a heavy water plant here in Argentina and uranium is being mined in Brazil from where we will be able to procure large quantities. Money won't be a problem. And talking about money: each of you will be paid a decent salary for your work. Please report to the administrative office after the meeting for your first installment. You haven't been paid since March and each one will receive a handsome sum of Argentinian bank notes and coins.

"Herr Doktor Knoll, will you please step forward?"

My colleague Klaus Knoll gets up: "Meine Herren! Our first task will be to construct a new nuclear reactor. We have chosen this spot here at Bariloche to do our development work and we were given the Spanish name of 'Comisión Nacional de Energía Atómica' (National Commission for Atomic Energy). We are supposed to be part of the government agency in charge of nuclear energy research and development that had already been established in this town. A number of Argentinian scientists will join us shortly.

"There are many German-speaking Argentinians in these parts. You must have noticed that downtown Bariloche has a distinct Bavarian flavor with German names on stores and businesses. We will be able to blend in here with the local population. While the construction of the nuclear reactor is getting underway you will be getting Spanish lessons so that you will be able to get along in this country. As Herr Ullrich told you, this is not a concentration camp and you will be able to wander around in your free time and mix with the locals.

"I want to appoint a deputy. Herr Doktor Willi Scholtz, are you available?"

I almost fall off my chair. "Herr colleague, this is very unexpected! I am not even a German. I only studied in Berlin and got caught up in the war. How can you expect me to fulfill that responsible position?"

"My dear Scholtz, your commitment to our cause has always been above the slightest doubt. I also have the fullest confidence in your abilities. Will you be my second-in-command? I cannot think of anybody more suited for that position. You were the right-hand man of Otto Hahn, as well as of Werner Heisenberg."

Reluctantly, I agree.

During the afternoon I and two colleagues decide to explore the town of San Carlos de Bariloche, to the west of our compound and on the edge of a huge lake. We find a Konditorei where we enjoy real coffee and Black Forrest Tart. The owner tells us that the first Germans to these parts already arrived during the previous century and that a steady stream of immigrants has turned Bariloche almost into a Bavarian town.

We see a local German newspaper on the rack: "Argentinisches Tageblatt" (Argentinian Daily Sheet). It contains local news but also international news. We see the names of Nazi officials in Germany who have been taken into custody by the Allies. Some of our colleagues who worked on the Uranium Club were grabbed up by the Russians and Americans – as well as other scientists and engineers.

We enquire with the Konditorei owner how we can get the newspaper delivered to our compound every day. He directs us to the local newspaper office and there we subscribe to the publication.

As we walk back, I remark: "It is almost as if we are back in Bavaria in peacetime without all the destruction that the war brought about. People here are relaxed, happy and peaceful. I suppose we will be able to fit in nicely as time goes on."

My companions agree.

Bariloche, Monday, 6 August 1945

Willie:

Today's news over the radio has all of us of the third Uranium Club very excited. The Americans have proved that an atomic bomb can work. They totally destroyed the Japanese city of Hiroshima and thousands of civilians have perished. The single bomb was delivered by a heavy bomber that flew over the city. As the aircraft turned and flew back a huge mushroom-shaped cloud rose up over the city.

Bariloche, Thursday, 9 August 1945

Willie:

A second Japanese city was obliterated by another nuclear device. This time it was the city of Nagasaki. Everybody expects that the Japanese will surrender after this.

Our Argentinian German newspaper contains photographs of the destruction of Hiroshima. Not a single building in the city was left standing or undamaged and it is estimated that the number of the dead will exceed one hundred thousand.

We are appalled by the enormity of it all. This is exactly what we have been working on for the past six years. We know that we will be able to succeed because the Americans have demonstrated that.

The leader of our team, Knoll, calls for a conference to discuss the news: "Dear colleagues, we can be sure that we have not toiled in vain. An atom bomb is possible. It is now only a matter of time before we get our own back on the Russians, British and Americans. They have smashed Berlin, Hamburg, Cologne, Dresden and many other cities. We have suffered tremendous losses. My deputy, Willi Scholtz, has lost his dear wife in Berlin. I am sure that everybody here has lost a relative or a friend through the bombing raids of the Allies. The time for reckoning is not far off."

He gets applause.

"It has become clear that our nuclear reactor, which is designed to work with heavy water, might also work with piles of pure graphite. We will have to look for sources. Anyway, we hope to have our reactor up and running early next year and then we can start enriching uranium. I thank you for your excellent work up till now."

Bariloche, Saturday, 1 December 1945

Willie:

A local construction company owned by German-speaking Argentinians is transforming our compound. They are erecting an office and laboratory block that is almost finished and they are also working on the urgently needed nuclear reactor.

We discuss the news from Germany on a daily basis. There is an international tribunal in Nuremberg that is prosecuting high Nazi officials, such as Hermann Göring, Rudolph Hess, the Generals from the OKW and other important leaders, such as Karl Dönitz who was C-in-C of the Kriegsmarine. They are accused of "war crimes", including the killing of millions of Jews and other people in concentration camps, atrocities against civilians and the execution of prisoners of war.

Karl Ullrich is adamant: "The swine! They accuse us of war crimes. If that is the case they are also just as guilty! Look at the vast numbers of German civilians that have been killed by their bombs. The Russians have driven millions of Germans from the eastern parts of Germany. I know of cases where they have shot prisoners of war. So – these trials are really a farce and history will prove that in due course. I am writing a book about my experiences of the war. In my Waffen-SS division I am aware of only one officer who was guilty of a so-called war crime when he shot a Russian prisoner who made him exceedingly angry. For the rest, my men fought with utmost bravery, but always within the rules."

We cannot agree or disagree because we never participated in battles. Nevertheless, I add: "I have witnessed how they set Berlin alight. My own home was demolished by an American bomb. And besides – concentration camps are a British invention. During the South African War at the beginning of this century they allowed thousands of women and children to perish in their concentration camps. And they have never apologized for their crimes! These trials are the zenith of hypocrisy!"

All agree.

Today, I have received the first letter from home. I was informed two months ago that it was safe to start writing letters, but using our aliases. I wrote my assumed name on the back of the envelope, together with the address of our compound, but I wrote the letter in such a manner that my parents would immediately know that the letter came from me. This is what I wrote:

10 October 1945

My dear Parents!

This is the first opportunity I get to write to you after more than six long years. As you can see, I am alive and well. I am with a number of my colleagues in Argentina where I am continuing my life's work. Please write back to me and use the name and address on the back of my envelope.

Unfortunately, I have to inform you of the death of my dear wife, Annemarie. She died in a bombing raid by American planes, together with my brother's wife. I am, therefore, a widower and I mourn the death of my beautiful wife still every day.

Have you had any news from my brother? I haven't heard from him for a very long time. If you have contact with him, please send him my love and inform him that I would very much

1 December 1945

like him to join me here. I can only continue with my work if he comes here.

Your loving son,

W

And today this letter arrived after having travelled halfway around the world:

6 November 1945

Our dearly beloved son!
Thank you for your letter. We reply immediately.
It is wonderful to know that you are safe, although we feel sad with you for your loss.
Your brother has written to us and it seems that he is somewhere in Austria where he is working to help sick people.
He will be overjoyed to hear that you are well, although you are on another continent. We informed him that you would like him to join you in Argentina.
He has already informed us of the deaths of your two spouses.
We are well and we are now living permanently on the farm.
The law practice in Kimberley has been sold.
Your loving parents,

Pieter and Isabella Scholtz

Bariloche, Monday, 3 December 1945

Willie:

I am having a chat with Ullrich and Wittman this morning: "I have received news that my twin brother, Herr Doktor David Scholtz, is alive and well and is practicing as a medical specialist somewhere in Austria. What's the possibility of getting him out so that he could come and join us? I am sure that he will be able to provide very valuable service to our community. He is a specialist surgeon and he was a medical officer in a Waffen-SS unit."

Ullrich's eyes widen: "It sounds as if he is a valuable man. I will see what we can do. In case you don't know, there is an organization that calls itself Die Spinne and they undertake the extraction of ex-SS personnel and other so-called war criminals from Europe and help them to reach Argentina and other South American countries. We will do what we can."

Knoll adds: "We surely need a medical specialist here. It is always tedious to send our people to doctors and hospitals in town."

Bariloche, Monday, 24 December 1945

Willie:

Karl Ullrich tells the whole group, scientists and German guards, during lunch: "It is Christmas Eve. We may expect Christmas Father to pay us a visit tonight after dark. Please be ready in the mess exactly at 21:00."

We are all curious to see what Father Nikolaus, the old saint, has to bring us tonight and we all sit ready in the mess, which is decorated with green branches and tinsel. It is almost as if we are in Germany, except that it is summer here, not winter.

The back door of the mess flies open and Ullrich shouts: "Achtung! Achtung! All rise!" We all obey and we turn around to see how Father Christmas looks. We cannot believe our eyes…

The Führer, Adolf Hitler, appears and walks to the front of the hall. Spontaneous applause erupts. Hitler smiles and grabs the hands of a few of the men. He is followed by Mother Christmas, his wife Eva. He still wears the German Army cap that he used to wear while still in Germany. When the applause dies down, Hitler starts speaking and I can understand why the German people adored him. He is a master orator

"My dear friends. Thank you for this wonderful reception. You will all wonder how it is that you can see me with your own eyes while the whole world believes that I died on 30 April. It was easy to stage a suicide.

"Berlin was in such a mess at that time that it wasn't a problem to find bodies of fallen comrades and dress them up in my and my wife's clothes and then to set them alight to prevent positive identification.

"We were taken through the tunnel network that was part of the Führer's bunker in Berlin and we reached a spot where we could board a light plane that took off during dark and flew us to Flensburg. which was still German territory. There the aircraft refueled and flew on to Denmark, which was still in our hands. It was a difficult flight in the dark because we almost bumped into church spires and high trees a few times. We flew very low so as not to be detected by the Allies. A Heinkel bomber took us further to Trondheim in Norway where we boarded a U-boat directly after the armistice was declared. And here we are! We are living at a secret location where we are guarded day and night and from where we can direct this project. The Wehrmacht may have surrendered, but we haven't surrendered. And neither have you! With your bomb we will bring Russia, Britain and America to their knees and resurrect the true Germany!"

When Hitler sits down after his short speech, the men start shouting: "Sieg Heil! Sieg Heil!"

After we have celebrated Christmas in an appropriate German way, Hitler and his wife depart to their secret place of abode.

Especially our SS guards are ecstatic about this wonderful Christmas present. This was the first time that I came in Hitler's presence and I could feel the magnetism of his personality.

Buenos Aires, Monday, 27 May 1946

David:

The Santa Isabella slides into the harbor of Buenos Aires and I get my first sight of South America. The voyage was quite uneventful. I and Pater Sepp had a few conversations with Captain Karl-Gustav von Lausewitz about his exploits during the war. He was also interested in our experiences. I wanted to hear everything he could tell me about Willie, which wasn't much, apart from the fact that he was a member of a party of scientists going to Argentina to continue their research there. I knew what this research was about but did not divulge my knowledge to the good Captain since it was supposed to be a secret. I did, however, trust Pater Sepp with this knowledge directly when hostilities ended, knowing well that he is good at keeping confidences.

We were both appalled at the horrible destruction brought about by the American atom bombs on Japan and we discussed the ethics of it. Pater Sepp explained: "The Americans justify their use of these bombs with the argument that many more people would have died if the war did not end last year in August and fighting kept going on for many more months. Japan would only have surrendered if America invaded the country with a huge loss of life to both sides."

I added: "That does, perhaps, make sense. But I don't know whether it will be justified when we use this type of bomb on New York, London or Moscow. The German Wehrmacht has surrendered and ceased to exist. We were beaten squarely and thoroughly. What will happen if we resort to the same tactics of the Allies by destroying their cities and killing countless numbers of American, British and Russian civilians after peace had been declared? It can be compared to a boxer who knocks his opponent out after the bell has rung for the end of the round. That is just not fair."

"Perhaps you are right. Let's see whether your brother and his team will be able to construct a number of those bombs – even if Germany has lost the war."

"I don't know. I got the idea that the team of scientists is not huge and that their resources are not limitless. Fortunately, I will not be required to work on the project because I know very little of physics. My job will be to treat sick people – and that's my life's calling."

Pater Sepp: "It will actually be a good thing if both of us prayed earnestly that almighty God in heaven doesn't allow this mad venture to succeed. The world has seen enough misery, pain, destruction and horrors. We don't need any more."

"Amen."

I had another interesting conversation with a German engineer on his way to Argentina. He introduced himself simply as Kurt Tank.

I retorted: "That name sounds familiar. Where have I heard it?"

"You may perhaps have seen my name in the newspapers. I designed aircraft for the Luftwaffe."

"Of course! You were the chief engineer at Focke-Wulf. You designed the FW 190 fighter, as well as the Condor. I had the opportunity of flying in the Condor in 1938. And what are you doing on this ship? Weren't you captured and prosecuted as a war criminal?"

"The Americans, Russians and British could not find anything against me. I worked the whole time during the war in our design office and never fired a single shot. I don't like the Americans nor the British nor the Russians and I declined all their offers to work for them. And then the Argentinians recruited me to design jet aircraft for them. I accepted."

"And why do they need their own jet aircraft? Can't they buy them from America or Britain?"

"I have the feeling they want their own bombers. There is gossip that the military leaders want Argentina to become a nuclear power, just as America. They seem to have a facility somewhere in the mountains where German expatriates are helping them to develop an atomic bomb."

I kept silent about what I know.

And now I and my friend Pater Sepp are standing on the deck of the Santa Isabella while the tugs are helping her to dock. Our luggage has been packed and we are ready to land. I have a new Swiss passport with my assumed name with which I will be able to enter the country without hitches.

I switch from Afrikaans to German: "I want you to meet my best friend – apart from you – Pater Joseph Heibl. He was the chaplain of my regiment and later of our whole division. We got reunited on board the Santa Isabella that brought us here. Pater, this is my brother Willi."

They shake hands and Willie assures him, also in German: "A friend of my brother is also my friend! Welcome. You sit there next to my brother and later we can get better acquainted. But I must warn you: we both are loyal Protestants and you must be a Romish priest. It is a deep mystery how you two got along all the time. But you cannot be too bad or too dangerous if David took a liking in you."

I laugh: "Willie, you will not believe it, but I was a novice monk for almost a whole year in an Austrian convent! But I am still a Protestant. The good Prior there just assumed that I was a good Catholic when he took me in. But let's eat first and then we can swop yarns."

Bariloche, Tuesday, 4 June 1946

David:

It took less than a week before I was given a clinic in the newly constructed office block. Herr Karl Ullrich, the camp commandant, asks me to give him a list of equipment and medicines I need. I also request him to find me a medical orderly or, even better, a trained nurse or two to help me with patients, especially when I have to perform operations. He promises to supply me with all those as soon as possible on condition that I supply proof that I am a qualified German Arzt.

"For the time being, you will only be allowed to treat patients here in our German compound. Then you will have to apply for registration with the Argentinian Medical Board to be able to practice in town, should you wish to do so. There is a well-equipped hospital and I believe that your services will be needed over there."

After dinner we listen to the radio news in Spanish. Most of the chaps in the recreation room cheer and clap their hands over the first news item. I don't understand anything, but afterwards Willie tells me what he has heard. He is already fairly fluent in Argentinian Spanish. The big news is that Argentina has a new president, military strongman Juan Peron. He was inaugurated today. He is very well disposed towards us Germans and our efforts to develop our bomb."

"You will not believe me, Willie, but I know that guy. He visited our regiment in November 1940 when he was only a Colonel and he even invited me to settle in Argentina after the war, should it become clear that I was unwelcome in South Africa. I forgot about that during the war but when I was approached to join you here, I suddenly remembered his offer."

"Well, well. My brother is moving in high circles! You will not believe it, but I am also moving in high circles. I met Adolf Hitler last Christmas!"

Bariloche, Monday, 17 June 1946

David:

Herr Karl Ullrich, our camp commandant, corners me after breakfast: "Herr Doktor, I have good news. All your equipment is to be delivered later today. Please be available to check everything and sign receipts for everything. I have also been successful to have found you a registered nurse. Unfortunately, she is not German, but I am sure that you will be able to get along with her. By the way, how are your Spanish lessons getting along?"

"I am making progress, but I am not yet able to hold my own during a conversation. Perhaps I will have to teach my new nurse some German."

He only laughs.

Just after lunchtime a truck stops in the compound with my supplies. Four of the guards, who have very little else to do, help me to carry everything to my clinic.

Only when the last items were piled up in my clinic and I have signed the receipt papers I notice a girl standing to one side. I walk to her and ask in my best Spanish: "Can I help you?"

I almost fall on my back when the girl answers me in Afrikaans: "Doctor Scholtz, I am your new nurse. I hope you will find me acceptable."

I almost give her a big hug but I decide that would, perhaps, not be quite appropriate. Instead, I shake her hand and reply in my mother tongue: "Wonderful! I am sure we will get along just fine. And what is your name, my dear?"

"Rebecca van Wyk."

"And where do you come from?"

"My family lives here in Patagonia, here in southern Argentina. My grandparents and parents came from Bloemfontein in the Free State in South Africa in 1905 because they refused to accept British rule. They are sheep farmers and we still speak

Afrikaans at home, although I had to attend a Spanish-speaking school. I trained as a nurse and I heard through the grapevine that a South African doctor was looking for a nurse to help in his practice. And here I am."

"My girl, this is a miracle from heaven. You must be an angel. Where are your wings? I was wondering how I would get along with a Spanish-speaking nurse and now I got this gift of a beautiful Afrikaans girl. I am sure that we will get along marvelously. While you were trained in this country, I am sure, you will be able to help me with local medical practices. Anyway, all these pieces of equipment and medicines have to be unpacked and stored. This is your first job to help me."

During dinner I asked Pater Sepp: "Do you have much work here? I don't see a church. And you cannot speak Spanish well enough to help the bishop in the local cathedral. Are there so many sinners in this compound who have the need to confess their sins towards you?"

Huapi Lake and Cathedral, Bariloche

"Actually, my friend, I am very bored. I am taking Spanish lessons and I have made contact with the bishop. But he can only use me on an ad hoc basis for the German-speaking Catholics here. But he cannot use me full-time before my Spanish is adequate. So, in the meantime, I am studying theology."

"My dear Father, from tomorrow you will be my medical orderly. My equipment has arrived and I hope to open my clinic later this week. I already have a female nurse. But beware, you are to keep your hands off her!"

"You know very well; I am already married. To the Church."

Fortunately, Rebecca is not the only female in the compound. A few German-speaking girls are employed as cooks, secretaries and drivers. They, however, live in town and that means that appropriate lodgings for Rebecca will have to be found. For the time being, she has to sleep in the clinic.

Bariloche, Friday, 20 September 1946

Willie:

Today is a great day. Our nuclear reactor is ready to become operational. Karl Ullrich calls for celebrations tonight.

We have been able to stockpile a large amount of uranium from Brazil, graphite from Mexico and heavy water from Argentina. We will experiment with the heavy water and graphite to find out which substance will give us the best results in our efforts to produce enriched uranium of weapons grade.

The operational reactor at the *Centro Atómico Bariloche*

The celebrations begin after dinner. The beer and Schnaps flow freely and the men sing one German song after the other. Somebody accompanies them on an accordion. Some of the men weep openly as they declare their longing for their ruined Fatherland.

Bariloche, Tuesday, 22 October 1946

David:

My clinic is running smoothly. I have a theatre for operations with anesthesia, an X-ray machine, all the instruments needed for serious operations and a whole apothecary full of pills, capsules, ampules and powders. Rebecca has taken over command of the practice and my only task is to tend to the patients – not that we have so many patients. So far, I have only operated on two men.

Brigadeführer Wilhelm von Grollmann

Just after lunch I am called to Karl Ullrich's office. He introduces me to a stern looking gentleman whose name is Wilhelm von Grollmann. He asks me to give him an interview in my clinic and we depart there.

"What is your complaint Herr von Grollmann?" I enquire.

"No, I don't have any complaints but a very important person under my care has a serious health problem. Can I speak to you in the strictest confidence?"

"Certainly. My medical ethics forbids me to discuss my patients with anybody."

"Well, thank you. Let me introduce myself first. I was a Brigadeführer and Major-General of the SS and the Police. Between 1942 and 1945 I was Police Chief of Leipzig, but also a deputy in the Reichstag. The Russians and Americans could not pin anything on me but I was nevertheless wary that you could perhaps invent some or other contrived complaint against me due to the fact that I was a prominent Nazi. An organization with which you are, no doubt, familiar, namely Die Spinne, chose me to take a very important job here in Argentina. I am in charge of the administration and safety of Adolf Hitler. Actually, he chose me as his personal assistant and manager of his administration. I am sure that you must know that he is still alive and lives at a secret location. He visited this compound last Christmas."

"I wasn't here at that time, but quite a number of the men here remember the occasion very well."

"Anyway, I am sort of Hitler's Prime Minister in his government of the Third Reich in exile, or – if you will – the Fourth Reich. You are aware of the fact that this facility will, hopefully, provide him with the means to again become the leader of a liberated Germany within a year or two. But now, Hitler is suffering from pains in his abdomen. He doesn't trust any of the Argentinian doctors. You are the only German doctor available."

"Herr von Grollmann, but I am not a German. I am a South African in exile."

"But you were a member of the Waffen-SS and you have received the Iron Cross First Class for the excellent service you rendered in Finland. You speak German with a Bavarian accent. You were trained in Berlin. That is good enough for me and, I believe, also for my Führer. Are you willing to treat him?"

This question catches me unawares. On the one hand, I don't have a great admiration for the man, but one the other hand, he is a suffering human being. I can remember how my comrades lost faith in the man towards the end of the war and even cursed him for all our misfortunes. But I cannot ignore the pain of a human being. And it is my duty to relieve suffering. After a few moments of silence, I manage to answer: "All right. This is a huge responsibility, perhaps too big for me, but I will try. But only on one condition: I must take my trusted nurse and my old medical orderly with me."

"Are these persons to be trusted?"

"Absolutely. My female nurse is very, actually extremely, loyal to me, although she doesn't speak much German. She speaks Spanish and Afrikaans. My medical orderly served with me in the Waffen-SS. Apart from being a medic, he is also an ordained priest and he was our division's Kriegspfarrer."

"Accepted. Can you leave immediately? There is haste."

"That can be done. I will just have to inform Herr Ullrich that I will be away for some time."

"I already have his permission to remove you from the compound for a few days. But we can only leave after dark. It is extremely important that your destination stays secret and you must not know where you are going."

"That gives me time to prepare and to tell my companions to get ready as well."

While I am packing a medical bag with all the instruments and medicine that I might need for a house visit to an important patient, I cannot help but to think that this will certainly prove to be the most interesting adventure I have ever had during my career as Arzt. I treated SS men, many civilians during my stay with my old regiment in Bavaria and later in Norway, American prisoners of war, simple Austrian folk in Styria and, now, members of this compound. But now I am to treat somebody who is, perhaps, the most hated man in the world, should it become known that he is not dead.

Residencia Inalco, Tuesday, 23 October 1946

David:

Since this is a secret mission, I didn't tell anybody where I and my two companions were going. We drove through the night and we slept as well as we could in the big sedan driven by a chauffeur. Herr von Grollmann sat in front with the driver and we three from Bariloche reclined on the back seat. Rebecca sat in the middle, between me and Pater Sepp. This is the first occasion in a long time that I had a female body in close proximity to mine and I decided that I enjoyed it.

We arrive at the edge of a big lake just after daybreak. A motor speedboat is waiting for us and it takes ten minutes for us to reach a jetty on the other side of the lake. A big mansion is to be seen among the trees and I guess that this is where Hitler is living. I see pill boxes along the shore and on top of the hill beyond the mansion. Those can only be machine gun bunkers for Hitler's guards. I gathered that we are in the north of the country to judge by the dense semi-tropical vegetation.

Herr von Grollmann leads us to the mansion where we are taken to the kitchen for breakfast. We are told to wait until the Führer wakes up.

After about an hour I am called to the Führer's bedroom. My companions are to stay behind. When I enter the bedroom, I am at a loss of words. How must I address this man for whom I have very little respect?

Before I can open my mouth a voice calls: "Guten Morgen, Herr Doktor Scholtz! Please step nearer. We are alone and from this moment on I am your patient. I appoint you as chief physician of the Fourth Reich with immediate effect!"

I laugh at this joke. "Mein Herr, thank you for this honor. But before I can accept that appointment, I will have to examine you first."

"Go ahead. I will answer all your health-related questions. But I refuse to discuss politics today. For that, I am in too much pain."

"Tell me more about the pain. Where exactly is it?"

He lifts his night shirt and shows me the spot on his abdomen. I feel around the spot and declare: "This feels like a tumor. How long have you suffered from this?"

"About two months. I took some pain killers but they don't really help. The spot only became worse."

"Mein Herr, I have brought my nurse and a medical orderly along. If it is a real emergency I can start operating within the hour. But I think it will be necessary to make one hundred percent sure what is going on inside you. And for that I need to take X-ray pictures to locate the growth exactly. It will also be necessary to take a biopsy that I will have to investigate under a microscope. I cannot see how we will be able to get an X-ray machine here in this remote spot with no roads leading to the place. You will have to come to my clinic in Bariloche. I will accompany you and my companions will help me to make you comfortable. How about it?"

"I don't like leaving this place."

"Then you must continue to suffer in pain. And if it is a tumor, it may bring your end about. It is your choice; I cannot force you, even if I am the chief physician of the Fourth Reich!"

"All right. But then we will have to leave after dark. Please call von Grollmann. He will have to organize an ambulance and an escort. In the meantime, you are welcome to enjoy your stay here. And I will very much like you to tell me about your career as Arzt in the Waffen-SS. I have been told that you earned an Iron Cross, First Class."

Suddenly I think I know how to address this man and I answer: "Your Excellency! If you want very good company, I will have to call my medical orderly. He was with me throughout the whole war and we became excellent friends. You will like him. He is actually more than a medical orderly. He is an ordained priest and if you have any sins on your conscience he will even listen to your confession. What do you say?"

"Please, give me some time to get dressed and then we can go to the living room. After lunch, I advise you and your companions to take some rest before we start our journey to your clinic."

Because I need to know as much as possible about my patient's health, I ask him on which medication he is. He shows me a few bottles on the table next to his bed. I inspect every bottle; there are sleeping pills, pain killers en 'n bottle marked Methylamphetamine. "Why do you use these pills?"

"Herr Doktor, oh, that's a wonder cure. If I feel downhearted, I swallow one. It restores my energy and I can face life again."

In think silently: "This drug is very addictive and the prolonged use of it may even lead to hallucinations. That may explain to me Hitler's reported bizarre behavior at the end of the war."

My patient continues: "I want to tell you a secret. Before and during the war I and my minister of health ensured that the whole of Germany was fed this stuff without realizing it. Minute quantities were added to coffee and chocolates. That lifted the morale of our people tremendously and that explains why we were able to endure so long against a terrible onslaught!"

I think further: "I and my brother, as well as our wives, must have been exposed to this stuff continuously. It is no wonder that I felt rather downhearted when I reached Stift Vorau because there was no coffee and chocolates available. I must have suffered bad withdrawal symptoms!"

I thank Hitler for this information and I go back to the kitchen where Rebecca and Pater Sepp are sitting. She is teaching him Spanish. I interrupt the lesson and announce: "Father Heibl, his Excellency, Herr Adolf Hitler, requests your company a little later this morning. He wants to hear all about our exploits during the war. I think he also wishes you to take his confession afterwards."

Pater Sepp smiles: "Please don't ever ask me what he confessed to me. That must stay confidential for all eternity."

"I know you as somebody who talks in his sleep. Perhaps I might hear something that way."

In the living room I tell Herr Hitler about my training as military Arzt and how our group made fun of Hauptscharführer Klaus Dralle. "He took revenge on us by making us jump around on our left legs. He promised us that this type of exercise will add ten years to our lives. One of my comrades shouted back: 'I already feel ten years older!'

"On another occasion he asked our group to complete a form providing details about the people who had to be notified in case of an emergency. Krebs, the gynecologist, wrote: 'A good doctor'. Dralle looked at the form and asked Krebs: 'And who is your doctor?' whereupon Krebs answered: 'That's me'. Dralle was not perturbed and he quipped: 'Krebs, I am sure that you were so ugly when you were born that the good doctor wanted to dump you into the waste paper bin or flush you down the toilet. I am sure that no doctor will ever want to treat you and, therefore, you will have to treat yourself'. For once, Krebs was at a loss for words."

Hitler exclaims: "I know that man! He was my driver during 1942. Actually, a good man, although he sometimes drank too much."

"Remarkable. What became of him?"

"While he was on leave in Berlin, he was killed in an air raid. Poor man. I liked him. He also told me about the impossible group of medical people he had to lick into shape at the end of 1939. He must have meant you, my dear Herr Doktor!"

Bariloche, Sunday, 27 October 1946

David:

We reach my clinic on this beautiful Sunday in Spring. There are flowers and blossoms everywhere. We deliver Hitler to my clinic with the ambulance drawn next to the entrance of the building. Since it is Sunday, nobody is working today and the place is more or less deserted. I suspect that many of them went to church.

I ask Pater Sepp to go and look for Karl Ullrich while I and Rebecca take Hitler inside the building. He struggles to walk due to all his pain, despite the pain killers that I have injected into him. He hides his face behind a wide-brimmed hat.

We make him comfortable on the bed in the clinic's recovery room while Frau Hitler, who accompanied us, sits next to his bed.

Karl Ullrich arrives and I tell him that I need a few guards to keep everybody away from this building. I am to operate on Adolf Hitler soon and he will have to stay here for a few days before he can go back. That means that nobody can be allowed to enter the office block. Nobody is also to know the reason for this extraordinary step. Ullrich understands and moves away to organize his guards.

To Pater Sepp I say: "The three of us will have to stay in this clinic for the duration. Will you please organize with the kitchen to have meals for five people to be sent here until further notice? We also need two extra beds for me and you because we will have to sleep in the operating theatre while Frau Hitler and Sister Rebecca are to sleep in the recovery room with our patient."

"Must I ask for arsenic seasoning for the patient's food? Or will he need foxglove or anaconda venom?"

"You evil man! You don't deserve to be called a priest. I have a sick person on my hands I will get him better, without your seasoning! If you aren't careful, I will report you to the Pope personally…"

An hour later the X-ray pictures have been taken. A cancerous growth has been located and the diagnosis was confirmed by the examination of a biopsy under my microscope. Hitler is made to lie down on my operating table, the overhead lights are switched on and I apply the anesthesia. Pater Sepp and Rebecca are at hand to execute all my orders. After thirty minutes the patient's wound is stitched up and he is transferred gently to the bed in the recovery room. I removed a tumor as big as an egg. Frau Eva Hitler and Sister Rebecca look after him as he slowly awakes.

Father Sepp asks Frau Hitler softly if she thinks he should perform the last rites. She shakes her head angrily: "My husband is certainly not dying! This good doctor will see to it, I am sure. Otherwise, his head will roll."

Pater Sepp retorts: "But the Führer has appointed him as chief physician of the Fourth Reich. How can you have so little faith in the man?"

Bariloche, Monday, 28 October 1946

Willie:

It is Monday morning and I want to go to my office. Two guards at the entrance to the office block stop me. Orders from Herr Ullrich. Nobody is to enter here. I notice other guards circling the building.

I find this strange. What is also strange is that the clinic was closed since a few days ago and David and his nurse have disappeared. Nobody knows what is going on and all look perplexed.

Fortunately, the mess is not closed and we are allowed to have meals. We all speculate on what is going on and various rumors are spreading through the compound. The going theory is that the good Herr Doktor David Scholtz, his nurse, sister Rebecca, and Pater Sepp have contracted some or other very dangerous virus and they are keeping themselves in quarantine. It is hoped that they will survive because we need them all. It is also hoped that the dangerous virus will not spread to the rest of the compound.

One of the wise guys declares: "I think the good Doktor is giving that priest sex lessons on his nurse. Just watch, in nine months' time there will be an addition to our compound."

I almost feel like giving the guy a good hiding. Nobody laughs at his sick joke.

Bariloche, Friday, 1 November 1946

David:

I deem it safe for the patient to be moved. Karl Ullrich comes to the clinic to hear about our patient's progress and I tell him: "It will be too dangerous to move him in an ambulance over the rocky roads. Is it possible to organize a floatplane to land on the lake next to us and to fly him back to the place where he came from? The plane must be big enough to take his stretcher, as well as four other passengers."

Ullrich frowns: "If that is the only way to take him home then it has to be done. His health is dependent upon your skills and orders. All right, I will see what can be done. But be prepared, it might perhaps only be possible tomorrow."

I report back to my important patient and his wife and they are satisfied with my arrangements.

Just after lunch we hear an airplane land at the air strip outside town. A motor cavalcade with sirens is heard approaching the compound. Hitler seems alarmed: "Herr Doktor, do you think that may be the Police coming to fetch me? Where can you hide me?"

"No, your Excellency. It cannot be the Police. The Argentinian authorities are well disposed towards our operation here at Bariloche. I don't think those sirens have anything to do with you."

I was wrong. A few minutes later Karl Ullrich enters the clinic with an important visitor. He calls: "Herr Doktor! Is your patient able to receive President Juan Peron?"

We all gape at him. This is totally unexpected. I hastily blurt out: "Of course! Please come in. But only the President is allowed in with the patient. His bodyguards, if any, are to stay outside. I don't want the public to come marching in here and spread all sorts of deadly germs!"

"That has already been ordered."

Juan Peron enters the clinic while I, Pater Sepp and Sister Rebecca stand at attention. He nods at us and asks where the patient is. I lead him to the recovery room where Herr Hitler is sitting up on his bed with Frau Hitler at his side. I leave the two politicians alone.

Our little medical team, together with Karl Ullrich, wait in the waiting room – too nervous to talk much. We can't even sit down and we march up and down. After thirty minutes the Argentinian President reappears and announces: "Herr Doktor Scholtz, I have to thank you for looking so well after your patient. He only has praise for you. He even told me that you were a military Arzt in the Waffen-SS."

"That is correct, Mister President. And may I remind you, please, that we have already met, many years ago. You visited our mountain artillery regiment during 1941 when you were still a Colonel."

Juan Peron smiles: "Si! Si! I remember clearly. Your regiment gave me a spectacular display of your readiness in the Bavarian mountains. You taught me much. I even remember visiting your field dressing station. And now we meet again. Remarkable!"

"Perhaps you cannot remember, but on that occasion, you suggested that I settle in Argentina if I cannot return to my own country, South Africa. And, here I am, as you proposed!"

While shaking my hand, the President continues: "I have already organized a floatplane to take your patient back home tomorrow. Farewell!"

After Peron and Ullrich have left the clinic, we three stare at each other. Pater Sepp is the first to break the silence: "By all the archangels in heaven! All the important saints up above there (and he points with his finger towards the ceiling) have held their protective hands over us! Well, I never! Nobody will believe if I tell them this…"

Willie:

The members of our research and development team are sitting idly around in the canteen, drinking coffee and discussing our plans. Suddenly we hear sirens wail and we rush out to see what is going on. Somebody shrieks: "The Police are coming. They are going to shut our facility down! Quickly, we must burn all our papers!"

Somebody else yells: "You fool!! Dummkopf! There won't be time for that. But who says it's the Police? Let's wait and see. We have enough armed guards here to protect us, should it become necessary."

President Juan Peron

A cavalcade of Police vehicles draws up at our gate and Karl Ullrich walks over. He orders the guards to let the visitors in. They drive through to the office block where the clinic also is. To our amazement a very important visitor gets out: President Juan Peron! He wears his military uniform and he is surrounded by bodyguards, but he waves at us with a huge smile. And then he disappears into the building, together with Karl Ullrich.

Pandemonium breaks out.

Herr Doktor Knoll, our leading scientist, asks for silence: "Meine Herren, there can only be one reason for the visit of the President of our adopted country. Herr Ullrich has to show him around. He wants to inspect all our facilities and see for himself what is going on here. It is a good sign that he came here. A very, very good sign. Let's give him a cheer when he comes out again!"

We already cheer in response to this sensible explanation for Juan Peron's visit. We all order Schnapps from the canteen to celebrate our good luck.

David:

I escort our important visitor through the front door of our building. I see it as my duty to accompany him to his vehicle.

A whole crowd has assembled outside the mess hall and everybody cheers and gives applause. The President smiles again and waves back before stepping into a Police car that drives away with sirens blaring and shrieking. The guards at the gate salute as the vehicles race back to the landing strip.

Willie sees me and runs to me: "What was that all about? I haven't seen you for a whole week! What the hell is going on? Why was the President here? "My dear brother, I am not allowed to answer any of your questions. Maybe later. Please excuse me, I have important matters to attend to."

Willie:

I haven't seen my brother act this strange in his whole life. He was actually rude to me. It is, though, a relief to have seen him alive and well.

I return to the crowd. They shower me with questions and exclamations.

"Men, unfortunately, I cannot tell you anything. My brother refuses to talk to me. At least, he seems to be in good health. If he and his medical team mates were in quarantine as we have speculated, then that theory has to be abandoned. He would never have dared to expose the President of our host country to a dangerous virus. But I agree with you, something very secretive and fishy is going on."

David:

After the departure of the important visitor, I go back to my patient: "Your Excellency! Before you are transported back to your residence tomorrow it is certainly necessary that I inspect your health thoroughly. We don't want all sorts of ailments and complications to plague you when you are no longer in my care. Do you mind if Sister Rebecca and Father Joseph assist me?"

Hitler does not mind and I start my examination. Sister Rebecca takes his pulse and his temperature. I peer into his eyes and examine his tongue and throat. With a spoon I tap against each one of his teeth. I light with a torch into his ears and declare: "I see a void in there. How is that possible, your Excellency? How can your skull be empty?" He only smiles.

I ask Pater Sepp to lift up his legs and I examine the soles of his feet and the nails on his toes. I listen with a stethoscope on his chest and his back while I ask him to breath in and out and cough. I take his blood pressure. He is required to swing his arms and to try to touch his toes, which proves to be very painful, due to the operation wound that is not yet fully healed. I take a small blood sample from his index finger and examine it under my microscope and I invite him to have a look. A few drops of his saliva are also inspected through the microscope. I also ask him to provide me with a sample of his urine and stool. After a while I get those and examine them under my microscope and put some in test tubes which I investigate by pouring acid and all sorts of other chemicals into the tubes. A horrible stench is given off.

The climax of the examination comes when I draw some blood with a syringe and let it drop into a test tube into which I have placed some anti-acid fruit salts. Of course, the liquid of the blood causes the fruit salts to form bubbles and froth. I show it to my patient and I murmur: "Oops. That doesn't look nice."

When all the tests have been performed my patient declares: "Herr Doktor Scholtz! Thank you for taking all the trouble of examining me so thoroughly. Something like this hasn't been done on me for a long time. What do you find? How is my health?"

"Your Excellency! I have a few worries. You realize that you are not so young anymore. I advise you strongly to take a tablespoon full of castor oil daily. It contains essential fatty acids. That will certainly prevent subanaemic mintropsia, for which you seem to be susceptible. It will also be a good thing if you take a table spoon full of Epsom Salts daily in a glass of lemon juice to keep the ventricles in your brain hydrated. If your brain ventricles become dehydrated it might cause dementia hysterica."

Hitler looks impressed.

I hand him a bottle with sugar pills: "These are sleeping pills. Don't wake them up by shouting or talking loudly in their presence."

Hitler grins.

Frau Hitler takes her husband to the bathroom for his first bath after his operation. Pater Sepp corners me: "What in heaven's name is 'dementia hysterica?' I know a little bit of Latin and it sounds like gibberish."

I smile wisely: "You are correct. It *is* pure gibberish. No such condition has ever been described in the medical literature."

"And subanaemic mintropsia? That is not even Latin or Greek."

"You are again correct. I just made it up."

"Poor ex-dictator. I don't want to be in his place with a daily dose of castor oil and Epsom Salts! And a glass of lemon juice. All those things must taste horrible…"

"Quite correct."

"And those pills you gave him – are they really sleeping pills?"

"Did they perhaps look awake to you?"

"No, they were certainly sleeping. Not one was moving!"

Rebecca wants to know what we are discussing and I tell her in Afrikaans. She starts laughing and holds her belly: "You naughty boy! Making the poor man suffer! How could you? Although, I understand he is the most hated man in the world and you are making some innocent fun of him. You horrible man! I think I must report you to the Medical Board for malpractice."

"Malpractice on a man who committed suicide more than a year ago? Come on…"

Pater Sepp asks: "Are there really ventricles in a brain? What are they?"

"Yes, there are hollow spaces in your brain and they are always filled with cerebro-spinal fluid. They can never become dehydrated, unless you become a mummy."

Bariloche, Saturday, 2 November 1946

David:

It is still early, shortly after sunrise. The work day has not yet begun and few people are around. Breakfast in the mess will only be at seven o' clock, somewhat later.

While my patient is being carried outside on a stretcher, we hear an airplane approaching. It is the floatplane that we have ordered and she "lands" on the water of the nearby lake. My patient is almost invisible under a blanket on a stretcher with a towel over his head and he is loaded into an ambulance, driven by Karl Ullrich himself. We – that is, I, Sister Rebecca, Pater Sepp, Frau Eva Hitler and Herr Adolf Hitler – drive off to the edge of the lake. A rubber dingy is ready to take the patient over to the floatplane, a civilian machine, no doubt chartered especially for the occasion.

Junkers W.34 bushplane on floats

The patient exclaims his joy at seeing the plane: "Ah, one of ours! A real Junkers! I will feel safe in her."

The pilot, who speaks German, welcomes us aboard and declares that the flight will take more or less an hour. I suspect that he must be ex-Luftwaffe and that he, somehow, also escaped from

Europe. We have hidden the patient well enough to prevent the pilot from recognizing his most important passenger. Hitler dozes off during the flight and he wakes up when we descend and float to the jetty in front of his residence.

Herr von Grollmann awaits us on the jetty: "How is our Führer?"

"Ask him yourself. He is awake."

Von Grollmann walks next to the stretcher that I and Pater Sepp are carrying. Hitler sees the manager of his affairs next to him: "My dear Grollmann, this Arzt is a magician. He has taken very good care of me and I am optimistic that I will be able to go for my daily walks fairly soon.

"We must remember to make him Minister of Health in the Fourth Reich. I believe he deserves such a position."

Pater Sepp winks at me.

Herr von Grollmann announces: "Breakfast will be ready shortly. Please be our guests."

I answer: "The floatplane is waiting for us. We cannot stay for breakfast, unfortunately. We will deliver the patient to his bedroom and then we will have to say good-bye. Anyway, thank you for the invitation."

"That airplane can wait. I will send somebody to fetch the pilot for breakfast in the kitchen. There he won't be able to see who the principal member of this household is."

We have little choice and we enjoy a hearty German breakfast in the big dining room of the residence. It is clear that the ex-Führer has taken a liking to us because he starts with an impassioned speech about his plans for restoring the Nazis to power in post-war Germany. The atomic bombs being developed in Bariloche play an important part in his planning and he is delighted to hear that my twin brother is the deputy leader of the team of scientists.

"I have instructed Herr Grollmann to organize a meeting with the chief scientists early next month to get a report on their progress. Then we can also plan the future. I foresee a glorious renaissance of Germany in the not-too-distant future!"

Willie:

It is lunch time and the mysteries surrounding the compound are never-ending. We were suddenly allowed into the office block this morning after breakfast and the guards were nowhere to be seen. However, the clinic of David was still closed.

The people discuss the fact that a seaplane landed on the lake this morning and returned later, before taking off again. Nobody knows where she came from and where she was going.

I was just taking my usual place in the mess hall for lunch when David and his priest friend appear. I remark: "Oh, you are still with us! We thought that you have fallen off the edge of the world into a deep abyss. Fortunately, I saw you when Peron made his appearance. But then you disappeared again. What on earth is going on? Or is it so secret that I may not know?"

David smiles: "Let's go for a short walk outside the compound after lunch and then I may perhaps be able to give you some information."

Lunch is enjoyed – or rather, only consumed – in silence.

And now we are taking a walk and David looks important when he takes me in his confidence: "President Peron visited us yesterday, as you very well know. He was very impressed with what he saw and he congratulated us with our work. He also asked me to inspect the site of a home for mentally unhinged criminals. It is situated very far from here and, therefore, we had to fly there. The place is very secure and I cannot see that any criminals will escape from that place, unless they are experienced swimmers who can stay in the cold water for hours on end."

"Wow. So, Peron is not going to shut this place down?"

"He never mentioned any intention of doing so."

David:

Without telling a single lie I have thrown my brother totally off the scent.

Just after dinner two engineers approach me: "Did we hear correctly? Is the President planning to convert our compound into an institution for mentally deranged criminals? What is to become of our hard work here?"

"You don't need to worry. The President was very impressed by what he saw here. We may continue our work. We won't see any lunatics being kept here."

Bariloche and Residencia Inalco, Monday, 2 December 1946

Willie:

The leader of our team, Herr Doktor Klaus Knoll, together with camp commandant, Karl Ullrich, approach me at breakfast. Ullrich says: "Dear Herr Doktor Scholtz, will you please join us in my office as soon as you have finished your breakfast?"

This looks important and I immediately agree.

In Ullrich's office, he asks us to sit down and he announces: "Meine Herren, things seem to be moving forward at a steady pace. The Führer has requested a meeting with the leadership of this project today, Monday. We are to fly by floatplane to his residence in thirty minutes time. Please get yourselves ready with all necessary paper work to be able to report on our progress. I have ordered transport for us to the lake where we will board the floatplane."

We get onto the floatplane and we are airborne within a few minutes. To judge by the position of the sun, we are flying in a northerly direction. After about an hour in the air we glide down onto a lake and float to a jetty. We get out and the pilot switches off his engine. Three gentlemen await us on the jetty.

The most senior man simply commands us: "Please follow me. Hermann, please take the pilot to the kitchen and serve him some coffee."

We enter a big mansion in the forest where our guide introduces himself: "Meine Herren, I am former Brigadeführer Wilhelm von Grollmann. I am the Führer's head of administration and you are to have a conference with him and Martin Bormann in a few minutes time. Please step into the Führer's office where we can hear what you have achieved so far."

The three of us enter a room with a huge desk, book cases and maps against the walls. Two gentlemen stand up to greet us: Adolf Hitler and his personal secretary, Martin Bormann. Hitler has aged visibly but his eyes are bright.

"Ah, you must be Herr Doktor Scholtz! You look just like your twin brother who nursed me back to life a few weeks ago. I found him to be a very capable man and I am sure that you are made of the same stuff."

I suddenly understand why David was so secretive. He had Hitler as a patient!

Bormann also greets us, but he keeps to the background.

Knoll delivers his report to the effect that our uranium machine or nuclear reactor is up and running and that we are steadily producing enriched uranium. We already have enough for three bombs.

Bormann speaks for the first time: "Thank you, meine Herren. You are doing splendid work. Unfortunately, you weren't able to get this far before the war ended. But the war will continue one of these days and you are the people who will make it possible."

He walks over to a big map of the world: "Our principal enemies are the Soviet Union, Great Britain and America. If we can drop bombs on Washington or New York, London and Moscow (he points at those cities with his hand) we can force these powers to give us back our country. They will have to pull back their forces of occupation, release all so-called war criminals still held captive and send back all prisoners of war. They will be forced to pay reparations for the damage they did to our cities, just as we were forced to pay damages after 1919. If they refuse, we drop some more bombs and that will scare them, just as Japan was scared into surrendering a year ago.

"They will not know where to find us initially and retaliation is, therefore, impossible. They will not dare to drop atomic bombs on the whole of Argentina. Only when they have fulfilled all our demands are we to enter our Fatherland in triumph. And you, gentlemen, are at this moment the most important people in the emerging Fourth Reich!"

I venture a few words: "Mein Führer, although I am not a German, I have a personal stake in humiliating the British and the Americans. An American bomber killed my wife in Berlin more than two years ago. The British have committed unspeakable atrocities against my people in our Second War of Freedom during 1899 to 1902. They have never acknowledged their guilt and I suggest that we force them to do so."

Hitler smiles: "We can always add that as another condition on the British. I like that idea!"

Karl Ullrich, the ex-military man, asks: "Herr Bormann, how do you envisage the dropping of the bombs on those cities? Where will we get the bombers for that?"

"That is something that we can sort out at a later stage. The important task is now to get those bombs assembled."

Hitler silences all of us: "Herr Knoll, can you please explain to me again how your bombs will work?"

"Mein Führer, certainly. It is actually very simple if you have the ingredients. When enough enriched or radio-active uranium is brought together it creates a big bang due to a chain reaction that will flatten everything in a radius of more than ten kilometers. Structures outside this radius will burn down due to the great heat given off."

"And how will you prevent your bombs from exploding when you assemble them?"

"We place two halves of the required amount of enriched uranium at two opposite ends of a metal tube. When the bomb is dropped a certain amount of explosive behind each half throws them together and as soon as the critical mass is reached the chain reaction occurs."

2 December 1946

Karl Ullrich stands up: "Heil Hitler! Sieg Heil!"

Adolf and Eva Hitler in the garden of the Residencia Inalco

After a lunch in the mansion's dining hall, we fly back to Bariloche. During our flight Ullrich remarks: "As you have seen, Hitler is an old man. He is actually sick, despite the check-up that your brother gave him. The real power is Bormann. He was the real big man in Germany during the last few weeks at the end of the war and it is actually he, with the help of the intelligence services, who created a network that enabled us to get to Argentina where we could reorganize."

David:

My brother was absent during lunch. I connect his disappearance with the floatplane that flew over the compound earlier today and again took off from the lake.

During dinner, I poke my brother in his ribs: "Did you enjoy lunch with Adolf Hitler?"

I can see that I touched a sensitive spot. He looks at me: "You are to stay silent, but, yes, I enjoyed the lunch there."

362

Bariloche, Friday, 10 January 1947

David:

During lunch, I browse through today's edition of the Argentinisches Tageblatt. My eyes fall on an item that I immediately read. My blood pressure rises the more I read. The first thought that arises in me, is: "This is the zenith of hypocrisy and injustice!"

The report gives details about an international tribunal, composed of judges from America, Russia and Great Britain, who found the former SS General Karl-Heinz Brenner guilty of so-called war crimes. He is given a twenty years prison sentence.

His crime was supposed to be the total destruction of the Finish town of Rovaniemi on 11 October 1944. He purportedly executed an order of General Rendulic to explode an ammunition train with the result that the town was destroyed and many people died

My blood boils. I was there myself. Everybody agreed at the time that it was the Finns who blew up the train with ammunition to deprive our division of supplies. Hundreds of German soldiers were killed by the explosion and I saw their bodies myself. There is no possibility that Brenner, my old commander, could have given such a criminal order.

Bariloche, Saturday, 5 July 1947

Willie:

It is almost a year since President Peron paid us a visit and that episode is almost forgotten. Much has happened in this time.

David has been registered as a specialist surgeon with the Argentinian Medical Board and his Spanish has improved to such an extent that he often assists with operations in the local hospital. He insists that his nurse, Sister Rebecca, always work with him. I smell a rat – they are far too friendly towards each other for a pure professional relationship. She even addresses him on his first name when they are speaking Afrikaans with each other.

David's friend, the priest, often helps the local bishop in the cathedral.

David:

Today is Saturday and we are not working. Snow has fallen on the mountains surrounding Bariloche on three sides and I and my brother are preparing to go skiing. I haven't had the opportunity to fly down a ski slope since 1941 when I was a medical officer in Sonthofen. Although there was much snow in Finland, there was no opportunity to go skiing down a mountain because the country is rather flat and filled with swamps and lakes.

Bariloche has a primitive lift system that takes people up to the start of the ski slope on a mountain called the <u>Cerro Catedral</u>. Our skiing skills were somewhat rusted but at the end of the day, after four runs downhill we feel confident again.

Rebecca is waiting for us at the bottom end of the ski slope. She looks excited: "David, tomorrow you must teach me how to ski. It looks so much fun."

"Swell, my dear, but that will come at a price. You will have to give me a first-class kiss before we can start tomorrow."

And I cannot help but to enjoy Rebecca's company more and more, although she is ten years younger than I am.

Ski lift on the <u>Cerro Catedral</u>

Bariloche, Monday, 20 October 1947

David:

We regularly write to our parents and receive replies from them. Unfortunately, the last letter from our mother, dated 9 October 1947, conveys the sad news of our father's death. We would have liked to be reunited with our family in South Africa but the possibility of having an appointment with the hangman's noose keeps us away. Anyway, we are busy with important work here and it won't do to abandon everything. Too much depends on us.

And – I and Rebecca have grown very fond of each other. My brother also seems to like her and we three Boers often drink coffee together. She is also saddened by the news of my father's death: "I have really hoped to meet your people. It is sad that your father was too sick to come and visit us here before he died."

Bariloche, Monday, 2 January 1948

Willie:

Three of our team of scientists and engineers are sitting in Karl Ullrich's office. Klaus Knoll has the word: "Herr Ullrich, our team has agreed that it is time to report to the Führer and his helpers that our first bomb is ready to be tested. Can you please organize a meeting at his residence as soon as possible?"

"That is wonderful news. It is almost three years since the end of the previous phase of the war. If I understand you correctly, the next and final phase is almost due, or am I not mistaken?"

"You are totally correct."

David:

This is the first workday of the new year. The German colony at Bariloche held a great Silvester feast two nights ago. Yesterday, those of us who had hangovers slept it off. I, my brother, and Rebecca rowed on the lake and enjoyed the lovely summer weather in the Southern Hemisphere.

Willie let it fall that the nuclear project was nearing its end. By this time both of us have confessed towards each other that we have held conversations with Hitler. Willie seems to admire him while I and Rebecca have very little respect for the man.

Willie comes to my office after lunch today and whispers: "We are going to meet Hitler tomorrow. Things are coming to an end!"

Residencia Inalco, Tuesday, 3 January 1948

Willie:

The floatplane delivers us again to the jetty in front of Hitler's residence where von Grollmann meets us and leads us into the house. Somebody is to take the pilot again to the kitchen where he is to await us after having been given a breakfast. He still doesn't seem to realize who the real inhabitants of this mansion are.

I, Knoll, Ullrich and Sebaldus Schwarz, our chief engineer, enjoy breakfast with Hitler and Bormann while we report about our project.

Knoll smiles broadly: "Meine Herren! You may congratulate us. We have assembled the first bomb and we have enough material to construct six more bombs. This first bomb has to be tested – if you agree."

Hitler, without his mustache, looks up from his boiled egg and waves his teaspoon: "Yes, please go ahead."

Bormann nods with a cup of coffee in one hand and a Brötchen with cheese in the other hand. His mouth is filled with bread and he cannot speak.

Schwarz proceeds: "It is my job to work out how we are to test the bomb. We cannot do it over an inhabited region where the Americans will notice what we have done. It can only be done somewhere in the Atlantic. I propose that we procure two innocent-looking sailing boats, preferably schooners, to take the bomb and our crews out onto the ocean. The bomb will be fitted with a time mechanism to go off six hours after we have activated it. The crew on that boat will then transfer to the second boat that will leave the area as fast as possible. From a safe vantage point about thirty sea miles away we can watch the explosion and take photographs for you to study."

Knoll adds: "We believe that this will be the safest way of conducting our test, away from the prying eyes of Jews, Communists and Americans."

Bormann smirks: "I like your plan. When will you be able to execute it?"

"As soon as we have bought two sailing boats and found dependable men to crew them. We have already identified a number of former members of the Kriegsmarine in our compound who may be able to help us. They will certainly know how to handle the schooners."

I open my mouth for the first time: "I and my brother, the surgeon, are experienced seamen when smaller sailing craft are concerned. Our late father owned a yacht in a small boat harbor near Cape Town and we frequently took the vessel out into False Bay.

Bormann looks at me: "Herr Doktor Scholtz, I believe that you and your brother have earned the gratitude of the German people for your wonderful efforts. You have also earned the opportunity of being crew members on the two schooners. Your brother can be the medical officer for the expedition. How about that?"

"Herr Bormann, thank you for the confidence you place in us. I am sure that my brother would like to participate."

Sebaldus Schwarz takes the word again: "Meine Herren, our way of testing the bomb will also provide us with the means to deliver the bombs undetected to their targets. We don't have bomber aircraft but we can sail the bombs unobserved to the target cities where the crews can activate the time switches and clear the area before the bombs go off. For that, we will have to get two more schooners with crews. Five men on a boat will be enough. Two of the boats will have to be crewed by men who speak English fluently if they are to disappear in America and Britain after placing the bombs. For the third boat we will need men who can speak Russian and who will be able to bluff their way from Moscow or another city to somewhere else."

Hitler listens attentively and holds up one hand: "All this sounds great. I approve of it. But since our last meeting, a little more than a year ago, I have thought again about our targets. It won't help to explode bombs in Washington, London or Moscow because we will have to intimidate the big bosses of these countries. They will have to be the people to accept our conditions and they will only be able to do so if they are still alive. So, we will have to choose other targets. While you are delivering your devices by sea it will have to be coastal cities. Any proposals?"

Schwarz requests that we look at a map of the world. We leave the breakfast table and retreat to Hitler's study where a map of the world is hanging on the wall. Schwarz takes the word: "Meine Herren! I have already thought about appropriate targets. I agree that we cannot take Washington, London and Moscow out. In America it might be New Orleans. If we flatten this city, we also obliterate an important air base of the American Marines. Here I have an aerial photograph of this facility for you to look at. There is also an important naval base.

"With all the destruction in New Orleans we will also bring all he traffic on the busy Mississippi River to the extensive harbor facilities in the Mississippi Delta on the Gulf of Mexico to a standstill. We will also destroy a large number of oil storage tanks and oil platforms in the Gulf of Mexico. The bomb can be planted somewhere in the Mississippi Delta. If we take New Orleans out, we will deliver a very serious blow to the American economy and force the White House to take us seriously."

Bormann looks ecstatic: "Mein Führer, this idea makes sense. I would like to give it the green light."

Hitler nods his head while he smiles: "When that happens, I will repeat my victory dance that I have given after my visit to Paris in 1940 when the Frogs surrendered to our forces. What will our target in Britain be?"

Schwarz points to Portsmouth in southern England on the map: "This is the most important naval base of the British. We will be able to smash most of the Royal Navy in one go. It will be easy for a sailing boat to drop anchor just outside the harbor. The crew can then easily activate the bomb and row to the shore, after which they can disappear."

Hitler cries out: "Great! Wunderbar! And which Russian city will be our third target?" Bormann nods his assent.

Schwarz continues: "At a later stage we can sail up the Volga and branch off into the Moskva if we want to target Moscow. But that will prove to be rather difficult due to the extreme length of the Volga. But a better interim target might be Tallinn in the Estonian Republic of the Soviet Union. It has an important naval base with access to the Baltic. We might also consider Leningrad, which we failed to take during the war. If our men leave the boat with the bomb at one of these cities, they will be able to reach Finland shortly afterwards with a motor boat that they can take along. That will not call for men who know Russian."

Bormann waves his hand: "Tallinn it will be. Gentlemen, we thank you for your wonderful planning. We will immediately order our contacts in Buenos Aires to look out for four schooners that will have to be purchased in different parts of South America and the Caribbean."

I interject: "With respect, Herr Bormann, but it is my considered opinion that each boat must be headed by a scientist or an engineer who exactly knows how to arm the bombs. That task cannot be left to crew members without the necessary technical skills and knowledge."

"That makes sense. Will you take one boat? I propose that Herr Schwarz takes another boat and that Herr Knoll commands the third boat. Agreed?"

We four shake our heads in unison.

Hitler looks serious: "Meine Herren, I actually have reason to be very angry. Why wasn't this bomb ready in 1944 when we could have ended the war before the Americans and British invaded France? I know, we should have allocated more resources to this project and I blame myself for not doing more to get ahead of the Americans with a nuclear bomb. We could have humiliated our enemies in 1944!"

I take the bait: "Mein Führer! I agree. If we had this bomb in time the destruction of so many German cities could have been prevented."

Hitler nods: "That is water under the bridge. Let's concentrate on the present and the future. Do you have any ideas about our destinations for a second strike, should the first one not deliver the desired results?"

Schwarz continues: "Yes, we have. We may target Glasgow in Scotland, which lies on the Clyde that may be reached from the sea. In America, I propose San Diego in California where there is a major naval base. The Russian port of Vladivostok could be our third target. It also contains an important naval base. We will have to send boats off from the coast of Chile for the targets in America and Russia, while the boat that will travel to Glasgow can leave from Buenos Aires."

"Good thinking. I like it."

Bariloche, Monday, 2 February 1948

David:

It is early morning on a Monday. Rebecca, the beautiful nurse, lies with her head against my chest. I feel her soft breasts pressed against my body.

"You wonderful creature. I have sad news. I should have told you earlier, but I did not have the heart. I will have to leave you today for a little while. I hope to be back in about three weeks. Will you wait for me?'

She gets tears in her eyes: "David, just as I thought that you belonged to me, I get the feeling that you belong to the Nazis. I also get the feeling that your absence has something to do with the secret projects going on around here. Are you still working for Hitler after you have operated on that evil man?"

"My dear, unfortunately, I cannot answer your questions. But I promise: I will come back. I am far too much in love with you to ever forget you or abandon you. All I can tell you is that I will be the medical officer on an important expedition. I won't be able to hide my absence from the compound and, therefore, you may confirm that I have left for a certain time. I have already spoken to the hospital in town and they have given me leave of absence."

Willie:

The train to take us to the coast is due to leave this afternoon. We have reserved a whole carriage for our team consisting of me, David, Knoll, Schwarz and six ex-members of the Kriegsmarine who are doing guard duty at our compound. We have already crated our bomb carefully to make sure that nothing can go wrong with it. It is to be loaded onto the freight car of the train and our crew members will take turns to watch over it unobtrusively. The crate is marked: "LAVADORA" (washing machine).

I cannot help but to feel very excited. I have worked for this moment for more than a decade as the associate of Otto Hahn and Werner Heisenberg. We are going to make history!

During lunch I ask my brother: "Are you ready for this trip?"

"I have already packed a bag with medical supplies and my suitcase with my clothes; they just wait to be grabbed."

Train at the Bariloche station

Southern Atlantic Ocean, Thursday, 12 February 1948

Willie:

We sailed out of the southern harbor of Buenos Aires, called Dock Sud, in convoy – two typical innocent sailing boats on an outing on a hot summer's day. This part of the harbor, located on the Rio de la Plata, was chosen because the railroad car containing the bomb could be taken right next to the place where the boat to be sacrificed was moored. A crane lifted the crate onto the boat and the crew stored it inside where it was securely fastened to prevent any undue movement.

The schooner Atalanta

It is fortunate that I and David have experience of sailing boats. We were able to get the hang of our schooner in a short time and the three seamen of our crew also seemed to know how to handle the boat. We were aboard the Atalanta, an old German boat built way back in 1901 but still in a beautiful condition.

That was a week ago and we have left any sign of land far behind us.

We latch the two schooners together just after breakfast and the crew of the other boat transfer to the Atalanta after Schwarz has unlocked the crate with the bomb and activated the timer. We set the other boat with its precious cargo adrift and we sail back in the direction where we came from. The timer was set for fourteen hundred hours and we are confident that we will be far out of reach of the explosion by that time. We also made sure that we leave the boat with the bomb far away from any known sea routes because we cannot afford anybody on a passing ship to observe our test.

David:

My services as medical officer of the expedition weren't needed until now. All ten members of the expedition are now aboard our schooner, the Atalanta. We fly the American flag to confuse any unfriendly person who might be watching us.

We all gather on deck a few minutes before 14:00. Willie takes the wheel and we fold all the sails where we are drifting in tranquil waters.

At exactly 14:00 we see a bright flash and a huge plume of smoke rising up into the sky. A few seconds later a shock wave hits us and rocks the boat. We also hear a far-away rumble.

We all dance up and down on the deck. The bomb works! We take shots of the event as fast as we can with a movie camera and two still cameras.

Sebaldus Schwarz races to the chart cabin and switches the radio on. Since this morning, we have kept radio silence but now we are ready to report to our colleagues at the compound, as well as the residence on the lake, that we were successful. Just to confuse any unwanted listener, he speaks English and not German.

Willie:

Portsmouth, here we come! I have arranged with my colleagues who are to take command of the other two boats that I will target Portsmouth. Through that, I will avenge all the thousands of women and children who died in British concentration camps.

Bariloche, Thursday, 27 May 1948

Willie:

The last of our three bombs to be used on our targets was finally assembled yesterday. The other two bombs were already crated and last night we also managed to pack this bomb securely into its crate. Each crate is stenciled "MOTOR DIESEL" (diesel engine) in Spanish. They are to be loaded onto the train today to be transported to the coast.

The extra seamen we have recruited to work one of the boats are to join us in Buenos Aires. They will only be told of the nature of our respective voyages when we are at sea.

David:

Our local German newspaper, Argentishes Tageblatt, carried a very interesting report this morning. In South Africa, General elections were held the day before yesterday. The government of Field Marshall Jannie Smuts, the old friend of our father, was defeated by the National Party, headed by ex-minister of religion Doctor Daniel Malan.

That is good news. The National Party was not in favor of South African involvement in the war in 1939 and it is possible that this new government may have another attitude towards South Africans who aided the Germans during the war. I feel sorry for Smuts, my father's friend, for being defeated but I know that my father did not favor the entry of South Africa into the war and that must have created a rift between them.

I greet a tearful Rebecca before I leave for the station. I cannot promise her when I will be back, if ever.

Buenos Aires, Friday, 28 May 1948

Willie:

Our train arrives at the main station in Buenos Aires where Wilhelm von Grollmann meets us. Our group is led to a waiting bus that takes us with our luggage, as well as the three precious crates, to a villa outside the city. This is to be our headquarters.

Von Grollmann feeds us lunch and then assembles the three boat skippers for a meeting outside in the garden, away from the house: "Meine Herren! I have your final orders. The boat that is to target Portsmouth, which is the slowest boat, is to depart first and sail to the island of Saint Helena in the middle of the Atlantic Ocean to take on provisions and fresh water. Thereafter, you are to sail around West Africa and enter the harbors of Dakar and Gibraltar where agents will help you to replenish your supplies. From there you are to cross the Bay of Biscay and enter the English Channel. Report to us every day on your position on the oceans. Lay at anchor outside Portsmouth until we contact you by radio to inform you that the other two boats are also ready. Wait for exactly twenty-four hours and then arm the bomb to explode six hours later and leave the scene thereafter to get to safety. It will be easy to catch a train to wherever. The three bombs have to explode on the same day, more or less at the same time.

"Boat number two, which is the fastest boat, is to proceed a day later to Recife in Brazil and from there to Dakar, Gibraltar, Antwerp in Belgium, Bremerhaven in Germany and from there to Tallinn. Our agents will await your arrival at all these destinations and aid you in any way that is necessary. Boat number one and boat number two are not to take the same route through the English Channel so as not to arouse suspicion from any quarter. And when you lie at anchor in the Baltic you report by radio your position and await the sign to activate the bomb exactly twenty-four hours later. Verstanden?"

"The third boat that has to target New Orleans, will sail the next day to Recife in Brazil and from there to Paramaribo in Surinam. And then you sail through the Caribbean and make a stopover at Kingston in Jamaica. Our agents will contact you at all these ports and help you to replenish your provisions and water. Your last leg is through the Gulf of Mexico, straight to New Orleans through the Mississippi Delta where you are to wait for the radio message that you are to arm the bomb exactly twenty-four hours later. Of course, you stay in touch with us and report on your progress daily at twelve hours GMT.

I ask: "May I suppose that we will have all the necessary navigational charts aboard?"

"Of course."

"We will also need passports and other travelling papers whenever we enter the different countries along the way."

"You will all be supplied with Argentinian passports with assumed names."

Schwarz wants to know: "We will need money along the way to buy supplies, to bribe corrupt officials and to pay for our journeys and voyages home."

"Of course. Here are your purses. Each leader is to handle the money, which comes in different currencies. When you travel back to Argentina after a successful operation, do not travel together but break up into two or three groups so as to avoid detection or arrest. And then you report back to us at this villa."

Knoll asks: "When do we put to sea?"

"Your boats are ready in the southern harbor and boat number one leaves the day after tomorrow at 06:00. We need tomorrow to load the precious cargo on to the boat and it will be guarded by trustworthy men, although these men will not know what it is they will be guarding. Any other questions?"

I ask: "How are we to be taken to the boats?"

"A truck has already been loaded with the first crate and the crew of boat number one will travel to Dock Sud on this truck. The other two crates and the other two crews will be taken the same way on consecutive days. By the way, here are the frequencies you are to use on the specified days to radio your progress to us here."

David:

Willie calls me and the three seamen of our crew to his bedroom and informs us that we are to leave in two days' time. We will sleep aboard the night before we sail and leave at 06:00 the next morning.

I wander around in the villa and its garden. In the kitchen, where I beg a cup of coffee, I find this morning's edition of the Argentisches Tageblatt. My eyes fall on an interesting report. Prime Minister Malan of South Africa has announced amnesty for all so-called South African war criminals who have aided the Germans, provided that they did not commit atrocities against civilians. Dr Attie Strauss, who worked for the Afrikaans section of the German Radio Zeesen's news service and who was imprisoned by the Smuts government for aiding the enemy, is to be released immediately and united with his German wife, Ursula.

That is the best news I have heard in a long time. That means that I and Willie will be free to return to our Fatherland!

Southern Atlantic Ocean, Monday, 31 May 1948

Willie:

Today is a very auspicious day to start our voyage to teach the British a lesson they will never forget. Today, exactly forty-six years ago, the two Boer republics had to surrender to the overwhelming army of Great Britain, sent to enlarge the British Empire. The Boers had never more than 50 000 men in the field, while Britain had almost half-a-million soldiers available. This gross injustice is to be turned around very soon by the two sons of a Boer warrior – with the help of some German exiles.

We sail out just before dawn on the Atalanta through the mouth of the Rio de la Plata into the wide open Atlantic. Our first destination is the island of Saint Helena to our north-east. We are keeping radio silence but we are to make radio contact every day at 12:00 GMT to report our progress.

Two of our seamen are able to navigate by means of a sextant, a chronometer and a compass and we are confident to find the tiny Island of Saint Helena in the middle of the ocean. The distance there is a little more than three thousand nautical miles and we will need more or less twenty-five days to reach our first stop-over. By that time, we will need new provisions and fresh water. We can only take supplies for more or less thirty days.

We take turns on the wheel and to man the galley to prepare meals. When the sails have to be hoisted or taken down, all help.

The Atalanta, despite her age, is a beautiful boat and easy to handle. She is fitted with a diesel engine to steer her inside a harbor or during a period of calm on the open seas.

Saint Helena, Monday, 28 June 1948

David:

I was the first to see signs of our first destination, Saint Helena Island. As is often the case, a cloud was hanging over the island and that was visible from afar in the clear blue skies.

During the past five weeks we had to be careful with our supplies. It was more than once possible to augment our supply of fresh water by stretching a piece of canvas to collect rain water, which we could use for washing. We also caught some fish and that was a welcome alternative to tinned food.

I had much time to think about what we are about to do – time that I didn't have previously since my medical practice in Bariloche kept me rather busy. I also spent much of my free time with Rebecca. But now, here on the open ocean with much time on my hands, I started to wonder whether we were really doing the right thing.

I share Willie's antipathy against the British and the Americans. The British committed horrible atrocities during the war in South Africa. An American bomb killed our wives four years ago. The British, the Americans and the Russians were just as guilty of so-called war crimes as the Germans, but that did not take the guilt of the Germans away – at least, not the guilt of the Nazis, because not all Germans were real Nazis, although many of them welcomed Hitler as leader of the country in 1933.

After my regiment's deployment to Finland, I almost never mingled with the general German population. I was always surrounded by SS fighters. But even they, who were supposed to be the most reliable supporters of the Nazi regime, turned their backs on Hitler during the final stages of the war. It became clear that it was a monumental disaster to start the war against three powerful nations, the British, the Americans and the Russians.

Hitler took a bite he could neither chew nor swallow and the German people had to pay for his follies.

But – detonating nuclear bombs within three cities filled with civilians didn't seem right to me anymore. Just as the Allies punished innocent civilians by bombing their homes and killing or maiming thousands of them in Germany, we were planning to do exactly the same. Should we go through with this, we will prove to be no better than Churchill, Roosevelt and Stalin who were just as guilty as Hitler of war crimes. Was that really what I wanted to do? Did I really want to heap more miseries on a horribly wounded world?

It was always my calling to heal people, to lessen pain and suffering, to preserve life and to uphold the dignity of people – even if it was a despicable figure such as Adolf Hitler who was lying on my operating table. But to be an associate and accomplice of Hitler was something else – I could not stoop to that low point.

Willie had quite another experience of the war than I had. He was constantly surrounded by fellow-scientists who became obsessed by this idea of developing an atomic bomb to take revenge on the Allies. He never experienced the horrors of war, except when he lost his beloved Annemarie. I saw enough of these horrors – boys who were wounded and crippled, who cried in pain, who had the most horrible nightmares about the fact that their friends were blown up around them and they had to kill people they didn't know. I didn't want any of that anymore. I was proud of our glorious division that performed heroic feats, but I never wanted to repeat something like that.

At night I often lay awake. I had seen the power of our first atomic bomb and I could imagine the destruction that the three other bombs could produce. I have seen pictures of Hiroshima and Nagasaki in the newspapers and magazines and it wasn't a pretty sight. Thousands of innocent Japanese were still dying from cancer and other ailments, due to the nuclear radiation they had been exposed to. No! I could not be an accomplice of a similar horror! War may be justified if one is attacked and defense is necessary. But it can never be justified to start a war as we are planning to do.

We sail towards Jamestown, the only sizable town on Saint Helena and we anchor amid a number of other small craft while we furl our sails.

"Willie," I address my brother: "I have a proposal. You take our three crew members in our dingy and row to the shore where you look up our agent who has to help us with fresh provisions. I will look after the Atalanta while you are ashore. Tomorrow I might go ashore with some of you while another crew member looks after the boat when we have to fetch barrels of fresh water."

"That is generous of you. All right, as soon as we get dressed in presentable clothes we will row over in the dingy."

I wait more or less an hour after my mates have left and then I weigh the anchor and hoist the sails. By this time, the others won't be observing our boat and that will enable me to sail away from them, unobserved.

Jamestown, Saint Helena, from the sea

Willie:
It is pleasant to be on terra firma again. We have left the dingy on the beach and secured it by pulling it away from the waves. I

approach the first person I see and enquire about the whereabouts of the address that was given to us.

We find the address easily and the agent tells us: "Before we can do anything, you must report to the immigration authorities, otherwise your boat may be impounded. I hope you have your passports ready?"

I assure him that we, indeed, have our passports and he accompanies us to an office where our passports are stamped. Thereafter, we proceed to buy all the victuals we need: fruit, vegetables, bread, butter, eggs, flour, milk powder etcetera. We get a wheel barrow to take everything to our dingy and we push off into the water after having transferred everything into the dingy.

One of the seamen exclaims: "But the Atalanta is gone! Where is she?"

I look around and confirm this observation, but I command: "Let's look better. Row around and look at every boat. Perhaps we didn't look properly enough."

But it is to no avail and we have to row back to the shore. I get out and go back to the agent. He takes out a telescope and asks me to look very well at all the vessels lying at anchor in the sea. The Atalanta is indeed gone!

The agent asks: "Do you think that your brother who stayed aboard could have been hijacked by pirates?"

"How will I know? You know these waters better than I do."

"The very last thing we can do is to go to the Police. They will want to know exactly what is going on and we cannot afford to do that. I don't know what your destination is and what you were carrying, but I can guess it must be something very sensitive."

"You are correct. But perhaps my brother decided just to have a look at the island from another side and taken the boat for a short trip. Let's wait and see what happens. I am confident that he will turn up, sooner or later."

Saint Helena, Thursday, 1 July 1948

Willie:

This is the third day on Saint Helena and still no sign of David and the Atalanta. Our agent, who goes with the name of Cornelius Niemann, suggests: "Perhaps he went on his own to complete your mission without you. He wants the glory all for himself."

I reluctantly agree: "You may perhaps be correct. But I think we must report his disappearance to our people in Buenos Aires. Most probably they are in radio contact with him and they will be able to tell us what has happened to him. How can we contact them?"

The agent shrugs: "I don't know. I have no idea who the people are who sent you out. All I know is that I am supposed to help you and I got my orders from people in Spain. It is perhaps possible that these people will be able to help you to get connected to Buenos Aires. I will put through a telephone call. I must be extremely careful what I say because the call goes through a series of exchanges where the operators can listen in. But I will try. Come back tomorrow morning."

I return to the guest house where I and the other three crew members have found lodgings. The agent could not provide us with accommodation and we had to look elsewhere. I report briefly to the other members of what the agent told me. They also think that it is possible that David went off on his own to place the bomb without our help.

Saint Helena, Friday, 2 July 1945

Willie:

I return to our agent. He has positive news: "You may phone this number in Buenos Aires, but only during the afternoon. It is night over there at the moment."

To kill time, I and the other three men go hiking through the hills of Saint Helena. It is not a big island and not much of its surface is suited for farming.

We visit the cemetery where Boer prisoners of war, who died on this island, were buried. They were caught by the British during the war of 1899–1902 and sent as far away as possible to prevent them from escaping. According to a notice at the cemetery, 180 Boer warriors are buried here.

We take a good look at the place and we stand with bowed heads next to the two monuments erected in 1913 to honor those men who gave up their lives defending their country against the colonialists and imperialists. I fervently hope that my brother is successful in bombing Portsmouth – the British deserve that.

During the afternoon we return to the Post Office in Jamestown where we put a call through to Buenos Aires. It takes an hour before we are connected and I hear the voice of Herr von Grollmann.

To confuse the telephone operators along the way we speak German and I ask: "Do you have any news of my brother? I haven't seen him for four days. The other four of us are still on Saint Helena."

"No, I have no news. I tried to raise you guys on the radio but nobody answers. Do you have any idea what may be going on?"

"No. All we can think of is that he went off northwards without us to complete the job all on his own. I cannot imagine that he would abandon the mission. Please continue and try to make contact with him by radio. I will phone back tomorrow to hear whether you have achieved anything."

"Will do so."

"I must say, I think it is rather nasty of him to leave us here without luggage."

"I agree."

Walvis Bay, Thursday, 8 July 1948

David:

Walvis Bay, at last! I am exhausted after sailing solo from Saint Helena. Instead of sailing north, I sailed in a southeasterly direction to the port of Walvis Bay, the main port of South West Africa, a place that we have visited in 1933 when the Usambara docked there.

The distance to Walvis Bay, as I have calculated on our charts, was a little more than 1 200 nautical miles and I hoped to reach it within ten days. Since I am alone on the boat the remaining supplies were enough for this time. I even caught some more fish. There was little time for sleep, especially when I crossed busy sea lanes with big ships that would fail to notice me.

Since leaving Saint Helena I, of course, haven't reported my position daily at 12:00 GMT as required, although I listened to the radio at those times. Herr von Grollmann became agitated after a while when he was trying to raise the Atalanta without success. After five days he started to threaten me with all sorts of ugly consequences because Willie has managed to reach him by telephone in Buenos Aires – most probably with the help of our agent in Jamestown. He warns me that I cannot plant the bomb all on my own and claim the glory for a successful venture. It has to be a team effort. Anyway, Willie has the purse with the money and without finances I will most probably be stuck in England – unless I have taken enough money of my own.

I never replied so as not to give von Grollmann any idea where I was and what my plans were. Herr von Grollmann's angry broadcasts stopped on day eight of my voyage to Walvis Bay.

I feel sorry for Willie and the other crew members because I have taken their personal luggage with me on the boat. But that could not be helped. There was no other way to sabotage Hitler's mad idea of taking revenge on his enemies.

The high sand dunes of the Namib Desert become visible as I approach the coast of South West Africa. I wasn't quite sure how to sail directly to Walvis Bay but it was impossible not to strike the coast of Southwest Africa at some point. I sail south after having caught sight of the sand dunes of the Namib Desert until Walvis Bay comes into view. I can also already smell the place due to the factory that processes whale blubber.

Sand dunes of the Namib Desert from the sea

Without any further ado I dock at a quay in the harbor and I walk to the office of the Harbor Police. To the policeman at the counter, I announce: "Good morning. I'm an illegal immigrant. I just got off my boat. I want to surrender myself to the chief of the Police here."

The constable gives me an incredulous frown: "Please repeat that, Mister. I don't think I've heard you correctly."

I repeat my exact words and I add that I have an atom bomb on my boat in the harbor, which has to be given to the authorities. While shaking his head, he picks up the telephone and asks the exchange to put him through to Major van Blerk at the main Police Station: "Hi Major, this is van Rensburg from the harbor here. Yes, I am OK. I hope you are also. Yes, my wife is also OK. Thanks. I have a funny guy here who wants to surrender himself to the chief of Police here in Walvis. He says he is an illegal immigrant and he has an atomic bomb on his boat that he wants to donate to us. He speaks Afrikaans like us Afrikaners and I cannot think that it is possible for him to be an illegal immigrant. OK, I will lock him up until you can send a van. No, he doesn't seem to be dangerous. No, he doesn't have a wild look in his eyes. Yes, his story is loony, but he looks quite normal, although he has lots of sunburn, perhaps from staying on his boat for a long time. No, he hasn't fled yet, he is standing quietly and listening to what I am telling you. Yes Major. Thank you, Major. Same to you. Yes, I agree. Good-bye."

He puts the telephone down and addresses me while scrutinizing my face for any signs of madness: "Major van Blerk says he will send somebody to come and pick you up. In the meantime, I must keep you here in our cell."

"I don't want anybody to steal the atom bomb aboard my boat. Can you please organize a guard to look after my boat? Her name is the Atalanta. It is a sailing boat, out there in the harbor."

"How will anybody know there is an atom bomb aboard your boat? Is it lying around on the deck?"

"No., it is inside the boat. But you never know when a Nazi from Swakopmund comes snooping here and steals the bomb. Or worse, activates the bomb! There will only be big hole where Walvis Bay once was if that happens."

Van Rensburg scratches his head and rolls his eyes. He picks up the telephone again and asks to be connected to Major van Blerk again. To the girl at the exchange, he says: "Yes, my luvvy, I am sorry to bother you so much. But this is urgent government business. The Nazis seem to be involved, somehow. Anyway, be a darling and ring that Major awake, pronto. Please."

A little later: "Hi Major, it's me again. Van Rensburg. This guy here says he is afraid that the Nazis will come to steal his bomb. Somebody must guard his boat to keep them away. No, I haven't asked him yet what his name is. All right, I will ask him and take a full statement. I will search him to see if he has any papers on him. Or dangerous weapons. But please, send enough men to come and fetch this guy and somebody to look after his bloody boat. I am nervous about this chap. So, hurry up! Please, Major. Yes, Sir! Good-bye. Yes, immediately. Thank you, very much."

"The major says you must give me your name and home address and show me papers you may have to prove who you are. And then I must take a complete statement from you, while you are sitting in my cell. No, I won't handcuff you."

"Constable, I have a passport with a name on it. But it is a forged passport with a name that doesn't belong to me."

Van Rensburg exclaims: "Hell! What else?"

"All I can tell you is that my late father was a member of Parliament and that I was a SS soldier during the war. My real name is David Scholtz, actually, David Johannes Philippus Scholtz. But I cannot prove it. I have sailed from South America and my home address is c/o The Medical Clinic, Nuclear Compound, San Carlos de Bariloche, Argentina. If you need references, I can name President Juan Peron of Argentina. He visited me there."

Van Rensburg yells: "Hemel! (heavens!). Next you will tell me that you and Adolf Hitler were also friends. And now you are afraid that some stupid Nazi will pinch your bomb. I refuse to take a statement regarding this silly story you are telling me. Anyway, come this way. After you. Into that cell."

As he turns the lock, I show him my right wrist: "Constable, do you see this tattoo? It proves that I was a member of the SS. All SS men had this type of tattoo."

"Which concentration camp did you guard?"

"No, I was in a fighting unit. We mostly fought the Russians."

Van Rensburg walks away, mutters under his breath and shakes his head.

A quarter of an hour later a truck stops with screeching tyres in front of van Rensburg's police station and I hear loud voices. A minute later van Rensburg unlocks the cell and hands me over to a sergeant and another constable.

"I am Sergeant Coetzee and this is Constable du Plessis. We are pleased to meet you, Mister Scholtz – if that is your right name."

I smile: "Yes, it is. Thank you for coming to fetch me."

"Okay, into the back of the van. No, no, you sit here in front with me and you show me where this blooming boat of yours with the atom bomb is moored."

I sit between Coetzee and du Plessis and we drive off to where the Atalanta is lying. We all get aboard and I show them the bomb.

Sergeant Coetzee gets red in the face: "Mister, don't waste my precious time. That's a crime. Obstructing the ends of justice. You can be thrown in prison for that. Look here, this sign says: 'Something Diesel.' I haven't heard of any atom bombs that work with diesel fuel."

"Dear Sergeant, of course that sign is only there to confuse people. It is Spanish. Please don't open that crate and fool around with the switches. You won't live to feel sorry."

"I thought the Nazis spoke German. Where is this Spanish coming from?"

"From Argentina."

"What next? Unfortunately, we don't have a spychiatrist here in Walvis. Perhaps we can arrange for you to go to Windhoek. OK, du Plessis, you stay here until you are relieved. Come, Mister Scholtz, into that van again. Perhaps I must handcuff you to prevent you from hitting me when we are alone."

"I promise to come quietly."

I am taken to Major van Blerk's office. He gets up from behind his desk and takes my hand (perhaps to prevent me from taking out a fire arm or something).

"Well, well. I have heard funny stories from people who try and stay out of trouble. But yours takes the cake. You are surrendering to the Police and admit that you are an illegal immigrant in possession of an atom bomb. Please! Come and tell me your whole story and don't waste my valuable time. Understand?"

"Major, I understand completely. And may I remind you that I was also a Major in the Waffen-SS. I commanded an artillery regiment and we fought against the Russians. In addition, I am a qualified medical practitioner and I specialize in surgery. You may call Field Marshall Smuts. He knows who I am. He and my late father were good friends. And – it is completely true that I brought an atom bomb along, which I want to present to the authorities. I don't know how to render it harmless and for that we need some experts."

Major van Blerk blurts: "Do you really want me to believe this rubbish?"

"Yes. And I think we have to inform the head of Police and the chief of the Defense Force and even the Prime Minister that two other boats are on their way to bomb cities in America and Russia. My boat was supposed to blow up the port city of Portsmouth in Britain, but I hijacked the boat and brought it here to prevent a major catastrophe. Some Nazis who have fled Europe after the end of the war are behind this, including my own brother who is an eminent scientist."

It suddenly seems as if a light switch is turned on somewhere behind van Blerk's eyes and he really looks interested. I continue: "Major, I want to make a complete statement, a long one, and it would perhaps be good if you could get a stenographer to take down my story in shorthand and have it typed. And then you can make me swear that it is the truth. You are a commissioner of oaths, I believe?"

Without further ado, van Blerk picks up his phone and barks: "Send Ansie to me. Immediately, She has to leave everything and get here with a sharpened pencil and a notebook."

A minute later Ansie appears. Van Blerk tells her: "This gentleman is to tell you his story and you are to type it immediately afterwards. It will have to be in the form of an affidavit. OK, Mister Scholtz, or should I say, Doctor Scholtz, you tell us everything. Yes, everything. Ansie will take it down in shorthand."

"I, David Johannes Philippus Scholtz, aged thirty-six, am a male person of sound mind. I wish to make this statement under oath out of my own free will and everything I say is the truth. I am a medical practitioner and specialist surgeon who studied medicine at the University of Berlin before the Second World War. My late father, Pieter Ernst Scholtz, was a member of Parliament between 1921 and 1933. He represented the electoral district of Barkly West for the South African Party and he was also a lawyer who practiced in Kimberley...." and so I ramble on, until I reach the point where I met Constable van Rensburg.

Major van Blerk growls at Ansie: "Now you go and type that affidavit as neatly as possible on the telex machine and send it through to Police Headquarters in Pretoria. For urgent attention of Major-General Palmer. And then you bring the print-out for this gentleman and me to sign. "

After Ansie has left the office, Major van Blerk lifts up the receiver of his phone and barks at the telephone exchange: "Get me Police Headquarters in Pretoria. I want to speak to Major-General Palmer, the Commissioner of Police, personally. It is extremely urgent. I repeat: extremely urgent!"

Two minutes later, the connection is made: "General, this is Major Gert van Blerk. I am the head of Police in Walvis Bay. My secretary is at this moment typing a telex to you, containing the statement by a certain Dr David Scholtz. He has uncovered a Nazi plot to explode three atomic bombs in England, the USA and Russia with the object of restarting the Second World War. This Dr Scholtz has hijacked one of the three boats with the atomic bomb on board and it is still on his boat here in the harbor. It is my considered opinion that this matter is so important that you ought to immediately send somebody to retrieve that telex and act upon it. I trust that you will know exactly what to do about this matter that could have very serious international consequences."

He stays silent for a minute and then says: "General, thank you for your time. Thank you for believing me. This story is so fantastic that it sounds like the product of a demented mind. But Dr Scholtz, who is sitting here with me, is certainly all there. I am not a doctor, but I think I can recognize a madman when I see one. His story makes complete sense. Thank you, General. Good-bye, General."

"And now, dear Doctor, or should I say, Major Scholtz, the ball is in the hands of the Commissioner of Police. I want to see that bomb myself, but later. I think somebody from Pretoria will phone back and I must be available to answer the phone. In the meantime, will you like some coffee?"

"Please."

My empty cup of coffee was scarcely cold or the phone rings on van Blerk's desk. He grabs it: "Van Blerk here. Yes, yes, yes. He is here, sitting opposite me. You can talk to him personally, General."

I stand up to take the phone. A voice on the other end asks: "Doctor Scholtz? You are speaking to Major General Matie du Toit. I am chief of staff of the South African Army. General Palmer has given me the gist of your statement and I think it is important to get to us as soon as possible. I will request Brigadier Jimmy Durrant, chief of staff of the Air Force, to send a plane to pick you up. That will perhaps only be tomorrow. Please hand the phone back to Major van Blerk."

I do so. Van Blerk listens and says: "Yes General. Yes, General. I will do my best. Thank you for your trouble. Yes, General. Good-bye, General. The same to you, Sir."

"The General ordered me to put you in a hotel for the night. The bill will be paid by the Defense Force. And now, go and show me that bloody bomb! I will put three men on guard in and around the boat."

"I prefer to sleep tonight on the boat."

"No, I don't want you to sail away in the middle of the night or get murdered by a crazy Nazi from Swakopmund."

We depart in van Blerk's van and arrive at the Atalanta. The one policeman on the boat, Constable du Plessis, salutes as the Major gets out of the vehicle. I show him around on the boat and show him the marks on the navigational charts how we sailed from Buenos Aires. If he had any doubt about the veracity of my story, this dispels it.

After forty minutes we arrive back at the Police Station after I have retrieved my personal luggage from the boat. Sergeant Coetzee awaits us with a message: "Somebody from the Air Force phoned. A plane is to land at our landing strip tomorrow at oh nine hours to pick up Doctor Scholtz and fly him somewhere. We have to organize a fuel lorry for them to refuel."

Van Blerk orders: "Coetzee, you are to pick up Doctor Scholtz tomorrow at half-past-eight and take him to the landing strip. He is staying in the hotel. I will organize the fuel truck."

I am taken to the local hotel where I am booked in personally by Major van Blerk. After I have dropped my luggage in my room, I decide to wander the streets of this town and I go back to the harbor to say good-bye to the Atalanta and the bomb. I go to the Harbor Police to thank Constable van Rensburg for believing in my story and phoning the Major.

Van Rensburg asks me: "So, your story is actually true?"

"Yes, I spoke to the Chief of Police in Pretoria, as well as the Chief of Staff of the Army. They are sending a plane to pick me up tomorrow. But this story is top secret. If you tell anybody, even your own wife, you will get into extremely serious trouble."

"Some people have all the fun in the world. And here I sit in this stinking place where nothing ever happens… Anyway, who is going to pay the bloody harbor fees for that blinking boat of yours?"

"Send the bill to the Government."

"And what happens to the food and drink on the boat?"

"If you want to get drunk on that, be my guest."

Cape Town, Friday, 9 July 1948

David:

The promised airplane of the Air Force is on time. Sergeant Coetzee brought me in the Police van to the landing strip. He assured me that three policemen are looking after the Atalanta around the clock, in shifts.

The pilot of the aircraft, a Dakota DC 3, kills the engines so that the plane can get refueled. A tank lorry approaches the plane and the refueling begins. The onboard technician uses a piece of bamboo as a dipstick in the fuel tank to gauge how much fuel is still needed. I am allowed to step aboard and it seems that I am the only passenger. The pilot introduces himself as Lieutenant Fourie and he informs me that we are to fly to the Ysterplaat Air Force base near Cape Town where somebody else will take care of me.

The co-pilot, a major, addresses me in German: "Guten Tag, Herr Oberstabsarzt! Wie geht es Ihnen?" (Good day, Surgeon Major. How are you?)

It is as if a bucket full of snow is thrown at me, here in the desert of Walvis Bay. After I've overcome the impact of the shock, I recognize Karl Krause, whom I met in Kufstein before the war and on whom I operated in Trondheim in 1941.

I manage to ask him: "And how on earth did you manage to get here? A major in the South African Air Force? Weren't you tried as a Nazi war criminal?"

"It's a long story how I got here. We can chat during the flight. Anyway, I am doing a conversion course on this crate. The captain of the aircraft is my junior, but he is also my instructor. And how did you land on this spot?"

"By boat. I escaped from the Nazis in Argentina. I already told the Police and the chief of the Army my story and that is why you have to take me somewhere. Let's chat when we are airborne."

After the process of refueling was concluded, we take off and after two hours we land at Bloemfontein where we refuel again. Another hop brings us to Ysterplaat with Table Mountain in the background. On our way here we flew over our family farm in the southern Free State and I wonder what my mother was doing there at this moment. There was, though, no way of informing her that I was flying overhead.

A sedan awaits me and I am taken towards the city. It is more than fifteen years since I and Willie last saw Table Mountain on our way to Europe. I remember suddenly that I have promised Josephine many years ago that I would take her up onto Table Mountain – a promise that I will never be able to fulfill.

It is already rather late on this Friday afternoon, but we manage to weave through the traffic and we don't go into the city, but turn away to the south. The driver, a colored man in a white dust coat, tells me that we are going to Groote Schuur, the residence of the Prime Minister. That comes rather as a shock, something I never expected.

The Policemen guarding the gate lets us through without any ceremony and I get out at the front entrance of the mansion. A man in a suit awaits me and helps me out of the sedan. I suddenly feel very inappropriately dressed in my working clothes and my unshaved face. The man introduces himself as the private secretary to the Prime Minister and he leads me to his boss's office.

Three men await me in the office. I immediately recognize Doctor Daniel Malan, the Prime Minister, because I have seen photos of him in the newspaper and because he was a member of Parliament in the time when my father also served. I greet him first. He introduces me to Mister Frans Erasmus, minister of defense, and General Sir Pierre van Ryneveld, Chief of the General Staff of the Defense Force.

When presented to the General, I can't help it but I have to stand stiff at attention and salute him. Before the Prime Minister could utter a word, the General asks me: "Young man, you seem to be a soldier. Am I correct?"

"General, I am proud to state that I was a Major in the proudest military unit of the war, the Sixth Mountain Division of the Waffen-SS. I was chief military surgeon of that division and I was also temporary commander of an artillery regiment and later also of an infantry battalion."

"Well, well. Pleased to meet you. I have had the opportunity of reading your statement that was telexed through to the chief of Police. I am, therefore, familiar with your military record. We were on opposite sides, but it seems as if you have switched sides and decided to join us. But I respect you as a military man. I was always an Air Force man, but I know of the reputation of the Waffen-SS."

General Sir Pierre van Ryneveld

Doctor Malan, who was silent up to this point, takes my arm and says: "Please, sit down. I was also privy to your amazing statement and it is clear that you performed a noble deed by sabotaging the effort to bomb England with an atom bomb. I was informed by the General just before you came that he had received intelligence from MI5 in Britain that they are aware of Nazi activities in Argentina that might include the manufacture of atom bombs. Your story confirms this intelligence. But I understand from your statement that there are two other boats with similar bombs on their way to America and Russia?"

"That is correct. And in this respect, I have two urgent requests. The first one is that you ask the governments of these two countries to be on the look-out for these boats. One of them will wait outside New Orleans for the signal to arm the bomb and the other one will pass through the English Channel on its way to Russia. If you could get the cooperation of the American and the British governments to apprehend these boats a great catastrophe can be averted."

"How will the Navies of these countries know which boats to stop?"

"They are small schooners, a sailing boat with two masts. The one on its way to New Orleans is called the 'White Pearl' and the other one is called the 'Noorderlicht'. Both are crewed by five men, all of them ex-Wehrmacht. My statement contains this information."

"And whose plan was it to bomb these cities to take revenge for losing the war? Your statement didn't make that quite clear, except to say that certain Nazi leaders who escaped to Argentina made this plan."

"Mister Prime Minister, you may perhaps not believe me, but the brains behind this fantastic venture are Adolf Hitler and Martin Bormann."

The Minister of Defense cannot help but to gape: "But they are dead! Hitler committed suicide three years ago. Bormann was shot while trying to flee Berlin."

"That is what the world thinks. That 'suicide' was staged. He escaped. I was in Hitler's company for a whole week. I operated on him at my clinic in Bariloche to remove a tumor and afterwards he convalesced in the clinic before I took him back to his residence, somewhere in the mountains. During his stay at my clinic, he was visited by President Juan Peron."

The General exclaims: "This is fantastic! Do you know where Hitler and Bormann can be found?"

"No. Unfortunately not. I was taken there to see him for the first time during the night and I haven't got the faintest idea where we went. When I took him back after the operation is was in a floatplane that landed on the lake next to his residence, somewhere at a secret location. I am sorry, but I cannot help in this regard. I can only guess that it is somewhere near the point where the borders of Argentina, Paraguay and Brazil meet."

The Prime Minister looks at Pierre van Ryneveld: "You have heard about these two boats. Can I leave it to you to contact the American Navy and the Royal Navy with the request to intercept these boats? Tell them that you are doing this on my behalf. I am certain that they will rather take notice of a General than of a former preacher."

"Consider it done. I will put through telephone calls to the respective chiefs and also send them each a telex. May I ask: May I mention the role that Major Doctor Scholtz played in this regard?"

I immediately respond: "Rather not, if you don't mind. I don't need that exposure. Please."

"All right. I will respect your wish. But I will anyway state that I have very reliable information from inside this organization about their plans and actions. I must say – it is a very ingenious plan to deliver atomic bombs by means of small sailing craft. Everybody would have expected a heavy bomber to deliver the bomb from the air, as the Americans did in Japan."

The Prime Minister looks at me again: "You said that you had two requests."

"Yes, Mister Prime Minister. My second request is that you notify the governor of the island of Saint Helena to take my brother and the other crew members of our sailing boat into custody and to deliver them to the South African authorities. I beg you not to prosecute or punish my brother. He has no idea of the horrors of war. I have seen what a war can do and that is the reason why I had to stop this madness."

The Prime Minister looks at the General: "What can be done in this regard? I will contact the governor through diplomatic channels, but how can we get these men to South Africa?"

"Mister Prime Minister, there is no regular mail service between Cape Town and Jamestown. We will have to send a Navy ship. Will that be all right, Mister Erasmus?"

Erasmus speaks again: "I believe so. Will you make the necessary arrangements with the Chief of the Navy?"

"Yes, I will contact Commodore Dean immediately after this meeting. May I have the use of an office and a telephone in this residence? I don't want to waste time to drive back to town, to the Castle, before I make these phone calls."

Doctor Malan picks up his phone and speaks a few words. His private secretary in his nice suit enters. "Will you please take the General to your office and give him privacy because he has to make a number of urgent telephone calls?"

"As you wish, Sir." The secretary leaves again.

I ask another turn to speak: "Mister Prime Minister, General, I think it will be necessary that I go along on this warship to pick up my brother. He will listen to me and see the folly of trying to revive the project of manufacturing an atomic bomb for Hitler."

"That's a good idea," the Prime Minister says: "And when both of you come back, I want both of you to report to me. Agreed?"

"Certainly, Mister Prime Minister. May I ask one other silly favor? My fiancée, an Afrikaner girl whose grandparents emigrated to Argentina earlier this century, needs to be united with me. It will be dangerous for me to show my face again in Argentina and I will not be able to go and fetch her. What can be done for her? (I stay silent about the fact the Rebecca is not yet my fiancée and that I haven't asked her to marry me, but I am sure that she will be willing to say 'yes' when the time comes)."

"I am sure that something can be done. But first of all: the General has a few urgent phone calls to make and you must be ready to report to the Naval Base at Simonstown. You may stay here in a guest room until our ship is ready to take you to Saint Helena. Gentlemen, thank you all for your time. If you have any other issues, please put it in writing and send it via my private secretary."

I salute the General a second time, which he returns and I greet the other two gentlemen with a handshake. Malan says to me: "Have you forgotten? You are to be our guest till further notice."

Saint Helena, Saturday, 10 July 1948

Willie:

We are bored stiff here on Saint Helena. There is nothing to do, except to wait. The agent contacted his people in Spain and they are making plans how they are going to get us off this island. Our dilemma is so unexpected that it will take time to get things organized. And still there is no news of David. By this time, he must be somewhere to the west of the bulge of Africa – unless he has had an accident and has sunk. I sincerely hope that this is not the case.

St James' Church, Saint Helena

It is Saturday today and I plan to go to church tomorrow. The only church here is the church of Saint James of the Church of England. It's clear that the names of the town and of the church are connected

– both are named after Saint James. My three mates don't understand English and they will keep themselves occupied somewhere else.

Shortly after breakfast our host calls the four of us to his drawing room. To my surprise, two uniformed policemen are waiting for us. One of them, a sergeant, asks me whether I am Doctor William Scholtz. I affirm my identity.

He continues: "Will you and your three mates please accompany us to the Police Station? We understand that you are stuck here on our island without any prospect of leaving. Am I correct?"

"Certainly." Secretly I wonder how this sergeant knows my real name since we registered with the authorities with our assumed names on our forged Argentinian passports.

"Then we must request you to accompany us to the station to complete some formalities. Please follow us."

I translate to the three German seamen and we follow the policemen. At the station we are led to the office of the chief of police where a stern-looking gentleman is awaiting us. He is extremely polite: "Gentlemen, I am very sorry to have inconvenienced you unduly. I understand that you are stuck here on the island against your will. Is that correct?"

"Indeed, sir."

"I must introduce myself. I am Sir George Joy, Governor of this Crown Colony. The Prime Minister of South Africa phoned me with the cooperation of our Colonial Office in London. I was urgently requested to take care of you. A ship of the South African Navy is on her way to come and pick you up and deliver you in due course to the people in charge in Cape Town. I am supposed to take you into custody, but since there is no way you can escape, I will allow you to stay at your present lodgings, provided that you report to the Police every morning before nine o'clock. Understood?"

I gape at him. How is this possible? How does the South African Prime Minister know of my whereabouts? Suddenly, it dawns upon me: David! He must have made contact with the South African authorities and spilled the beans. The traitor! And I am powerless to do anything.

Sir George asks me again: "Do you understand what I am saying, dear Sir?"

"Ah, yes, Sir. Hmm, yes, Sir! Thank you for allowing us to stay at our lodgings. When is this Navy ship expected here?"

"Within a few days, or so I was given to understand. Sergeant, will you please accompany these gentlemen back to their lodgings and also confiscate their passports, which are, no doubt, forgeries."

"Will do so, Sir!"

"Dismiss!"

The Police Station and Prison on Saint Helena

On our way back to our lodgings I explain to the three Germans what this was all about: "Men, unfortunately, the game is up. I gather that my brother took our boat and fled to South Africa where he told the authorities about our plans. We will have to inform our agent of this development so that he can spread the word that our secrets have leaked out. I just cannot believe that my own twin brother would turn traitor and betray us."

Southern Atlantic Ocean, Monday, 12 July 1948

David:

While being a guest at Groote Schuur, the residence of the Prime Minister, since Friday night, I was left very much to my own devices.

However, yesterday was Sunday and Malan, being a former minister of religion, invited me to accompany him and his family to church. This invitation amounted to an order and I dressed myself in my best clothes for the occasion. The Malan family attended the Dutch Reformed Church in Rondebosch where a pew in the front of the church was reserved for them. This was the first time that I heard an Afrikaans sermon in fifteen years and the preacher was Dominee (Reverend) Willie Conradie, somebody whom I knew from my days as a student in Stellenbosch.

I was a guest at Sunday lunch, although I was seated at the lower end of the dining table because there were other guests, including Defense Minister Frans Erasmus, his wife Cora and their son.

And now, it is Monday morning and the private secretary – again in his neat suit – comes to my room and informs me that the Prime Minister's driver is taking me to the naval dockyard in Simonstown in half-an-hour's time. I hastily get my belongings together and go to the front entrance where the chauffeur takes my bag and drives off with me. I suppose that the Prime Minister was too busy to see me off – not that I expected anything of the sort.

At the entrance of the dockyard a naval policeman lets us through after seeing the pass of the driver and I am taken to one of the South African Naval Service's ships, the frigate HMSAS Natal.

I am shown to a cabin by a sublieutenant who introduces himself as Botha. The ship's horn is sounded and she is pulled away from the quay by a tug.

I am on my way to Saint Helena, again! But this time in a spectacular mode. After we have reached the open sea in False Bay, before turning at Cape Point to enter the Atlantic, sublieutenant Botha comes to fetch me to meet the captain on the bridge.

I am introduced to Commander Fanie Bierman. I salute him as a superior officer and he returns my salute with a wry smile: "Oh, so you are that SS Major we have to take to Saint Helena? Prime Minister's orders? Well, well, I never. I wasn't informed what the reason for this hastily organized voyage is, but it must be something important. We were told that we have to pick up four men – a South African citizen and three Germans, and you are to lead us to them. Did I hear correctly?"

"Indeed, Captain."

"All right, when we get to Saint Helena, I am to radio the Governor, a chap called Sir George Joy, and tell him to expect us. And then you are to be rowed ashore to do your job."

"Yes, Captain. I will need at least four men to accompany me in case the four men over there refuse to come along with me. You are also requested to ask for Police assistance, just in case."

"Sounds all tight. And, Major, please keep out of the way of my men when they are doing their work. You are, however, free to talk to them when they are off-duty. You may move around on the ship but this bridge is off-limits. You take your meals in the officers' mess, of course."

Saint Helena, Sunday, 18 July 1948

David:

We were cruising along at a steady eighteen knots and at last the silhouette of Saint Helena rises over the horizon.

Commander Bierman sends for me: "Look here, Major, or whatever you are, we are going to drop anchor in a few minutes' time. I have detailed Chief Petty Officer Olivier and four of my biggest seamen to take you to the shore. They will row the whale boat. I have radioed this chap, Sir George, and he says you must come to the Police Station where he will wait for you. Then you handle everything from there until you come aboard again. I must also tell you that the Chief of our Naval Forces has instructed me to go to Walvis Bay after this to pick up a certain item there that must somehow be defused and then be brought back to Cape Town. Do you know anything about it?"

"Yes, I do. When we get to Walvis Bay I will handle this parcel, together with – I hope – the people we are to collect here in Saint Helena. And I will also like to thank the local Police chief, Major van Blerk for all the trouble he took over this item. Maybe you can recommend him for a medal of some sorts."

Willie:

Our landlord has provided us with a pack of playing cards and that keeps us occupied during the long days. We report to the police station every morning after breakfast. We donated the supplies that we have bought and could not deliver to the Atalanta to our landlord and he prepared our breakfasts from those. The Chief Constable at the police station informs us every time that he has no news about our future.

We have very little contact with the outer world. Our landlord has a radio and he often listens to the BBC World Service. No news about nuclear explosions in America or Russia was ever mentioned and I come to the conclusion that David was able to wreck the whole program on which I have been working for the last twelve years. I feel furious, yet also powerless. It is very frustrating. Extremely frustrating.

One of the Germans, Oberleutnant zur See a.D. (sub-lieutenant, retired) Siegmund Stinkel, calls us outside. There is a warship dropping anchor outside Jamestown. It looks like a frigate. I ask our landlord whether he has a telescope or binoculars. He has binoculars. I aim them on the ship and I see the South African flag fluttering on the stern.

I tell my mates: "This looks like trouble. This ship is here to arrest us and we will be taken to South Africa or maybe Britain where severe sentences await us. We will be charged with conspiring to blow up the Royal Navy. Does anybody have a plan?"

Before anybody can answer, two policemen appear. The sergeant announces: "Gentlemen, the Governor requires your presence at the Saint Helena Police Station. You are to come forthwith and without any resistance, otherwise force will – unfortunately – have to be applied."

"Does this have any connection with that warship anchoring out there?" and I point at the sea.

"Sir, I am sorry. I am not at liberty to divulge any details. You are to follow me. Immediately." I translate his words for the benefit of the three Germans.

When we reach the Police Station the Governor, an upper-class Englishman with a monocle, exclaims: "Ah, here you are, you chaps. I am exceedingly grateful for your cooperation by coming here willingly and speedily. We are to proceed to the prison building. Please follow me as I lead the way. Be carefulat the treacherous steps."

Alarm bells start ringing in my head. Prison? Are we to be locked up? Will we be dragged from here in chains to stand trial somewhere?

Sir George Joy

The Governor stops in the antechamber of the prison: "Chalmers," he addresses the guard: "We need some privacy. Do you mind?"

Chalmers leaves his chair and Sir George says: "Well done, old chap. Please be a sport and bring us five cups of tea, will you? And then you leave us alone. I have some important matters to discuss with these gentlemen."

Chalmers disappears and the Governor continues: "Gentlemen, I sincerely hope that you will have fond memories of our beautiful island after you have left. I really hope that you don't have any serious complaints about the treatment that you have received. I believe that you have been treated better than Napoleon Bonaparte who was also exiled to this Island. I trust that you have utilized the opportunity of visiting the place where he stayed. It is a jolly interesting place, even with a somewhat French flavor.

"You, Doctor Scholtz, would have found it interesting to take cognizance of the fact that he drank South African wine during his stay here. It is interesting how fallen dictators change into simple common folk once they are removed from their countries, don't you think?"

I nod in agreement and I cannot help to think of Adolf Hitler living in exile in a remote spot in Argentina. I also ask myself: when is this guy coming to the point of his long-winded speech?

Chalmers enters with a tray, five cups, a milk bowl, a sugar bowl and a teapot. He dumps them on the table in front of Sir George. The Governor looks at us: "Milk? Sugar? How much?'

I nod again and he pours the milk, and then the tea into each cup. Chalmers leaves us again."Where was I before this rather welcome interruption? Ah, yes, gentlemen. I trust that you have noticed the naval vessel out there on the ocean?" and he indicates vaguely with his hand.

"That will be your mode of transport away from our Island. I expect a landing party to join us at any moment. I was requested to indicate to you that resistance will be quite futile, in fact, utterly useless. This landing party is to take you away and our policemen will assist them, should the need arise.

"Of course, you will be allowed to gather all items of a personal nature from your lodgings. And, please, do remember to pay your bill to the good landlord who took you in."

I am still sitting with my cup in my hands when my brother David steps in. The Governor smiles: "Ah, welcome. Dear Sir, you are the splitting image of this gentleman sitting here, enjoying his cup of English tea. I gather that you two must be related, in fact, brothers? Twins?"

I nod in the affirmative, too perplexed to speak up.

David speaks up: "Am I to suppose that I am in the presence of the governor? Sir George, compliments from the prime minister of South Africa. He is very grateful for the role that you have played. You will never know how important your part in this whole affair was."

"I was merely doing my duty for king and country, dear Sir. Since South Africa is part of the British sphere of influence, I graciously assisted in any manner that was appropriate and within my power."

"Sir George, is there any possibility that I can speak with my brother in privacy?"

"Oh, certainly. I cannot think of a more private space than the last cell there in this row of cells. Fortunately, this island is a tranquil spot and we have almost no crime. The result is that this prison is mostly empty, as is the case at the present moment. I will leave you now. If you need anything, please call the Chief Constable. I wish you all a good day, gentlemen! Bon voyage!" With that, he rises and leaves the building after shaking hands with every man.

David takes me to the last cell. I know it is useless to yell at him, but I, nevertheless, hiss: "You traitor! You betrayed us! I have been working on this project the last twelve years and you have utterly and totally demolished it. I can throttle you. Our comrades will certainly come after you. You can be sure of that!"

David listens to my outburst with half a smile. After a while he says: "You can be very grateful that I came to your rescue. Do you really think that Hitler and Bormann could have held the world hostage with their nuclear bombs? You could perhaps have killed thousands of innocent people, but what would have happened after that? Your other bombs are still in Argentina and it will take ages for these Nazis to get them ready for a second strike. But in the meantime, all of you will have been hunted down. It is well-known that Argentina teems with Nazis. I heard personally from the Prime

Minister and the Chief of Staff of our Defense Force that the Brits know much about the operations of the Nazis in Argentina. Juan Peron would not have been able to withstand the international pressure if atomic bombs started to explode and he would have expelled all of them."

My stomach gets tied in a knot.

David continues: "Just this morning, our ship's Captain showed me a signal that he had received from Naval Headquarters in Simon's Town. The other two schooners have been intercepted by the American Navy and the Royal Navy. Their atomic bombs have been seized and the crews arrested. They will look forward to lengthy prison sentences for conspiring to commit mass murder. We have also received the news that the nuclear facility in Bariloche has been hastily abandoned before some sort of retaliation takes place. It is surmised that they all fled across the border, to Chile or perhaps Paraguay. Including Hitler."

I can only shake my head in disbelief.

"Anyway, that madman Hitler has caused enough misery in this world. Of course, Churchill, Roosevelt and Stalin are also very much guilty of war crimes. But Hitler is stark raving mad, while the others were perhaps not. I, as a medical practitioner, can certainly classify him as a nut case. When I told you in Bariloche that I was requested by Peron to look at an institution for mentally deranged criminals, I had Hitler's hideout in the wilds in mind. Can you remember that?"

I agree: "Hmm."

"You were blinded by the success of producing nuclear weapons, but you never thought about the unnecessary destruction and death you would bring about. Have you seen what the Americans did to Nagasaki and Hiroshima? Do you want that on your conscience?"

I shake my head again.

"Can you remember how horrified we were when the Nazis burnt books, smashed the windows of Jewish businesses and killed millions of Jews in their concentration camps? Is that the sort of world you wish for?"

I shake my head.

"Now you have a choice. You can come willingly with me to South Africa. We have an appointment with the Prime Minister. He has promised not to charge us with treason for aiding Germany during the war. We will actually be granted amnesty, although we continued to aid the Nazis even after the end of the war. You may choose that, or extradition to Britain. Which option do you choose?"

I hold my head with both hands and I sob: "You don't really give a man a choice. Actually, I would love to go back to South Africa. That is where we really belong. I almost started to think of myself as a German. We were surrounded by Germans for the past fifteen years, almost half a lifetime. Perhaps it is time to make a new start."

"You need not worry about retaliation by the Nazis. They have fled. Their treasure of gold ingots that came on the ship with me has been seized and it will most probably be transported back to Germany where it belongs. Germany is on the point of becoming an independent republic – that is, the parts of the country that are not occupied by the Russians. They will need that gold to build up their country again."

Southern Atlantic Ocean, Tuesday, 20 July 1948

David:

Today is the fourth anniversary of the assassination attempt on Hitler and I find it is a fitting day on which to continue my debate with Willie aboard the HMSAS Natal on our way to Walvis Bay and Simonstown. We stand at the bow and look at the water passing below us.

Willie contends that Hitler did much for Germany. The Germans have regained their self-confidence and national pride after his ascension to power. Unemployment has dropped and the wealth of ordinary people improved markedly. "He must be given credit for all this."

I frown: "And look at what became of Germany after the war he had started. A smoking ruin. Millions died. Millions are homeless. Millions maimed for life. Millions psychologically wrecked. And, besides, has it ever occurred to you that the real supporters of Hitler, the hardline Nazi's, were usually members of the lowest classes? They were mostly uneducated people. Often with criminal tendencies. The civilized Germans and those with Christian convictions, could not bring themselves to support him."

"His fight against Communism and Bolshevism has to be applauded and needed all our support. That is why I was willing to go along with the development of the bomb."

"Do you really think that Hitler would have been able to eradicate Communism with his few atomic bombs? It is impossible to force Soviet Russia with its wide expanses and millions of inhabitants to submission with two atomic bombs. You cannot bomb the whole country and kill everybody. It just won't work. I was involved in fighting the Russians. Both Napoleon and Hitler have tried to conquer that country and both failed dismally. They broke their teeth on a hard piece of ice "

"One cannot but admire Hitler for fighting till the end, against all odds. He deserves a place in history as a good statesman."

"Do you really think that the Germans will take him back after his followers have exploded atomic bombs on three cities and killed thousands of innocent people? The Allies have done their best to smoke out all the Nazis who have been guilty of crimes against humanity, including the indefensible persecution of the Jews. I was witness of this crusade, barely a month after the end of hostilities when a British Major and a few soldiers came to the convent where I was hiding to hunt out Nazis and SS men. The closest associates of Hitler have been hanged. Other Nazis, who haven't fled to South America or did not commit suicide, are behind bars. Hitler will have absolutely no support base should he ever venture to return to Germany. He will have the whole country united against him – or what's left of the country. His ideal of becoming the Führer of the Fourth Reich is nothing but a bad dream. It is so far divorced from reality that it is actually a mystery why some Nazis in Bariloche and elsewhere could think that they can resurrect the Nazi empire and take on the whole world. Your project was doomed from the beginning."

Willie tries again: "You know, if it wasn't for his steadfast leadership Germany would have given up the fight long before the time."

"If they had but done that. The Generals who tried to assassinate him on the twentieth of July 1944 had exactly that in mind. I want to tell you something that I heard myself from Hitler. He and his minister of health fed the whole of Germany with a dangerous drug by spiking our coffee and chocolates. The goal was to improve our morale, but when we no longer got this stuff after the war, we all sank into despair and depression."

"Perhaps you are right. There is one positive point, though, connected to this whole saga. Both of us have received our doctorates from a world-class university and we have had experiences that money cannot buy. We can build our own future on that."

Cape Town, Wednesday, 28 July 1948

David:

I and Willie are sitting the private office of Prime Minister Malan in Groote Schuur. Defense Minister Frans Erasmus and Finance Minister Klasie Havenga are also present.

The prime minister looks stern and glares at us through the lenses of his spectacles: "Look here, men, I believe this horrible piece of history is now finally behind us. Under the previous government, you would have been thrown in prison for aiding the country's enemies during the war. Fortunately for you, our new government has decided to grant amnesty for people in your position. If you have broken any laws during your stay in Argentina, we cannot do anything about it because it didn't happen within our borders. You were on your way in the Atlantic Ocean to wipe a British city off the face of the earth, but it did not come to pass. That is also outside our jurisdiction. So, you cannot be punished for that, either. It just won't do to try and prosecute you. Well, what must we do with you? Any suggestions?"

Willie takes the bait: "Mister Prime Minister, we both are extremely thankful that you have given us this chance and that you are prepared to spend some of your valuable time with us. We are eager to serve our country in whatever capacity."

The prime minister nods: "I must say, both of you have actually achieved much. David, you became a respected surgeon. Willie, you are an expert on nuclear physics, or so I am told. David, in addition, you have saved the world from a terrible disaster. I have some proposals to make to both of you. Are you ready to listen?"

Willie: "Mister Prime Minister, we have left these shores more than fifteen years ago. We spent a long time in Germany and, after the war, we lived amongst Germans in Argentina. But we never forgot our roots. We proudly attended the laying of the foundation stone of the Voortrekker Monument ten years ago. It was our desire to take revenge on the British for what they did to our people. But I now realize that it won't do to fall so low as they did by obliterating one of their cities from the face of the earth. David has convinced me that war is terrible.

"I've seen very little of the destruction and suffering brought about by the war, but he has experienced it, as it were, from a ring-side seat. My brother wants to spend the rest of his life helping people who suffer. I want to devote the rest of my life to develop the peaceful generation of energy by means of nuclear power. I am really curious to hear what you want to tell us."

Prime Minister Dr D.F. Malan

Doctor Malan looks impressed: "Well, men, we must do something to keep you here in our country. We need your knowledge and skills. You have declared your eagerness to help this country of ours. Look, I am the Chancellor of the Stellenbosch University. I have spoken to Professor Raymond Wilcocks, the Rector. He is willing to establish a chair in nuclear physics and he is convinced that he will be able to get the University Council and the Senate to back him. Mister Havenga, our Minister of Finance, has been able to dig out the funding for such a chair from somewhere in his budget. Am I correct, Klasie?"

Klasie nods.

"If we don't do that, some other country such as America or Great Britain will grab you. We must do something to hold onto you."

Willie retorts: "Mister Prime Minister, you don't know me. I will never work for those two countries."

I agree: "Me, neither."

The Prime Minister looks at me: "And, you, David, you have proved to be a capable surgeon. Unfortunately, the University of Stellenbosch doesn't yet have a Faculty of Medicine, otherwise we could have placed you there out of gratitude for what you did. How about a job as a military surgeon? Frans, am I right in assuming that a senior position in one of our military hospitals can be found?"

It is the turn of Frans to nod and grunt an affirmative.

"You were a major during the war. We can appoint you with the same rank and promote you within a year or so to lieutenant-colonel. Our military surgeons can learn much from you with your extensive experience of war-time conditions. How about that? You may even become head of a military hospital or even Surgeon-General in time."

Minister of Defense, F.C. Erasmus

The Minister of Defense interrupts: "But first you must undergo training as a South African soldier. You must be able to salute properly without shouting 'Heil Hitler'. I also advise you not to wear the Iron Cross that was awarded to you. It won't go off very well."

I smile: "I only shouted 'Heil Hitler' during my training at the SS Academy. Never after that."And I know how to march, how to salute properly, how to shoot with a gun and aim a howitzer. In case you have forgotten, I was temporary commander of an artillery regiment."

"Unfortunately, you will have to receive our type of training. During this retraining you will have the rank of candidate officer, but after three months of basic training you will receive your commission on a certificate signed by the Governor General."

I smile: "Mister Prime Minister, Mister Erasmus, thank you for that job offer. Fortunately, we are not at war anymore and I think that I will like a military environment. I became used to that during the war. Although – I wonder whether I will be able to shake off all of my German habits. But this will be a good start. Thank you."

Willie looks relieved: "Mister Prime Minister, your generous offer almost takes my breath away. Not so long ago I thought that the hangman's rope was awaiting me somewhere. I gratefully accept the offer to teach nuclear physics. When do we start?"

"As soon as possible. I think you will need some time to prepare your lectures and then you can get going early next year. I advise you to make contact with the dean of the Science Faculty as soon as your job has been approved by the University Council. You, David, can start as soon as you can deliver proof of your qualifications so that you can register with the Medical Council as a specialist surgeon. And, of course, after your basic training as a soldier of the Union Defense Force."

He gives a sly smile while looking at me: "And, by the way, our Ambassador in Argentina has made contact with a certain Miss Rebecca van Wyk. She denies that she is your fiancée.... (he stays silent for a few seconds for effect and then continues) but she also says that she has the fervent wish to become your fiancée. The Ambassador then said that you seem to be eager to make her your bride by calling her your fiancée. He thought that it would then be a good thing to propose to her on your behalf and she also accepted his proposal, of which he took note of with gratitude, also on your behalf. So, our ambassador has actually proposed to her in your stead and he has also received her acceptance in your stead. You ought to write to him a serious letter of thanks for what he did to aid you by making sure about the young lady's feelings and intentions towards you. Through his good intervention you may now really call her your fiancée. She is at this very moment on her way on a freighter as a special passenger because there isn't any regular passenger service between us and South America."

I get tears in my eyes and I can only nod in gratitude.

"But you will somehow have to find the money to pay for her passage. The Government cannot pay for her because she wasn't part of this operation."

I manage to respond: "All right. I am sure I can work something out. After all, Willie still has a purse full of money which the Nazis in Argentina gave us to cover our expenses. I don't think they will insist on a full report on how we spent their money."

The three politicians smile and the Prime Minister continues: "She also told the Ambassador that she is expecting your child."

I cannot help but to get a smile on my face in response to this rather unexpected message, although it is no real surprise to me. The fact that precisely the very prim and proper Prime Minister of our country imparts this important, yet delicate, news to me may be regarded as rather unusual.

The minister of defense speaks again and changes the subject: "The fact that we warned the British and the Americans about the danger that some of their cities could be flattened by atom bombs made them very, very grateful. Representatives of the CIA and MI5 will like to meet both of you in the foreseeable future. Are you willing to tell them all you know?"

Before I can answer, Willie states with a clear voice: "Certainly! If it helps the cause of peace, I am more than willing."

He adds: "I suppose they will also want to talk to these three Germans who came with us."

"I believe so. It is also possible that the Yanks and Brits will reward you in some way. Let's wait and see. And… that bomb that you have delivered to us – we can't use it and after we have defused it, it was donated to the British for their safekeeping. They wanted to pay for it, but we were only too thankful to get rid of it."

Willie smiles: "Fortunately, my name isn't on it. Therefore, I cannot get into trouble, although I did work on it."

The prime minister takes the word again: "Gentlemen, listen carefully, very carefully to me: this meeting never happened, as far as the world out there is concerned. Everything that we've discussed here stays between these four walls. You two men may mention your studies in Germany, your war-time experiences and that you worked and did research in Argentina, but nothing else, absolutely nothing else. The only other person, apart from us, who knows the full story is General van Ryneveld. And I know I can trust him to keep his mouth shut.

"In other words (and he again stays silent for a few seconds to emphasize his words, while staring at us): You never met Adolf Hitler. You never saw Martin Bormann. You never tried to bomb Portsmouth. You never helped with the development of atomic bombs for the Nazis. You never had a clinic at a Nazi compound in Argentina. Do I make myself clear?"

EPILOGUE

Stellenbosch, Monday, 31 January 1949

Willie:

My work as professor in nuclear physics at the Stellenbosch University started officially today when the departmental head welcomed me this morning and assigned an office to me. The lectures only start in a fortnight's time, but I have to be at my post already today.

Shortly after I have started to arrange my books on the shelves and organize my stationary in the drawers of my desk the department's messenger enters my office: "Professor, here's your mail."

I think: "This is fast. From whom did it come?" The address on the envelope is in type script and reveals nothing about the sender. I open the letter. It is also written on a type writer and it was written by my distant cousin, Gerrit Scholtz, and it is dated a fortnight ago, namely 17 January 1949. I start to read:

```
Dear Willie,
Please accept my congratulations on your appointment
as professor in nuclear physics at the Stellenbosch
University. I saw a report in the newspaper regarding
your appointment and I gathered from that that you
have managed to survive the war. I have heard a
rumour that you were prevented from leaving Germany
after war had broken out. If that is true, as a
foreigner you must have experienced a difficult time.

    I have not been able to find out what has
happened to your brother David. Please inform me
about his circumstances.

    However, I am working as journalist since my
return from Europe and presently I have the position
of deputy editor of a daily newspaper in
Johannesburg. My connection with our newspaper is the
most important reason for writing to you.
```

Our newspaper's correspondent in Windhoek visited Swakopmund and Walvis Bay during the December holidays. Because he is constantly on the look-out for a good story (especially during December, which is known as cucumber time) he engaged in a conversation with a policeman in the Walvis Bay harbour. After he had treated the man on a few beers in a bar he heard a very curious story.

According to this policeman, he witnessed a sailing boat that entered the harbour a few months ago, purportedly with an atom bomb on board. The man who sailed the boat into the harbour was afraid that a group of Nazis in Swakopmund would hear about the bomb and try to steal it. Why he was afraid of the Nazis is unclear because he presented himself as a former major in the German SS. The commander of the Police in Walvis Bay thereupon ordered three policemen to guard the boat. They were too afraid to go on board out of fear of detonating the purported bomb, which could blast Walvis Bay from the face of the earth.

The man who brought the boat was taken away by the Police and was apparently arrested. The next day he was taken under Police escort to a military aircraft. Nobody knows what happened to him afterwards.

Something that makes this story still stranger is that a South African warship removed the purported bomb three weeks later, leaving the boat just there. Nobody knows who owns the boat. The harbour dues are accumulating and the harbour captain threatens to auction the boat off to regain the money owed. According the ocean maps on board, this boat apparently came from South America (of all places!).

Our correspondent tried to talk to other policemen who apparently were also involved but all of them denied any knowledge of an atom bomb in the harbour. The correspondent visited the harbour himself and saw a boat that could have contained the purported bomb. It was impossible to go aboard and to look for clues.

Do you perhaps know something about these strange events? I wondered whether you may have heard a rumour in this regard since nuclear physics is your field of specialisation and you ought to have knowledge about atom bombs.

Repeated enquiries at the Department of Defense were met with silence, which makes us believe that there must be something in this strange story. If there is any truth in this tale my newspaper is eager to publish a report. Your help will be greatly appreciated.

Your longing cousin,

After I have read the letter, I tear it up. The pieces of scrap are the first trash to be deposited in my wastepaper basket. There is just no possibility that I can answer Gerrit's letter and disclose my involvement with the nuclear bomb in question. I agree with the wise advice of the prime minister to forget about all this.

Later, I start to wonder: what will happen if the newspaper is, after all, able to dig up the truth and publishes a report about it?

After an hour I decide to relent and I retrieve the pieces of paper from the wastepaper basket to find Gerrit's address. I write a short letter to thank him for his interest in me, to mention that David is working as a surgeon in Cape Town and to assure him that

I haven't heard any rumors about an atomic bomb (which is totally true). I place the letter into an envelope and write the address on the outside. I hand it to our messenger and give him three pennies for a postage stamp.

Cape Town, Friday, 13 December 1957

David:

It is now four years since I have been given the post of commander of the military hospital in Wineberg, Cape Town, with the rank of colonel. There is the prospect of being promoted to the position of Deputy Surgeon General.

Only last week, I saw a patient who reminded me of my days in Germany and Bariloche. I saw Colonel Karl Krause of the Air Force Base Ysterplaat near Cape Town in my consulting room before he was operated upon. After that we renewed our old acquaintance from our respective holidays in Kufstein and our meeting in the Lazarett in Trondheim.

With our shared background of the war, we could speak freely – alternatively in Afrikaans and German.

Through the years I stayed interested in events in my adopted second fatherland, Germany. Therefore, I subscribed to the weekly magazine *Der Spiegel*. When I arrived home on this Friday, the thirteenth, I greeted my beloved wife Rebecca, and our offspring. Pieter, Johannes and David Junior. I grab the mail lying on a table in the entrance hall and settle comfortably in a chair in the living room while Rebecca places a mug of coffee next to me. She joins me with her own mug of coffee.

After we have told each other what we have experienced during the day, I grab the newest number of *Der Spiegel*. Rebecca understands my world because she occupies the position of matron of another hospital – without me being in any way responsible for her appointment.

To my amazement my eyes fall on the photo of a retired Austrian general, a certain Lothar Rendulic – the man from whom I have received the Iron Cross, First Class, thirteen years ago. He has written a few books about his war experiences and his newest book is announced: *"Die unheimlichen Waffen: Atomraketen über uns. Lenkwaffen, Raketengeschosse, Atombomben*" (Monstrous Weapons: Atomic Rockets over us. Guided Weapons, Rockets, Atom Bombs).

According to the review, he provides a detailed description of the Nazi efforts to build nuclear weapons, including the atomic bombs that were manufactured in Argentina. I wonder how accurate his information is, which sources he used and whether he mentions Willie as one of those involved.

I emit a long whistle and Rebecca becomes curious: "What are you reading there?"

"I will tell you shortly. But I must phone Willie first." I pick up the telephone's hand set, dial number "0" and request the operator at the exchange to connect me with my twin brother's home number in Stellenbosch.

GLOSSARY

The greatest part of this story is situated in Germany or in a German environment. Therefore, many German words and terms are used. They are given their English equivalents the first time they occur, but for the benefit of the reader a complete list of such words, terms and abbreviations is given here:

Abteilung	Department
Abwehr	The German Intelligence Organisation
Achtung	Attention
Alm	Mountain pasture
Anschluss	Joining
Artzt	Medical practitioner
Autobahn	Freeway
Bitte	Please
Blitzkrieg	Lightning war
Bratwurst	Grilled sauage
Brötchen	Breakfast roll
Dame	Lady
Danke schön	Thank you very much
Dirndl	Folk dress
Divisionsarzt	Divisional physician or surgeon
Donnerwetter	Lit: Thunder; a common German way of expressing anger or amazement
Drachenzähne	Dragons' teeth
Dummkopf	A stupid person
Fahneneid	Banner oath
Fahnenjunker	Officer cadet
Fähnrich	Ensign

Feldlazarett	Field hospital or sick-bay
Feldwebel	Sergeant
Formular	Application form
Frau	Married woman, Missus
Fräulein	Unmarried woman, Miss
Fregattenkapitän	Commander (navy)
Freiherr	Knight
Frohe Weihnachten	Happy Christmas
Führer	Leader, guide
Gau Province	Gebirgsjäger Mountain troops
Gebirgsdivision	Mountain division
Gestapo	Geheime Staatspolizei or
Secret State Police Gefreiter	Senior rifleman
Gleis	Rail or platform on a station
Glückliche Neujahr	Happy New Year
Glühwein	Cheap red wine heated on a
log fire Gnädiges Fräulein	My dear lady (to an
unmarried woman) Gottesdienst	Church service
Graf	Count
Großadmiral	Admiral of the Fleet
Grüßgott	Greetings in the name of God; the Bavarian way of saying "good day"
Guten Abend	Good evening
Guten Morgen	Good morning
Guten Tag	Good day
Hauptbahnhof	Main railway station
Hauptmann	Captain (army)
Hausarzt	Family physician
Heer	Army

Heimat	Fatherland, alternatively the region where one has grown up or home town.
Herr	Mister, gentleman or sir
Herzliche Glückwünsche	Hearty congratulations
HWA	Heereswaffenamt or Munitions Office of the Army
Idiotenhügel	Easy ski slope for beginners
Imbißstube	Refreshment bar
Immobiliengeschäft	Property agency
Kampfgruppe	Battle group
Kapitän	Captain (of a ship)
Kapitän zur See	Captain (navy)
Kapitänleutnant	Lieutenant (navy)
Keks	Cookies
Kittel	Overall
Kneipe	Bar, canteen
Kommillitonen	Fellow students
Korvettenkapitän	Lieutenant commander
Krankenhaus	Hospital
Krebs	Cancer
Kreuzitürken	Crucify the Turks (a common German way of expressing anger)
Kriegsmarine	German Navy
Kriegspfarrer	Military chaplain
Kriegswichtig	Essential for the war effort
Kübelwagen	Bucket wagon"; the nickname given to the Volkswagen military sedan

GLOSSARY

Lametta	Long thin strands of golden paper to decorate a Christmas tree
Lazarett	Military hospital
Lebe wohl!	Live well!
Leibstandarte	Unit of body guards
Leutnant	Second Lieutenant (Army) or Ensign (Navy)
Luftwaffe	German Air Force
Oberbett	Eiderdown
Oberfeldwebel	Senior Sergeant
Oberleutnant zur See	Sub-lieutenant
Oberst	Colonel
Oberstleutnant	Lieutenant-Colonel
OKW	Oberkommando der Wehrmacht – the high command of the German Armed Forces
ODESSA.	The abbreviation for 'Organisation der Ehemaligen SS Angehörigen' (Organization of former SS members)
Panzerfaust	Bazooka; a missile fired from a tube and used against armor
Pater	Father; the title with which a Catholic priest is addressed
Pension	Guest house
Personalausweis	Identity document
Pionieren	Sappers. military engineering troops

Privatdozent	Tutor, lecturer
Prost!	Cheers!
Putch	Coup d' etat
Rathaus	City hall
Ratsaal	Council hall
Rechtsanwalt	Lawyer
Reich	(German) Empire
Reichsbahn	Railways of the Reich
Reichsforschumgsrat	Council for Research of the Reich
Reichskanzler	Chancellor of the German Reich
Reichsmark	The German currency
Reichstag	Parliament of the Reich
Reichswehr	The Germn armed forces after the First World War
Rosenkohl	Brussels sprouts
SA	Sturmabteilung – the organization of storm troopers of the Nazi Party
Sanitäter	Medical orderly, medic
Sanitätsdienst	Military medical corps/service
Schaffner	Conductor on a train
Schar	Squad or troop
Scheise	Shit
Schilauf	Skiing downhill
Schwalzwälder Kirschtorte	Black Forrest Tart
Sekt	Champagne
Selbstverständlich	Of course
Sondergerät	Special Tools
Spazieren	Hiking
Spinne	Spider

SS	Schützstaffel or protection squadron; initially, this was Hitler's bodyguard, but it was later expended to become a second military force alongside the regular Army
Stadtbummel	A walk through the city
Stammtisch	A table reserved for regular customers to a bar or restaurant
Standarte	Regiment in the Waffen-SS
Standesamt	Registry office
Stift	Convent or priory
Stollen	Cake with raisens and almonds, traditionally enjoyed at Christmas-time
Straße	Street
Straßenbahn	Tram
Silvester	New Year's Eve
Tiergarten	Zoo
Treppenhaus	Stairway
Tschüss!	Good-buy!
Unternehmen	Military operation
Unteroffizier	Corporal
Uranverein	Uranium Club
Verstanden?	Do you understand?
Versuchsstelle	Testing station
Waffen-SS	Armed Schützstaffel or protection squad
Wehrmacht	The German armed forces during the Nazi rule
Wissenschaft	Science

Wochenschau	Cinema newsreel
Zwiebelturn	Onion-shaped tower

RANK STRUCTURE OF THE WAFFEN-SS

It is necessary to explain the rank structure of the Waffen-SS and give the English equivalents since most of these are used in this story:

Collar	*Shoulder strap*	*Sleeve on combat dress*	*Rank*

General Officers

			SS-Oberstgruppenführer und Generaloberst der Waffen-SS (Colonel General)
			SS-Obergruppenführer und General der Waffen-SS (General)
			SS-Gruppenführer und Generalleutnant der Waffen-SS (Lieutenant General)
			SS-Brigadeführer und Generalmajor der Waffen-SS (Major General)

Officers

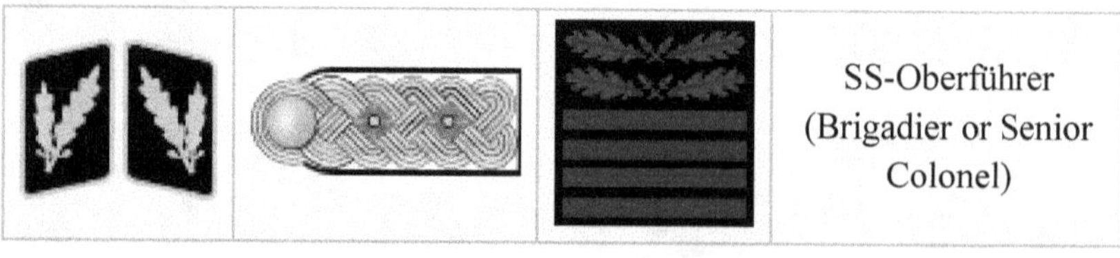

			SS-Oberführer (Brigadier or Senior Colonel)

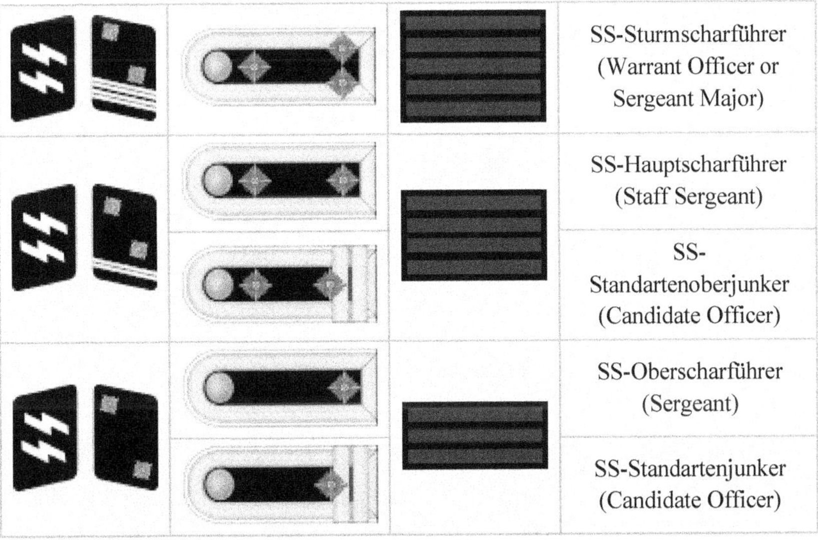

			SS-Standartenführer (Colonel)
	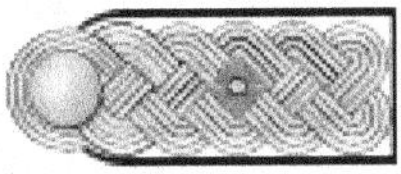		SS-Obersturmbannführer (Lieutenant Colonel)
			SS-Sturmbannführer (Major)
	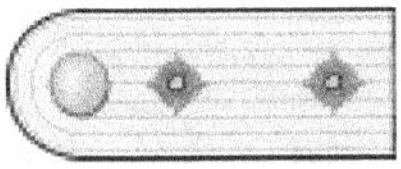		SS-Hauptsturmführer (Captain)
	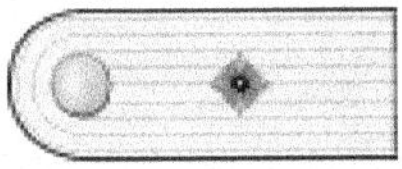		SS-Obersturmführer (Lieutenant)
	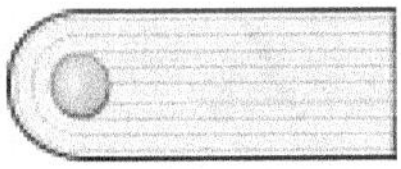		SS-Untersturmführer (Second Lieutenant)

Non-Commissioned Officers and Candidate Officers

			SS-Sturmscharführer (Warrant Officer or Sergeant Major)
			SS-Hauptscharführer (Staff Sergeant)
			SS-Standartenoberjunker (Candidate Officer)
			SS-Oberscharführer (Sergeant)
			SS-Standartenjunker (Candidate Officer)

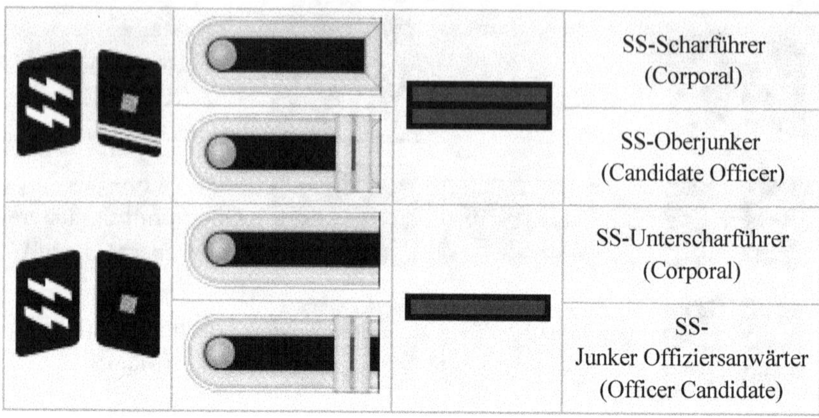

| | | | SS-Scharführer (Corporal) |
| SS-Oberjunker (Candidate Officer) |
| SS-Unterscharführer (Corporal) |
| SS-Junker Offiziersanwärter (Officer Candidate) |

Enlisted Men

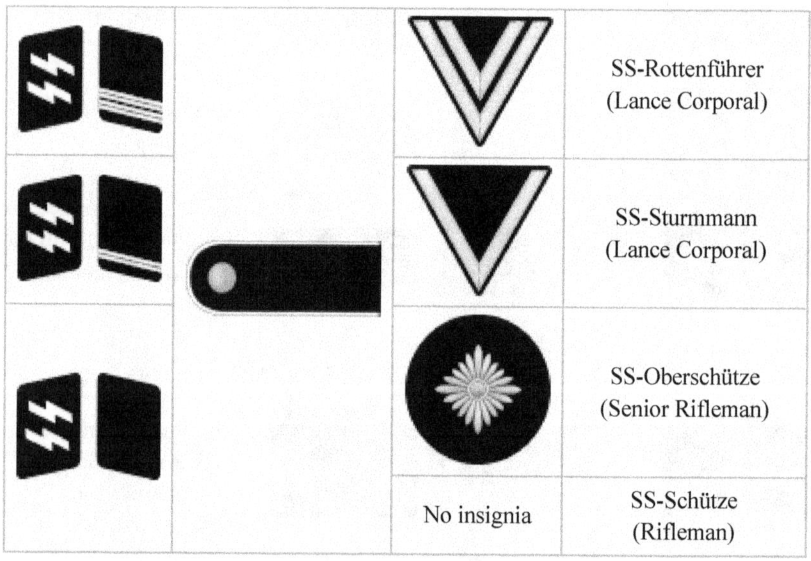

| | | | SS-Rottenführer (Lance Corporal) |
| SS-Sturmmann (Lance Corporal) |
| SS-Oberschütze (Senior Rifleman) |
| No insignia | SS-Schütze (Rifleman) |

Source:

https://en.wikipedia.org/wiki/Ranks_and_insignia_of_the_Waffen-SS

RANK STRUCTURE OF THE SANITÄTSDIENST
(MILITARY MEDICAL SERVICE)

449

Generaloberstabsarzt	Surgeon General
Generalstabsarzt	Surgeon Lieutenant General
Gencralarzt	Surgeon Major General
Oberstarzt	Surgeon Colonel
Oberfeldarzt	Surgeon Lieutenant Colonel
Oberstabsarzt	Surgeon Major
Stabsarzt	Surgeon Captain
Oberarzt	Surgeon Lieutenant
Assistenzarzt	Surgeon Second Lieutenant

PICTURE CREDITS

PART 1
BERLIN

Brandenburg Gate
https://sv.m.wikipedia.org/wiki/Fil:Berlin_Brandenburger_Tor_BW_1.j
pg

3 January 1933
The SS Usambara leaving Table Bay with Table Mountain in he
background
https://i.pinimg.com/originals/47/5a/2e/475a2ea87429a0b1a8947b87e1
e60d3f.jpg

5 January 1933
The Adolf Woermann, sister ship of the Usambara, at Walvis Bay
http://www.travelnewsnamibia.com/news/walvis-bay-harbor-
multifaceted-port-call/

18 January 1933
The main building of the Humboldt University
https://www.colourbox.com/image/the-humboldt-university-of-berlin-
germany-image-2914261

Logo of the Von Humboldt University
https://en.wikipedia.org/wiki/Humboldt_University_of_Berlin

22 January 1933
The Reformed Church in Berlin
https://www.reformiert.de/berlin.html

23 January 1933
Otto Hahn

https://www.nobelprize.org/prizes/chemistry/1944/hahn/biographical/

30 January 1933
Hitler, at the window of the Reich Chancellery, receives an ovation on
the evening of his inauguration as chancellor
https://commons.wikimedia.org/wiki/File:Bundesarchiv_Bild_146-
1972-026-11,_Macht%C3%BCbernahme_Hitlers.jpg

27 February 1933
Firefighters struggling with the flames
https://en.wikipedia.org/wiki/Reichstag_fire

21 March 1933
Hitler and von Hindenburg
https://en.wikipedia.org/wiki/Adolf_Hitler

15 April 1933
Sanssouci Palace in Potsdam
https://www.flickr.com/photos/13877445@N06/3733363410

14 July 1933
Adolf Hitler
https://nypost.com/2018/09/04/book-claims-to-have-uncovered-the-
real-story-of-hitlers-death/

24 December 1933
Interior of the Katharinenkirche in Brandenburg an der Havel
https://en.wikipedia.org/wiki/Brandenburg_an_der_Havel#/media/File:I
nnenansicht-katharinenkirche-brb.JPG

31 December 1933
Goslar in the Harz
https://www.uncommon-travel-germany.com/harz.html

9 June 1934
Stendal: St Mary's church and Town hall

https://www.landkreis-stendal.de/de/stadtportraets/stendal-kurzportrait-20009090.html

Scholtz crest of arms
C:\Users\User\Documents\Scholtz\Coat of arms.mht

28 June 1934
The Rappenseehütte, with the Mädelegabel peak in the background.
https://www.oberstdorf.de/en/hiking/huts-and-climbs.html

31 December 1934
Arnsberg in the Hochsauerland
https://en.wikipedia.org/wiki/Arnsberg

20 June 1935
The Semmering Pass
https://www.britannica.com/place/Semmering

6 August 1935
The Kaiser Wilhelm Institute in Berlin-Dahlem
https://alchetron.com/Kaiser-Wilhelm-Society

1 August 1936
Hitler at his seat of honor at the Summer Olympics of 1936
http://time.com/4432857/hitler-hosted-olympics-1936/

31 December 1936
Ski lift at the Nebelhorn, Oberstdorf
https://www.skiresort.info/ski-resort/nebelhorn-oberstdorf/

3 July 1937
Brandenburg an der Havel: Rathaus
https://www.brandenburg-
live.com/Sehenswuerdigkeit_Highlight_29_Rathaus-mit-Roland.html

8 February 1938

Krankenhaus Moabit

https://www.ansichtskartenversand.com/ak/91-old-postcard/5309-weitere-Ansichten-Bezirk-Tiergarten/7735820-AK-Berlin-Moabit-Krankenhaus-Moabit-oekonomie/?&lang=2

15 March 1938

Lise Meitner during a lecture

https://commons.wikimedia.org/wiki/File:Lise_Meitner_(1878-1968),_lecturing_at_Catholic_University,_Washington,_D.C.,_1946.jpg

14 July 1938

Neuberg an der Mürz

https://www.neuberg-muerz.gv.at/

16 December 1938

The tent village outside Pretoria during the laying of the foundation stone of the Voortrekker Monument, December 1938. People wore the clothes of a century ago

http://www.eggsa.org/documents/main.php?g2_itemId=1552189

27 December 1938

FW 200 Condor

https://www.airvectors.net/avfw200.html

3 July 1939

The Hardanger Fjord

https://en.hardangerfjord.com/

5 September 1939

Generalstabsartzt und SS Gruppenführer (Lieutenant General) Ernst-Robert Grawitz, head of the SS medical corps

https://en.wikipedia.org/wiki/Ernst-Robert_Grawitz

30 August 1940
Shoulder straps of a Assistenzarzt
https://www.aboutww2militaria.com/wehrmacht-heer-medical-officers-
shoulder-boards-in-rank-of-arzt-medical-lieutenant-matt-grey.html

PART 2
SS SURGEON

Waffen-SS soldiers
https://www.super-hobby.com/products/German-Infantry-1941-1945-
Cold-Wind.html

10 September 1940
Sonthofen in Bavaria
https://en.wikipedia.org/wiki/Sonthofen

14 November 1940
Mountain troops shooting with a gun
https://www.flamesofwar.com/Default.aspx?tabid=108&art_id=3650&
kb_cat_id=100

4 February 1941
Mules pulling a 105mm howitzer through a Bavarian village
https://www.flamesofwar.com/hobby.aspx?art_id=2486

The Edelweiss badge of Gebirgstruppen
https://epicartifacts.com/product/ss-gebirgstruppen-sleeve-edelweiss/

15 May 1941
U-boat bunkers at Trondheim
https://en.wikipedia.org/wiki/German_U-
boat_bases_in_occupied_Norway

Karl-Maria Demelhuber
https://alchetron.com/Karl-Maria-Demelhuber

28 June 1941

Crest of the 6th Waffen-SS Gebirgsdivision Nord

https://en.wikipedia.org/wiki/6th_SS_Mountain_Division_Nord

30 September 1941

Gebirgsjäger on skis

https://www.gebirgsdivisionnord.com/history.html

25 December 1941

Captured Soviet equipment in Karelia

https://en.wikipedia.org/wiki/Operation_Silver_Fox

A Junkers Ju 52 ambulance aircraft on the snow

https://picgra.com/media/1994327716213420690

25 December 1942

Brigadeführer Matthias Kleinheisterkamp

https://en.wikipedia.org/wiki/Matthias_Kleinheisterkamp

Volkswagen Kübelwagen

https://za.pinterest.com/pin/1900024822897759/

Junkers Ju 88 bomber

https://en.wikipedia.org/wiki/File:Bundesarchiv_Bild_101I-363-2258-11,_Flugzeug_Junkers_Ju_88_(cropped).jpg

25 December 1943

Gruppenführer and Lieutenant-General of the Waffen-SS Lothar Debes

https://www.tracesofwar.com/persons/7668/Debes-Lothar.htm

A field dressing station in the forests of Karelia during winter

https://commons.wikimedia.org/wiki/File:RIAN_archive_662767_Army_hospital._Volkhov_Front,_1943.jpg

1 May 1944

Waffen-SS soldiers with their camouflage summer outfits

https://www.militaryimages.net/media/waffen-ss-marching-to-battle-2.21692/

Tante Ju taking on a wounded soldier with medical personnel looking on
https://za.pinterest.com/pin/321092648405633788/?lp=true

22 July 1944
SS Soldiers
https://www.nationstates.net/page=dispatch/id=316164

4 August 1944
Ilyushin Il-2 Shturmovik.
https://aircraft.desktopnexus.com/wallpaper/1210794/

19 September 1944
Gruppenführer und Generalleutnant der Waffen-SS Karl-Heinrich Brenner
https://en.wikipedia.org/wiki/Karl-Heinrich_Brenner

Opel Blitz WWII German truck
https://za.pinterest.com/pin/506373551825760775/?lp=true

23 September 1944
Mercedes Benz type L 1500 E ambulance
https://i.pinimg.com/originals/33/3a/94/333a94c4b2a0d2969a9a94bd05876792.jpg

24 September 1944
Armored half-track
http://www.wardrawings.be/WW2/Files/1-Vehicles/Axis/1-Germany/08-Halftracks/Sd.Kfz.251/Sd.Kfz.251-8.htm

1 October 1944
Frozen soldier
https://za.pinterest.com/pin/338614465729707605/

12 October 1944

75 mm Mountain Howitzer 36

https://en.wikipedia.org/wiki/7.5_cm_Gebirgsgesch%C3%BCtz_36

---

30 October 1944

Generaloberst Lothar Rendulic

https://en.wikipedia.org/wiki/Lothar_Rendulic

Shoulder straps of a Obersstabsarzt

https://www.philipp-militaria.com/archivartikel/Ein-Paar-Schulterstuecke-fuer-einen-Oberstabsarzt-Sanitaetstruppe-der-Wehrmacht--1459747832.html

27 December 1944

Young SS soldier

https://za.pinterest.com/pin/178736678948043038/

1 January 1945

Ruins of the Château du Grand-Geroldseck near Wingen

https://en.wikipedia.org/wiki/Vosges

Interior of the church at Wingen

https://throughmyfatherseyes.wordpress.com/2013/10/05/wingen-sur-moder/

7 January 1945

Storckenkopf in the Vosges Mountains, covered with patches of snow

https://en.wikipedia.org/wiki/Vosges

16 January 1945

Frozen soldier

https://za.pinterest.com/pin/309129961920878828/

14 February 1945

Tank traps on the Westwall

https://en.wikipedia.org/wiki/Siegfried_Line

3 April 1945
Standartenführer Franz Schreiber
https://www.valka.cz/Schreiber-Franz-t125595

8 April 1945
SS Gebirgsjäger in the Alps, 1945
https://www.flickr.com/photos/farinihouseoflove/4050506964/

13 April 1945
Soldiers in the mountains
https://za.pinterest.com/pin/132222939035694661/

8 May 1945
Stift Vorau
https://www.teuschler-mogg.at/en/leisure/places-of-
excursion/327_167_company_Augustiner-Chorherrenstift-
Vorau.aspx?LNG=en

9 May 1945
Interior of the church at Vorau
https://www.pinterest.es/pin/146296687871882928/

1 May 1946
Library of Stift Vorau
https://www.steiermark.com/en/vorau-abbey_p154392

10 May 1946
Santa Isabella
https://picclick.co.uk/Deutsche-Ost-Afrika-Linie-PD-Usambara-RP-
Postcard-392248140089.html

PART 3
THE URANIUM CLUB

Members of the Uranium Club
https://www.mirror.co.uk/news/world-news/hitlers-top-nuclear-scientists-dubbed-7734885

30 September 1939
Werner Heisenberg
https://en.wikipedia.org/wiki/Werner_Heisenberg

4 June 1942
Albert Speer
https://prabook.com/web/albert.speer/1345317

8 December 1942
Professor Abraham Esau
https://en.wikipedia.org/wiki/Abraham_Esau

5 February 1943
Vermork heavy water plant at Rjukan, Norway
https://en.wikipedia.org/wiki/Norwegian_heavy_water_sabotage

June-July 1943
The entrance of the tunnel at Haigerloch, known as the "Atomkeller"
https://mimisadventuresineurope.blogspot.com/2010/07/atomkeller-museum-in-haigerloch-germany.html

16 November 1943
Entrance to the tunnel with the reactor, Haigerloch
https://de.wikipedia.org/wiki/Atomkeller-Museum#/media/Datei:Eingang_Atomkeller_Haigerloch.JPG

11 March 1944
The Kaiser Wilhelm Institute in Berlin-Dahlem

https://www.berlinexperiences.com/the-battle-of-berlin-april-25th-1945-berlin-is-encircled/

23 March 1945
FW200 Condor bomber
https://en.wikipedia.org/wiki/Focke-Wulf_Fw_200_Condor

PART 4
PLANTING THE BOMB

San Carlos de Bariloche
https://www.rutaschile.com/Destino-Detalle.php?D=51

21 May 1945
View of the Nahuel Huapi National Park landscape surrounding Bariloche
https://en.wikipedia.org/wiki/Bariloche

22 May 1945
Karl Ullrich
https://stabswache-de-euros.blogspot.com/2013/08/blog-post.html

2 July 1945
Cemetery of Boer prisoners of war, St Helena
https://sthelenaisland.info/boer-cemetery/

24 December 1945
Adolf Hitler
https://en.wikipedia.org/wiki/Adolf_Hitler

30 May 1946
The railway station at Bariloche
http://www.railwaysofthefarsouth.co.uk/04fsanantspareph.html

17 June 1946
Huapi Lake and cathedral, Bariloche

https://www.pinterest.co.uk/pin/286752701248253973/

20 September 1946
The operational reactor at the *Centro Atómico Bariloche*
https://en.wikipedia.org/wiki/Bariloche

22 October 1946
Brigadeführer Wilhelm von Grollmann
https://www.worthpoint.com/worthopedia/wilhelm-von-Grollmann-
photo-signed-137871358

1 November 1946
President Juan Peron
https://en.wikipedia.org/wiki/Juan_Per%C3%B3n

2 November 1946
Junkers W.34 bushplane on floats
https://en.wikipedia.org/wiki/List_of_seaplanes_and_amphibious_aircr
aft

Adolf Hitler
http://themillenniumreport.com/2016/07/hitler-escaped-to-argentina-
died-old-photos-docs-and-dna-analysis/

1 December 1946
Residencia Inalco
http://robscholtemuseum.nl/humans-are-free-hitler-escaped-to-
argentina-died-old-pictures-of-him-after-the-war-fbi-documents-dna-
analysis-of-skull-pictures-of-his-house/

5 July 1947
Ski lift on the Cerro Catedral
https://en.wikipedia.org/wiki/Bariloche

3 January 1948
Adolf Hitler

https://truth11.com/2019/04/10/hitler-escaped-to-argentina-died-old-pictures-of-him-after-the-war-fbi-documents-dna-analysis-of-skull-pictures-of-his-house/

2 February 1948
Train at Bariloche station
https://bariloche.org/la-llegada-del-tren-a-bariloche/

12 February 1948
The schooner Atalanta
https://za.pintcrest.com/pin/237142736608540823/

28 June 1948
Jamestown, Saint Helena, from the sea
https://en.wikipedia.org/wiki/Saint_Helena

8 July 1948
Sand dunes of the Namib Desert from the sea
https://www.sailingtotem.com/2016/02/cruising-namibias-skeleton-coast.html

9 July 1948
Dakota DC 3
https://www.aviationcentral.co.za/tag/saaf100/

General Sir Pierre van Ryneveld
https://en.wikipedia.org/wiki/Pierre_van_Ryneveld

10 July 1948
St James' Church, Saint Helena
http://sainthelenaisland.info/stjames.htm

The Police Station and Prison on Saint Helena
https://www.tripadvisor.co.uk/LocationPhotoDirectLink-g1767153-i133870715-St_Helena_Island.html

12 July 1948
Groote Schuur
http://travelsfinders.com/groote-schuur-rondebosch-cape-town.html

18 July 1948
HMSAS Natal
https://en.wikipedia.org/wiki/HMSAS_Natal

Sir George Joy
http://sainthelenaisland.info/governor.htm

20 July 1948
HMSAS Natal
http://blogs.sun.ac.za/antarcticlegacy/2016/01/10/visit-of-the-h-m-s-a-s-natal-to-marion-island-april-1950-a-personal-account/

28 July 1948
Prime Minister, Dr D F Malan
https://en.wikipedia.org/wiki/D._F._Malan

Minister of Defense, F.C. Erasmus
https://en.wikipedia.org/wiki/Frans_Erasmus

Rank Structure of the Waffen-SS
https://en.wikipedia.org/wiki/Ranks_and_insignia_of_the_Waffen-SS

www.ingramcontent.com/pod-product-compliance
Lightning Source LLC
Chambersburg PA
CBHW060302100726
47907CB00002B/249